Saving

the

Scot

HIGHLANDERS
OF
BALFORSS

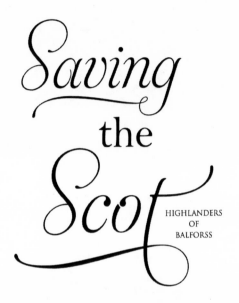

Saving

the

Scot

HIGHLANDERS
OF
BALFORSS

JENNIFER
TRETHEWEY

Entangled Publishing, LLC
2614 South Timberline Road
Suite 105, PMB 159
Fort Collins, CO 80525
rights@entangledpublishing.com

Amara is an imprint of Entangled Publishing, LLC.

Edited by Erin Molta
Cover design by Yellow Prelude Design, LLC
Cover photography by Shutterstock and Deposit Images

Manufactured in the United States of America

First Edition March 2019

This book is dedicated to all the rescuers, the men and women and animals who put their lives on the line daily to save others. To the soldiers, fire fighters, police, EMTs, nurses, doctors, rangers, coast guards, disaster relief workers, rescue dogs, wildland firefighters, ski patrol, and more, I dedicate this book to your bravery and sacrifice. And to the people with no training or super strength who see someone in trouble and step in without reservation to help—thank you for your courage. It gives us all hope for humanity. None of these people would call themselves heroes, but they are. And to some, they are guardian angels.

Prologue

Louisa Robertson didn't think anything was more thrilling than wearing men's trousers, with the possible exception of wearing men's trousers on stage. One had the sensation of being altogether naked. It was the most freeing thing she'd ever done.

It was also the *wickedest* thing she'd ever done. Wicked and dangerous. If her tyrannical father, General Robertson, discovered what she'd been doing while he was away, he would put a swift end to her assignation with the stage, for that was what she believed her relationship with the theater to be—a love affair. And this evening she would consummate that love affair by playing the role of Viola—a young girl who disguises herself as a boy—in her favorite Shakespeare play, *Twelfth Night.*

Louisa stepped into the wings and inched closer to the stage. From there she could peer out and spy on the audience. As the stage manager, Ronald, had said, the house was full this evening.

"Stand by for your entrance, lass," Ronald whispered.

Louisa nodded and made a last-minute adjustment to her trousers. They had a habit of riding up her bottom.

"Ye ken your lines?" he asked.

"Oh, aye." A tremor of nerves fluttered up from her belly. She shook out her hands and slowed her breathing. For weeks, she'd lingered around the theater, performing odd jobs whenever she could, and her persistence had paid off. Two nights ago, without notice, the actress playing Viola had left the tiny Edinburgh theater for a better part in London, causing the biggest stramash Louisa had ever seen—costumers swooned, stagehands wept, and managers vomited. Louisa went straight to the director and told him she knew all Viola's lines and as she and the actress were of a size, she could fit into her costumes, as well. Out of desperation, he had agreed to let her stand in for the actress until they found another.

"If you lose your place," the stage manager said, "Sam's in the pit wi' the book."

"I ken it," she whispered back. He was beginning to make her nervous.

Her previous scenes had gone well this evening. The audience was laughing uproariously at the actor playing Malvolio who was, as the other actors knew, in love with his own performance. His tendency to languish in laughter only added to her nerves. Would he never finish?

At last, Malvolio exited, nearly knocking her over on his way through the wings, uttering a terse, "Have a care, lass."

Ronald poked her in the side. "Right, then. Here comes your cue."

From on stage, the actress playing Olivia announced, *"Give me my veil: come, throw it o'er my face. We'll once more hear Orsino's embassy."*

Louisa strode into the scene imitating the swagger her brothers would use and spoke in a tenor voice. *"The honorable lady of the house, which is she?"*

"Speak to me: I shall answer for her. Your will?" Olivia craned her head to the side, as if trying to see something behind Louisa, which was odd. Olivia had never done that before.

Nevertheless, Louisa declared Viola's lines in her young man's voice. *"Most radiant, exquisite and unmatchable beauty, I pray you"*—Louisa hesitated for a moment. Behind her, there was some disturbance in the audience and she was tempted for a half second to look out and see what it was, but she picked up her line and went on—*"tell me if this be the lady of the house, for I never saw her: I would loath to cast away my speech, for besides that it is excellently well penned..."* There was definitely something amiss. A few men shouted for someone to sit down, and a lady expressed her indignation. Olivia and her attendants shuffled away from Louisa as far upstage as the scenery would allow.

Louisa turned gradually toward the audience on her line. *"I...have...taken...great...pains..."*

A large red-faced uniformed officer of the Royal Highland Regiment stormed up onto the stage.

Louisa stiffened. "Hallo, Da," she said in her little-girl voice. "What are you doing here?"

General Sir Thomas Robertson wrapped an iron arm around Louisa's waist, hoisted her onto his shoulder like a sack of grain, and marched out of the theater to riotous laughter and applause.

Humiliating.

What was her father doing in Edinburgh? He was supposed to be in Ireland. And how had he known where to find her? By all God's glory, if her doaty maid, Mairi, had been the one to tell, she would sit on that girl. *Bonnets.* The costume mistress would be in a right state if she failed to return her trousers.

Outside the theater, the general tossed her into a waiting carriage. She scooted into the corner and made herself as small as possible. A mass of kilted muscle and fury launched himself inside, slammed the door, and banged on the roof for the driver to go. She remained perfectly still on the bumpy, jangling carriage ride. Any minor movement might further incur his wrath. They didn't refer to her father as the Tartan Terror for nothing.

The general did not say a word all the way from Grass Market to their town house on George Street. He wouldn't even look at her. The silence was worse than shouting. She could bear the shouting. What she couldn't bear was the look on his face. She had shamed him. She hadn't meant to. Louisa only wanted the same freedoms her older brothers enjoyed but that she was most unfairly denied.

A sickly feeling gnawed at her bowels. The last time she'd provoked the general with "behavior unbecoming a lady" he had leveled a disturbing threat. Would he remember that warning? Worse, would he follow through?

Once inside the house, he rumbled an ominous, "Go upstairs and change into decent attire. I will speak to you in the parlor."

Her young maid waited at the top of the stairs wide-eyed. "I'm sorry, I am. Truly." She wrung her hands in her apron. "The general come home in a rage. You ken he can be a right fright when he's got his blood up. Your brother tellt him aboot the acting and…" Mairi deflated. "I tellt him the rest."

Mairi's eyes were puffy. She'd obviously been weeping. At the sight of her overwrought maid, Louisa's anger melted into despair. She hadn't been any less afraid of the tyrant. How could she fault Mairi? "It's all right. I'm no' angry. Could you help me change?"

A half hour later, Louisa entered the parlor wearing a subdued gown of gray muslin and with her hair wound into a missish braid. The general stood by the fire with a whisky in hand. His coloring had returned to normal.

"You wanted to speak to me, Da."

He turned and stared at her as if he'd never seen her before. It had been months since he was home last, for Hogmanay. It was mid-March now. He looked as dashing as ever in his uniform and despite her apprehension, she was glad to have him home even for a little while. Unable to stomach her father's disapproval, she let her gaze drop to the delicate painted china figurine of a French courtesan. It had been her mother's.

She reached for the figurine, but flinched when her father shouted at her.

"Disgraceful," he bellowed. "If one of my men had done anything half so reprehensible they'd be pilloried for a week." He tossed the rest of his whisky down, set the glass on the mantel, and began to pace in front of the fire, head lowered, hands behind his back. He paused. "I blame myself. I thought after your mam passed, your granny would take you in hand. Instead, she let you run wild like some savage. Do you ken what they call you when my back is turned? The General's Daughter from Hell." Father looked up at heaven as if appealing for some divine power to intervene. "Daughter from Hell. That makes Tartan Terror sound like a crabbit spaniel." He closed his eyes and shook his head. "What in damnation were you doing on that stage?"

Had he watched her? Hope gave her heart a squeeze and she gasped. "Oh, Da. Did you see me? Did you like it?"

He went red in the face again and shouted, "Do you suppose I like seeing my daughter on *stage* in *trousers*!"

Is it me being on the stage that dismays him or the trousers? "Da, please sit down. You're making yourself sick."

"I'll tell you what makes me sick. What makes me sick is your willful disobedience. Your undisciplined character. Your intractable temper. And since you cannae control yourself, it is left to me to save you from what will surely be your ruination."

Her heart lurched. "No, Da. I'm sorry."

"You mind what I told you the last time."

"Please, Da. Please dinnae do it." Tears sprouted from the corners of her eyes.

"I will not be moved."

"I promise, I'll never—"

"Aye. That's what you promised last time you disappointed me, and the time before that, and the time before that. You broke your promise every time."

She needed air. She was suffocating and the room had started to spin. "I willnae...you cannae. *You cannae make me.*"

"Yes, I can. You, Louisa Robertson, Daughter from Hell, will be married by the end of summer."

Chapter One

Ian Sinclair untied the knot in his neckcloth and began retying it again. It had to be perfect. Everything had to be perfect today.

He called to his quartermaster. "Mr. Peter!"

Peter appeared at his cabin door instantly. He must have been hovering again. "Aye, Captain."

"Are the passengers ashore?"

"Aye, Captain."

"The cargo?" he asked, his chin lifted while he worked at the cloth.

"Unloading as we speak, sir."

"Supplies?" He still couldn't get the bloody knot right.

"Cook's gone ashore with the list."

"And the topsail—"

"Topsail's being mended, masts are oiled, and the guns are cleaned."

"And the—"

"Everything's done, Captain."

"To hell with this blasted thing." It was hopeless. He tore at his neckcloth again. "Bloody, buggering bastard."

"Want some help with that, Captain?"

Ian dropped his hands and barked, "Peter, you're not my damned valet."

Peter smiled at his outburst. "Aye, but I tie a handsome neckcloth." He stepped forward and, in no time, took control of the situation.

Ian endured Peter's attention while he listened to the familiar sounds of the crew, their conversation relaxed now that they had made Leith Docks.

Peter finished and stepped back to inspect his work. "There now. You look smart."

He admired the knot in his glass and somehow it irritated him that Peter had done it so effortlessly. "Thanks."

Peter held out his best wool coat, tailored to a nicety, brushed clean, and buttons polished. "Sure you don't want to wear your uniform?"

"Too presumptuous," Ian said, slipping the coat over his gray waistcoat and starched white shirt. "I havenae been offered the commission, as yet."

"What else could General Robertson want to speak to you about?"

What else, indeed. Ian wanted that commission, more than he liked to admit. He needed to be back in the army—needed the order, the discipline. He was a soldier and soldiering was what he did best.

"Did you send word ahead?" Ian asked.

"Aye, Captain. They'll be expecting you." Peter smiled that knowing smile of his.

"I'm not nervous," he growled.

Peter shrugged. "Didnae say you were."

He closed his eyes and breathed in, taking that moment to

gather himself, master his nerves. Nothing rattled Ian Michael Sinclair, former Captain of the 42nd Royal Highlanders of Foot and second son of Laird John Sinclair.

"Ask Murphy to find me a hack. I need to be at Edinburgh Castle by the noon hour."

"Aye, sir." Peter dashed off.

Ian took another look in the glass. Outwardly, he looked ready, but was he mentally prepared for this meeting? He'd been summoned by his former superior officer, Lieutenant Robertson, now General Sir Thomas Robertson, having earned the rank and the knighthood for his valor at Waterloo. Robertson was known informally to some as the Tartan Terror. He had acquired the name in Flanders for his ferocity. It was used by his men out of respect and admiration. Ian owed the general more than his respect. The man had saved his life at Quatre Bras seven years ago. Robertson had carried him off the field to a dressing station, alive and in one piece, but for the gaping saber gash on his thigh. For that, Ian owed him his service and whatever else the general asked of him.

"Right then," he said to his reflection. "To Castle Rock."

An hour later, Ian and Peter strode across the esplanade to Edinburgh Castle and were waved through the gatehouse. A guardsman met them at the portcullis and escorted them to the Governor's House where they were hustled inside and asked to wait in a dimly lit hall until they were called.

"I hear they'll let you see the Honors of Scotland for a shilling," Peter whispered.

"The crown and scepter, ye mean?"

"Aye, and the sword. I'd like to see the sword." Peter glanced around as though he might spot the object nearby.

"Maybe. We'll see." Raised voices somewhere in the building distracted Ian. The argument spilled into the corridor and a group of six men trying to outshout each other trailed behind a harried-looking General Robertson clad in red uniform jacket and tartan trews. At the door to his office, the general rounded on his assailants bellowing, "Enough. No more of this until tomorrow." He turned to Ian and ordered a curt, "Sinclair. Inside."

Ian followed the general into his office leaving Peter in the hallway, defenseless. Hopefully, the general's assailants weren't after blood.

The general looked a few pounds heavier and many years older than the mere seven years that had passed since their last acquaintance. He collapsed into his chair, put his elbows on the desk and his head in his hands. Ian waited patiently at attention because he didn't know how else to stand before the man. At last, the general sighed and raised his head, his eyes red with fatigue.

"It's a bloody nightmare, Sinclair."

"Is it war, then, sir?"

"Worse. His Majesty King George IV is visiting Edinburgh, the first time a monarch has set foot on Scottish soil in nearly two hundred years, and all of Scotland has gone mad." He added bitterly, "The King claims blood ties to Stuart and suddenly everyone's a Jacobite." He pointed to the door. "Those sharks you saw out there, MacDonell and Glengarry? They're threatening a clan war over who takes precedence in the plaided pageantry nonsense." The general raked a hand through his snow-white hair. "On top of that, the King has ordered his Highland regalia from his tailors, therefore, all peers of Scotland attending the King's Grand Ball must appear in traditional Highland costume." He laughed to himself and his voice pitched higher. "The only thing comical about the debacle is watching the lowlanders desperately search for their Highland ancestry and a suitable tartan."

"Is there something I can do to help, sir?" *Something like a commission, perhaps? A regiment to lead? A garrison to command?*

The general regarded him for an uncomfortably long time, then pointed. "Have a seat, Sinclair."

"Thank you, sir."

"I hear you've been captaining your own ship these last years."

The general's mood had shifted and Ian eased himself back into the chair. "Aye, sir. The *Gael Forss*. It's fine work, the shipping trade, but as you know, I prefer the life of a soldier."

"A passenger vessel?"

"We can accommodate a few passengers, but mostly we ship goods up and down the coast and to and from the Continent." Ian relaxed into a comfortable conversation with the general, confident the meeting was going well.

"And America?"

"The *Gael Forss* will sail for Boston next month, sir."

"I...have a favor to ask of you." The general looked unsure of himself, something Ian had never witnessed in the Tartan Terror.

"Of course, sir."

"It's a personal favor, really."

Personal? Alarms went off in Ian's head. Had an ill wind shifted the meeting off course? "Anything, sir."

"Good. I knew I could count on you."

Shite. He'd just agreed to do whatever the hell the general had on his mind. He hoped it had nothing to do with treason or murder.

"I need you to escort my daughter to Connecticut to meet her fiancé."

Disappointment rose up the back of Ian's throat and he swallowed hard. "You want me to take your daughter to Connecticut aboard the *Gael Forss*, sir?"

"Aye."

Bloody frigging hell. A goddamned child minder. That's the commission the general had in store for him. His daughter's chaperone. Sweat beaded on his forehead and the knot in his neckcloth Peter had tied so perfectly was beginning to choke him. "I see."

"Now, I know you were hoping for a commission. Do this favor for me, deliver my daughter into the hands of her fiancé, and there will be a choice assignment waiting for you when you return." The general rose and held out his hand. Apparently, everything was settled and the meeting was over.

Dazed, he stood and shook hands. "Thank you for this opportunity, sir," he said, as a matter of form.

"I'm afraid I won't be present to see my daughter off. I'm leaving today for Belfast. Her brother Connor will take care of the arrangements. She'll have a companion, of course. I trust that's no problem."

"Not at all, sir."

"Good," the general said. "Again, my thanks. I have complete confidence in you. Good day, Sinclair."

Ian saluted, turned on his heel, and exited the office.

Peter waited in the hallway looking expectantly at him. "Did you get the commission?"

He blinked. "Aye, but first I must complete the Thirteenth Labor of Hercules."

"Sir?"

"Never mind. I need a drink."

• • •

Louisa sat on the edge of her bed and read the note her father had left before his hasty departure for Belfast. It couldn't be true. Surely there was a way to stop this madness before it was too late. She sighed a stage-worthy, "Ah, me. What am I to do?"

Mairi removed Louisa's shoes and *tsk*ed with disapproval. "The bow on your left slipper has come loose."

Louisa sighed again. "It's tragedy, pure tragedy."

"Och, it's no' so bad. I'll give it a stitch and it'll be good as new."

"Not my shoe. This." She thrust the offending note at Mairi.

"What? The letter from the general?"

"He's gone and done it. He's sending me to America to marry. The contracts are signed and passage has been arranged."

Mairi's eyes flew open wide. "America," she gasped. "You're goin' to America?"

"We both are. I wouldnae leave you behind," Louisa assured her.

"Me?" Mairi put a hand to her chest.

"A' course you're going wi' me. I cannae go alone, can I?"

"Oh, oh, miss. Is it really true? We're going to America?" Mairi fanned herself, her face a portrait of rapture. Louisa had never seen such a reaction from her normally levelheaded maid. Excitement seemed to be building inside her at an alarming rate and Louisa worried the girl might swoon.

"Bonnets, Mairi. This isnae good news. It's a disaster. He's making me marry some…" Louisa struggled to get the word out. "*Man.*" She stood and paced the room, angry with the general, irritated with her maid, and furious that events had brought her to this precipice.

"Who?" Mairi asked, startling Louisa out of her vigorous pacing.

"What?"

"Who is it you're to marry?"

Louisa referred to the letter again. "A Mr. Edward Kirby. Oh, God." She flung herself backward onto her bed, lifted the letter in the air, and waved it like a flag of surrender.

Mairi took the letter then and read. When she'd finished, she looked at Louisa quizzically. "Whatever is there to fash aboot? This Mr. Kirby sounds like a good sort of fellow. He's a young man, got his own business—a foundry—and he's doing fine by it. He's even got a big house and servants, forby."

"I dinnae care if he's the Prince of Egypt, I willnae marry. Ever."

"Ye want to be a spinster all yer life?"

The mere sound of the word sparked Louisa's fury. She sat up and pointed an accusing finger. "Dinnae ever use that word in front of me, Mairi. You ken I hate it. It's a nasty, dirty word people use to shame women for not finding a husband, as if that's the only way for a woman to live, to attach herself to a man like his favorite hound, dependent upon him for food and shelter, left begging at his feet for an occasional pat on the head, and then forgotten in some corner of the house. Well, that's no life for me. Ever. I'll not be someone's hound and I'll not be called a spinster. I'll be my own woman. I'll run away if I have to."

"Go an' boil yer heid, ye dafty. Ye cannae run away. What would you do?"

"I could do lots of things. I could teach or run a shop or be a lady's companion. I could even be an actress," Louisa said with some reservation. She hadn't really had an opportunity to prove herself a competent actress, but she thought she could, given the chance. "I thought to run away to London and try to be an actress there. The problem is, no matter what I do, Da would just send one of my brothers to drag me home again."

"You ken very well the stage is no place for a proper young lady such as yerself. That's what got you into this mess, is it not?"

Louisa reached for Mairi's hand and pulled her down to sit next to her on the bed. The girl was her maid, yes, but she was also Louisa's only confidante and, as they were equal in age, both being twenty-two, the one person who understood her completely. She let her head rest on her friend's shoulder.

"Oh, Mairi. I wish you had been there. It was the most glorious feeling to be standin' on that stage in front of hundreds of people, everyone watching you, listening to you, loving you. If only Da had watched me just a wee while, he might have loved me." She corrected herself. "I mean, he might have liked my performance."

"Och, he's worried for ye, is all. Things will be fine. You'll see. No doubt Mr. Kirby is a worthy fellow." Mairi rose and collected the slippers for mending. "Lord knows, I'd give my eye teeth to trade places with you." She chuckled and said more or less to herself, "Aye, that'd be heaven, it would."

The ghost of an idea tickled at the back of Louisa's brain. "What did you say?"

"Pah," Mairi flapped a hand. "I was talking havers."

"No. You said you'd trade places wi' me." Perhaps she had read too many Shakespeare plays but... "Were you serious?"

Mairi straightened, her brow buckled. "Wed a rich man like that and never have to work again? Have servants wait on *me* for a change? A' course I'd want to be you." She shook her head and continued toward the door, still laughing to herself. "Who wouldnae want to be you?"

In the next moment, a fully formed plan popped into Louisa's head and unfurled like a rug. She jumped to her feet and called, "Wait."

Mairi paused at the door. "Yes, miss?"

"Come here." Breathless with excitement, Louisa pulled out the chair to her dressing table. "Sit." When Mairi didn't move, she ordered, "Sit *down*."

The maid sidled toward the chair and lowered herself. "What's got into you? I dinnae like the look on your face."

"Hold your wheesht and close your eyes." She whipped

off Mairi's mobcap and the maid's mess of auburn ringlets spilled over her shoulders. Louisa scooped them up and pinned them on top of her head, allowing a few ringlets to feather the sides of her face. Next, she clipped a pair of glittering earbobs into place, and pinched her cheeks into rosy peaches.

"Ouch."

"Keep your eyes closed." At the last, she buttoned a white lawn chemisette with a high ruffled collar around the girl's neck. "There," she said. "Take a keek."

Mairi stared into the mirror spellbound. Even Louisa had to admit, the transformation was astounding. Given the right adornment, Mairi was undeniably beautiful. The corners of her maid's mouth curved up. "Oh, miss." Then her eyes flicked from her reflection up to Louisa and her smile disappeared. "Oh, miss." The timbre of her voice had changed from awed to appalled. "Oh, no." She shook her head. "Oh, no-no-no-no-no."

Louisa arched a brow. "Oh, yes-yes-yes-yes-yes."

. . .

The bell above the door *ting*ed as Ian entered the bookshop on St. Mary's Wynd. He removed his hat and inhaled the familiar smell, that heady combination of leather with a trace of vanilla and printer's ink. This was his favorite place in Edinburgh, the one spot where he could set aside his cares and silence the thing in his head that constantly demanded order.

He exhaled, let his shoulders loosen and his mind slow.

The bookseller acknowledged him from behind his counter with a raised hand.

"My order's come in, then?" Ian asked.

"Only yesterday, sir."

Good. And just in time. The *Gael Forss* was set to leave in two days. At least he'd have something enjoyable to read during the crossing. He should purchase the book and be on his way, as there was still much he must accomplish yet this afternoon. Plus, he'd promised to stop at his sister Maggie's house to say goodbye to her and the children.

Ian gazed longingly at the shelves, bowed in the center, laden with treasure waiting to be excavated. And the golden letters embossed on the soft leather spines called to him, daring him to peek inside their covers. Well, maybe he could spare a few more minutes. What would be the harm? In any case, his sister would forgive him for being late if he arrived with gifts of books for his niece and nephew.

He asked the bookseller, "Have you a recommendation for a lad of twelve years?"

"The American author, Washington Irving, is popular. I have one copy of *The Legend of Sleepy Hollow.*"

"I've heard of it. A ghost story, aye?" Ian smiled to himself. Young Malcolm would love it. Ian located the book, checked the binding, and tucked it under his arm. Now to find a suitable story for his nine-year-old niece, Belinda. He took a leisurely stroll down the first two aisles of shelves, randomly pulling down books to examine their fly pages and check the publication dates, but mostly for the sheer pleasure of holding them in his hands, testing their weight, and running his fingers over the textured leather.

The rustle of skirts made him lift his head. Peering through the books to the next aisle, he caught a flash of pink. Pink was a young woman's color. And was that lavender he smelled? Those three things—skirts, pink, and lavender—fired Ian's need to investigate. He strolled to the end of the aisle and poked his head around the corner.

He staggered backward upon seeing her. That she was young and pretty didn't surprise him. He had a nose for beautiful women. What did surprise him was the look on her face. She stood smiling down at the pages with a dreamlike quality Ian had only seen on women in the throes of passion. Unmistakable carnal delight.

"What the devil are you reading?" The question was out of his mouth before he could censor his words.

Her head snapped up and wide green eyes, as bright as any gemstones he'd ever seen, stared back at him. And for a moment, he thought he'd been stabbed in the heart.

"I beg your pardon?" Her response to his rude question sounded more like a challenge.

"Forgive me." He fumbled for something to excuse his impertinent behavior. "I...you seemed to enjoy...I mean, you were smiling and...I wondered what book could bring you that kind of...em, pleasure."

She clapped the book closed and hugged it to her breast. "What I read is none of your concern, sir." Her eyes darted to the left. Was that guilt?

Ian tilted his head to the side to examine the spine, which she promptly covered with her thumb, but not before he'd gotten a good keek at the title. "*Moll Flanders*," he said, unable to check the surprise and, admittedly, the disapproval in his tone. A novel recounting the numerous lovers taken by a notoriously promiscuous woman was not a book a young and— Ian absently hoped—unmarried woman should be reading.

The green-eyed lass—belay that—the very, *very* pretty green-eyed lass lifted her chin. "Not that it's any of your business..." She glanced about the shop and lowered her voice to an angry hiss. "But I happen to enjoy Daniel Defoe."

Did she know the pink patches blossoming in her cheeks counteracted her attempt at defiance?

"As do I, but—"

"But what?" she demanded, her chin lifting another quarter of an inch.

"*Moll Flanders* is awfy scandalous, is it no'?"

"Indeed, it is." She gave a sharp schoolmarm nod, as if

she'd just smacked the back of his hand with a ruler. "And that is what I like about it." She swept her skirts around and turned on her heel. "Good day, sir."

He didn't understand why, but something compelled him to stop her, to keep her from walking away, walking out of his life. "Miss, if I may beg a favor?"

She paused but didn't face him.

"Would you suggest a book to please a nine-year-old lass?"

She spun. "Your daughter?" He thought he detected disappointment in her question.

"My niece."

Her head wobbled as if deciding whether she should indulge him. "You might try *The Nutcracker and the Mouse King* by Mr. Hoffman. You'll find it at the end of this aisle."

Ian bowed. "My thanks."

She dipped a quick curtsy.

It took Ian less than a minute to retrieve *The Nutcracker and the Mouse King*. Maybe because she was pretty, or because she was shockingly interested in *Moll Flanders*, or maybe because she had challenged him so boldly, whatever the case and for whatever reason, he had every intention of continuing his conversation with Miss Green-Eyes. Perhaps, after introducing himself properly, she would meet him for a stroll in King's Park tomorrow morning. The bell over the door jingled, sending a jolt of alarm up his legs. He rushed to the front of the shop and glanced about. *Moll Flanders* was left behind, forgotten on a table near the door.

"Where did she go?" he asked.

The bookseller frowned. "Who?"

"The young woman with the green eyes and the cloak and the…" Damn. Why hadn't he asked for her name?

"I dinnae ken the lady, sir," the bookseller said with a blank look. "Will you be adding those books to your order?"

No matter how carefully Ian planned, nothing ever turned out as he envisioned. He'd expected to die on that field in Flanders seven years ago. He'd expected General Robertson to grant him a commission when he strolled into his office two weeks ago. And he'd anticipated spending his last two evenings with a saucy green-eyed lass he'd met in the bookshop this afternoon. No surprise to him, none of his expectations had been met. Fortunately, life had taught him to accept disappointment like a man and move on.

But nothing, *absolutely nothing*, could have prepared Ian for what awaited him at the Leith Docks this afternoon.

His niece and nephew had loved their gifts and thanked him with kisses. His sister Maggie had grumbled that the ghost story would surely give Malcolm nightmares, but she'd thanked Ian, fed him, and had sent him on his way with a tin of ginger biscuits, his favorite. He ate half of them in the carriage on the way back to the ship while contemplating the green-eyed lass he'd met at the bookshop—a strange, intoxicating mix of bold and bashful.

Upon reaching the docks, he paid the driver, collected his purchases and his half-empty biscuit tin, and headed toward the ship. A stout elderly woman stood before the gangway blocking his passage. She jammed her fists on her hips and demanded to know, "Are you Captain Ian Sinclair of His Majesty's Royal Highland Regiment?"

He smiled genially at her scowling face. "I am," he said, trying his best to coax the woman out of her bad humor. "I mean, I was. I'm no longer in His Majesty's service."

"I've been looking for you for six years," she said, her expression still accusatory.

His effort at charm had no effect. He must be losing his touch. "And now you've found me. What can I do for you, madam?"

"Will you be claiming the child?"

Child? What child? "I beg your pardon?"

"Did you no' receive my daughter-in-law's letters?"

"I'm sorry—"

"My son's widow, Alice Crawford. She wrote to tell you she was with child—your child. Did you no' receive her letters?"

Alice Crawford. The name sounded familiar but...a sickly feeling crawled up the back of his legs and settled in his stomach. He remembered spending several nights with a war widow named Alice the week before he'd left for Flanders with his regiment.

"No, I received no letter from... Are you saying she's borne a child by me?"

"Aye. A son."

The initial shock having receded, Ian grew skeptical. "Why did Alice no' come to find me?" he asked, his voice having hardened.

The fire in the older woman's eyes went out. "She's dead," she said dully. "Died in childbirth."

"I'm sorry. Truly. But how—"

"How do you ken the lad is yours?" she asked, still bitter.

"Aye, madam." He'd known several men who had been approached by women claiming to have borne children by them. They were, of course, all men of means. The claims were often suspicious. In some cases, they were downright spurious. But Ian always held a measure of sympathy for the women and, in particular, the children. They had almost no chance of proving their claims, yet some of them must be telling the truth.

Mrs. Crawford turned and barked in the direction of a waiting carriage about ten yards away. "Rory!"

The carriage door opened and a boy around six years old

hopped out—the age a child would be had he fathered one with Alice Crawford. He ran to his gran's side. Tall and lank, to Ian he would look like any other lad his age but for his eyes. The lad had the Sinclair eyes, and when he smiled he looked so much like Ian's brother Alex, it made his heart stutter.

Mrs. Crawford put an arm around the boy's narrow shoulders. "This is Rory. Rory, say hallo to Mr. Sinclair."

He lifted a hand and waved. "Hallo, sir."

Ian cleared his throat twice before he could respond with, "Hallo, Rory."

Rory pointed and asked, "Is that your ship?"

Oh Christ. It was Alex's voice. Or maybe it was his own. In any case, it was Sinclair. "Aye. That's the *Gael Forss*." As if needing to give himself some importance, Ian added, "I'm its captain."

Rory smiled with appreciation, and Ian felt a rush of pride. Just as quickly, doubt flooded his sensibilities. This couldn't be his son. It was impossible. He was always so careful to…except that one time. And that one time had been with Alice Crawford.

The old woman must have seen the change in Ian. She patted Rory's back and said, "Back to the carriage and wait for me, laddie."

As though in a dream, Ian watched the child version of himself skip away.

"Satisfied?" Mrs. Crawford asked.

"Aye," he said.

"Well? Will you claim the lad or no?"

As if he hadn't yet experienced the full spectrum of human emotion, anger surfaced next. Ian grit his teeth. "Six years?" he asked. "You waited six years to find me?"

Mrs. Crawford had the decency to look guilty. She'd lied. She hadn't been searching for him for six years. If she had, she would have found him. He hadn't been that hard to find.

"Why now? After all this time, why do you want me to claim him now?" he asked.

"I'm an old woman. When I'm gone, he'll have no one."

Ian regarded her closely. She wasn't that old. No older than his own mother and she wasn't about to expire anytime soon. Mrs. Crawford was hiding something from him.

"Aye. I will claim him. He's mine, I've nae doubt, but I leave for America the day after tomorrow."

Mrs. Crawford turned and muttered, "Bastard."

"No. I'll be back in three months' time. You have my word."

She made another sound of disbelief.

He resisted the urge to curse. "Where do you live?" he asked.

She folded her arms under her considerable bosom. "Number 5 St. David Street."

"My solicitor's name is Andrew Carlisle. Can you remember that? Andrew Carlisle. I'll see him tomorrow and instruct him to provide you with a monthly stipend. Enough for you and the boy—rent, food, anything you need. But please, dinnae do anything rash, aye?"

He was a good foot taller than her. Still, she tipped her head back and stared down her nose at him. Gray tendrils of hair had escaped her kertch and floated about her rounded shoulders, making her seem less formidable. At last she gave him a curt nod. "Aye. Andrew Carlisle. Three months."

"Wait," he said when she turned to leave. There must be something else he could do, some gesture of assurance before she and the boy left him, some way of communicating that he took his responsibilities seriously. Ian remembered the parcels he clutched under his arm. He held out the tin of ginger biscuits. "Give these to Rory. Tell him they're from his Auntie Maggie."

Chapter Two

For two days, Louisa had brooded about the bookshop man. How dare he—whatever the man's name was—ask her what she was reading? How dare he tower over her and comment on her choice of books? How dare he speak to her with his handsome face when they hadn't even been *introduced*? Their meeting had rattled her so, she'd left the shop without purchasing the book, and now she had nothing new and thrilling to read on the long boring voyage across the ocean. Six weeks. Blast that bookshop man and blast his blue eyes.

Louisa stomped down the stairs and stormed into the parlor. Midmorning sun streamed through the windows casting a swath of pulsing white light across the room. Her cat, Barnabas, lay bathing in the warmth, and her mood softened the instant she peeled him off the carpet and held her face to his brindle fur. Barnabas had been with her twelve years, more than half her life. Would he miss her after she'd gone?

As soon as Mairi bustled into the room, Barnabas wriggled out of her arms and trotted away, tail in the air, without a backward glance. Why would the cat care if she was leaving the house forever? Why would anyone care? Her older brother didn't. Nathan was too busy to tear himself away from business even for a few minutes to wish her well. The last she heard, he was somewhere on the Continent. Her da hadn't even come to see her off. He'd simply sent a messenger with her marching orders. No words of farewell. Not even so much as a goodbye kiss.

"Is ought amiss?" Mairi asked. "Are you still whinging aboot the man in the bookshop?"

"Dinnae be daft." Louisa was beginning to regret having told Mairi anything about her encounter with the bookshop man. "Did you remember to pack the pistols Gran gave me?"

"A' course. They were the first things I put in your trunk. I ken you value those more than your pearls."

"Aye, well, pearls are fine but they'll no' protect us from pirates."

"Pirates." Mairi shivered.

Louisa paced. Questions about the wisdom of their plan still plagued her. What if there was something she forgot, something that would give them away? She let out a long sigh.

"What now?" Mairi asked.

"If Gran hadnae died, none of this would be happening."

Mairi gave a sympathetic tilt of her head. "Och, who's to say. If your gran was still alive, she might be coming along with us." Mairi's tone was obviously meant to cheer her. In fact, her maid was visibly vibrating with excitement. She was thrilled about going away forever. If she had no qualms about leaving, why should Louisa?

"You are absolutely right, Mairi— Sorry." She held up a hand to correct herself. "You are absolutely right, *Miss Robertson*. We must get used to our new roles."

Louisa's brother Connor would arrive in a matter of minutes to escort them to the Leith Docks. If they could pass muster upon boarding the *Gael Forss*, she was certain her plan would work. Her chief concern was whether Mairi could keep up her end of the charade.

"Shall we go over it again one more time?"

Mairi cast her a troubled look. "A' course, miss."

Louisa huffed her frustration. "No. I'm not your mistress, remember? I'm your companion. I'm Miss Mairi MacQuarie. You can address me as Miss MacQuarie or Mairi when we're alone. But never *miss* or we're sunk."

Mairi broke out in a grin. "Fooled you."

"Bonnets. Stop your nonsense. This is serious."

"Right, then." Mairi extended her gloved hand and spoke in a prim, almost overly correct, Midlothian burr. "Good afternoon, Captain. My name is Miss Robertson." She swept her hand with a graceful flourish toward Louisa. "And this is my companion, Miss MacQuarie. We are happy to make your acquaintance. If you would be so kind, please direct us to our cabin."

Louisa relaxed and let out her breath. "Fine. And if anyone should inquire about your destination?" she quizzed.

Mairi snapped her fan open and canted her head a demure degree to the left. "I am on my way to meet Mr. Edward Kirby of New London, Connecticut. We are to be married, ye ken."

"Excellent. And if someone asks after me?"

Mairi leaned toward her invisible conversant. "Oh, aye. This is my dearest friend and boon companion, Miss MacQuarie. You may have heard of her. She is an actress of the highest caliber." She punctuated the last bit with a bat of her eyelashes. The girl was a shameless flirt.

Louisa frowned. "Yes, well, ye dinnae need to lay it on quite so thick, aye?" Her maid had taken to her new role as Louisa Robertson rather quickly. A part of her feared she had created a monster.

They'd rehearsed for weeks in the privacy of Louisa's bedchamber. The other household servants had looked at them askance, but no one had caught on to their plan, bold as it was. Louisa had been skeptical at first, but Mairi seemed as determined as she to follow through. It made perfect sense. How else was Mairi to elevate her circumstance but to exchange places with a well-bred woman? Likewise, how else was Louisa to free herself from the confines of her suffocating existence but to become someone altogether different?

Mairi played the role of Louisa Robertson, daughter of General Robertson, newly affianced to Mr. Kirby. It hadn't been too difficult for Mairi. She knew Louisa's history, her likes and dislikes, she even knew all her mannerisms, right down to her speech. With the exception of a few grammatical missteps, Mairi had proved to be a competent mimic.

Louisa, on the other hand, created an entirely new persona for herself. Simply swapping identities and taking on the role of maid was not appealing to her. The work would be tedious and, more importantly, too restrictive. Even Mairi agreed she'd never make a convincing servant no matter how skilled she was as an actress. And since she had every intention of pursuing a career in theater, Louisa reinvented herself as the multitalented singer, dancer, and actress Miss Mairi MacQuarie. Indeed, the name had a stage-worthy ring to it.

"Right then. I hear Connor's carriage outside." Louisa took Mairi's hands in hers and squeezed. "Are you ready?"

Mairi's eyes sparkled. "Aye. I can hardly believe it. We're going to America. This is the best day of my life."

"Lou!" Connor shouted from the entry.

"Be there in a trice," Louisa called. Mairi reached for Louisa's bonnet. "Nae. That's no longer your job. We must put our own bonnets on now."

Mairi whispered, "Just once more, miss. After all, we

havenae boarded the ship, yet."

Unexpected tears pricked at the corners of Louisa's eyes. She nodded and allowed Mairi to place her sunbonnet on her head, adjust it, and tie the ribbons in a perfect bow under her left ear. "Thank you, Mairi," she whispered.

"There you are, Lou." Connor swanned into the parlor looking his usual wind-tossed and rumpled self. No matter what attire her youngest brother sported, he always looked as though he'd slept in his clothes. Unlike Nathan, Connor didn't care about what he wore and refused to hire a valet.

"I half expected you to bolt. At the very least I expected to see you wearing trousers." He gave her a teasing grin, one that had not changed since childhood. One that she adored and resented at the same time. One that said, "I put up with you even though you are a bothersome girl."

"You look a fright. Where did you find that reeking frock coat?"

Connor feigned indignation. "You hurt my feelings. This is my best coat, I'll have ye know."

"*Hmph.*" Louisa lifted her chin. "You'll no' have to worry about me hurting your delicate feelings after today."

"Steady, now." Connor placed a gentle hand on her shoulder and aimed a pair of sincere green eyes at her. "Ye ken I'll miss my little sister. Always. But Da says this is for the best."

For the best? Best for who? How could sending her away to a foreign country to marry a complete stranger be best for her? No. This could only be best for Da. He was sending her away because she was an embarrassment to him.

"Do *you* think it's for the best, Brother?"

"I cannae say." Connor stuffed his hands in his pockets and made a valiant attempt at reassuring her. "Nathan says Mr. Kirby will treat you well. If he doesnae, write to me and I will come and personally show him the error of his ways. Do ye catch my meaning?"

"Aye. Thank you, Connor." She smirked. "And I will miss your ugly face, as well."

Mairi erupted into giggles. Connor, a notorious rake, hadn't an ugly square inch on him.

Noticing Mairi for the first time, Connor aimed an appreciative smile her way. "My, you're looking fine this morning, Mairi. Like a real lady." He shot her a flirtatious wink, which she returned, much to Louisa's chagrin.

During their weeks of rehearsal, Louisa hadn't had time to address Mairi's tendency to flirt with members of the opposite sex—*any* member of the opposite sex. She was going to have to do something to curb the girl's incorrigible behavior.

"Come on then," Connor said. "Your trunks are already on their way to the ship and I've got your traveling papers. We dinnae want to miss the tide."

It took forever to wind their way through the heavily trafficked areas of the city. As they neared the harbor, the fecund smell of the sea overtook the smoky stench of Edinburgh. A flock of seagulls screamed and turned above a fishing boat laden with the morning's catch. The dockside teemed with people, carts overloaded with goods, and stray dogs dodging in and out of traffic. The going was agonizingly slow, as the Leith Docks were still undergoing major repairs in anticipation of the King's visit, something else she was going to miss.

Gradually, a tall ship loomed into view and Louisa's stomach took a turn.

Mairi leaned over her to look out the carriage window. "Is that it?"

Connor stuck his face next to Mairi's. "Aye. That's the

Gael Forss." He banged on the roof and the carriage rattled to a stop.

Louisa stared at the ship tied about twenty yards down the Leith Docks. Her heart reared and leaped to a gallop. The ship was huge, yes, but at the same time, much, much too small. She would be trapped aboard that vessel for upward of six weeks with no escape. Worse, she'd be expected to sleep below, locked in a small dark cabin.

Connor clambered out of the carriage and helped Mairi down. But Louisa continued to stare out the window at the *Gael Forss.*

"Louisa?" Connor called. "Lou? Something the matter?"

"Em...no."

"Come on, then."

She stepped out, careful to brace herself on Connor as her legs had gone wobbly like jellied fruit.

Connor peeled her fingers off his arm. "I need to see the harbormaster. Wait for me here."

Louisa stumbled forward when a group of pedestrians almost bowled her over.

Mairi steadied her. "What's amiss?"

"Nothing," Louisa lied.

"Is it the old problem?"

By old problem, Mairi meant Louisa's fear of small places. Her maid was one of the few people outside her immediate family who was aware of her fear of being trapped. It had plagued her for as long as she could remember. Da had told her once that her mam had the same problem. When they were children, her brothers had only to level one simple threat—to lock her in the closet—and she would comply with whatever they asked.

Louisa thought she'd outgrown that fear years ago. More fool her. She'd only learned to avoid places that made her uncomfortable—narrow alleys and dark wynds, attics and basements with low ceilings, and she was always careful never to enter a room with a door that might lock behind her.

Mairi touched her arm. "Are you afeart of the ship?"

"Give me a second, and I'll master it," Louisa said. She closed her eyes and recited slowly to herself what Gran had taught her.

Bobby Shafto's gone to sea, Silver buckles at his knee;
He'll come back and marry me, Bonny Bobby Shafto!

She breathed in deeply once more, exhaled, and opened her eyes. "There. I'm ready now."

• • •

It was Sunday, the day they were to make sail for America, and to say that Ian was out of sorts would have been an understatement. He hadn't slept at all on Friday night, spent all of Saturday with his attorney drawing up a contract providing for Rory's maintenance during his absence, and had managed only a few hours of sleep that night. The sudden fact that he was a father—the father of a six-year-old boy—had kept him awake. Most men had nine months to adjust to the idea. Ian had been ambushed with fatherhood, a most unfair way of discovering his change in status.

He'd considered visiting the Crawford house on St. David Street this morning, but thought better of it. His brief appearance, the second in as many days, might confuse the lad. And so, he'd forced himself to stay put.

It wasn't until after breakfast that he'd remembered the commission the general had promised. Ian plummeted into a most foul temper. He had been hoping for—no, he'd been counting on—a commission from his former commander. Instead, he'd unwittingly been saddled with the man's "personal favor," his daughter, whom he'd recently come to find out was commonly known as the "General's Daughter from Hell." He wondered what outrageous thing the woman had done to deserve the title.

A trip to the bookstore, an encounter with an attractive young lady, and a visit to his sister's home had done much to soothe his irritation with General Robertson. And then, like a stone dropped from above, he'd found out he had a son. He'd been a father for six years and hadn't known until two days ago. The timing couldn't have been worse.

Jee-*sus*.

The thing inside Ian's head that sensed approaching chaos, the thing that compelled him to check and re-check, straighten and re-straighten, count and re-count, the thing that he had worked for so many years to quiet, sent him a loud signal. *Order!* Ian must have order or he may lose what limited control he had over his life.

He squared the objects on his desk until he achieved a satisfying balance, evened out the spines in the bookcase until they were flush with each other, and counted the quills in the pen box. Six. There must be six. Only once he'd finished these tasks did his mind quiet and his shoulders relax.

He removed the twine from his package of books, looped it around his fingers, tied it into a neat bundle, and placed it in his davenport desk drawer with other similar oddments he'd retained for future use. Having unwrapped the books, he smoothed the paper and folded it into a precise square. He was not one for waste.

The door to his cabin was tied open to encourage a cross breeze as the days were growing ever warmer. His was a competent crew, one that no longer needed his constant supervision. Still, he listened to their progress. The cargo, the goods for trade that would make their transatlantic voyage a profitable one, had to be stored and secured with care, able to survive a summer squall without damage. Additionally, his men loaded food, fresh water, whisky, ale, fuel, and medicines—provisions sufficient to supply crew and passengers for the duration of their passage with enough in reserve for disaster. A good captain should always be prepared for disaster.

Familiar footsteps rang outside his cabin and he called to them before their owner could knock. "Come in, Mr. Peter."

"Our, em, passengers have arrived, Captain. We're stowing their trunks below now. Will you be wanting to welcome them aboard, sir?"

"Miss Robertson and her companion?"

"Aye, sir."

If Miss Robertson was the Daughter from Hell, no doubt her companion must be an old battle-axe with a face like a bulldog and a voice that could cut stone. Ian sighed and asked, "And what about Mister...Bottom something?"

"Reverend Wynterbottom?"

"Wynterbottom, aye."

"No sign of the reverend as yet, sir."

Damn. A clergyman and two women. Ian stroked the buttery-smooth cover of his latest acquisition, longing for the hour when he could crack the binding, cut the pages, and delve into Robert Southey's latest biography, *Life of Oliver Cromwell*.

"Right, then. I'll be there in a trice."

Peter's footfalls trailed away.

Ian didn't like passengers. Aside from the added responsibility and their constant complaints that this wasn't right or that should be different—as if he could change anything in the middle of the Atlantic—as captain, he was obliged to dine with them on occasion, which meant engaging in their invariably dull conversation. Or maybe it was he who was dull. He sighed. *When did I become such a curmudgeon?*

He pulled the ribbon from his hair, gathered the stray locks back into place and redid his queue. The knot of his neckcloth needed retying. He gave it thirty seconds of his time, then pulled on his jacket, checked that his boots were free of road dust, and tugged his cuffs down to show a quarter inch below his sleeves. He was no slave to fashion like some addled Englishmen he'd met but, like any good soldier, he was trained to be precise. Nothing vain about that. In any case, it was good manners to appear one's best when greeting passengers. Especially ladies.

Bloody hell. Female cargo. He'd conveyed women before, mostly members of his own family or near relations, but never across the Atlantic, a six-week passage. None of his crew were fanatical, but Scots did tend to be a superstitious lot. If anything went wrong...

He wouldn't think about that. Nothing would go wrong. He would navigate the Atlantic without incident, deliver Miss Robertson to her fiancé, the unlucky sod, unload his cargo in Boston, and return to Edinburgh for his choice assignment. And his son.

Christ. I have a son.

Every time he remembered, his heart paused for a moment, as if determining if it was safe to beat. He stuffed thoughts of fatherhood into his boot and practiced a welcoming look in his glass. His image reflected a man plagued with a severe case of the piles. Sour and pained. Like he felt.

"God help us all." He jammed his hat on his head and strolled out onto the deck to greet the "Daughter from Hell."

• • •

"Is that the captain, do ye think?" Mairi lifted her chin in the direction of the *Gael Forss.*

"Aye. I'd wager that's Captain Sinclair." Louisa experienced a flutter of excitement, a sensation completely different from her earlier tremor of apprehension. She'd already spotted the tall, broad-shouldered man. Who wouldn't? He stood at attention, one hand crooked behind his back, the other grasping the ship's railing, surveying the goings-on below him like an emperor. Even at this distance and with the sun at his back, she could make out the strong line of his jaw, his long straight nose, and arrogant brow. Had she not known any better, she would have thought he was...

"Devil take him!" Louisa gasped.

"Who? The captain?" Mairi asked.

"Aye. He's the Bookshop Man. The one who was so rude."

"The one you fancy?"

"Dinnae be daft," she snapped. "I dinnae fancy him at all."

"Oh, aye. I can tell by the way ye stare at him wi' your gob hangin' open. You must hate him something fierce," Mairi said.

God, Louisa hated it when Mairi took that *I know everything* tone.

"Fine ladies do not use crass expressions like *your gob hangin' open*," Louisa chastised. "Ladies dinnae have *gobs*. They have *mouths*."

"Sorry." Mairi looked adequately repentant. At least enough to satisfy Louisa.

She glanced back up at the captain and met his eyes. Her heart tripped and tumbled around in her chest for a moment. Had he recognized her? Would he know who she was? No. She hadn't revealed her name in the bookshop. And thank goodness for that.

Again, she experienced that flutter in her belly. Her father had mentioned something about dining with the captain being a perquisite of their packet. She'd be trapped aboard this vessel for six weeks or more with the impertinent Captain Sinclair. She'd have to see him every day. She'd have to dine with him, too. Louisa resolved that if he dared trifle with her again, she would have to set him straight immediately and in no uncertain terms.

"Lou!" Connor shoved his way through a mob of people like a fish swimming upstream. He waved something in the air. "Everything's in order. If you're ready, I'll see you on board and introduce you to the captain."

Louisa heard Mairi gasp. They hadn't planned for this complication. If Connor introduced them, their plan would be ruined.

"No!" She hadn't meant to shout.

Conner's head jerked up, his smile replaced by confusion.

"I'd rather you said goodbye to us here, dear brother. I dinnae want to have a teary farewell in front of the captain." She put a calming hand on his arm and let her eyes fill. She'd become quite good at crying on demand. "And after all, we must set out on our own at some point. Might as well be right here, right now." She withdrew her hand and placed it over her heart for dramatic effect.

Connor blinked twice, cast a look over his shoulder at the captain, then back at her. He grinned again. "Ye wee bizzum. You cannae fool me."

Mairi stifled a squawk with a gloved hand.

Heart pounding at a furious rate, Louisa said, "Wha-what do you mean?" She furrowed her brow into a mask of innocent perplexity.

"Planning to jump ship and swim to shore before it sets sail?"

"Of course not. You're talking havers. And you've upset Mairi, too."

Connor laughed out loud. "A joke. But seriously, Lou, dinnae try anything foolish. You'll drown in that rig," he said, indicating her skirts. "Wait here. I'll give the captain your papers and come right back to say goodbye."

Mairi let out her breath. "Oh, God. I thought we were done for."

Fueled by residual panic, Louisa rounded on Mairi. "You have to learn to keep your head. This willnae be the last time we find ourselves in a pickle. You must relax and think fast."

"I'm not as practiced a liar as you," Mairi huffed.

"It's no' lying. It's acting. There's a difference."

Mairi grunted. One of her many sounds indicating she neither believed nor trusted Louisa.

Louisa glanced up at the *Gael Forss*. Captain Sinclair laughed at something Connor said. Probably some disparaging remark about "his daft sister" that she'd have to endure. Then she remembered, *she* wouldn't have to endure the remark. The woman standing at her side acting the part of Connor's sister would be the target now.

Connor shook Captain Sinclair's hand and trotted down the narrow gangway as deftly as a mountain goat.

"Look lively, Miss Robertson," Louisa said, nudging Mairi's arm. "This is our cue."

• • •

Ian spotted them below on the docks amid the crowd of seething humanity, the two well-dressed women standing near the carriage—bonneted, gloved, corseted, and cloaked—fully armored in their female regalia. Which one, he wondered, was the Daughter from Hell? No matter. He wasn't going to tolerate nonsense from either of them. The sooner he established that, the better. A good captain ran a tight ship.

He cast another discreet glance in their direction. The brim of one bonnet lifted and he saw her face—her pretty oval face, with pink pursed lips, sun-kissed cheeks, delicate dark winged eyebrows, and—

Ian uttered curse words that would make members of his crew blush. He recognized those eyes. It was her. The lass from the bookshop. Miss Green-Eyes. Jee-*sus*. Was that the general's daughter? The one from hell? If so, he'd been far too forward with her in the bookshop. She might report his conduct to her father and Ian could kiss his choice commission goodbye.

His heart skidded to a halt and he had to rub at his chest to get it going again. Shite. Had he truly allowed those green eyes to unsettle him? Again? He was a man, a soldier, a Highlander for bloody hell's sake. He was merely surprised, is all—surprised that he could make out the color of her eyes from this distance. They were indeed unusually green for him to see them so distinctly from up here.

"Captain Sinclair?"

A gentleman sauntered up the gangway with his hand extended. Was this that reverend fellow?

"How do you do," the man said. "Connor Robertson. Pleased to make your acquaintance."

"Ah." Ian shook Robertson's hand. "And I you. The general said you'd be making arrangements for your sister's passage."

"Indeed. I have my sister and Miss MacQuarie's papers here stamped by the harbormaster. I would appreciate it if you would keep them until you reach Connecticut."

"Of course." Ian tucked the parcel of travel documents into his waistcoat pocket.

"I would introduce you myself, but my sister has requested that we make our goodbyes dockside. Doesnae want any tears, aye."

"I understand."

"Em, you may have heard, Louisa's a bit of a handful, to say the least. Consequence of growing up with no mother and two hellions for brothers, I wager." Robertson laughed nervously and, to be polite, Ian joined him. "My brother Nathan and I tended to indulge her. She may be strong willed, but she's a delight, actually."

Connor Robertson loved his sister. This was his way of saying as much. His way of saying *Go easy on her, please.*

To set the man's mind at rest, Ian said, "My brother and I were wont to spoil our sister, as well."

"My thanks." Robertson smiled his relief. Good. They understood each other. "Well, I'll not keep you any longer. Please find me when you return to Edinburgh. I'd like to buy you a pint."

"I look forward to it." Ian nodded and Robertson trotted away. He did look forward to a drink with Connor Robertson, but somehow the exchange had only served to add to the already crushing responsibility of ferrying these two ladies across the Atlantic safely. Miss Robertson wasn't simply the General's Daughter from Hell. She was also a beloved sister.

"Shall I put the documents in the safe for you, sir?" Peter asked, always anticipating his needs.

"No. Thank you. I'll take care of it." He turned back to watch Robertson take his leave of the two women. He'd thought he'd be able to determine from the exchange which one was the sister, but they seemed to carry equal weight with Robertson's affection. So, the companion wasn't a battle-axe after all. But which one was Miss Robertson?

"Mr. Peter?" he asked, keeping his eyes fixed on the two bonnets making their way toward the gangway.

"Aye, sir?"

"Are the ladies' effects stowed in their cabin?"

"Aye, sir."

"Towels and—"

"Fresh linens and a decanter of brandy in the cupboard, a tin of biscuits, and a basket of raspberries. Everything is exactly as it should be, sir. I've placed lavender on the pillows like Miss Lucy instructed and left an invitation for them to dine in the captain's mess this evening."

Ian gave Peter a hard look, one that might have other men reaching for their dirks, but Peter never flinched. "Have I become completely superfluous?"

Peter grinned, revealing the tiny chip in his right front tooth. "Nae. I'm just very good at my job."

"*Humph*. Well then, remember to give yourself a rise."

"Aye, sir." Peter looked beyond his shoulder and chucked his chin. "Here they come."

The two women toddled up the gangway, one hand on the rope railing, the other grasping a fistful of skirts. Peter reached out to help the first woman aboard. Not the green-eyed beauty. This one was a pretty blue-eyed lass with dark red hair.

Ian reached for the gloved hand of Green-Eyes. He was hoping—no, praying—that Miss Green-Eyes was not the General's Daughter from Hell. Partly because she might spoil his chances for a commission and partly—mostly—because she had captured his attention in a way no other woman had and he couldn't take his eyes off her.

She grasped hold of his hand and he felt a powerful tremor of tension sing through his body. She was nervous. Very nervous. Perhaps even terrified.

"I am...em..." What the devil was his name? "I, em..."

His quartermaster saved him. "Welcome aboard the *Gael Forss*, ladies. I'm Mr. Peter and this is Captain Sinclair."

The blue-eyed one stepped forward. "How do you do. I'm Miss Robertson and this is my companion, Miss MacQuarie."

Green-Eyes was not the general's daughter. Good. He could breathe again. Yet, he was still attached to her. She had clamped onto his hand as if it were a lifeline and would not let go. With each second they remained connected, another drop of self-possession seeped out of his brain. Her eyes, as round as shillings, darted around the deck. He had to make his mouth work or the woman was going to bolt.

"Uh...em...Welcome aboard, ladies."

"We are happy to make your acquaintance," Miss Robertson said. "If you would be so kind, please direct us to our cabin, sir." Ian tore his eyes away from Miss MacQuarie to acknowledge Miss Robertson. There was something forced or arch about her words. He followed Miss Robertson's gaze down to where his hand joined with Miss MacQuarie's.

"Of course," he said, and transferred Miss MacQuarie's hand to Miss Robertson's.

"Ladies, if you'll follow me," Peter said.

The three strolled toward the hatch leading to the cabins below. What the bloody hell had just happened? He shook his head like a dog hoping to rattle himself back to his senses. He'd lost his bloody frigging mind, is what happened.

Ian hadn't fully recovered from the shock of meeting Miss Green-Eyes when a commotion on the dock grabbed his attention. A dour-looking clergyman carrying a walking stick barked his impatience at a boy of about fifteen.

"Keep up, or I'll return you and find another."

Reverend Wynterbottom. He must have purchased the boy's passage and now the lad was indentured to him. How many years would that poor loon have to endure Wynterbottom's temper?

"And if you drop that bag in the harbor—"

"Reverend Wynterbottom," Ian called, hoping to deflect the man's ire away from the boy. "We've been looking forward to your arrival. Welcome aboard the *Gael Forss*."

Now, why couldn't he have been that articulate with the ladies?

"Very inconvenient, this whole..." Wynterbottom waved his stick in the direction of the dock, the harbormaster's office, and the *Gael Forss*, indicating that everything was to blame for his crabbit disposition. Ian noticed a distinct odor surrounding the clergyman, a miasma of alcohol and cologne.

"I do apologize, Reverend." Ian waited until the clergyman was aboard before reaching past him to help with a travel bag that weighed more than the boy carrying it.

"Here now," the reverend said. "Leave that to the boy. That's what I bought him for."

Ian turned a sharp eye on Wynterbottom. "Last I checked, it was illegal to own another human being in Scotland."

The reverend, looking chagrined, said, "I mean to say, that's why I bought his passage, to act as my manservant."

Ian turned to the boy. "What's your name?"

The grubby youth removed his tattered hat. "Danny Sinkler, sir."

"You from Caithness?" Ian asked incredulously. The name Sinkler was a variant of his own name, and most Sinklers he'd ever met were from Wick or thereabout.

"Oh, aye. We moved here when I was a wee one. My parents died last year of the fever. I tried to find work, but—"

"I beg your pardon, Captain," Wynterbottom interrupted irritably. "I'd like to settle into my cabin now, if you please."

Ian spotted his young porter emerging from the hatch. "Will, come take Danny Sinkler below. He can bunk with you. I'll show Reverend Wynterbottom to his cabin."

"Aye, Captain."

The skies suddenly darkened and thunder boomed in the west. Bloody, bloody hell. Two unpredictable women and a dyspeptic God-botherer. Ian was known for his cool composure, his calm under fire, his ability to sort out difficult situations using reason rather than emotion, but he suspected this voyage would test the limits of his self-control.

• • •

Louisa balked at the stairway leading below deck. It was dark and there was no way of telling how small or how cramped her quarters would be. When someone closed the hatch door behind her, would she be trapped? Would she panic and embarrass herself?

Damp coated her palms and fear swelled into an unmanageable-sized ball inside her chest. It pressed against her lungs, making it difficult to catch a full breath.

At the bottom of the steps, Mairi's smiling face shone up at her. "It's no' so cramped as I feared, Miss MacQuarie," she reassured. "The passage is wide and there's plenty of light inside the cabin."

From behind her, Mr. Peter said, "Everything all right, Miss MacQuarie?"

"Once we go below, do you close this hatch? I mean, do you lock it?"

"No, miss. The hatch closes so that no one accidentally falls down the stairs, but the grating allows in light and it's never locked. The only time the opening is fastened is in the case of storm to keep the lower decks from flooding."

Louisa glanced back down into foreboding darkness. "I see." She didn't see. Mairi had disappeared.

"There's naught to be afeart of, miss," Mr. Peter said.

"I'm not afraid," Louisa snapped. She took a deep breath and chanted "Bobby Shafto" to herself on the way down the steps. The passageway was dark but for the checkered square of light on the floorboards—the sun shining through another grate in the deck above. Shadows flickered through it as crew members walked overhead. Mr. Peter had followed her down and stopped on the last step, unable to pass as she remained at the bottom gripping the railing and blocking his way.

Mairi emerged from one of the cabin doors, the light from within illuminating her figure. Good. It was brighter inside the cabins.

"Come." Mairi beckoned. Louisa made a brisk march to the cabin door. Mairi was right. It was a large room. Much larger than she had expected. The cabin wasn't deep, but it was wide. A berth on either end, made with linens and what looked like matching embroidered counterpanes. Their trunks were stowed at the foot of each berth. Situated just inside the door, a washstand, ewer, basin, and towels.

Unfortunately, there were no windows, no source of air, light, or escape. The lantern hanging from above provided light, but once the door to the cabin was shut...

"This is your porter, Will," Mr. Peter said, introducing a lad of about fourteen or fifteen years.

Will made an awkward bow. "At your service."

"Whatever you need, just ask Will. He'll see to it." Mr. Peter made a graceful bow with a flourish. "Until supper, ladies." He smiled a rakish smile and Mairi giggled, blast her.

Will opened a latched cabinet. "Brandy and biscuits, compliments of the captain. I'll bring fresh basin water in the mornings when you ring for it and change your linens when you like. The head—" Will's eyes slid sideways. "I mean, the necessary is under the stairs and to the right."

"What time will you be serving dinner?" Mairi asked.

"I'll bring your tea at six bells and supper is at three bells. But I'll serve your breakfast whenever you like. Is there aught I can get you in the meantime?"

"Nae—" Mairi and Louisa spoke at the same time.

"That'll do, Will." Mairi gave Louisa a look, one that said, *I'm better at this game than you.*

Will started to dash off but returned instantly. "Och, I almost forgot. Shall I tell the captain you'll be joining him for supper?"

"Yes, of course," Mairi said. "Three bells?"

"Aye, Miss." And he was gone.

Louisa untied her bonnet and tossed it on her trunk, then

lowered herself onto the berth. "You need to stop flirting."

"I didnae flirt," Mairi protested.

"Aye, ye did. Mr. Peter smiled at you, and ye giggled like a daft schoolgirl."

"I was jess bein' friendly."

"Servants can flirt and be friendly, but you're no' a servant. You're a proper lady now."

"Forgive me," Mairi sassed back. "I thought I was playing the role of Louisa Robertson and we both ken there's nothing proper aboot—*about* her."

"Keep your voice down," Louisa hissed.

Mairi started to close the door.

"Leave it open."

Mairi's sassy demeanor shifted to one of concern. She sighed and lowered herself to her berth across from Louisa. "I'm sorry."

"I'm sorry, too." The ball of fear inside Louisa's chest began to unravel, releasing floating bits of panic. "I dinnae ken why I thought I could do this. I mean, what will happen tonight when it gets dark and the walls close in and—"

"Dinnae fash yourself. You're braver than anyone I know. If you can stand on a stage in front of all those people in trousers and spout lines from Shakespeare, you can make a trip across the ocean. And, like you said, the ship is no' so bad." Mairi leaned forward. "I can ask for another oil lamp, if you like."

Louisa suddenly became desperate for a lungful of fresh air. "I need to go above."

She dashed out of the cabin and down the passageway toward the stairs leading to the upper deck. As soon as she landed on the bottom step, a pair of tall shiny black Hessians pounded downward. She stepped back and took in long, long legs wearing what looked like doeskin britches that had been painted onto muscular thighs. As the figure descended, so did a well-tailored navy coat fitted to a narrow waist and broad shoulders. The wearer carried a large leather travel bag in one hand and when his handsome face came into view, the panic that had threatened to overtake her reason made a swift departure.

"Captain Sinclair," she said.

The captain seemed momentarily surprised to find her at the bottom of the stairs but recovered quickly, removed his hat, and gave her a slight bow. "Miss MacQuarie."

"I trust your niece appreciated *The Nutcracker and the Mouse King.*"

"Oh, aye. Very much." He waited there, his gaze unwavering, until another gentleman descended, a clergyman. "Reverend Wynterbottom, this is your fellow passenger, Miss MacQuarie."

"How do you do." Louisa bobbed a curtsy.

Wynterbottom grumbled something unintelligible, then added, "I do not approve of women traveling on their own."

Before Louisa could answer, Captain Sinclair said sharply, "She and Miss Robertson are under my protection." She detected a warning in the captain's words.

Reverend Wynterbottom asked, "Where's my cabin?"

"First door on the left." Captain Sinclair remained at the bottom of the stairs. He'd looked at her in a similar way when she'd boarded the *Gael Forss,* but she hadn't taken much note of it at the time, as she'd been preoccupied with moving forward rather than turning and running away. "Is there something I can help you with, Miss MacQuarie?"

My goodness, he had a pleasing voice. Deep and smooth and, well, soothing. "I need some air," she said.

"If you wait here, I can—"

"Captain," Reverend Wynterbottom shouted. "My bag, if you please."

The captain's demeanor darkened and he glared at the unpleasant man. Released from his riveting gaze, Louisa took the opportunity to dash up the stairs.

Above deck, she inhaled a deep, full breath and let it out. The sky had turned gray, a darker gray than its usual Scottish daylight gray, but for now the sky, any color sky, was a comfort.

She heard heavy boots on the stairs behind her and moved away from the hatch opening toward the nearest railing. Maybe Da had come to wave goodbye. Or Nathan? She heard someone call for her maid. Louisa answered absently, "She's gone below," and continued to search the dock for a familiar face. Even Connor had left. He must have been in a hurry to get rid of her.

"Miss MacQuarie?" a pleasing male voice asked from close behind her.

"I said she's gone—" Good Lord, had she forgotten already? The voice was addressing her. *She* was Miss MacQuarie. "Yes?" She turned to stare directly into a man's neatly tied neckcloth. She darted a look upward and met the captain's blue eyes. *Bonnets.*

"It's no' safe for you to be on deck at this time. We're preparing to sail and the men—well, you dinnae want to get in their way or distract them."

"Yes, but…" She looked around her, at all the men rushing to and fro. There must be somewhere she could stand. "I find I need to be above deck at this time."

He gave her a puzzled look, one that made her extremely self-conscious. Louisa realized then that she'd forgotten her sunbonnet and gloves. She clasped her hands behind her back to hide them from the captain.

Please go away and leave me be. Find someone else to bother. Just for a little while.

His shoulders lowered an inch or so and his expression changed to something like resignation. Dear Lord, the man was beautiful.

• • •

Ian caught the look of desperation in Miss MacQuarie's eyes, so like a horse about to bolt. If she did, Miss Robertson would leave the ship, as well. No Miss Robertson, no commission. The woman had been so distracted, she hadn't even understood him properly when he called her name. He had to act before his carefully constructed plan turned to shambles.

Think, man. How does one calm a skittish horse? He remembered what his father had said. *If ye want the horse to calm, you must be calm.* In a gentling tone, Ian said, "There now, Miss MacQuarie. Look at me—nae, dinnae look at the dock—look here, in my eyes, ken?"

Her wide green eyes flashed in his direction.

"There's no danger aboard the *Gael Forss*. I'll no' let anything harm you or Miss Robertson, but it's best we get out of the way of the crew, aye?"

She gave a jerky nod.

"I'll show you back to your cabin."

"No!"

Bloody hell. "All right, then. We'll take the steps up to the quarterdeck." He moved toward the stairs, never breaking eye contact with the lass. She seemed marginally calmer, but until she got her breathing under control and was able to speak to him, he'd not let her out of his sight.

When she made no move toward the stairs, he held out his hand. "It's easy. Only six steps."

She slapped his hand away. "I can do it myself," she said, her words clipped with irritation. She stomped up the steps. At the top, the ungrateful chit shouted down, "And you dinnae need to talk to me like I'm a child."

Ian resisted the temptation to tell her to stop acting like one. He supposed he should be happy she seemed more like herself—or at least a little more like the woman he'd met in the bookshop. "Sorry." He joined her on the quarterdeck and watched her patrol the perimeter, hands clasped behind her back. She was calmer now, moving about with ease. Perhaps she would be fine on her own. He had work to do. They'd be pulling up anchor soon and he couldn't fanny about on the quarterdeck with a female, no matter how green her eyes might be. He gestured to the housing covering the skylight to the captain's mess. "Have a seat."

She plopped herself down.

"Are you comfortable here, Miss MacQuarie?"

She lifted her chin as if challenged. "Yes, thank you." She indicated the bustling deck. "Dinnae let me keep you. Feel free to go about your business. I'm quite content."

Oh-ho, aye. Here is the lass from the bookshop.

"Miss!"

Jee-*sus*. It was the other one.

"Miss!"

Miss MacQuarie sprang to her feet and called down. "I'm up here, Miss Robertson."

Ian leaned over the railing to find Daughter from Hell holding a bonnet and a pair of gloves in one hand while her other hand had clapped over her mouth as if she had said something she should not.

"My bonnet and gloves. How very kind of you, Miss Robertson. Please join me. There's a marvelous view of the harbor from up here."

Chapter Three

Louisa experienced a fit of pique when Mairi crested the quarterdeck smiling sweetly, batting her lashes, and extending her hand to Captain Sinclair for assistance. *Devil take her.* She'd seen Mairi haul two full water buckets up three flights of stairs. She didn't need help to reach the damn quarterdeck. And a woman engaged to be married should not be flirting with Captain Sinclair.

She waited until the captain excused himself before rounding on Mairi. "What were you thinking?" she whispered. "You cannae fetch my hat and gloves and follow me about like a servant."

"Sorry, miss."

"And for all God's glory, stop calling me miss." Louisa batted the bonnet away when Mairi tried to place it on her head. "Have you forgotten everything we practiced?"

"Sorry. There's a gentleman passenger below causing the most awfy—awful racket, yelling at some poor sod who cannae do anything right. He beat the lad with a stick, too. It get me—got me all upset."

"Probably that sour clergyman with the doaty name. Pay him no mind. If I catch the blackguard at it again, I'll put an end to it."

"That's why I come—*came* looking for ye. It's no' my place, but I ken you'd know what to say."

Obviously off balance, Mairi was struggling with the grammar they had practiced. Louisa had asked the impossible from her, yet she was trying very hard. She had to give her that.

Louisa plucked the bonnet from Mairi's grasp. "I'll do it myself." She fumbled for a moment, turning the bonnet in her hands trying to determine which way to face the bloody thing in order to get it on her head straight.

The wind had plucked several pins from her hair. Trying to fasten her curls back into place proved fruitless so she jammed the bonnet over the unholy mess and fumbled with the slippery, fluttering ribbons, muttering a curse with each attempt at tying a bow.

"If ye dinnae stop, you'll knot the ribbons and I'll have to cut the thing off your head," Mairi said.

Louisa let her hands drop to her side. "Bonnets. Will ye help me?"

Mairi pressed her lips together, no doubt stifling an *I told you so,* and tied the ribbons in a neat bow.

When she finished, Louisa gave her a contrite thank-you and pulled on her kid gloves. After collecting her patience, she said, "You need to stop thinking in terms of 'your place.' You're no longer a servant and even if you were, you'd be within your rights to protest when seeing someone badly used." Louisa checked her frustration, and added, "No one can give you the sack."

That made the tension in Mairi's posture loosen.

"And if you want to consider your position in relation to others," Louisa continued, "I would say you're the most important person on this ship. Precious cargo, as they say."

Mairi tilted her head to the side. That notion had clearly never entered her thoughts. The slow grin spreading across her pretty face indicated the idea pleased her. Perhaps a little too much.

They sat on the box covering a skylight to the room below, the captain's quarters, she imagined. Shoulder to shoulder, Louisa and Mairi wordlessly watched the crew untether the ship and raise anchor. Louisa swallowed back tears as the Leith Docks floated away.

Cast out. Banished by her own father. She'd only herself to blame. She'd behaved so abominably, Da had no choice but to send her away. Her unruly behavior was jeopardizing his reputation as well as her own. No doubt her brothers worried she would tarnish theirs, too. That was the way of it. One bad apple spoiled the bunch. And she was a very bad apple. At least, that's what her father thought.

Gran had never seen her as bad. Gran had loved her exactly as she was—headstrong and determined to do exactly as she pleased. She'd say, "Life is like a great banquet, lass. If you dinnae take what ye want, you'll end up with the scraps others leave behind."

If Mam and Gran hadn't left—died—none of this would be happening. They would have defended her right to be who she wanted to be, what she wanted to be. They would have insisted she had a right to choose whether she wanted marriage or not. They were strong, in spite of the fact that most women had little control over their lot in life. Men decided the future of their female relatives and women obeyed or were cast out.

Gran had said her mam had been a strong woman, that she had chosen Da even when her English parents had forbidden the union. Gran had said, "Yer mam's kin didnae want a bloody Scot in their family, so they turned their back on her." She was cast out of their English family, which was the reason why Louisa had never met any of them.

"I miss Gran," Louisa said, sniffing away another tide of tears.

"It feels like she's been gone such a long time, but it hasnae even been a year since she died." Mairi smiled. "I 'member when she first arrived—after your mam passed—I was only twelve then, hired to work in the scullery, and I was so afeart of her. She threatened to cane your da if he didnae take his cheroots outside to smoke 'em."

Louisa chuckled at the memory.

"And then she told yer brothers to stop tormenting you or she'd roast them and eat them for supper. Good God, the look on Connor's face. I ken he believed her."

The memories served to cheer Louisa, and she took Mairi's hand in hers. "We're stuck on this ship for six weeks or more. What are we going to do with ourselves?"

"You can help me finish my weddin' gown."

A twinge of guilt niggled at Louisa's conscience. She scrunched her nose. "I ken it's a little too late to ask, but are ye sure about this?"

"Aboot—about what?"

"Are ye sure about marrying Mr. Kirby?"

Mairi inhaled sharply and shot Louisa a startled look. "Ye dinnae want to change yer mind now, do ye?"

"Nae. Only, I was worried *you* might be having a change of heart."

Her former maid gazed off at the retreating shoreline and made the face she always did when puzzling out a difficult problem. "At first, I thought the whole idea was daft, and that you'd change yer mind. I didnae say anything as I was having fun playacting I was someone else. Then I started thinking, why not? Why not me? I could be a fine lady. All it takes is good manners and pretty frocks. And if I were to marry a wealthy man, well then, my sons and daughters would be real. They wouldnae have to act a part."

Louisa patted Mairi's hand. "It takes more than good manners and pretty frocks to be a lady."

"Like what?" Mairi asked, irritated that her judgement would be called into question.

"Like not flirting. Gran says women who flirt cannae be taken seriously. You dinnae want to get a reputation as a flibbertigibbet, do you?"

"That's calling the kettle black. What do you care aboot reputation? You dance on stage in men's trousers."

"Of course I dinnae care about my reputation as a marriageable young woman. I dinnae want to get married. I seek a different kind of notoriety. I plan to be a great actress— or a great teacher. I dinnae ken. But, something great. You, on the other hand, need to look after your reputation if you want to be the wife of a gentleman. You must present a picture of respectability, domesticity, and chastity."

"Chastity?" Mairi seemed to rear up like an animal sensing danger. "Ye mean like...never bedded a man?"

Louisa shifted to get a better look at her former maid. She'd always known Mairi to be a horrible flirt but hadn't imagined she'd actually...had a man in her bed. Oddly, the realization didn't bother her so much as intrigue her. "Who?"

Mairi cast her a worried glance and chewed at the corner of her lower lip.

"No point keeping a secret now, ye dafty. Tell me," Louisa urged.

"Well, ye 'mind the lad what delivers the coal?"

Louisa recalled a vague image of a tall, lanky figure covered from head to toe in sooty black coal dust. "Aye."

"It turns out, he washes up quite well." Mairi suppressed a smile as best she could but lost the ability to contain her mirth when she said, "He's very handsome and talented, forby."

"Talented? Ye mean he can sing and dance?"

Mairi smirked and slid her a sideways glance. "I dinnae ken I should tell an innocent such as yerself."

Louisa pinched Mairi's arm.

"Ow."

"Tell me now."

Mairi checked to see if anyone was within hearing, then leaned in close. "He has a great big todger." She indicated the size like she would the length of a fish. "And he kens how to use it to give a lass pleasure."

Louisa knew about men's bodies. She had two brothers who, when they were boys, found it enormously amusing to display their parts at the most inappropriate times. And she knew how those parts fit together with a woman's parts. She'd seen bawdy drawings. But how in bloody hell would a "great big" part be anything but painful? Her thoughts circled back to Mairi whose mischievous brow had buckled into a frown of concern. "What's the matter?"

"Do ye ken Mr. Kirby will mind?"

"What? That you're not a virgin?" At Mairi's nod, Louisa said, "For all God's glory, dinnae tell him. And besides, how would he know? Men make such a fuss over that delicate bit of tissue that can be easily lost in so many other ways than, than...great big todgers."

Mairi laughed, her eyes glittering. Was it the wind, or did Mairi feel true affection for her? Certainly, Mairi was the closest thing to a friend Louisa had ever known. Perhaps now that the gap in status between them would be erased, they could be real friends.

Just then, a gust of wind caught their bonnet brims and knocked their heads back with force.

"I'm going below." When Mairi stood, another gust picked up the hem of her skirts and lifted them, revealing her shapely stocking-covered legs all the way to the garters at her knees. Louisa helped her fight her skirts back into place, but not before the men on deck got a tantalizing keek at Mairi's goods. At least six men had frozen in place with mouths agape.

Including Captain Sinclair. To his credit, he snapped out of his trance first and barked at the others to get back to work. Louisa felt mortified on behalf of her friend. Mairi, however, was exceedingly pleased with herself. She posed at the top of the stairs laughing a musical laugh, not at all like her usual cackle, and said, "My thanks, Captain. Such a blustery day. Is it always so?"

Louisa had a sudden urge to push the trifling wee bizzum down the stairs.

. . .

Bloody hell. They'd barely left the shores of Scotland and already the Daughter from Hell was teasing his men. He had a mind to turn back and deposit the bothersome female on her father's doorstep. She was his making. Let him deal with her. If Ian hadn't wanted that commission so badly, he'd do just that.

But he'd waited seven long years to regain his position in the army. What was another three months? He'd have to put his foot down, is all. And he might as well start now.

"Miss Robertson." He extended a helping hand. "I believe it would be best if you and Miss MacQuarie returned to your cabin and remained there until supper."

"You are so kind," she said sweetly.

Just like the devil, he thought, to look and sound angelic. She disappeared down the hatchway, but not before she gave the crew a broad smile. He ground his teeth and whirled on the other green-eyed she-monster still lingering on the quarterdeck.

She lifted a challenging eyebrow at him. "I'm not ready." She turned and marched to the railing.

Bloody frigging hell. He would have to kill her. Taking the stairs in two furious bounds, he debated whether he should push her overboard or simply break her neck. A good dunking might soak the sass out of her. Then again, it would be far more satisfying to slip his hands around her slender, silky neck, feel her rapid pulse through his fingertips and... and...and kiss her. Just under her left ear, perhaps? Maybe bare one of her shoulders and kiss her there, too.

Damn. She's looking at me.

"Captain Sinclair? Are you well?"

"I'm fine," he bit out. "I would be better if you would please get yourself below deck and remain there until supper."

"That's hours from now. You cannae expect me to spend half the day cooped up in that suffocating cell."

"Are you unsatisfied wi' your accommodations, Miss MacQuarie?" He heard the nasty edge in his voice and willed himself to remain in control.

"On the contrary. I find my accommodations more than satisfactory, but I dinnae want to spend the better part of six weeks trapped within those four walls."

She lifted a haughty chin and he simultaneously wanted to kiss her and pull a burlap sack over her head. What on earth had made him think to pursue this woman when he'd met her in the bookshop? She was nothing but a bag of trouble.

"It is for your safety that I ask you to remain below."

"It is for my health that I wish to remain above. I need fresh air. I am a paying passenger not a prisoner. I should be able to move about as I wish."

It was everything he could do not to reach out and shake her.

"I am the captain. My word is law aboard this ship. I

dinnae like it when people challenge my authority."

She jammed her fists on her hips and leaned toward him. "And I dinnae like it when people tell me what to do." She straightened and gave him a cursory glance from head to toe. "Especially someone who is not my blood relative."

"Then think of me as your bad-tempered cousin and heed me when I say, get below deck before I pick you up and carry you there."

She narrowed her eyes at him. If she was thinking about testing his resolve, she was in for a big surprise. His mind flashed on scooping her into his arms and holding her tight, her plush body writhing against his. He felt a tightening in his britches and shook himself free of the image. *What the hell is wrong with me?* He pointed to the hatchway. "And if you make me carry you, I'll lock you inside your cabin and throw away the key."

The color in Miss MacQuarie's face drained. He'd genuinely frightened her but the threat worked. She practically bowled him over on her way toward the hatchway. He'd won. Strange. Instead of feeling victorious, he felt guilty, like he'd kicked a dog.

Peter emerged from the captain's quarters. He'd probably heard the entire exchange.

"Crew's ready for the ceremony, sir."

"Coming."

Sailors were superstitious. Scottish sailors doubly so. He and his brother Alex, his cousins Magnus and Declan, and Peter had salvaged this vessel five years ago when they'd rescued a gaggle of kidnapped women. At the time, it had been a pirate ship called the *Tigress* operated by villains who traded in flesh and stolen goods. Rather than sell the ship, the five Scots had decided to try their hand at the shipping industry.

As Ian had been released from service two years earlier

and had no occupation at the time, he was elected to captain the ship and Peter to act as quartermaster. They'd found a competent crew and a seasoned navigator, and Ian and wee Peter had learned their positions as they went.

Not wanting any trace of the former denizens to taint their new enterprise, they had refitted the ship to accommodate a small number of passengers and renamed it the *Gael Forss*. That had been their first mistake. Apparently, renaming a ship was bad luck. They'd had to conduct an *unnaming* ceremony before holding a *renaming* ceremony to rid the ship of any bad luck. The renaming of a ship, Ian had learned, was only the first of many superstitions surrounding sailors and their relationship with the sea.

It seemed every time they set sail, he was apprised of yet another bad omen. For instance, certain days of the week were bad for sailing. Thursday because it was Thor's Day, god of thunder, and Friday because…well, Ian had no idea why it was bad, nor could any of his crew remember. It was just bad. In addition, no whistling on board, no gingers on board and, of course, no women on board. Unless they were naked. Naked women on a ship were a good thing. But then, for most men, naked women in general were a good thing. Ian didn't think he could induce either Miss Robertson or Miss MacQuarie to oblige.

He had one thing working in his favor. Today was Sunday, the best day for sailing. The ceremony he was about to perform with his crew was essential and perhaps as good as a church service. Before each journey, he and the crew drank a tot of whisky—a sacred drink to the Scots—and recited a prayer for safe passage. Today, more than any other, he hoped God was listening.

• • •

Louisa growled her exasperation with the horrid Captain Sinclair and stormed past him. She was not happy—*not happy at all.* They had yet to pass one hour aboard this reeking, creaking ship and she wanted to scratch the man's eyes out. How dare he order her about like she was his, his… something. She was in her cabin before even noticing she'd descended into the bowels of the ship. Distracted by her tangle with Captain Sinclair, she'd forgotten to panic.

Mairi had her sewing out, embroidering flowers on the cuffs of her wedding gown. "What's got you in a twist?" she asked without looking up. Louisa supposed her stomping had announced her state of temper.

Pointing in the general direction of the captain's quarters, she sputtered, "That-that-that *man* is far too…too…too—"

"Handsome?" Mairi asked.

"Yes. *No.* He—he thinks he's the king of everything and he's not. He's just a bloody sailor and I do not like being ordered about like one of his crew."

"You really ought to mind your language," Mairi said, taunting Louisa with her own advice.

"Dinnae test me, friend," she warned.

Mairi laughed. She was a perpetually good-natured person. Not like Louisa who was always in a snit about something. "Sit down and sort yourself afore ye fall down," Mairi said. "I'll get us a brandy. You'll feel better after you've had a tot."

Louisa was more than out of sorts. She had spiked a temper tantrum as hot as any she'd had as a child. How could she let that bastard Sinclair rile her so?

Mairi handed her a glass containing a swallow of brandy. She started to relax the instant the fumes reached her nose.

"All's you have to do is tell the captain about your fear. I'm sure he'll understand."

"I am not afraid. All that's under control. I dinnae care

to be bullied is all." She tossed the brandy back and let the sweet burn sail down to her belly where it blossomed.

"Better?" Mairi asked.

Louisa gave her a weak smile. "Aye."

"Good. Lie back and shut your eyes. I'll wake you when Will brings our tea."

That was another of Mairi's qualities she admired. The girl always had the ability to make people around her feel at ease, a characteristic common to all gentle ladies. Mairi would be a great success as Mrs. Kirby.

Louisa did as she was told and relaxed back on her berth. Like always, Mairi was right. She probably should have told the captain she didn't like it below, but now she was so angry with him and he with her, she didn't think they would be able to have a civil exchange. At least, not for a while.

Mairi tried to wake her for dinner, but her stomach had gone sour. She continued to sleep until a knock on her cabin door woke her. Mairi opened the door to Will.

"Supper will be served in the captain's mess in thirty, Miss Robertson."

"Thanks," Mairi said.

From down the passageway, they heard a crash followed by the bellowing complaint of Reverend Wynterbottom. Will's face contorted with concern.

Mairi poked her head out the cabin door and her body tensed. "Oh, no."

Will shouted, "Please, sir. Dinnae go do that."

The distinct sound of wood smacking against flesh echoed in the passageway. Louisa flung herself out of bed and shoved Mairi and Will aside. At the end of the dark hall she saw Reverend Wynterbottom, his face a shadowy mask of rage, lifting his cane to strike Danny Sinkler again. The boy was on his knees covering his head.

"Stop that this instant," she shouted.

Wynterbottom lifted his red jowls and bared his teeth. "Shut your mouth, you interfering bi—"

"Reverend!" roared Captain Sinclair.

Everyone went quite still, including Louisa. The only sounds were the footsteps of the captain calmly descending the stairs and poor Danny's desperate breathing.

Indicating Danny, Wynterbottom explained, "This incompetent wretch dropped my—"

Captain Sinclair cut him off short when he snatched the cane from Wynterbottom. "I'll ask you nicely once, dinnae strike the lad again." He rested the cane against the passageway wall. "Come wi' me, Danny. We'll have the ship's surgeon look at you."

Danny got to his feet, flinching slightly.

Reverend Wynterbottom protested, "The boy will never learn without discipline."

"And you'll never teach him without patience." Captain Sinclair placed a comforting hand on the back of Danny's neck and guided him toward the stairs.

"I should clean up the mess first," Danny whispered.

"Dinnae fash. Will will see to it," the captain said gently. His voice sharpened. "I'll see you all at supper." Then to Wynterbottom he said, "In the meantime, gather your temper, sir."

Captain Sinclair and the boy went up to the main deck while Reverend Wynterbottom returned to his cabin with a slam. Louisa listened to his sour rumblings from behind the door and waited for her heartbeat to slow.

She jumped when the porter, Will, stepped into her view. "Sorry, Miss."

"Dinnae be sorry. Your captain is a good and just man," she said, and felt a sudden twinge of shame for her earlier behavior. What she saw as overbearing, domineering conduct on the part of Captain Sinclair had been warranted. He'd been concerned for the safety of his passengers, and she had reacted in a childish manner. The truth was, she hadn't been afraid. She hadn't even been angry with Captain Sinclair. She was unhappy. Da had not come to say goodbye.

A half hour later, Mr. Peter helped Louisa and Mairi into their places at the captain's supper table. Captain Sinclair stood stiffly at the end. He introduced them to his navigator, Mr. Purdie, seated at the far end. When the shy man blushed at his praise, Captain Sinclair's posture softened and he smiled fondly at the fellow.

"I am truly the most fortunate of captains to have Mr. Purdie aboard the *Gael Forss*. He has more experience at sea than all our crew combined and has generously schooled me with patience—more patience than I deserve, at times." Captain Sinclair and Mr. Purdie laughed at what Louisa guessed was some mutually remembered incident. "But it is because of his great knowledge of the sea that I and the crew sail with courage and confidence." Captain Sinclair lifted his tankard.

Louisa and the others lifted theirs.

"To Mr. Purdie and a safe voyage. *Slainte*."

Their friendly chorus of "*Slainte*" died when Reverend Wynterbottom entered the room, his face pinched with disapproval. "You should have waited for me to bless the meal before imbibing. Is this what I can expect from your crew? Drunkenness and undisciplined behavior? It's a wonder we should ever make it—"

"Welcome, Reverend." The warm light went out of Captain's Sinclair's eyes, replaced now with a dull and lifeless stare like in ancient marble statues she'd seen in kirk. The dim glow of the oil lamp hanging overhead illuminated the flex and jump of the captain's jaw muscle, the only aspect of his countenance that gave away his irritation with the clergyman. "Please, sir. We've not yet begun our meal and would appreciate your blessing."

Louisa wondered how much it cost the big Scot to speak pleasantly to such an unpleasant man. As captain, it was his responsibility to see that his passengers had a safe passage. She doubted, however, that he was responsible for the comfort of his guests. He'd delegated that task to the porter, Will. And yet, he had demonstrated with Wynterbottom the kind of restraint Louisa didn't think possible in a man. At least, no man she'd ever known. Had he employed this level of patience when dealing with her earlier today? And had she been so selfish not to notice?

The table occupants mumbled a collective "Amen" and she realized she'd missed the reverend's blessing altogether. No matter. Captain Sinclair's kind words to Mr. Purdie were adequate blessing for her.

Reverend Wynterbottom and Mr. Purdie served themselves from the center platter containing chunks of tender beef, roasted potatoes, sugared carrots, and buttery peas. Mr. Peter kindly heaped a good amount on Mairi's plate before filling his own. Likewise, Captain Sinclair moved to serve Louisa.

"Just potatoes if you please, Captain," she said.

"Does your stomach trouble you, Miss MacQuarie?" The concern in his voice pecked at her conscience. How could he be so kind to her after she'd given him such a difficult time?

"Only a little. No cause for concern, but thank you."

His eyes, the most sincere blue she'd ever seen, searched hers. *What is he looking for?* Was he assessing her health? Did he think he could discern another meaning behind her words? That old English proverb came to mind, "Thine eyes are a window to thy soul," and she tore her guilty gaze away lest he see what she would not admit to herself.

After a mercifully short pause, Mr. Peter and Mairi struck up a conversation in which Mr. Peter told the story of how the

Sinclairs of Balforss had acquired the *Gael Forss*. Originally a pirate ship, the crew had kidnapped the young woman betrothed to Captain Sinclair's cousin, Declan. Fortunately, the pirates' departure had been delayed by their own greed.

"Had they not stopped to steal Mr. Declan's whisky, we might never have gotten a chance to save Miss Caya," Mr. Peter said.

"Mr. Peter is too modest to tell you that, although he was only fourteen at the time, we owe our success entirely to his courage and cunning."

Throughout his tale, Mairi made gasps and sighs of awe and approval, which seemed to please Mr. Peter and spur him on. Louisa doubted any man was immune to Mairi's charms. Her friend had only to aim her wide, worshipful eyes at a fellow and she could bend him to her will. Her beauty had an additional benefit. It seemed to mask any gaffes in her use of etiquette or speech. After all, how could anyone question the rank of such an obviously charming woman?

"And you did battle with the pirates?" Mairi asked.

"Oh, aye, but they were no match for the Sinclairs. Laird John and his men are warriors, former soldiers blooded in battle, skilled swordsmen."

Reverend Wynterbottom lifted his head from his plate and proclaimed, "Lord, how long shall the wicked triumph? How long shall they utter and speak hard things? And all the workers of iniquity boast them—"

"Thank you, Reverend Wynterbottom," Captain Sinclair said, interrupting his recitation.

But the clergyman continued, his voice growing in volume with the tremolo of rage. "And he shall bring upon them their own iniquity, and shall cut them off in their own wickedness." He aimed his daggerlike glare at Mr. Peter. "Yea, the Lord our God shall cut them off."

"Enough," the captain shouted. "There is a time and

place for your sermon, Reverend, and you shall have it next Sabbath morn. Until then, I ask you to keep your preaching to yourself."

Wynterbottom sent his fork clattering to his plate and rose from the table. "Blasphemy," he roared, and stalked out of the captain's mess.

Though the light was dim, it was plain to Louisa that Mr. Peter's face had lost its usual florid color and had taken on an ashen hue at the clergyman's awful condemnation.

"Mr. Peter," the captain said. "You took one man's life that day, only one. The five lives you saved more than wash away that sin."

"Five?" Louisa blurted.

The captain flicked his gaze her way only for a moment before he returned to Mr. Peter. "We saved five kidnapped women from the hold of the *Tigress* that day, five women the pirate O'Malley had planned to sell God-knows-where for God-knows-what purpose. They owe their lives to a boy of fourteen, now a man, one I call brother."

The color returned to Mr. Peter's face and he gave the captain a crooked smile. "Thank you, sir."

After supper, Mr. Purdie and the captain excused themselves—Mr. Purdie to check on the helmsman and Captain Sinclair to his cabin. Mr. Peter offered to escort Louisa and Mairi below.

"You go on ahead," Louisa said. "I just remembered something I want to ask the captain."

• • •

Ian shut the door on his passengers, his ship, his world. He needed the quiet and order his cabin offered. He shrugged off his coat and tore open his neckcloth—both were suffocating him. Standing in front of the open transom window, he breathed in the sea air and, with more care, he unbuttoned his waistcoat and laid it over a chair.

A briny breeze caressed his neck like a woman's touch, and his shoulder muscles unclenched. He pulled the tie from his queue and let the air riffle through his hair. For the first time that day, he found some peace. The window was right over his berth. Bracing himself with both hands, he leaned against the sill and let his head dip to stretch the back of his neck, a sweet, welcome ache. The ladies had been fine company at supper, but that bloody dog-collar Reverend Wynterbottom had tried his patience thrice today. It was only going to get worse. He had best address it directly and soon. Tomorrow.

He answered the light rap on his cabin door. "Come!"

The door creaked open behind him. "Shut the door," he barked, assuming it was Peter come to have one more word. The door clicked shut. Ian gave his face a scrub with both hands, turned, and went perfectly still. "Miss MacQuarie."

"May I have a private word with you, Captain?"

All his senses went on high alert as if he had an intruder. Here. In his room. The captain's private quarters. And he wasn't dressed—well, not completely. What did she want, why was she here, and how fast could he get rid of her?

He made himself say, "Yes. Of course." He would have asked her to sit down, that would have been the polite thing to do, but then she might stay longer. Jee-*sus*. She was in his bedchamber, the place where he slept. He watched in horror as she stepped farther into the room, her gaze aimed at his bookshelf.

"You wanted to speak to me?" he prompted.

She reached for one of the books—*his* books. He tensed. His books were precious and he kept them in order, a system of his own making, very precise. Pulling a volume of Shakespeare from the shelf, she said, "*Twelfth Night*. It's my favorite." She opened the book and smiled at the pages as if the words pleased her. They had pleased him, too, but they were *his* words in *his* books and he rarely shared them. His fists clenched and unclenched, wanting to grab the volume from her hands.

"I've played the part of Viola, you know."

Viola? Of course, she played Viola. A woman who disguises herself as a man and causes major mayhem for everyone in the play. Just as she was doing now.

She aimed a disconcerting smile at him. Not the usual coy or flirtatious smile he received from ladies. In fact, her smile had nothing to do with him and everything to do with what she was holding in her hands—*his* book.

"It was at the Grass Market Theatre." She dipped her head. "It was only one performance. I replaced another actress." She lifted her face to appeal to him again. "But the director said I was quite good. Have you ever seen *Twelfth Night*? On the stage, I mean?"

"No," he said in a manner he hoped would convey that he did not wish to talk idly about Shakespeare and plays and stages.

She shut the book and replaced it on the shelf...*in the wrong spot.*

He lunged forward and reached over her head. "Not there," he said, taking the book from her hand. She backed away from the bookshelf, somewhat startled. "Sorry," he said. "It goes here. I have a system."

"A system?"

"Aye. A system."

She dipped her chin and cast him a suspicious sideways glance. "I see," she said and sidled toward his desk. *His desk.* Before he could steer her away, she picked up the leaded crystal paperweight in the shape of a selkie, the one his mam had given him, expensive and valuable and *his*. She tossed it from hand to hand testing its heft.

"That, that's…" he sputtered, and she set it down…*in the wrong place*. When her back was turned, he moved it to its rightful spot. No sooner done, she plucked a feather quill from the pen box and absently stroked the feather while she casually strolled about his room—*his* room—looking at *his* things. Was she doing this on purpose?

"Miss MacQuarie, please tell me what I can do for you."

She dropped the quill on the top of his chest of drawers, just dropped it there, and his eyes remained fixed on the pen, riveted on the quill lying where it should not be. The intense desire to put it back where it belonged made his teeth itch. He knew it made no sense, but he couldn't help himself. He kept his things in order. Everything had a place in his small cabin. Neat and tidy at all times.

She was talking to him but his focus was not on her words, as they should be, but on the feather quill. She'd come to his cabin to unearth his weakness. Having discovered it, she had begun her slow assault on his sanity.

"Captain Sinclair, did you hear what I said?"

"I beg your pardon?"

She examined him for an uncomfortably long time, then collected the quill off the chest of drawers and handed it to him.

"Thank you." He put it back into the pen box and the tension that had been balling into a fist between his shoulder blades released. He could breathe again. "Sorry. You were saying?"

"I came to apologize. We got off to a bad start today. I let my feelings rule my temper and, unfortunately, you bore the brunt of that. I realize now you were simply doing your job. So, I'm sorry." She clasped her hands together and the corners of her mouth curled into the most pleasing smile he'd ever seen.

He'd expected a lecture, or a complaint. At the very least, he'd anticipated a request for something impossible to provide. He hadn't expected her sweet apology, words spoken in a honeyed tone that melted over his head and slid down over his shoulders. His heart gradually slowed to an audible *thump* every fifteen seconds and he had to consciously drag in a lungful of air to say, "The fault was mine, I'm sure." The words came out of his mouth, but he didn't recognize them as his own. They sounded like some daft loon, not a grown man.

Miss MacQuarie's smile broadened, and her eyes half closed. "Well, you were rather demanding, but thank you. I accept your apology. Good night, Captain." And she was gone.

Ian fell back into his skin with a jolt. What had just happened?

The next thing he knew, Peter was at his side. "You all right, sir?"

He stabbed his finger in the direction of the door. "That, that, that woman, that MacQuarie person, she was in here, stormed through my room like a cyclone, leaving chaos and, and, and...whatnot in her wake. Apologizing and touching my things and..." He sat down hard in his chair. "Who *is* she?"

"Touched your things, did she?" Peter asked, grinning out of one side of his mouth.

Ian recognized that look. "Quiet or I'll kick your arse into next week."

Chapter Four

Who *was* he?

That's what Louisa kept asking herself on the way back to her cabin. Contrary to her earlier assessment, Captain Sinclair wasn't the arrogant bully who gratified himself by ordering about the occupants of this small ship. Men did that sort of thing. They liked establishing their personal empires where they were in complete charge. The more powerful the man, the larger his empire. Her father, for instance, commanded an entire division of the King's army. Lesser men lorded over the few people they employed. The powerless had only their wives and children to dominate. But the captain was something different.

A true tyrant would never have compromised his law. And yet he'd allowed her to remain above deck—for a short time and under his supervision, of course, but he had been sensitive to her discomfort. A true bully would never have stooped to defend Danny Sinkler. Yet Captain Sinclair had. Not only had he intervened, he had treated the lad with kindness, and he'd put that sour Reverend Wynterbottom in his place right quick.

The most recent business in his cabin had been puzzling. Louisa definitely got the feeling she'd caught the man unawares. He'd become particularly agitated when she'd touched or shifted items in his office. Odd for a man of power and grace to be so unsettled by little things like that.

His library pleased her, and she would have liked to have perused his collection further. She respected persons who appreciated the knowledge and entertainment books offered. She suspected he shared her love for theater, as well. He had several volumes of Shakespeare's plays. Perhaps if he showed her his "system" he might allow her the freedom to select a few books to read. Maybe he'd even spare the time to discuss the books. She'd like that.

Someone had left an oil lamp burning in the corridor to light her way back to her cabin. From behind his closed door, Reverend Wynterbottom's fervent whispers to God made her shiver. No doubt he was asking the Lord to smite his enemies for him, the awful man. Mairi had left their cabin door open. The soft glow of the lamplight within spilled into the corridor.

"There you are," Mairi said. She was already dressed in her nightgown and robe. Both articles were among the many items Louisa had selected from her own wardrobe to outfit Mairi. Once again, guilt struck Louisa squarely in the chest. What if Mr. Kirby was a tyrant? What if he was unkind to Mairi? Or worse, what if he was the sort that beat his wife?

"Is something wrong?" Mairi asked. "You looked flushed. Did Captain Sinclair say something to upset you?"

"No. I ken it was me that upset him."

"What, then?"

Louisa sat next to Mairi on her berth and took the embroidery hoop from her so that she could hold her hands. "You must promise to tell me if you have any qualms about Mr. Kirby. If you fear that he would mistreat you in any way, you must say something *before* you marry him. I willnae leave you with someone who would not treasure you. I couldnae live with myself if—"

"Dinnae be daft. Did you not read the letter Mr. Kirby sent?"

She had a vague recollection of a letter Da had included with his last message, but she'd been so distressed by the fact that he hadn't changed his mind and that he wasn't coming home to say goodbye, allowing her one last chance to appeal the life sentence he'd placed upon her, that she'd set aside the note from Mr. Kirby without reading it. "Nae. I didnae. Why?"

"I have it here." Mairi took the letter from her sewing box, the place where she kept a lock of her mother's hair and other things of sentimental value. She carefully unfolded it and held it out to Louisa. It had been sealed. Traces of the broken wax still clung to the parchment. With all that had passed, the letter somehow felt too personal for her to read, as though it had been intended for Mairi all along.

"No. You read it to me," Louisa said.

Mairi smiled down at the letter. "I ken he wrote it afore he knew for certain I was—you were—" She glanced up at Louisa, searching for the right way to explain it.

"Go on," Louisa said. "The letter is for his intended. That's you."

A look of gratitude passed over Mairi. She read:

"Dear Miss Robertson,

The general has given me reason to hope that you might consider my offer of marriage. You may think it unusual that I would offer for your hand without ever having the pleasure of making your acquaintance, but I feel as if I know you well.

I have the distinct honor of calling your brother Nathan my friend. As schoolmates do, he often related stories of his family. It was with particular fondness he spoke of his beloved sister, her beauty, her kind heart, and her sweet nature. I decided that one day I should like to marry a lass such as that.

Years later, I have yet to meet another who compares. And so, with your father's consent, I make my offer to you. Come to America and I pledge you my troth, I will make it my life's work to see that you never regret choosing me.

Awaiting your kind reply, Mr. Edward R. Kirby"

Mairi sniffed and wiped her cheek, Mr. Kirby's words having obviously moved her to tears. Though he seemed sincere and his sentiments genuine, the letter did not have a similar effect on Louisa. On the whole, the message reinforced her determination to avoid marriage altogether. Kind heart and sweet nature? Her brother Nathan had never referred to her as anything but a bothersome addlepate. What stories had Nathan dreamed up to tell his friends?

"It's romantic, is it not?" Mairi said.

"Aye. Very romantic," Louisa lied. More like idiotic. Then again, maybe not. Louisa may not resemble anything like what Edward Kirby imagined, but Mairi did. Mairi *was* kind and sweet and beautiful. She was all those things and more. Fine then. She wouldn't feel guilty about her decision. She'd chosen to do the right thing, even if she'd made that decision for selfish reasons.

Mairi refolded the letter and held it to her heart. "I think I will love him," she said more like a prayer to God than to anyone in particular.

On impulse, Louisa said, "Let's hope he doesnae resemble a toad."

Mairi snapped out of her trance. "Oh no. He sent me—you—this." She took a painted miniature framed in gold from her sewing box. A somber-looking man with regular features and light brown hair cut in the shorter fashion gazed directly back at Louisa. "You see? He's quite handsome." Mairi stroked a finger lightly over his painted hair. "And Mr.

Nathan says he's a fine-looking gentleman, tall and well-set."

"When did you speak to Nathan?" She didn't think her brother had been to the house since before the general had informed her about the marriage contracts.

Mairi's eyebrows drew together. "I cannae remember. You werenae home when he visited."

"Why did you no' tell me?" Louisa asked, unable to disguise her surprise and irritation.

"I thought I had. Sorry. If you'll recall," Mairi said, equally irritated, "I had much on my mind with packing us both to go to America and practicing to be someone I was not, plus all my regular chores on top of that. It must have slipped my mind."

"Well, did he say why he visited?"

Mairi's eyes slid to the right as if trying to recall. "Nae. He didnae say. He seemed sorry about something. Sad even. He asked were you angry about having to go to America and I said you didnae mind. It was the marrying part you didnae like and he said not to fash because Mr. Kirby was a good man. 'A perfectly creditable fellow,' he said. And I asked was he handsome and that's when he said he was a fine-looking gentleman."

Nathan had come to say goodbye, after all. "What put you in mind that he was sad?"

"Dunno. He had that look in those green eyes of his— you ken the one—like someone shot his dog."

Louisa's smiled and swallowed a lump in her throat. Maybe her big brother did care about her. Just a little.

. . .

Ian was a soldier. He'd trained himself to wake alert and ready at the first sound of alarm and to sleep when it was time to sleep. But he'd lain awake for hours pondering the whirling dervish that had upended his thoughts. The part of his brain that was in charge of rational thinking seemed to have shrunk to the size of a pea, leaving only the ever-swelling irrational, obsessive portion of his brain with which to puzzle out his opinion of Miss MacQuarie.

If she hadn't entered his room whilst he was distracted, if she hadn't moved his personal possessions, if she hadn't smelled like lavender, if she didn't have those damn fiery green eyes, then maybe, *maybe* he wouldn't have noticed her pink lips, or her shiny hair, or her bosom. God, those breasts. How cruel to keep them all bound up in that corseting when they should be free to bounce about.

Bloody buggering bollocks. *Stop. Just frigging stop.*

Ship's bell rang twice, then once. Christ. Half one in the morning. He threw the sheet aside and pushed out of bed. If he couldn't sleep, he might as well make a circuit around the deck. Perhaps the fresh air might clear his mind of her and allow him a few hours of rest before dawn.

Ian pulled on trousers and buttoned the fall. He collected yesterday's shirt, sniffed the oxters, and fought his way into it. He didn't bother with boots or a coat. No one but the night crew and the stars would see him. The stars didn't care and his crew were a forgiving lot.

He stooped through his cabin door, and stepped out on the deck. Ocean spray misted over him, as he arched his back and stretched his face upward. The moon hid behind streaks of benign-looking clouds. Good. No sign of bad weather. The deck was dark but for the navigation lamps. A few shadows moved about, the night crew keeping watch.

"Trouble sleeping?"

Ian spun around and exhaled relief when he recognized the outline of Mr. Purdie's compact frame at the ship's wheel.

"Aye. You?"

"Will came to my cabin, said a crew member reported a

ghost prowling the quarterdeck. I came topside to see what's what." Whatever the man meant to investigate must be worth noting. Mr. Purdie had just strung together more words all at once than in the entire time Ian had known the man.

"And what did ye find?"

Mr. Purdie jerked his head toward the steps leading to the quarterdeck as if to say, *See for yourself.*

Ian cautiously crept up the stairs until the quarterdeck was at eye level. A slight figure leaned against the ship's railing, loose hair and long robes floating in the sea breeze. He crested the quarterdeck and strode toward the lass. She turned a startled look his way, eyes so wide he could see their whites. The one thing he'd been trying to escape was standing before him.

He should be angry. Instead he experienced a gush of pleasure as if he'd just come across some rare treasure he could claim as his own. Her name rushed out of his lungs in a whisper. "Miss MacQuarie."

She hugged her long dressing robe around her middle. "If I could stay here just until sunrise, I would be much obliged, Captain." Her voice shook in a way that made him ache to calm her. "I willnae get in anyone's way. I promise."

"Were you frightened?" If that bampot clergyman gave her a difficult time he'd—

"No," she was quick to answer, then made a little huffing sound. "Yes. Sort of. Small spaces, em, bother me." He could tell by the tone of her voice it had been difficult to reveal this weakness. Now that the secret was out, the floodgates opened and she rushed to tell the rest. "It's the cabin, you see. It's smaller than I had anticipated. And darker. At night, the walls and the ceiling close in on me and my heart starts to beating and I cannae control my breathing and I needed to be where I can see the sky."

"It's all right, Miss MacQuarie."

"I ken it makes no sense—"

"Nae. I understand. Better than you may think." Though why anyone afraid of confined spaces would embark on a voyage across the Atlantic Ocean was beyond him. "I'll allow it, but only temporarily until I can find another solution. You cannae spend every night for the next month and a half prowling the quarterdeck. You're making the crew nervous."

"Sorry."

"I'll bide with you until dawn."

"That's hours away. I dinnae want to keep you awake. That'll make you more crabbit than you already are."

Ian resisted the urge to laugh. How did this slip of a girl make him lose track of himself so easily? "I cannae sleep anyway. If ye dinnae mind, I'll sit wi' ye." There was just enough room for them to settle back to back on the skylight cover without touching. Some vestige of civility embedded in him by his mam, no doubt, made him ask, "Are you warm enough?"

"Oh, aye. It's a lovely evening."

The wind picked up slightly and tossed a lock of her hair across his cheek. Rather than follow his boyish impulse to pull the silky tress, he closed his eyes and allowed it to linger there, tickling him under his nose, and teasing his lips.

"You have an interesting collection of books, Captain Sinclair."

"I like to read. It relaxes me."

"I do, too. What kind of books do you like?"

"I enjoy Robert Southey's poetry and biographies. Walter Scott, of course. I read *Ivanhoe* to the crew the last time we crossed the Atlantic."

She swiveled around. "You read to the crew?"

He shifted to meet her question and they were sitting side by side, shoulder brushing shoulder. "Aye. They enjoy good stories." He saw the white flash of her smile. "Does it surprise you?"

"A little—oh!" A gust of wind from the south whirled her hair into a tornado of wavy locks. She gathered them together and tamed them into a braid as she spoke. "Ye seem so..." She shrugged her shoulders. "Regimental."

He couldn't tell if she meant it as a compliment or a criticism. "Aye, well, I suppose that's owing to the fact that I am—or I was—a soldier." He was going to tell her about the commission the general promised when something on the deck floor distracted her. "What is it?"

"Good Lord, you have the biggest feet I've ever seen."

Only then did he remember he'd left his boots and coat in his cabin. *Shite.* "I didnae expect to find a lady on deck at this hour, did I? You keep catching me in various states of undress. I'd hate to guess how you'll find me next."

Miss MacQuarie gave a sudden burst of laughter, which seemed to startle her. She clapped both hands over her mouth. Still, her shoulders bounced up and down. God, he remembered this feeling from when he was a lad. Making a girl giggle felt so good, so right. Like he was taller, stronger, and smarter than he really was. He hadn't made a lassie laugh like this in years.

Miss MacQuarie sobered. "I wasnae laughing at you, Captain."

"I know.

They were quiet for a few minutes. Then she asked, "Where are we?"

He inhaled and leaned his elbows on his knees. Odd to feel this relaxed with a relative stranger, and a woman, no less. "Aboot a mile and a half off the east coast of England, I ken. We'll pass the southern tip of Cornwall in another few days. After that, we sail south, well away from the coast of France and Spain. There's no' as many pirates as there once were, but I dinnae want to take chances. Then we'll catch the Canary Current southwest, down the coast of Northern Africa and wait for the trade winds to take us west."

"Pirates?" she asked with undisguised alarm.

"Dinnae fash. We've an experienced crew, we're well armed, and the *Gael Forss* is a swift and nimble ship. We've never had trouble before. Still, we're prepared for anything."

There was another long silence between them, an easy one. He looked down at his big, bony feet glowing like phosphorus in the night. He was barefoot, sitting shoulder to shoulder with a woman in her sleeping attire. Reports of his outrageous behavior would reach every crew member by breakfast. And he didn't frigging care.

"If I learned your system, could I borrow books from your library?"

"You can borrow a book anytime you like. You dinnae have to learn my system."

"How does it work?"

"Simple. I have a shelf for poetry, one for biographies, one for fiction, and a shelf for references. The first three are arranged alphabetically by the author's last name, and the references are arranged by subject."

"Very smart and sensible."

"I think so." He scratched the back of his neck. "Would you feel comfortable in the room where we dine? You could choose a book to read by lamplight at the dining table and I'll get you some tea, if you like."

She tipped her head to the side at a charming angle. "Do you have any brandy?"

He led Miss MacQuarie down the steps, into the captain's mess, and lit an oil lamp. "Have a seat. I'll fetch a book and a brandy for you. I'd let you choose but it might look bad," he said, stumbling and stuttering over his words. "You entering my cabin at this hour and—and in your—your—" He gestured to her robe.

"I understand."

He started out the door and paused. "Any requests?"

"I would like you to choose something for me, please."

Ian stopped breathing. On the surface, her request was innocuous. Select a book for her to read. Pull from his shelf an interesting one and hand it to her. Anyone else would perform this task in less than a minute with little thought and even less effort. But to Ian, she might as well have asked him to take her to his bed. She'd asked him to choose a book *for* her. It was, for him, a more intimate gesture than any act of lovemaking.

His mouth flooded with saliva at the thought of Miss MacQuarie in his bed and he swallowed to keep from drooling. "Yes. Of course."

Ian flung himself into his cabin and caught his breath. Jee-*sus*. What the bloody hell was wrong with him? It took him twice as long as usual to light his oil lamp because his hands were shaking. Once lit, he held the lamp up to his shelves. What would she like? Poetry? Biography? A novel, perhaps? Whatever he gave to her, whichever book he chose, she would be reading the same words he'd read and she'd know that. What would she think? He had to be careful with his decision. She may take the words in the book as a message, misconstrue them, interpret them to mean more than what he—bloody hell. Had he lost his mind?

She just wants a book to read, ye loon.

He set down the lamp and poured two brandies. He drank his, and poured himself a second, and a third. Fortified, he returned to the task at hand. The histories, no. Nothing in the law or philosophy section. Skip the reference shelf altogether. He swept past the volumes written in Latin and in French. Chaucer, God, no. Tragedy? *Romeo and Jul*—hell no. Comedy-comedy-comedy. Farquhar? George Farquhar. Yes. She's an actress. She would like a play. *The Beaux' Strategem*, of course.

"Captain?"

He jumped at her voice. She was at his door. Again. He wanted to shout, *Dinnae come in.* Too late, plague take her.

"I thought you'd forgotten me." She took the book from his hand and held it to the lamp to read the title. "*The Taming of the Shrew.* Shakespeare. I've never read this one."

What? How did that—

She beamed her brilliant smile at him and his knees threatened to buckle. "This is perfect. Thank you." And she was gone.

The Taming of the— Bloody hell. That play was filled with bawdy jokes and risqué talk. And would she think he thought of her as a shrew? But it was too late to tell her it was a mistake.

He poured himself another brandy.

Bloody buggering hell. What would she think of him? And what would she think he thought of her?

• • •

Louisa sat at the dining table with a lamp, a book, a wee glass, and the bottle of brandy Captain Sinclair had left her. She read the fly page out loud, "*The Taming of the Shrew.*" A tiny flutter stirred just below her ribs. She'd heard of this one and had wanted to read it, but never had an opportunity. She had half expected Captain Sinclair to choose some moldy old play by Farquhar. After all, how many times can one read *The Beaux' Strategem*? But this play was different. Charming and refreshing. How had he known she would like this play?

She sipped the heady brandy, the fiery sensation in her throat lessening with each swallow. Captain Sinclair was a curious fellow. Tall and rakishly handsome, but his personality didn't match his outward appearance at all.

He was so particular, so serious. She'd seen him give an affectionate smile to Mr. Peter. And, of course, he had used his "pleased to meet you" smile on her and Mairi, but she hadn't seen him really laugh. Not even a grin.

Very well. Before this voyage was complete, she would see Captain Sinclair laugh. Even if she had to stand on her head to do it, she would make him laugh. Laugh until his teeth rattled. What would make the oh-so-serious Captain Sinclair laugh? Perhaps the answer was in this play. The tiny words began to swim around on the page. The volume had been published long ago and though it had been gently handled, the yellowing paper showed its age.

Captain Sinclair had left the aft window open a crack. He'd left the door to the captain's mess tied open, as well. Just knowing she wasn't completely enclosed eased her irrational fear of being trapped. What was it he'd said when she'd tried to explain? *I understand…better than you may think.*

Louisa yawned so wide her jaw cracked. She should close her eyes, just for a little while. Give them a rest and then continue reading until right before dawn when she'd slip below to her cabin without being seen. That's what she'd promised Captain Sinclair. And he had said, *Good night, Miss MacQuarie.* Captain Sinclair had a very nice voice. Not too high. Not too low. Soft and rumbly. She would like to hear him read to the crew. She yawned again and, folding her arms on the table, rested her head in the crook of her arm to think. What would she like to hear Captain Sinclair read aloud in his rumbly-just-right voice?

"Miss? Miss?"

Louisa lifted her head and wiped the damp from the side of her mouth. It was daylight. *Bonnets.* She'd fallen asleep and drooled.

Will stood before her peering down into her eyes. "Are you all right, miss?"

"I'm fine." She got up and bustled toward the door, stopped, collected *The Taming of the Shrew*, and hurried out...smack into Captain Sinclair.

He made an exclamation of surprise that sounded like, "*Ooof.*"

"Sorry." The deck was littered with crew members all staring at her as if she'd grown horns. Had she? She scrambled down the stairs to the lower deck, a trail of laughter following her. How embarrassing.

Just her luck, the awful Reverend Wynterbottom was coming out of his cabin. "Devil take you, girl," he growled, as she fled past him. Apparently, she *had* grown horns. Oh, if only a big wave would wash the bloody clergyman away, this voyage would be much improved. God forgive her for thinking such a dreadful thought.

Inside her cabin, Mairi was just waking. She sat up in bed rubbing her eyes, her night cap askew. "Were you in the privy?"

"Em, no. I was..." Her chance for sneaking back to her cabin unnoticed had come and gone. She'd slept through it. Louisa had no other alternative but to tell Mairi everything. Well, almost everything. She would save the bit about his naked feet to herself. Surprisingly arousing, those feet. Of course, she'd seen a man's naked feet before, but they were her brothers' and those didn't count.

Louisa also didn't mention wondering what he would look like had he forgotten his shirt. The light in the captain's mess was rather dim, but she had seen how the soft fabric of his shirt molded to his muscled chest. And she would bet a guinea he hadn't worn his smalls underneath his shirt and trousers because she could clearly make out the dark brown disks of his nipples through the fabric.

Mairi leaned close and whispered, "Did he kiss you?"

Louisa acted shocked and appalled by the question when, in fact, she had been thinking about kissing Captain Sinclair herself. "Of course not. The captain is a gentleman—"

"A very handsome gentleman," Mairi said, and poked her in the ribs.

"Stop that right now. I dinnae want to hear any more about Captain Sinclair and his handsomeness. I've had quite enough. And you ought to stop your saucy behavior."

"And you ought to start your saucy behavior." Mairi stepped into her day dress.

"What do you mean?"

"You're me—I mean to say, you're not you. You're free of your da's prim and proper expec...expec..."

"Expectations?"

"Aye, expectations. You can flirt with whomever ye like. Kiss whomever you like. If the captain fancies you, and I ken he does, there's naught to stop you from enjoying his attentions." Mairi finished tying the closures of her gown.

"You're being ridiculous. And besides, he's not..." She searched for a word but didn't find one. "He's not *doing* anything. There's no attention to be enjoyed. He's simply being...accommodating."

"Is that what they're calling it now?"

"Stop baiting me or I will sit on you. And stop your laughing right now."

For the next three nights, Captain Sinclair left brandy and a lamp burning in the dining room. When the walls began to close in on Louisa, she would quietly make her way to the mess with her book. She was careful not to fall asleep again and always made it back to her cabin before dawn.

During the day, she took catnaps, wrote in her diary, took in some air after each meal, and played cards with Mairi. She saw very little of Captain Sinclair and spoke to him not at all. Which was, of course, a minor disappointment as she had wanted an opportunity to make him laugh.

On the fifth night of their journey, she discovered Captain Sinclair seated at the dining table when she entered the captain's mess.

He bolted to his feet. "Evening, Miss MacQuarie."

"Good evening, Captain. This is a pleasant surprise."

"Aye, well, I've been thinking about how small spaces bother you." He held his neckcloth in his hand as though he'd just removed it. She chanced a look at his feet. *Bonnets.* He'd worn his boots. But he had left his coat behind and he did look a braw sight in the white shirt with his collar open. Captain Sinclair fidgeted. She wanted to tell him to be at ease but thought it might make him even more nervous.

"You recall, that first night, I told you I'd try and think of a solution?"

"Aye."

"I have an idea. It's an experiment I'd like to try—if you're willing." Her heart twisted around inside her chest. This somber man, who barely knew her, was trying hard to help her. She would have explained that there was nothing to be done, her da had tried all sorts of remedies, nothing had ever worked, but she didn't want to disappoint him.

"Do you trust me?" he asked.

Did she trust him? She trusted him to carry her safely to America, how much more trust did he need? It was herself she didn't trust. Alone with this tall, graceful, powerful man, she might do something embarrassing like throw herself at him, or beg him to kiss her, or ask him to remove his shirt, please.

"Yes. I trust you completely."

. . .

She trusted him. More fool, her. If she'd known what indecent thoughts were going through his mind at the moment—every moment for the last five days, she would keep as far away from him as possible.

"Good. Leave the book here and follow me," he said, before he changed his mind. Before she changed *her* mind. He led the way out onto the deck. The wind had picked up. According to Mr. Purdie, they were headed into a storm tonight, hence the urgency for him to find a solution to Miss MacQuarie's issue.

"Where are we going?" she asked, her voice loud enough to be heard over the snapping, creaking racket the rigging was making.

"To the fo'c'sle—the housing at the bow of the ship," he shouted. Halfway down the gangway, the ship pitched forward into the trough of a rolling wave. Unprepared, Miss MacQuarie stumbled into him just as a wave crashed over the bow, sending spray onto the deck. He hunched over her body to protect her from the worst of it. The storm was approaching faster than he'd anticipated.

"Quick. Take my hand. We need to get under cover."

She slipped her fluttering hand into his big rough paw. It was like holding a live bird, so delicate, so fragile, her palms smooth like fine satin. Jee-*sus*, what would they feel like on other parts of his body?

When they reached the fo'c'sle, he coaxed her into the open portal, a covered corridor too short for him to stand upright, at the end of which were two doors. One to Mr. Purdie's cabin and the other to the surgery.

"Are you ready, Miss MacQuarie?"

"Yes."

He held up his neckcloth. "I'm going to blindfold you."

"Why?"

"Do you trust me?" he asked again.

They stood together in that cramped corridor. She'd placed a hand on the wall behind her to brace herself from being tossed about by the ship's movement. Face turned up to his, her eyes searching, she said. "Yes. I trust you."

"Turn around."

At his command, she turned away, both hands on the wall. He slipped his neckcloth around her head, covering her eyes like a game of blind man's buff. He tied it tight enough that it wouldn't slip off. She touched it, adjusted it for comfort. "All right?"

She nodded.

Ian leaned down to her ear. "Let me lead you." He opened the door to the surgery and guided her inside the tiny windowless space. "I'll be with you the entire time. I'll not allow anything to happen to you." He pushed the door shut and the latch clicked.

Miss MacQuarie spun around. Her once-calm demeanor instantly became panicked with the sound of the latch. Her breathing turned to panting. Though it was pitch black in the closet-sized room, he was close enough to sense her reaching for the blindfold and he stilled her arms.

"Easy," he said. "I'm here and nothing can harm us."

"The door, is it locked? Can you open it?"

"It's not locked. I can open it at any time. We can come and go as we please. I keep it closed to keep out the storm." And to have you all to myself, he thought, and felt his trousers tighten around his privates.

"Where are we? What is this room?" Her voice, her entire body was lit up with fear. He could feel the heat coming off her. He knew that kind of fear, the kind that seized upon your mind, convinced an otherwise rational being that he would die, soon, and badly.

He held her shoulders, his grip gentle yet firm. "You cannae see the room, so I will describe it to you and you can imagine it in your mind's eye."

She continued to pant. "I ken we should stop the game now," she pleaded.

"It's a big room," he said. "Filled with light."

"No. No, I can tell by the sound. It's too small. I cannae breathe. My heart, my heart."

This skittish mare was going to bolt. He leaned closer to her ear. "Nae. The room is as big as a ballroom and lit with a hundred candles. Can you no' see it, lass?"

He'd thought of the blindfold this morning when he'd recalled how she reacted when she'd boarded. She'd reminded him of a panicked horse about to kick its way out of its stall. They blindfolded horses to keep them calm. Perhaps the method would work on this filly. He sensed a change in her breathing. Was it working?

"Have you never been to a ball, lass?"

"Of course," she panted. "Of course, I have." She caught her breath again. "I've been to many balls."

"Then you ken what it looks like. Can ye hear the music, too? Can you hear them playing…what is that? A waltz?" He hummed a waltz he remembered from a time so long ago, it hardly seemed like his own life.

She made a little puff of amusement. He supposed he was behaving foolishly, but he had gotten her mind off the thing that plagued her.

"Are you laughing at my singing?"

"No." She made a nervous titter. "Yes."

He felt a surge of gratification. His method was working.

"Dance with me," he said, and took her in an embrace.

Catching her unprepared, she sucked in a great gulp of

air. He continued humming, sounding nothing like the tune in his head and everything like what a lunatic might drone. Her body continued to shiver, but she settled her arm on his shoulder, slipped that silky birdlike hand in his and let him sway her from side to side. Thank God he had good sea legs because the ship's pitch and yaw did not match the rhythm of a waltz.

They couldn't *really* dance. The room was barely large enough for two people. Cupboards on one side for equipment and supplies. A surgical table secured to the wall on the other.

"Is there a storm?" she asked.

"I only hear music," he said, drawing another laugh out of her.

After another few bars of his abysmal humming she said, "You're thinking. What are you thinking about?"

"I was remembering the last time I waltzed. It was five years ago, the first time we sailed the *Gael Forss* to England. We carried goods to sell, but the real reason for the trip was to take my brother Alex's family to visit his wife's father, the Duke of Chatham."

"Your brother is married to the daughter of a duke?" she said incredulously.

"Aye." As she grew warmer in his embrace, her perfume, a light scent of lavender, filled his nose.

"Did she teach you to waltz?"

"Nae. It was her brother, the duke's son, Bulford, who taught us all—me and Alex and Peter and Magnus. On the surface, Bulford is like most English nobility. Fopdoodles, Magnus calls them. But in the end, Bull turned out to be a surprisingly good fellow, in spite of his silly beaver hat and ruffled cravat."

"Who is Magnus?" He felt her breath tickle his neck and adjusted his hold on her, drawing her closer, dangerously close to his hardened body.

"My cousin. There are five of us who own the *Gael Forss*. Cousins Magnus and Declan, my brother Alex, me, and Mr. Peter."

"Is he a cousin, too?"

He dipped his head next to hers so that they whispered into each other's ears like lovers. "Nae. He was my da's groom, but as I told you, he's the reason we acquired the ship."

"And you all live in Edinburgh?"

"Och, nae. My da is Laird of Balforss. We live in Caithness on the northern coast of Scotland. Have you ever been there?"

"Nae. What's it like?"

He inhaled a deep, shuddering breath. "Caithness is a wild place with wide flat moors filled with red deer and grouse. My three times great-grandsire, James Sinclair, built Balforss House of stone and wood and…love. You can feel them when the house is quiet, my ancestors, brave men and women." He smiled. "The River Forss runs through our property and at night, with the windows open, the falls sing you to sleep. To the west, mountains separate us from Sutherland, not the most neighborly folk, but they're Highlanders like us. From the coastal cliffs of Balforss you can see the Orkney Isles like huge green rocks floating in the sea. Just about any time of the year, you'll find sea otters and gray seals frolicking about just off the shore and along the shingle beach."

"You miss it," she said.

"Aye. Every day." He pulled her even closer and breathed her in.

• • •

Louisa had waltzed before. Gentlemen had held her with gloved hands at arms' length from their bodies and she'd been swept around ballrooms at a dizzying pace, but this was altogether different. This was more like a lover's embrace. He held her close, so close her chest brushed lightly against his. Without his coat, the warmth of his body seeped through his light linen shirt. His shoulder muscles flexed and rolled under her left arm, and their hands, their bare hands, fit together as if they were made for each other.

He spoke softly into her ear, that rumbly just-right tone that made her insides stir. His breath riffled her hair and bathed her ear in heat. Something at the bottom of her belly, even lower, awakened like a flower opening to the sun. Now. Now would be the perfect time for her first kiss. And his were the perfect lips, those full, strong lips that never smiled.

Please, please. Kiss me now.

He pulled his head back and she floated to her tiptoes, waiting, waiting for him to kiss her.

"Miss MacQuarie," he whispered.

"Yes."

"Are you quite at ease?"

"Yes."

"Do you think you are ready to take the blindfold off?"

She lowered her heels to the ground and the ballroom he had created in her mind dissolved. What she thought were violins was really the high-pitched howl of the wind. The sickly sensation of the ship tossing up and down on the ocean tugged at her insides making her queasy. She let go of his hand and backed out of his embrace. The shock of fetching up against something hard made her heart leap.

Louisa tore off the blindfold and blinked. "Where's the light?" Her voice bounced around the tiny cell.

Something touched her, tried to grab her. It said something.

"The door. Open the door," she said.

It said something again, but she couldn't make sense of it. She flung her arms out searching, clawing aside the bulk that stood in her way. "I have to get out. Let me out."

Hitting a solid surface, she searched for a handle, a latch, anything to get out.

"Miss MacQuarie, no!"

Louisa flung open the door and staggered out into black wind, sea spray, and the shouts of men. The thing that had kept her in the small space grabbed at her again. She twisted out of its grip and ran into a wall of water that sent her sprawling face first onto the deck. She coughed up seawater, gasped, and scrabbled to her feet again only to be violently swept sideways into something hard. The dark thing grabbed hold of her and lifted her into the air. The sudden change made her dizzy. Lightheaded.

Louisa opened her eyes to blurry lamplight and Mairi patting her cheek. "Miss. Miss. Wake up, please."

She was lying in her cabin below deck soaking wet. "How did I get here?"

"The captain." Mairi moved aside, revealing Captain Sinclair, also soaked to the bone, standing in her doorway.

"Are you all right, Miss MacQuarie?" he asked.

There was a ringing in her ears that nearly drowned out the storm raging outside. She touched her head gingerly.

"You hit your head on the mizzenmast. It's my fault. I'm sorry."

With his dark hair plastered to his head, ringlets lashing his cheeks, and water dripping from his nose, he looked worse than she felt. She managed a reassuring smile for him. "It's all right, Captain. I'll no' be going above deck in a storm again."

He blew out a breath and, without looking directly at her, said, "Good. Get some sleep and I'll…I'll check on you in the morning." He shut the door behind him gently.

"Poor man. You must have given him a fright." Mairi helped peel off her wet clothes.

While she did so, Louisa wondered if someone was peeling Captain Sinclair's clothes off. "I don't remember how I got to the cabin."

"The captain carried you." Mairi dropped the last sodden stocking in the hamper. She handed Louisa her night rail with a yawn. "Put this on and sit. I'll comb your hair." Louisa gave a weak protest then sat and gratefully allowed Mairi to remove what pins still clung to the mess, now looking and smelling like seaweed, no doubt. "Whatever were you doing out on deck in the storm?" Mairi asked.

"The captain tried to cure me." The brush caught on a tangle. "Ow."

"Sorry. Cure you of what?"

"The problem I have with small places."

"How?"

Louisa smiled. "He took me dancing."

. . .

Idiot. Ian banged his head against the inside of his cabin door two more times as if he could take away her pain by inflicting his own. Jee-*sus.* She could have been swept over the side. He'd heard stories of the sea taking men twice her size into the deep. Why couldn't he have left well enough alone? His experiment was working. He'd had her calm, completely at ease, but oh, no. He had to push it, had to make her take off the blindfold.

Of course, she bolted, ye clot-heid. She's a woman, not a damned horse.

He shivered in his cabin, seawater puddling on the floor. When he attempted to pull the soggy shirt over his head it stuck to his skin. After several tries, he ripped open the front and tore it off his body. More stupidity, but it appeased him. Momentarily. His boots were another matter. They refused to budge, held to his feet with suction. Fine then. He'd sleep in his wet trousers and boots, die of pneumonia for all he cared.

He flopped back onto his berth. The scene on the darkened deck kept running through his mind—the black wave, her head, the mast—all connecting, all at once, all just out of his reach. A lightning bolt of fear had lanced through his heart the moment she'd fallen, sapping him of what strength he possessed. It was a wonder he managed to collect her from the deck and carry her to her cabin.

He held up his hands. They were shaking. *Get control of yourself, man.*

The pain throbbed with his pulse, hammering from the inside of his skull, right behind his eyes which were shut tight at the moment because the spiteful sun was trying to get inside his head and burn his brain. It was the kind of migraine he had frequently experienced after Quatre Bras, the kind that crippled him for days on end. Nothing would give him relief. No amount of alcohol or willow-frigging-bark tea would shake it. Only time. Time and suffering.

He hadn't had one this vicious for years. He'd thought they'd gone away forever. Apparently, they simply stockpiled venom and waited until the most inopportune time to strike.

"Sir?" Peter said, his voice barely above a whisper. "Is it the migraine, again?"

Shite. It hurt too much to answer him.

A knife shot up the back of his neck directly through the top of his head when he tried to nod. The pitch and roll of the ship added to his nausea. Death might be a better alternative.

Peter covered the cabin window with a blanket and set a

bin beside his berth. Ian was known to vomit when stricken with a blinding headache. "I'll get Turk to look in on you after breakfast."

Turk served as cook and surgeon aboard the *Gael Forss*. He was an excellent cook and a good enough surgeon, but aside from cracking open Ian's skull and allowing his brains to seep out, there would be nothing the man could do for him. Ian's objection came out as an inarticulate grunt. Too late. Peter had already left him to his misery.

The rest of the day he spent in a kind of delirium. Peter and Turk made visits to his bedside dressed as a golden retriever and a giant walking turtle respectively. Turk got him to swallow some vile concoction that made him vomit so hard he thought he'd started bleeding from his eyes. It was only tears, Peter reassured him. They managed to remove his boots and trousers with no help from him.

Twice he thought he heard her outside his door, the green-eyed voice with the breasts that should be freed of their corseting. The lady with the lavender body whom he would like to play like a drum, hard and fast. When he pictured her, the monster pulled away from the shore, revealing her lying naked on the beach like a selkie.

"The captain cannae see anyone today," Peter said in a hushed voice.

The migraine came rushing back like the tide. Someone made a bleating sound. To his eternal shame, it came from him.

Minutes later, hours later, seconds later—what did it matter—he heard Green Eyes talking again. She was arguing with Peter, the feisty wee bizzum. The door opened allowing the evil daylight inside his cabin. With it came swishing petticoats.

"Miss, I dinnae think—"

"It's all right, Mr. Peter. I have experience with this. You can go now. I'll call out if I need you."

The door clicked shut leaving them in blessed lavender

darkness. She was at his bedside, her skirts brushing his shoulder—his bare shoulder. Shite, he was naked, covered only by a blanket. He was, of course, very little threat to her in this state, but she shouldn't see him like this, weak and crippled, struck down by a stupid headache. "No. Go away," he rasped, his throat raw from vomiting.

"Captain Sinclair," she said in a low voice. "I'm going to help you to sit up just a little so you can lay your head in my lap."

Lay my what in her what?

She slipped her hands, her silky-smooth birdlike hands behind his neck and shoulders and pulled him up. The room tilted. He hoped he wouldn't fall out of his berth. More delicious rustling sounds. If he was not mistaken, she was sitting where his pillow was. Or maybe he was just delusional.

"You can lie back down now," she said and cradled his head until it reached her plush lap. With the change in position came another angry wave of pain. He pressed his mouth shut to keep from whimpering like a baby. She should go. She shouldn't see him like this.

The lavender lady brushed his hair away from his face and if his hair didn't hurt so much, he would have enjoyed the feeling. A moment later, fingertips as soft and cool as rose petals made slow, seductive circles at the sides of his forehead. Light, swirling, sensuous circles—had anyone ever touched him there? On his temples? Did people know how wondrous it felt to have one's temples stroked?

"Breathe," she said. "Just breathe." Her fingertips glided over his forehead, met in the middle and smoothed a cool path down the bridge of his nose, circled around his eyes and paused at the top of the orbit. She gently pressed and as she did, the evil ache behind his eyes eased up. He released an involuntary sigh. "That's it," she said, and repeated the process starting with the swirls on his temples. She did this over and over again until his face muscles loosened and slid off his head.

Next, she reached her deceptively strong hands under his stiff neck, alternately kneading it into the consistency of bread dough, and sinking her fingers into his bunched shoulder muscles eliciting more pain—not the torturous, punishing kind but the good kind, the healing kind.

"Breathe," she said.

He did. He'd do anything she asked of him for the migraine was in retreat. Like a good soldier, she had marched into his cabin, planted her flag, and begun her attack on the enemy.

After the long battle, she asked, "Better?"

"You're winning," he said drunkenly. She raked her fingernails across his scalp, a glorious feeling. A feeling so sensual that if she kept it up, other things would go up.

"How did you know how to—oh, God, that is heaven."

She chuckled. "My gran would have spells. This always worked for her. I thought it would help you, too."

"It did."

"Do you think you can sleep now?"

"Aye."

She cradled his head again and slipped out from under him. As she withdrew her hands, he took hold of one and kissed it. It was a crazy, impulsive thing to do, something a loon would try with a lass. "Thanks," he said.

"I was only returning the favor."

Feeling reckless, he ventured a joke. He lifted his blanket just enough to peer down at himself. "You caught me completely undressed this time. Do you do it on purpose?"

He made her laugh. Christ, he'd begged for death this morning and now he was flirting with a pretty lass. A miracle.

"You're smiling," she said.

He was. He must look a complete fool and yet, oddly, he didn't care. He'd made her laugh and he felt good. That was all that mattered.

Chapter Five

Louisa hurried back to her cabin, not wanting anyone to see the triumph ready to burst from inside her. She had eased her grandmother's pain on many occasions. Gran had often said, "You have a healing touch, *a nighean.*" Whether her ministrations were efficacious or merely a distraction from what had troubled her gran, she never knew for certain. Until today. *She* had been the one to heal him. What was more, she'd made him smile—one step closer to her goal of making him laugh.

She hesitated at the bottom of the staircase. The corridor below deck had grown dark, and Will had not yet lit the oil lamps hanging overhead. From behind the door on the left, she heard the crabbit reverend mumbling something that sounded more like an incantation than a prayer. No one had spoken to the man since the captain had chastised him at supper that first night. They'd heard him shouting, but he hadn't come out of his cabin.

Bobby Shafto's gone to sea...

She sidled past the reverend's door, her back against the

opposite wall, careful not to make any sound.

Silver buckles on his knee...

Felt for the handle to her cabin door and opened it.

He'll come back to marry me...

The cabin was dark. Where was Mairi? From down the corridor came two sets of footsteps, a man's chatter, and Mairi's intermittent laughter. Louisa released her breath. Mairi and Mr. Peter lingered in the corridor chatting, while Louisa fumbled for the flint to light the lamp. Once glowing, she hung the lamp from the ceiling and reclined on her berth.

She'd half expected to be chased away from the captain's door for the third time that day. Mr. Peter must have been powerful worried about Captain Sinclair to have let her in. Good thing, too. He'd been in agony. Too weak from the pain to object, he'd put his head in her lap, let her smooth away the trouble from his brow, melt the tension in his body, chase away the demons. It had taken a long time, longer than with Gran. Eventually, she'd replaced his pain with peace. But unlike with her gran, the encounter had been shockingly arousing.

Not only had she been acutely aware of his nakedness under that thin blanket—thank goodness, the light in the cabin had been dim—but the sighs and moans he was making, dear Lord in heaven, they were sighs of pleasure, not pain. Odd how the two sounded so similar.

"You're winning," he'd said. She would have interpreted the kiss of her hand as a simple gesture of thanks had he not embellished the moment. He'd flirted with her. Captain Sinclair, the stodgy, rule-making, never-smiling grown man, had actually made a joke. For her benefit, no less.

"There ye are." Mairi removed her bonnet and closed the cabin door. "Mr. Peter said you were helping the captain with a medical problem?" Mairi's comment was a taunt more than a question.

"Stop that," Louisa spat. "Captain Sinclair was in great pain. You know very well I helped Gran with her migraines. I simply offered the captain the same release."

Mairi laughed. "I'm glad our captain found his release."

Louisa shook her finger at Mairi. "Dinnae think I dinnae understand that bawdy reference."

"Sorry." Mairi wasn't sorry at all.

The humor grabbed Louisa by surprise and she giggled. Those giggles grew into laughter. Mairi's face contorted with her own seizure and the moment quickly got out of control.

Reverend Wynterbottom bellowed hellfire and brimstone from down the hall, turning their moment of mirth into something chilling.

Staring at each other wide eyed, Louisa asked, "What did he say?"

"I ken he called upon the sea to open up and swallow the witches," Mairi whispered. "And I suppose we're the witches."

Reverend Wynterbottom continued his incoherent ravings on into the next evening. Louisa and Mairi were sitting in their cabin listening when they heard Will knock on the reverend's door.

"Reverend Wynterbottom, sir. I've got your supper."

Louisa rose and peered down the dim corridor in time to see the reverend unlatch his door and wordlessly take the tray from Will.

"Is there ought else I can get for you, sir?" Will asked. No answer. "Are you well, sir? Would you like the—" Will jumped backward and the reverend slammed his cabin door.

Louisa whispered Will's name and gestured for him to come to their cabin. He entered and she closed the door behind him. "What's wrong with him?

"Dinnae ken, but he didnae look well."

"How do you mean?"

Will shifted uncomfortably and glanced at the closed door. "I oughtn't to say."

"Do you think he needs a physician's attention?"

Will shrugged. "I'll tell the captain. He'll ken what to do."

"Perhaps you should tell Mr. Peter instead. The captain is indisposed."

"Och, nae." Will brightened. "He's just sent me. The captain invites the ladies to dine with him. Shall I tell him you accept?"

"Of course," Louisa said.

"You go on without me," Mairi said. "The sea has soured my belly. I'll have toast and tea in my room, if you please, Will."

"Yes, miss." Will opened the door. "I'll be back wi' your tea in thirty. Will you be ready for supper by then, Miss MacQuarie?"

"Yes, of course."

Will dashed away.

Louisa folded her arms under her bosom. "Why?"

Mairi, the picture of innocence, sat on her berth batting her eyelashes sweetly. "Whatever do you mean, Miss MacQuarie?"

"Why are you so determined that I should"—she searched for the right word—"liaison with the captain?"

Mairi cocked her head. "Lay a son?"

Louisa huffed. "Tryst."

Mairi batted her silly eyes again.

"Stop pretending you dinnae ken what I mean."

"Fine then." Her friend looked contrite. "You fancy him, do you not?"

Louisa's cheeks heated.

"Aye, you do. And he fancies you. So, why not?"

Louisa glanced at the floor, considering whether to lie or not.

Mairi gasped. "You've never been kissed afore, have ye?"

"*Aaah!* You are infuriating."

As Will had promised, he returned to their cabin and escorted Louisa to the captain's mess. Captain Sinclair met her at the door and helped her to sit at a table with only two place settings.

"Where are Mr. Peter and Mr. Purdie?"

"On duty." Captain Sinclair sat across from her rather than at his usual spot at the head of the table. "How is Miss Robertson's health?"

"Better." The table was lit by candles instead of an oil lamp. Good beeswax candles. Though the light was dim, she saw ruddy patches on his freshly shaved cheeks. "As are you, I think."

Danny Sinkler appeared, balancing a tray containing a soup terrine and two bowls. The lad's face puckered with concentration as he ladled out two bowls of rich leek and chicken soup, his tongue protruding from pinched lips in increments. Slowly, and with excruciating care, he placed a bowl first in front of her and then in front of the captain. Without the least indication of impatience, the captain waited, his attention on her rather than the struggling boy. Task completed, Danny heaved a deep sigh of relief that made one think he'd just escaped the hangman's noose.

"Well done, Mr. Sinkler." His praise was not in any way patronizing. He'd made the comment offhandedly like he would to any adult member of the crew.

Danny Sinkler grew another inch before her eyes. "Thank you, sir," he said and disappeared with the tray and terrine.

Perhaps Captain Sinclair saw a question in her eyes because he answered without her asking. "With Mr. Sinkler's permission, I purchased his indenture papers from the reverend. He prefers to work on the *Gael Forss,* and my cook is in need of an assistant."

"That's very kind."

Captain Sinclair collected his spoon. "Not kind. Practical." He tasted the soup and nodded. "Good. Try it."

The soup was indeed good, as was the wine. According to Captain Sinclair, they were drinking the last bottle of wine he'd commandeered when they'd captured the pirate ship five years ago.

"This ship has brought great wealth to the Sinclairs of Balforss," she said.

"The *Gael Forss* brought us something far more valuable than goods. Something priceless. Of the five women rescued, two have married into our family."

Louisa's heart plummeted to the bottom of her stomach. Before she could school her question, she gasped, "One of them is your wife?"

The captain's features lightened for a moment, and then returned to his usual inscrutable expression. "Nae. Miss Caya is married to my cousin Declan, and Miss Virginia is married to my cousin Magnus."

"Forgive me. That was a very personal question."

"I dinnae mind talking aboot my family." He finished the last spoonful of soup and leaned back in his chair. "But I'd rather talk aboot you this evening, Miss MacQuarie."

Danny Sinkler entered with a platter and set it in the center of the table. "The men caught flounder today. Turk made this one wi' stuffing just for you and the lady, sir."

"Give Turk my compliments."

"Yes, sir." Danny collected the empty soup bowls and hustled out of the dining room.

"And shut the door, Mr. Sinkler."

The door clicked shut, and Louisa's pulse skyrocketed.

Captain Sinclair shot her a look of sheer misery. "I'm sorry. I forgot." He leaped to his feet. "I'll open it."

"No. There's no need. I'm not affected," she assured him. Indeed, her pulse had soared at the idea of being alone with him rather than her "old problem."

He lowered himself into his chair. "What is it then?"

Dear Lord, must she say it out loud? Confessing that she'd never dined alone with a man would reveal far more about *everything* she'd never done than she was willing to admit. Captain Sinclair was used to worldly women, not missish girls. "I was…I was reminded of the last time I dined alone with a gentleman."

. . .

The last time? Ian could have sworn she was thoroughly unschooled in the ways of love. The night before last, while the storm raged outside, the blindfolded Miss MacQuarie had trembled in his arms like a…well, like a debutante at her first ball.

"What happened?"

"What? Oh"—she flapped a hand—"I hardly remember. It was so long ago."

"So long ago? How old could you be?"

"I beg your pardon."

He floundered in front of the flounder. "I only mean, you seem so young."

"I assure you, I am much older than you may think, Captain." Changing the subject, she said, "Would you like me to filet?"

"Thanks. I can manage." Normally, he was quite good at filleting a whole fish. His father had taught him. If he was alone, he could have done it with his eyes closed. Unfortunately, Miss MacQuarie's most recent revelation had put him off balance. The knife slipped from his hand and clattered on the table.

"Allow me." Miss MacQuarie collected the fish knife, rose, and began a quick and efficient dissection. At least, he assumed her movements were efficient. His eyes were fixed on her décolletage, poised over the fish plate and aimed directly at his face, plague take her. This was his night, his opportunity to take back the control that had slipped away yesterday, replace her vision of him laid low by a headache, and redeem himself in her eyes. Instead, she had him by the bollocks, and they hadn't even started the main course.

"There," she said, having finished serving them both. She sat, snapped open her serviette, and placed it back on her lap, the lap that had cradled his head only a day ago. A heavenly pillow. If he had been himself at the time, if he had had possession of his wits, he would have turned his head and buried it—

"Captain Sinclair?"

His head snapped up, and he practically yelped, "Aye?"

"Is anything wrong?"

He collected his cutlery and addressed the fish on his plate. "I was remembering you said something about being an actress."

"You are correct. I'm on my way to New York with recommendations from my previous employer. I seek an acting position with a new theater company there."

"Why did you leave your former employ?"

She paused for a moment. "I've always wanted to work in America and when Miss Robertson offered to pay for my passage in exchange for my companionship, I could hardly say no."

"You have a lot of experience? On the stage, I mean."

Miss MacQuarie took another sip of wine before answering. "What I lack in experience I more than make up for in talent."

"Your granny doesnae mind you leaving her?" He saw his mistake immediately. She looked as though he'd kicked her in the stomach. "Please forgive me."

She recovered her poise, but she couldn't hide the shine of tears in her eyes. "Not at all. You had no way of knowing."

"Recent, was it?"

"Gran passed last autumn. I miss her very much. She was the only one who believed in me."

The Sinkler lad scratched on the door and entered. He placed a plate of cheeses and apples on the table and took away the remains of the flounder. The door clicked behind him, and Ian's confidence soared at the sound. He collected the paring knife and began peeling the apple.

"I ken ye dinnae need it, you have enough self-confidence to make good on your own, but I believe in you, Miss MacQuarie." He kept his eyes on the business of peeling the apple, intent on removing the skin in one piece, but he sensed her smile. When he finished peeling the apple, he held it out to her. She would know the custom: drop the peel behind her back and whatever shape letter it formed foretold the name of the lad she would marry. "It's not yet midnight. Do you want to give it a try?"

She tilted her head and smiled. "I have no intention of shackling myself to a man. I'm an actress. I have a career to think about."

"All right then, I'll give it a try."

This was a maiden's game, not a man's, but his absurdity elicited the desired response—bubbling laughter. As long as he made her laugh, he didn't mind playing the fool for her. He spun the peel over his head and let go. Miss MacQuarie took the candle from the table and held it close to the peel now lying curled on the cabin floor.

"Is it a *J*?" she asked.

"Nae. It's an *L*." He smiled down at her startled face. "What's your Christian name, lass?"

For one terrifying moment, he thought she might produce a name that started with an *L*. Did that mean he had to marry her? And would that be a tragedy?

"M-Mairi."

That was curious. He'd made her stammer again. "Mairi," he repeated. "Mairi. It's a pretty name." He collected the peel off the floor and stood. "But I'm sorry to say, you're no' the lass I'll be marrying," he teased.

She teased him back. "Thank you. I'm much relieved."

They returned to the table for sweet cheese and tart apple slices.

He pretended to be occupied with removing the rind from a piece of cheese and quietly said, "My name is Ian, by the way."

"Pleased to make your acquaintance, Ian."

He looked up to find her holding out her right hand as if to shake his. He took it, and like the day she boarded the ship, he couldn't let it go. She sensed the connection, too. He could see it in her eyes. Surprise but also…recognition. Danny scratched on the door again, and they snatched their hands away.

"Come."

The lad entered burdened with a platter of boiled pudding smelling of cinnamon and molasses.

Mairi clapped her hands and let out a sigh. "Clootie dumpling."

He'd asked Turk to make this meal special, but the man had outdone himself. Even Ian was impressed. "Aye. And it's not even Hogmanay."

She dug into the sweet treat, a dark molasses raisin cake dowsed with an obscene-looking cream custard dripping down the sides.

Ian paused to watch Miss MacQuarie slip a forkful of pudding into her pouty mouth, her eyes closing in ecstasy. A drop of whisky sauce clung to her lip and the urge to leap over the table and lick it off had him by the balls. When, how, why had he become so stupidly besotted with this woman, who by all accounts was one giant contradiction? She insisted she was older than she looked, but by his estimation, she could be no older than twenty. She suggested she was a woman of experience and yet she'd trembled in his arms like a virgin. She claimed to be an actress and yet he would swear she was of good stock, Scottish gentry at the very least. Miss MacQuarie would also have him believe she was intrepid, yet he knew for a fact she had at least one debilitating fear.

And those hands—those magic hands that had defeated the raging monster in his head no other medical man, no healer, huckster, or witch doctor had ever been able to tame—he wanted those hands, needed them, required them. She could have been a harpy and he'd have wanted to capture her and stow her away in his sea trunk. But she was no harpy. Miss MacQuarie—Miss Mairi MacQuarie—was a beautiful enchantress. Mairi MacQuarie. Mairi MacQuarie. The name danced in his head like a waltz.

Jee-*sus*.

"Aren't you having any, Captain?"

He wiped his sweaty palms on his britches. "Em, you have…" Ian pointed to his own bottom lip. "Some sauce, uh…"

Her eyes shuttered, and she dipped her head. Using her left index finger, she swiped the drop away. The tip of her pink tongue slithered out from between her lips, and Ian lost his restraint. He reached across the table, wrapped his big hand around her slender wrist, and drew her finger into his mouth. His lips closed and he swept his tongue in circles around the slender digit. Miss MacQuarie's sticky sweet lips formed a perfect *O* right before green-eyed fury swept her gorgeous face.

In that half second, he realized he may have overstepped.

She pulled her finger free, and his lips made a rude smacking sound.

"Captain Sinclair." She exhaled his name with an indignant huff.

He swallowed. Oh, aye. He *had* overstepped.

Miss MacQuarie popped up from the table. By the time he'd found his feet, she was already at the door.

"I forgot myself. I beg your forgiveness."

She paused without turning around. Was she waiting to hear more?

"It's just that you're so…so…"

She turned a startled look his way, not like the one before, the one filled with outrage. This one was expectant.

The door swung open revealing Danny Sinkler standing at attention.

Miss MacQuarie dipped a low curtsy. "Thank you for a perfectly lovely supper, Captain Sinclair."

He jerked a stiff bow. "You're most welcome, Miss MacQuarie."

"Good evening," she whispered and slipped away.

Ian fell back in his chair like a stunned beast. *What the hell was that?*

• • •

What the devil was that?

Louisa stumbled blindly back to her cabin, completely forgetting to be frightened by the darkness. Inside, Mairi was seated by the oil lamp in her night rail cradling a bundle of something.

"What have you got there?" Louisa asked. A tabby cat

squirmed free of Mairi's arms and yowled.

"Will brought her to me. Said she must have stowed away while they docked in Edinburgh. We're calling her Brandy, as he found her tucked among the casks in the hold."

Brandy rubbed up against Louisa's skirts. She bent for a closer look. "She's filthy but well fed and doesnae have any fleas. I ken she may have been someone's pet."

"Aye, that's what Will thought. Anyway, he's asked us to keep her for the noo—for now."

Louisa closed the door and flung herself on her berth. Brandy hopped up and nestled next to her. She stroked the cat, and it purred loud enough for the next cabin to hear.

"How was your supper with the captain?" Mairi asked. When she didn't answer, Mairi added, "Something happened. I can see it on your face. Did he kiss you?"

"No." She heard the disappointment in her answer. "I mean, not exactly."

A dismayed Mairi shook her head. "Either he kissed ye or he didnae. There's no in-between, friend."

"He kissed my finger."

"Ye mean he kissed yer hand?"

"Nae, he kissed—" Louisa lowered her voice to a whisper. "He sucked my finger."

Mairi's brow furrowed, and she leaned back to take her in, as if assessing whether Louisa had gone off her nut.

"After, he said 'sorry' that he forgot himself because I was so..."

"So what?"

"I dinnae ken. Danny came to the door, and I said good night afore he finished."

Mairi switched berths to sit next to her. "I think you best start from the beginning."

Louisa sighed. She told Mairi everything they talked about, everything they ate, and everything he said, no matter how insignificant. Because she remembered it all. When she finished, Mairi—the irritating bizzum—laughed. Louisa had to swat her several times to get her to sober. "For all God's glory, I swear I will sit on you if you dinnae stop. What is so funny?"

"Oh, Lord. Poor Captain Sinclair. He's got it bad."

"What do you mean? Tell me this instant, you vexing piece of old baggage." She swatted Mairi one more time. The cat left the berth and hit the floor with a soft *thu-thud*.

"You're a siren and you dinnae even know it."

She narrowed her eyes at Mairi.

"Lass," Mairi explained. "You made him forget himself. He even said so. No man in control of his reason would suck a lady's finger at the supper table." Mairi leaned in and whispered, "You drove him mad with desire."

Louisa drew in a breath and exhaled on, "Oh."

Mairi chuckled. "Get yourself to bed," she said, and kindly helped her out of her gown and into her nightclothes.

"You really have to stop helping me in and out of my clothes," Louisa said. "Eventually, I'll have to do it myself." She snuggled under the bedding as the night had taken on a chill quite uncharacteristic for late June, but then she'd never been in the middle of the English Channel before. "And your speech is much improved. You sound like a real lady."

"Thank you." Mairi gave her a satisfied smile. "Are you going up to read this evening?"

"Nae. I ken I best stay out of Captain Sinclair's way for a while." She suppressed a giggle. "Lest I drive him mad wi' desire again."

It was no use. They both bubbled with laughter for a good long spell.

Mairi and Louisa took their jobs as cat-minders seriously, and for the next three days, they occupied themselves bathing, grooming, and entertaining Brandy Cat. Will offered to take what they had for laundry, but rather than hand over their smallclothes for who-knows-who to examine, they chose to wash their things and hang them to dry in their cabin.

Worry over Reverend Wynterbottom's health and sanity had grown, as it had been a week since he'd last shown himself. Will said he wasn't eating well, and his distemper had reached unprecedented pitches. By their tenth day at sea, and well into the Atlantic Ocean according to Will, Louisa heard Mr. Peter outside Reverend Wynterbottom's door.

"Will you open your door, Reverend?" Mr. Peter asked politely. "I'd like to know you are well, sir."

She was worried about the reverend. As distasteful as the man had been, she wouldn't like him to come to any harm. Louisa whispered from her cabin door, "We havenae heard him raving to himself since yesterday."

Mr. Peter nodded and turned back to the reverend's cabin. "The captain would like a word with you, Reverend. Shall I ask him to come to you?" Still no reply. "Right then. I'll tell the captain you await his visit."

Mr. Peter said in a low voice meant only for her, "Best you and Miss Robertson remain in your cabin until after the captain sees the reverend, aye?"

"Of course," Mairi replied from behind Louisa. "Thank you for your concern, Mr. Peter."

From the abashed look on Mr. Peter's face, Mairi had no doubt batted her blasted eyelashes at the loon. But Louisa had no intention of missing the exchange between Captain Sinclair and Reverend Wynterbottom. She hadn't but a few brief sightings of the captain since their supper. Once or twice she'd caught a glimpse of him on the quarterdeck. Each time he quickly averted his gaze. Another time they'd collided as she'd entered the galley in search of Brandy Cat, who had turned out to be quite the escape artist.

She'd smacked into his big body full on, front to front, nearly knocking the wind out of her. Captain Sinclair had gathered her in his arms reflexively, steadying her. He'd looked as shocked at their intersection as she felt.

"I do beg your pardon," she'd gasped.

"My fault. I wasnae looking where I was going," he'd said, still holding her and staring intently into her eyes with a look she couldn't interpret.

After a moment, she'd said, "I think I can stand on my own now."

"What?"

"You may release me."

"Och!" He'd dropped her like a box of hot coals.

That was the last she'd seen of him since yesterday. So, she remained at her cabin door, half hidden, watching his tall Hessians tromp down the stairs.

Captain Sinclair rapped on the cabin door. "Reverend Wynterbottom, this is Captain Sinclair. May I come in, sir?" No answer. "Just a wee word. It's important, Reverend. I would like to ascertain that you are well." No answer. "I'll have to force the door open, then. Stand back."

Captain Sinclair rammed the door with his shoulder once, twice. The frame splintered on his third try. Louisa waited, expecting a shout or protest from the reverend, but nothing. The captain emerged and called up the stairs, "Mr. Peter, send Turk down right away. Reverend Wynterbottom is ill."

Louisa hurried down the corridor to the reverend's door.

"Dinnae go inside, Miss MacQuarie."

"But I might be able to help."

"That's kind of you. I'll let Turk see him first, and then perhaps you can assist." He guided her back toward her cabin. "Go inside. I'll let you know what Turk says after he's examined the man."

· · ·

Ian thought he knew what the problem was but wanted confirmation from Turk. Wynterbottom appeared delirious, unfocused, and his body gave off a sour odor he recognized. The man clutched at Ian's sleeve mumbling over and over, "I failed them. I failed them."

Once Turk arrived, Ian waited outside in the hall. He let Turk examine the reverend while Will cleaned up the unholy mess that littered the man's cabin. Aside from an overflowing chamber pot, moldy scraps of food, and vomit, Reverend Wynterbottom had pissed himself.

Turk staggered out of the cabin, took in a breath of air, and began washing his hands in a clean basin of water.

"What do ye think?" Ian asked.

"It would seem our passenger has decided an ocean voyage would be the best place for him to dry out."

As Ian suspected, Reverend Wynterbottom was a habitual drunkard. He'd known other men to suffer from this affliction and had once witnessed the contortions one's body must endure while ridding itself of strong spirits. For whatever reason, the reverend had chosen the *Gael Forss* to use as his sanatorium.

Fortunately, the man had seen the worst of it and was coherent enough to help Turk and Ian bathe and dress him while Will changed his bedclothes and tidied the cabin.

"Gentlemen," Reverend Wynterbottom said, "I have asked God to forgive me for my weakness and I ask you for the same. Please allow me to apologize to my fellow passengers, and…and to that poor young man whom I misused."

"Apology accepted, Reverend. Miss Robertson and Miss

MacQuarie will be relieved to know you are mending."

"Yes, indeed, Reverend."

Ian turned to find Miss MacQuarie at the door. She'd ignored his direct order once again, the blasted wee bizzum. Yet his irritation was tempered by the kindness of her gesture, forgiving a man who had been unspeakably rude to her.

"Do you think you're well enough to take your dinner with us?" she asked. "Miss Robertson and I would welcome your company. Some tea and toast, perhaps?"

The reverend smiled gratefully at her generous offer. "I would like that very much."

"That's grand. Will can set the table here in the corridor. I'll come for you when it's ready."

When Miss MacQuarie walked away, Ian followed her down the corridor. "Miss MacQuarie."

She spun and shined a smile his way. "Yes, Captain."

"Thank you for that."

"For what?"

"For forgiving him."

"Of course."

The heat, the exertion, and the close quarters had made him sweat through his coat and the starch in his collar chafed his neck raw. "And do you forgive me?" He held his breath.

She stepped closer. "My dear Captain, whatever have you done that needs my forgiveness?"

"When I...em..."

She whispered a low seductive, "When you licked my finger?"

"Then you didnae forget?"

"I will never forget that particular moment, sir." Her genuine chuckle dissolved his discomfort in an instant.

"Nor shall I." Something stirred below his belt and he cursed his traitorous body.

Jee-*sus*.

Later that night he lay naked on his berth, unable to sleep. His skin was too hot and too sensitive for bedclothes. Everything was wrong. Before he'd gone to bed, he'd straightened and squared everything on his desk, evened every book in his library so that the spines aligned, and refolded every article of clothing in his trunk. Still, something was out of place. He could feel it, sense it with an internal faculty for which he had no name, but was as powerful and as essential as any of his other senses.

Something was out of place. And it was female.

Miss MacQuarie.

From the moment she'd come aboard, she'd upended everything she came in contact with: his ship, his crew, his library, his things, his-his-*his frigging mind*.

Damn it to hell.

Even now, lying here, thinking angry thoughts, she made him hard. Jee-*sus*. He fisted his cock. Fine. Just this once, just to get her out of his mind, over and done with, and then no more. No more talking to, looking at, or dining with Miss MacQuarie. Mairi MacQuarie. He closed his eyes and stroked. Mairi. Mairi. Frigging gorgeous green-eyed Mairi.

He scanned the quarterdeck for signs of Miss MacQuarie. He'd managed to avoid direct contact with her for the last week and a half. Which was remarkable given the size of the ship and the amount of time she spent roaming the deck. He'd had no complaints from Peter or any of the crew, so she must know how, when, and where it was safe for her to be. Still, it rankled him that she wouldn't abide by his word. If she was a member of his crew, he'd discipline her, give her bare arse a good tawsing—the thought made his cock stir. He scrubbed it from his mind and strode toward the ship's bow.

Learning to navigate by instruments—sextant, chronometer, compass, and charts—had come easily to Ian. He had a keen interest in math and had quickly grown confident when establishing longitudinal coordinates. Yet he'd much to learn about reading the ocean, the wind, and the skies. That, Mr. Purdie said, came only with time.

According to Mr. Purdie, they were nearing the Canary Current, the ocean stream that would whip them south-southwest to where they would catch the trade winds and eventually the Gulf Stream up toward the eastern coast of America. He'd made this trip only thrice before. Each time he'd tried to detect the moment when the Canary Current took hold, and each time he'd failed. Purdie knew, though. He had an uncanny relationship with the sea, a sort of sixth sense for the subtle changes in the ocean.

What was it that Purdie saw or felt or sensed that foretold the change? Ian closed his eyes. Had the temperature dropped? He opened his eyes again and stared out at the vast sea. He let his focus blur and saw a definite line of differentiation: lighter on the eastern side and dark on the western. He spun around seeking confirmation from Purdie. The man stood behind the wheel with a wide smile. He'd done it. They were in the Canary Current and he'd actually become aware the moment when it happened.

He thundered down the fo'c'sle stairs and took the forward hatch down to the crew's quarters. He'd ask Turk to prepare a celebratory dinner for Purdie, Peter, and himself and order extra ale for the crew. No sooner had he reached the bottom step than he heard a deep, but not unfamiliar, feminine voice.

"Here, sirrah Grumio, knock, I say."

And in a lighter voice, *"Knock, sir! Whom should I knock? Is there any man has refused your worship?"*

"Villain I say"—in the deep voice—*"knock me here*

soundly."

Ian hurried forward to investigate. Seated around the crew's mess, the oil lamp shone down on eight of his twelve crew members leaning forward in rapt attention, all eyes worshipfully riveted on Miss goddamned MacQuarie. She was reading to his crew. He recognized those lines. Shakespeare's *The Taming of the Shrew.*

"*Knock you here, sir!*" In her Grumio voice. "*Why, sir, what am I, sir, that I should knock you here, sir?*"

"*Villain, I say*"—as Petruchio—"*knock me at this gate and rap me well, or I'll knock your knave's pate.*"

A burst of laughter from his crew. And then he saw the traitor. Peter. How could Peter have allowed this to happen? He knew damn well that—well, maybe Peter didn't know, but he *should* know that this was not the place for Miss MacQuarie, sitting here being ogled by his crew and—

Mr. Peter bolted out of his chair. "Captain, sir."

Miss MacQuarie stopped her reading and the rest of the crew stood. They all looked guilty, and Ian knew why. He knew what must pass through any man's mind when they focused on Miss MacQuarie.

"Miss MacQuarie has favored us with a dramatic reading, sir," Peter said. "*The Taming of the—*"

"*Shrew*, yes." Ian looked pointedly at Miss MacQuarie. "I'm certain everyone found your reading diverting, but I must insist my men return to their duties." He knew them all by name, but at this moment, he was too angry to speak directly to any of them.

He simmered impatiently while they took turns mumbling their compliments and thanks to the woman he was going to strangle as soon as he got her alone. When her admirers had dissipated, he growled, "A word with you in the captain's mess, please, Miss MacQuarie."

"A' course, Captain," she said sweetly. "Would you please

hold this." She handed him the book, plucked up her skirts and began walking up the staircase. When her boots reached the step level with his eyes, he blinked. In place of the lovely turn of ankle—a treat he had anticipated—he glimpsed the bottom of, of, of...was she wearing trousers under her petticoats?

He bounded up the stairs after her and followed hot on her heels, straight down the gangway, through the portal, toward the captain's mess. On the way, he recollected the last time he'd visited home. It was Beltane and Ian had met his cousin Declan on the fairgrounds in Thurso. Declan had told him about a dream he'd had. He was always having daft dreams. The trouble was, Declan's daft dreams had a habit of coming true.

It had been an unscheduled visit. He'd surprised his family. His cousin Magnus had asked if the reason for his sudden appearance was to announce his plans for marrying. When Ian had denied any such plans, Declan had frowned and said, "What aboot the girl in the breeks?"

"What girl in breeks?" Ian had replied.

"The one you love. I dreamed you married her."

Damn.

Inside the captain's mess, he shut the door behind him, suddenly aware he was gripping the book so hard he thought he might leave marks on the cover. He placed it on the table.

"Is something wrong, Captain?"

Something was wrong all right.

Miss MacQuarie put a hand on his arm, and he shook his head like a dog.

"Captain Sinclair?"

He swallowed audibly and pointed to her boots. "What are you wearing under there?"

"I beg your pardon?"

"Trousers," he demanded, knowing he sounded like an

imbecile but needing to know. "Are you wearing trousers? Under your skirts, I mean."

She turned away from him and circled the table. "I fail to see what trousers have to do with me reading Shakespeare to your crew. But yes, I'm wearing trousers."

He closed his eyes and raked his fingers over his scalp, accidentally pulling strands of hair free of his queue.

"You look unwell, Captain. Is it the migraine again?"

Ian shook his head vigorously. "No. You're not in the right spot. You're out of place."

"Do you mean I shouldnae be in the crew's mess?"

"No. Yes." He pointed at her boots again. "What is the purpose of the trousers?"

"You."

"*Me?*"

"Yes, well, it gets windy on deck and you were rightfully angry when the breeze took Miss Robertson's skirts. So, I put them on to spare your sensibilities."

He staggered backward. "My sensibilities?"

She took a step closer. And another. And another. His heart rate slowed, and the muscles in his chest released their suffocating hold on him. The closer she came, the more he calmed until she stood directly before him.

"You should sit." She put her hand on his shoulder, and for a moment, everything fell into its proper place again. Even Miss MacQuarie. The threat of imminent doom flew away and the bundle of tension fisting in his stomach unfurled. He felt two stones lighter. The only thing tethering him to the floor was the look in her eyes.

He gathered her in his arms and kissed her. Placed his rough, wind-chapped lips on her innocent-looking pink ones, and ground his unshaven beard against her rose petal-soft skin. She didn't stiffen or resist. Instead, her whole body softened and molded against his hard edges. Her arms slipped over his shoulders and those slender fingers played with the back of his neck. She tasted of tea and honey and strawberry jam. But he needed more. He put a thumb on her chin, pulled her mouth open and dove inside with his tongue. The act seemed to surprise her, like she'd never been possessed by a man in this way. But hadn't she said…hadn't she implied that she was experienced? He released her lips to look for the answer.

Her eyes fluttered open. "Oh. Is that how it's usually done?"

He inhaled a moment of confusion. "Have ye never been kissed before, lass?"

Her mouth formed that perfect *O* again. "Of course, I have. Hundreds of times." Then she laughed as though they'd had a big misunderstanding. "What I meant was, is that how *you* usually kiss, Captain?"

Doubt crept into his belly and took up residence. "Aye. Most of the time." Bloody hell. Had he done it wrong? "I'm a wee bit rusty, though."

"I am, too. Shall we give it another go?"

• • •

So, this is what kissing was. She'd always imagined she would feel awkward pressing her lips to someone else's. The whole idea of it seemed silly to her. But this wasn't silly at all. Captain Sinclair's kisses were anything but. They were…they were like wearing trousers on stage. Only better. Much, much better.

Am I doing this right?

His tongue, it was in her mouth, slipping over her teeth and tangling with her tongue. She tried to follow, but it was like trying to keep up with one's dance partner when one didn't know the steps. Dizzying, but thrilling.

Oh God, am I doing this right?

He was trembling, but not from nervousness. He didn't seem at all nervous. He seemed sure of himself. His whole body vibrated with life. Was this...was this?

She pulled free of his kiss. "Is this passion?"

Captain Sinclair was breathing hard and his eyes had a sort of glazed look, like she'd woken him from a dream. "What?"

"Is this the passionate part? Are you feeling desire for me?"

"Aye. Aye. I-want-you-oh-God." The last bit ran together before he claimed her mouth again. He backed her against the wall. And that's when he placed his hand on her left breast. Dear Lord. She'd done it again. She'd driven him mad with desire. Common sense told her to stop everything, push Captain Sinclair away, and march out of the room before she lost her dignity, her maidenhead, and her trousers. Not necessarily in that order.

But kissing Captain Sinclair was deliriously wonderful. Her whole body hummed with a warm, tingly sensation like a big swallow of brandy. Only brandy had never made her nipples ache. Nor did it make the private spot between her legs tighten.

He released her lips again and thank goodness. She needed air to clear her head. He dragged his bristly cheek across hers and his heavy breathing roared hot in her ear.

"Say my name," he whispered. "Say my name."

A simple request but by the way he'd asked, she thought he must need it to live.

"Captain Sinclair," she whispered back.

He nuzzled her neck, the bristles tickling. "No." He shook his head. "Say my name."

They'd shared their Christian names at supper, normally a shockingly intimate thing to do, but as it had been couched in a game, she hadn't thought it too outrageous at the time, yet now…

"Ian." She drew his name out like an incantation.

He uttered a soft groan and dragged a kiss from under her right ear all the way down to the top of her left breast.

She let out a gasp of her own which only fueled his determination. His head rose up and he straightened to his full height, towering over her, then slipped his hand down the front of her bodice and scooped one breast into his palm. She cried out when he squeezed her nipple, but he smothered her cry with another demanding kiss.

Her corseting seemed to frustrate him because he released her lips and her breast with a growl. He cupped her bottom with both hands and drew her belly up against a rock-hard lump in his trousers. He pressed his forehead to hers. "Mairi. Oh God, Mairi."

She shuddered. That wasn't her real name. That was her pretend name. The part she was playing aboard the *Gael Forss*. It sounded wrong and upsetting when he said it, as if he were thinking of someone else while he made love to her. He ground his hips against her and moaned the name again, and like snuffing out a candle, the fire inside her died.

"Stop."

He froze instantly. "Is something wrong?"

"Let me go."

He eased away from her and moved his hands to her shoulders. "I'm sorry. I was too forward."

"No-no. Just let me go. I need to go back to my cabin."

Slowly, reluctantly, he released her and stepped back. She couldn't look at him. Tonight, her acting felt more like lying and it sickened her.

"Good night," she whispered and fumbled with the door. He reached over her and turned the handle.

As she fled, he called after her, "You forgot your book."

But she couldn't go back. She didn't dare. She might confess her lies and that would ruin everything.

Mairi and Reverend Wynterbottom were engaged in a game of draughts at the table Will had set up in the corridor for their meals. Louisa didn't think clergymen played games like draughts, but then she didn't think they drank spirits, either. Certainly draughts were the much lesser of those two evils.

They barely noticed her when she squeezed past the table into her cabin. Grateful not to have to speak to Mairi, Louisa closed her door and undressed. Mairi would have read her disquietude immediately and pressed her for the reason. Rather than share the reason with her friend, she wanted to keep this particular pain to herself. She'd keep the kiss to herself, as well. Tuck it away in the corner of her memory and take it out later, when she'd gotten past this uneasy feeling.

Odd. She was perfectly happy being Miss MacQuarie to Captain Sinclair, but when she'd heard Mairi's name on his lips spoken with such passion, it had upset her beyond reason. She didn't want to be Mairi to him. Just like he wanted to hear her say his name, she wanted to hear him breathe, "Louisa," in her ear.

Louisa left the lamp burning and crawled into her berth already occupied by Brandy Cat. Once she closed her eyes, she was back in the captain's mess, his hand cupping her breast and his beard scrubbing her neck. Brandy Cat's deep purring echoed his just-right voice rumbling, *Say my name.*

Chapter Six

That was a close call. He'd very nearly debauched Miss MacQuarie in the captain's mess. He should ask Turk to check him for fever. He was not himself at all. Then again, maybe he *was* himself. Maybe he'd been the same self-indulgent, reckless sod all along. Maybe the sober man, the rational man who was always in control, was just an act he maintained to hide the real Ian Sinclair, the destructive monster that had gotten a young woman pregnant and forgotten, and a child fatherless for six years. Jee-*sus*. Alice Crawford had lost her life giving birth to his son.

He staggered into his cabin and shut the door. A cursory check told him nothing was out of place, yet that sense of total disorder continued to plague him. He'd encountered a severe bout with the compulsion to square and count things after he'd recovered from his wounds at Quatre Bras. He'd thought he'd finally rid himself of the bothersome and sometimes bizarre behavior. Now it was back again. It became particularly pronounced whenever he was reminded that he was a father. A frigging father. He was the last person on earth who should be entrusted with the care of a child.

Back in the captain's mess, just for a moment, while he'd had her in his arms, everything had been right. Everything had been in its place. Then... He gritted his teeth. Then Miss MacQuarie had upended his cart once again, blast that woman. He fell into his desk chair.

Trousers. Frigging trousers. Blast his cousin Declan and his doaty dreams.

A knock on his door brought him to his feet again. "Come."

Peter swung the door open and leaned inside. "Mr. Purdie would hae a word wi' ye, sir."

Ian jammed his hat on and moved to the door. "Anything wrong?"

"Dinnae ken."

As soon as he went out on deck, he sensed the change in pressure.

"Ye feel it?" Mr. Purdie asked, standing on the starboard rail.

"Hurricane?"

"Could be."

"I thought it was too early for hurricanes."

"Rare, but not unheard of."

"When?"

"I'd say four, maybe six hours. It's coming in from the east. If the wind kicks up, we may be able to get south of it before it catches us."

"Mr. Peter," Ian said, trying to disguise the panic welling inside his guts. "Crowd all sail she can carry. We're going to outrun this."

"Aye, sir."

"And have the men ready the ship for gale-force winds."

"Right away, sir."

This was the inevitability he had prepared for and

dreaded. A severe summer storm could toss them off course and cause them the loss of a week or more. A hurricane could sink a ship. Well-stocked longboats would hardly do them any good, as they'd be impossible to launch in a storm if they needed to abandon ship. But all those concerns were for six hours from now. His most immediate concern was to minimize Miss MacQuarie's inevitable panic when they battened the hatches.

He encountered the reverend and Miss Robertson seated at the table in the corridor engaged in a game of draughts.

"Ah, Captain," the reverend said. "Care to take my place? Miss Robertson has beaten me three times already this evening."

"Thank you for the offer and I'm glad to see you feeling well. I came down to tell you to expect bad weather. It would be best if you remained in your cabins until Will gives you the all clear. Meanwhile, I suggest you stow your valuables. Things could get rough. Where's Miss MacQuarie?"

"Asleep, I think." Miss Robertson looked a shade paler. "Shall I wake her?"

"Best leave her sleep."

Miss MacQuarie opened her cabin door and poked her head out, her hair in a long braid over her shoulder. "Will you lock the hatches?" she asked, already sounding alarmed. "Will we be trapped down here?"

"We dinnae lock them, Miss MacQuarie. We batten them—cover them with tarpaulins so the water doesnae flood the lower decks. You'll be able to get out anytime you like, but I ask you, for your own safety and for the safety of my crew, to please stay below."

Even in the dim corridor lit only by a single lantern, he saw the look in her eyes, like a horse about to bolt. He squeezed past Miss Robertson and reached for her, knowing full well she was dressed only in her nightgown. She didn't retreat. "Miss MacQuarie, look at me." Her eyes flicked his way and focused. "I will come for you. I promise. If there is any danger, I will come for you. Do you understand?"

She blinked. "Aye. You'll come for me."

He attempted a reassuring look, one like his father had used when he was a lad and had been afraid of lightning. "It'll be windy. Perhaps you should wear your trousers then. For me."

She managed a quivering smile. "Thank you, Ian," she whispered and he felt the blood shoot up from his limbs to his crown.

Jee-*sus*.

He was going to have to bed this woman or lose his mind.

• • •

After being tossed from their berths several times, they chose to huddle together on the floor of their cabin. Louisa wrapped one arm around Mairi and clutched Brandy Cat in the other. From above: thumping feet, crashing waves, howling wind, and shouting crew members. All around her, the ship's timbers screamed protests at the sea as it rolled and pitched. Most disturbing was the yawing, the side to side movement as if the ship's prow, like a snake's head, was turning left and right searching for a way out.

Captain Sinclair might have been joking about the trousers. Nonetheless, she chose to wear them. Mairi shook violently, and Brandy Cat dug her claws deep into Louisa's chest. She would have marks to remember this night, if they lived through it.

"Dinnae fash, Mairi. Captain Sinclair promised he would come for us if there was any danger."

"Well, he's no' here, so there must be no danger, right?"

"Do you ken Reverend Wynterbottom's all right?"

Louisa asked more to make conversation than because she really wanted to know.

"Will's with him." She laughed then. "I can hear the reverend praying. Poor Will."

They both laughed, until a long wide stream of seawater seeped in under their door. Brandy Cat saw it and scrambled out of her grasp. "Ouch! Have a care, you wicked thing." The cat leaped up onto the berth with her back arched and her fur standing on end.

Louisa and Mairi scooted out of the way, but there was no escaping the onslaught of water. Then she heard the thump of boots and a sharp rap on the cabin door. "Misses Robertson and MacQuarie?"

"Come in, Will."

He swung open the door and leaned his drenched head inside. He shouted over the dull roar of the storm. "Captain wanted I should check and see how you ladies fared."

"Tell Captain Sinclair we're doing fine. We have complete confidence in him," Louisa shouted back.

Will flashed her a smile. "Aye, miss." He pointed to their lantern swinging wildly from the ceiling. "You'll have to put that out, miss. Dinnae want any accidental fires." He shut the door, and Louisa almost called him back just for the comfort of his additional company.

Mairi started to rise, but Louisa stopped her. "No, I'll get it. I'm closer." She reached up, but before she could close the flame, the door banged open, and Brandy Cat shot out of the cabin into the dark corridor.

Mairi cried out. "Will's left the door off the latch!"

"It's all right." Louisa stumbled sideways once, then lifted the lantern off the hook. "I'll go get her."

"I dinnae think you should leave."

She lurched toward the door, bracing herself against the jam. "I willnae be long. The cat cannae have gone far."

Keeping one hand on the wall and the other holding the lantern aloft, Louisa crept toward the galley. "Here, kitty. That's a good Brandy Cat. Come to Lou— Come to Mairi."

A flash of cat tail disappeared into the dark storage room that led to the galley. Damn, someone had left the door open. She lifted her lantern inside the storage room and called to the kitty again. The door through to the galley was shut tight, but someone had left open the hatch to the lower deck. The ship took a steep pitch to the side, and her lantern went out. *Bonnets.*

She set the lantern on the floor and called into the abyss. "Are you down there, Brandy Cat?" The ship took another hard roll, and Louisa lost her balance, her boots slipped on the sea-washed floor, and as her arms churned for something to grab onto, she tumbled down the steps, banging her elbow, her knees, and scraping her back. She landed in a heap at the bottom of the steps, staring up at darkness. A moment later, she heard the hatch slam shut with a crash.

Dark. Everything dark. No air. Oh, dear God. She had to get out. Get out now. She scrabbled to her knees and groped for the stairs. Which way was up? With no light and the ship tossing about, she became disoriented. She crawled up two, three steps, but the ship pitched forward and, as there was no railing, she slid sideways off the stairs and ended up sprawled on the floorboards. She picked herself up and tried climbing again. At the eighth step, she banged her head. Using all her might, she pushed up against the hatch covering. Either it was locked or something was holding it down. Something heavy must have fallen on top of the hatch. She banged and shouted, "Help! Let me out! Please, let me out!"

She called, and called, and called, and called. Nothing. Her elbows hurt, her knees stung, and the scrape on her back might be bleeding. The ship pitched again and she clung to the steps to keep from tumbling off. Reasoning it was safer to remain on a level surface than risk breaking a limb in a fall, she climbed back down into the abyss.

A furry thing jumped on her lap and she screamed. "Damn it to hell and back, Brandy Cat." The cat dug its claws in her arm. "This is all your fault." She hugged the cat tight, glad for its company and not wanting to lose her again. She was trapped, but she wasn't alone.

"It's going to be fine, cat. Captain Sinclair will come for us. You'll see. He promised and he is a very stubborn man, which makes him impossible. But the good thing about stubborn men is that they always do what they say they are going to do. I know this for a fact."

He would. He would come for her, but what was she to do in the meantime? She closed her eyes tight. If Ian was here with her, she wouldn't be so afraid. If he held her in his arms, like he had the night he'd taken her dancing…

Easy. I'm here and nothing can harm us.

His words—that night he'd tried to cure her, the night he'd taken her dancing—came back to her. That soft, rumbly, just-right voice of his that made her insides quiver.

It's a big room. Filled with light. Can you no' see it lass?

She'd been panicked, ready to flee, but he'd held onto her tight. Even now, she could almost feel his big arms wrapped around her, pulling her close, his warm breath in her ear.

Have you never been to a ball, lass?

She'd lied to him, told him she'd been to many balls, when she'd only been to two. And they could hardly have been called balls.

Then you ken what it looks like. Can ye hear the music, too? Can you hear them playing…what is that? A waltz?

He'd started to hum some unrecognizable melody, tuneless and off key. She laughed at the memory. His singing had been dreadful, but the sound of it had calmed her then and, she realized, it calmed her now.

He'd wanted to cure her. Well, maybe he had. Ian's words rumbled in her ear as if he were with her at that very moment. *Dance with me.* He swept her into his arms and they waltzed, turning and whirling around the dance floor. One hundred candles hung from chandeliers illuminating the couples spinning dizzy circles around them.

Do you hear the storm, lass?

"I only hear you, Ian. Only you."

. . .

The wind seemed to have abated some and the waves no longer washed over the deck. Even the pitch and yaw of the ship had evened. Off to the east, he saw the blessed sun shoot its first rays of dawn across the horizon. They had lived to see a new day, thank Christ. Ian eased his grip on the rail and chanced a look at Purdie still steady at the helm. The old seaman pulled a half-toothless grin at him.

They'd done it. They'd outrun the goddamned storm. Still, he had a niggling feeling that something or someone was out of place. He searched and spotted the lean form of his quartermaster lashed to the fo'c'sle railing.

"Mr. Peter, see that all crewmen are accounted for."

"Aye, sir."

The winds continued to howl, and he had to shout to Purdie. "I'm going below to check on our passengers."

Purdie gave him a sharp nod.

He untied and tore away the batten, then pounded down the staircase. The hallway table and benches had shifted during the storm, blocking the stairs. In the future, he would have them nailed down. For now, he shoved them aside. Will, Reverend Wynterbottom, and Miss Robertson had gathered in the corridor. Miss MacQuarie was probably cowering inside the cabin sick with fear, poor lass.

"Captain," Reverend Wynterbottom called. "I've been praying to God for the safety of the ship and all its crew."

"Your prayers are answered, Reverend."

"We're out of danger?" Miss Robertson clutched Will's arm, steadying herself. He detected alarm in her voice—understandably so. They'd lived through a harrowing ordeal.

"Aye. We seem to have outrun the storm. Anyone injured?"

"Miss Robert—I mean Miss MacQuarie," Miss Robertson stammered.

"What?" Ian stiffened, that internal sense that something was not in its place, not straight, not true, spiked razor sharp. "What's happened?" He strode down the corridor to the ladies' cabin door. "Where is she?" He spun around and fired a look at Will. "What's happened to her?"

"The cat ran off and she went to look for her, sir. We called for Miss MacQuarie, but we cannae find her."

"Which way?" he shouted.

Miss Robertson pointed forward, toward the passage to the mizzenmast, a passage that should have been lashed shut. He'd have Will's hide for leaving it unattended right after he took Miss MacQuarie over his knee for not being where he had ordered her to be.

He lurched toward the darkened passage and, finding the door open, ducked inside. Turk kept supplies in this area. It should have been sealed up tight to keep things dry. The door on the far side that led to the galley remained sealed. He felt his way around. "Miss MacQuarie," he called. Nothing. He banged his knee on a sharp edge in a place that should be clear of items, and bent to feel. Damn, a crate containing provisions had toppled, blocking his way through. She must have gone in a different direction. If he couldn't get through, certainly she couldn't.

He backed out of the storage area and was about to

rethink his search when he remembered the hatch in the floor leading to the lower deck, one Turk rarely used, but that crate had fallen on top of it. Shite. He raced back inside and practically fell over the crate. "Reverend Wynterbottom," he shouted.

He heard the distant echo of, "Yes, Captain."

"Bring me a lantern!"

He tried to shift the crate. Bloody hell, what was inside the thing and why hadn't it been lashed down? He shoved and pulled and, damn, the thing would not budge. His heart pounded in his chest. If some bampot had left the hatch open, she could have fallen to the deck below, hurt herself. Shite, she could have broken her neck, the blasted wee bizzum.

"Miss MacQuarie!" He heard a faint cry. "Dinnae fash, lass. I'll reach you soon."

Reverend Wynterbottom arrived with the lantern.

"Hang it above and give me a hand with this, aye?"

The old clergyman was stronger than he looked and together they raised the crate back up on its end. He found the rope dangling on the wall that should have held the thing in place and handed it to Wynterbottom. "Fasten that on your side, sir."

Ian flung open the hatch door and called down, "Miss MacQuarie."

"We're here, Captain," she called back.

We? He snatched the lantern from above and took the steep steps down backward. Halfway, he lowered the lantern, casting light on Miss MacQuarie sitting on the floor in her trousers, the cat attached to the front of her like a barnacle. He reached the bottom step and knelt at her side.

"Are you injured?" It was then he saw the tracks on her dirty face, evidence she'd been weeping.

"I—*hic*—knew you'd come for us."

He gathered her in his arms. She buried her face against

his neck and sobbed. The itching feeling that something was not in its place eased.

After a few minutes, Reverend Wynterbottom called down. "Everyone all right?"

"Aye, Reverend. You can return to your cabin and let Miss Robertson know Miss MacQuarie is well."

The blasted cat made a yowling protest and scampered up the stairs. Miss MacQuarie pulled away from him. "You're all wet. You should get into some dry clothes before you catch your death."

He had been drenched in seawater for so many hours, he was no longer aware of his waterlogged state. Until now.

At her insistence, he allowed her to climb the steps on her own. When they reached her cabin, she said, "Please let me out on deck. I cannae bear to be down here—"

"Aye, lass." He understood. After a night in what would have been her personal hell, she needed the air. She needed the sun. As they made their way out onto the deck, he could see that she was favoring her right leg. He swept her into his arms and headed toward the fo'c'sle.

"Where are you taking me?"

"The surgery. I'll fetch someone to see to your injuries."

"Turk, the cook? Absolutely not!"

"Lass, ye've got some bad scrapes and I need to know you've no broken bones."

"If you let me walk on my own, you'll see it's just bruises and scratches."

He reluctantly set her on her feet.

"Go put on dry clothes. I'll be on the quarterdeck for only an hour or so, then I'll go to my cabin and sleep, aye."

What she proposed didn't feel right, but then Miss MacQuarie often jumbled his usually calm state of mind. She hobbled toward the aft. It was then he saw at least six of his men stop what they were doing and gape at her. Shite. They were staring at her frigging trousers.

"What are you looking at?" he shouted. "Go about your duties, men." His eyes fell back to her fine-looking rump, and he felt his cock thicken inside his uncomfortably soggy drawers.

• • •

Still reeling from the hours she'd spent trapped below deck in the dark, Louisa sat for some time on the box housing the skylight. She thought of this place as her personal perch. After all, Captain Sinclair had allowed it. He hadn't given anyone else leave to spend time on the quarterdeck.

Mairi visited her once. She'd tried to convince her to go below and dress decently. But Louisa couldn't find the strength to stand, nor did she want to leave the sun at that moment. She'd promised Mairi she'd "be along soon." That had been when the sun still hovered over the eastern horizon.

Now it was halfway to noon, yet she continued to reflect on her night spent trapped in the dark hull.

Though the ship had been in danger of being swamped by the storm, she had assured herself that Captain Sinclair would come for her. She'd seen the look in his eyes when he'd told her so. She knew the look of a stubborn man when she saw one. Her father and her brothers Connor and Nathan all had that look when they were most determined and they'd never failed. Only death would keep them from succeeding once they'd set their minds to something. Blasted pigheaded men. Impossible most of the time, but when it came down to it, she knew she could count on them, just as she knew she could count on Captain Sinclair.

She'd never spent so many hours trapped in a dark space. Even when her brothers had locked her in the closet, their boyish pranks had only lasted minutes, though they'd felt like an eternity. Someone had always answered her cries to be released. Louisa had screamed until she'd made herself hoarse last night, but no one had come.

Yet she hadn't been alone. Ian had been with her in spirit, holding her, dancing with her, rumbling in her ear and making her laugh. Ian, the antidote to her irrational dread. Big, tall Ian with his dark wavy hair and his blue, blue eyes. He'd taken her dancing in their pretend ballroom and her paralyzing anxiety had, for the first time, dissipated on its own. He hadn't cured her. But Ian had taught her how to manage her panic, how to conquer her own fears.

The storm last night had been twice as strong and had lasted twice as long as the first storm they'd encountered in the channel. Mr. Peter assured her that no one had been seriously injured—like her—just a few scrapes and bruises.

"Nothing a plaster and a tot of whisky wouldnae fix," he said, holding out a wooden cup and cloth bundle. "I brought you a cup of tea and bannocks for your breakfast."

"That's very kind of you, Mr. Peter."

"Dinnae thank me. Captain Sinclair asked I should bring it to you," he whispered.

She found her smile. "Why are you whispering?"

He pointed downward at the captain's mess below them. "He told me not to tell you he sent the tea," he rasped, and screwed up his face in a smirk. He was trying not to laugh.

She lowered her voice to match his. "Why would he no' want me to ken he sent the bannocks and tea?"

Mr. Peter leaned back on his heels, folded his arms, and cocked up an eyebrow. "Did he tell ye aboot his cousin Declan?"

"He hasnae talked much about his family."

Mr. Peter lifted his chin. "Ask him aboot Declan's dreams." He swooped off his hat, made a ridiculous bow, and sauntered down the stairs to the deck, jamming his hat back on his blond head as he went.

Louisa waited a moment before taking the stairs down to the deck and entering the captain's mess. Captain Sinclair bent over the dining table with a map spread out before him. His head popped up and he straightened, his expression carefully schooled into that blank stare Scotsmen wore when confronted with imminent death.

"Miss MacQuarie." His eyes dropped to her trousers and bounced back up to meet hers.

She lifted the tea and bannocks. "Were these your idea or Mr. Peter's?" she asked, testing him.

He returned to studying his map. "I asked Mr. Peter to bring you something," he said as if the gesture were of little consequence.

"Thank you," she said.

"It was nothing."

"I havenae properly thanked you for finding me—"

His head jerked up, lips flattened into a tight line and eyes flashing ice-blue anger. "You were in the wrong place—I specifically—why—" He took a deep breath. "Why can you not do as you're told?" His brow buckled, taking on a truly puzzled expression.

"I'm sorry." She really was. It had been her own fault for thoughtlessly dashing after the cat, putting herself in danger and Captain Sinclair through needless worry. "Will you forgive me?"

He stared at her without moving for an uncomfortably long time. At last he swallowed and nodded. "Yes. If you promise to do as I say for the duration of the voyage," he added.

She stopped grinning and said, "Yes. I promise." And she really did mean it. She would do exactly as he said...unless it was impossible.

He pointed the compass he was holding at her bottom

half. "And take off those trousers before you distract my men. You're a walking catastrophe."

"Yes, of course."

She had already turned to leave when he added, "You know, I was prepared for a bucket of nonsense from Miss Robertson. Even her brother warned me she was a handful. I didnae expect any trouble from you. But you've been twice the bother."

Apprehension seized her by the shoulders and spun her back around. Did he know? Did he suspect? Louisa examined his face for any clue. He remained still for several moments, and then a broad toothy smile stretched across his handsome face that nearly reached his ears. He chuckled and shook his head. "You certainly have made this trip interesting, Miss MacQuarie."

Louisa smiled back. "I do what I can." Victory. She'd made him laugh. Genuinely laugh. And it had only taken a hurricane and a pair of trousers.

"I get crabbit when I have no sleep," he said by way of apology. "Please sit and eat your breakfast." He moved the map to the other end of the table to make room for her, then pulled a chair out for her to sit. He continued to examine the map, walking the compass point across the complex markings.

She washed a bite of grainy bannock down with a mouthful of tepid tea and asked, "What are you doing?"

"Trying to determine our location."

"You dinnae ken where we are?"

He gave her a look of mock indignation. "A' course I ken where we are. We're in the Atlantic Ocean."

She laughed. He could be very charming when he wanted to be.

"Where exactly in the Atlantic Ocean is what I'm trying to establish," he said.

"How do you do that?"

He regarded her for a moment, as if measuring her sincerity. "Would you like me to explain it to you?"

• • •

Once again, Miss MacQuarie had surprised him.

"How do you do that?" she'd asked.

She wanted to know how to determine their position. He need only answer with vagaries like using the sun and the stars. But there was something so desperately eager in her eyes.

He knew life was difficult for women, especially clever ones like Mairi MacQuarie. Once, many years ago, when his mother had overheard him question the need to educate women as they could never understand concepts that came easily to men, she had blasted him with, "So, you think yourself smarter than women, laddie?" She'd locked him in the parlor with nothing but a basket of knitting for the entire day—ten hours of mind-numbing boredom.

When she'd fetched him for supper, he'd asked, "Why did you do that?"

She'd said, "That was one day, Ian. Imagine spending the rest of your days in that room. That's what life is like for intelligent women."

And so, he made the offer he knew his mother would have expected him to make. "Would you like me to explain it to you?"

"Oh, yes please!"

Her face lit up like it had when he'd given her *The Taming of the Shrew*. Staggering, he thought, how much it pleased him to please her. Demonstrating the instruments would likely throw off his schedule and leave him disorganized in the head for days, but he tried not to let it disconcert him overly much.

Just enjoy the moment, ye cloth-heid.

"Fine then. I have duties and then I need some sleep. As do you. We'll begin tomorrow after breakfast. But do wear your skirts. I cannae do the explaining to a woman wearing trousers."

"Thank you, Captain. You are correct. This is turning out to be a most interesting journey."

The next morning, Miss MacQuarie appeared at the door to his mess before he had finished his breakfast. She was looking refreshed with sleep, her hair in a tidy bun-thing and her eyes brighter than he'd ever seen them. She bounced on her toes a few times until he put on his coat and collected his hat. He made himself appear casual when, in truth, he was as excited as she.

As promised, he began teaching Miss MacQuarie the basics of navigation. And as he suspected, she was a serious student. She absorbed everything he said with a kind of desperate interest and keen understanding he'd never witnessed in anyone but young Peter.

He showed her the binnacle where the ship's compass was housed. He demonstrated how to use his sextant, an elaborately adorned brass instrument he'd purchased in Amsterdam three years ago—one that he valued even more than some of his books. And then he showed her the most important piece of navigational equipment aboard the *Gael Forss*.

Ian took the cherrywood box down from the cupboard and set it on the dining table.

"You use this box to navigate?" she asked.

"I use what's inside." He unlatched the top and lifted

back the lid.

Miss MacQuarie leaned in for a better look. "But that's just a clock."

"No' just any clock. It's a chronometer, a precision instrument able to keep within seconds of Greenwich Time."

"What does telling the time have to do with navigating?"

"It's just part of it. I use the compass for direction. I use the sextant for finding latitude, and I use the chronometer to accurately determine longitude, give or take a mile or two. It's when I have all three pieces, I can chart where we are on the map."

Miss MacQuarie's eyes roamed toward the map still spread out at the end of the dining table and anchored at each curly end with books. She was thinking, reasoning out what he'd just told her. Watching her face, witnessing the moment when the puzzle came together, filled him with...pride?

Her head popped up. "It's like in the city, isn't it? It's easier to find where you are when you ken the cross street."

God, she was amazing. Or maybe not. Maybe she wasn't unusual at all. Maybe all women were this smart and men simply didn't know it, or hadn't bothered to find out. The thought was a little unsettling, really. So many men unwittingly married to clever little women all squireling away their intelligence until one day...

"Am I right?" she asked, the light burning bright in her eyes.

"Aye, you've got the right of it, Mairi."

The light in her eyes extinguished. "Please. Dinnae call me Mairi."

He'd been too familiar, overstepped again. Damn. He looked away, not willing to let her see the color rush to his face. "Sorry," he said.

"Dinnae be sorry, Ian. It's just I never liked the name. I'll be changing it anyway."

"But Mairi is such a bonnie name."

"I need a better stage name. One that no one will forget."

Danny entered with supper, creamy smoked haddock soup and a loaf of rye. He hadn't known how hungry he was until he smelled the soup. "I'll be back with the ale, sir."

"Thank you, Mr. Sinkler," he said. "Please." He gestured for Miss MacQuarie to sit. "Are you hungry, lass?"

"Famished."

They were quiet while they ate. After Danny left the ale, Ian lifted his and saluted, "To clever women."

She lifted her tankard, and tapped his. "To clever women and wise men."

"*Slainte*," they said together.

If only he were a wise man. When it came to women, especially this woman, he had the brain of a potato. He set down his tankard. "So, if I cannae call you Mairi, what can I call you?"

"I like it when you call me lass. Once I decide what my stage name will be, you can call me that."

"You want very much to be an actress."

She closed her eyes, inhaled deeply, and tilted her head back. "It's wonderful, you know, to be acting a part in a play with everyone watching you, hundreds of people all listening to you, to everything you say. Laughing when you say a funny line and crying when there's a sad bit. And clapping at the end, shouting *bravo, bravo.* It's like the whole theater loves you."

"Will you be an actress all your life?"

"If you're asking will I ever marry, the answer is no. The theater is my love. I willnae shackle myself to a man."

There seemed to be something lacking in her conviction. Was she trying to convince him or herself? "What's wrong with men?"

"They," she huffed with frustration. "They're always

gone. They take no notice of their wives. And when they do, they're always ordering them around and telling them what they *shouldnae* do and who they *shouldnae* talk to and what they *shouldnae* wear."

He leaned back in his chair. "Like me?"

Her mouth hung open for a moment, then she closed it and looked down at her lap. "Well, maybe a wee bit." She sat up and added, "But you're much, much better."

"Better than who, lass?"

She shrugged. "Dinnae ken. My da, I suppose. But when I become a real actress, I'll be famous and travel all over the world and my da will—" She stopped herself, as if she'd said too much.

"What will your da do?"

"Nothing."

"I thought you said you were already a real actress."

Her face went the prettiest shade of pink he'd ever seen. She chewed on her lower lip, the one he very much wanted to kiss. "I might have exaggerated."

God, what it must have cost that proud woman to tell him that. He shook his head. "Nae, lass. I heard you reading the Shakespeare to the crew. You dinnae overstate your talents at all. You're a fine actress."

She leaned forward. "Do you think so? Do you *really* think so?"

"Aye, I do." And he wasn't lying to make her happy. She had commanded the crew's attention well. What he hadn't told her was that she was half cracked to want to be an actress. No woman as beautiful and intelligent and just plain lovely should throw her lot in with criminals and degenerates like actors. But he wasn't daft enough to tell her that at this particular moment. When things seemed to be going so well.

"And, what about you, Ian?" Louisa asked.

His name on her lips felt like a caress. "What about me?"

"You're a braw captain of a beautiful ship. Your first love must be the sea. Or would you give up life aboard ship to be married?"

"What makes you think I'm no' married?"

She startled. "But I thought you said…"

He shook his head. Did the lass have no guile? Every single thought in her head appeared on her face. "Nae. I dinnae have a wife. And, though I enjoy captaining the *Gael Forss*, it's not my life's ambition."

"What do you mean?"

"I am, at heart, a soldier. I was one until the war with France ended. I've been waiting for seven years to be reinstated."

Her demeanor had taken a dark turn. Many women had a sour attitude toward the profession. Women were such contradictions. As much as they were drawn to a smart-looking uniform, they had no taste for what soldiers actually did.

"Do you think that will ever happen?" she asked.

"It already has. General Sir Thomas Robertson, my former commander, has promised me a coveted position when I return from America. All I must do is safely deliver his daughter into the hands of her fiancé."

Chapter Seven

Louisa's heart reared up and took off at a gallop. Had she heard him correctly? Her father had promised him a commission if he delivered her to her fiancé? His future, his dream, his one ambition hinged on making happen the very thing Louisa was determined would not happen.

"Are you all right, lass?"

"Em, no. It's been a long day. I think I need to lie down." She rose from the table.

Captain Sinclair stood immediately. "Shall I escort you—"

"Nae. I'll be fine. Thank you for today, Captain Sinclair. It was very informative."

She found her way below without falling, though she wobbled on her pins like a drunkard. Reverend Wynterbottom, Mairi, Will, and Danny were all having their supper at the table. The boys bolted to their feet and before the reverend could struggle to his, she insisted they continue with their meal. She'd interrupted them. As a result, she felt separate, like an outsider.

"Did you have a nice time learning to drive the boat?" Mairi asked.

The boys snickered at Mairi's crude terminology. Men learned to discount women so early. How could they ever unlearn it? Yet, Captain Sinclair hadn't discounted her. Initially, she'd thought he'd agreed to teach her how navigation worked to prove that a woman could never understand such a complex concept. As the day wore on, though, it had become clear that he enjoyed showing her what he did. He'd even said she was clever.

"Yes, thank you. Very interesting, but exhausting. I think I'll find my bed."

She lit the oil lamp, turned up the flame, and shut the cabin door on the table conversation. Mairi's wedding dress hung on the wall. She'd nearly completed all the embroidery work, the tiny flowers so lovingly stitched along the cuffs, hem, and bodice. Mr. Kirby probably wouldn't even notice Mairi's hours and hours of labor. But she had made what might have been a plain gown beautiful because marrying Mr. Kirby was the most important event in her life. It was everything to her.

Just as a career in the King's army was everything to Captain Sinclair. Was becoming an actress the most important thing to Louisa? The sad answer was, she didn't know. She did know that if she reneged on her promise to Mairi and went through with the marriage to Mr. Kirby as her father had intended, she would crush Mairi's hopes and dreams and lose a good friend in the process. If Mr. Kirby married Mairi instead of Louisa, eventually her father would find out their deceit and Captain Sinclair's career would end in disgrace.

Mairi's laughter echoed in the corridor. She was so happy. A future she'd only dreamed of was about to come true. In less than a month's time, Mairi MacQuarie, a ladies' maid from the ugly part of Edinburgh, was about to become a lady of importance and the wife of a wealthy man.

No doubt this game of changing identities was still fun for her. It had become something altogether different for Louisa. It had become a nasty trick played upon two unsuspecting men. One braw and handsome and honest and generous. And the other...well, she didn't know the other, but he was her brother Nathan's friend whom he thought acceptable as a brother-in-law, so he must have a good character or Nathan would not have agreed.

She changed into her night rail, dimmed the lamp, and climbed into bed. Louisa rarely prayed. She was not a sinner of the first order but she was a sinner, and an unrepentant one at that. Tonight, Louisa whispered into the dark, "I've made a mess of things and I dinnae ken what to do. One way, I hurt Mairi. The other way, I hurt Captain Sinclair."

If Gran was here, she'd tell her to choose carefully. *Every choice you make has consequences—some good, some bad— you just have to learn to live with them.*

"I dinnae want to choose. I want to make everyone happy. Mairi and Mr. Kirby must wed, and Captain Sinclair must get his commission. But I dinnae ken how to make both happen without everyone discovering I'm a terrible person."

Louisa didn't think she could bear Captain Sinclair's look of hurt and scorn should he ever find out she'd played him a fool. He would never understand that it wasn't her intent to harm him. She simply didn't want a husband and Mairi did. Her plan had begun as a way to make everyone happy. Now, it had the potential to ruin lives.

• • •

Ian tugged his neckcloth loose and tossed it in the pile of washing for Will. Miss MacQuarie's exit had been abrupt.

It must have had something to do with what he'd said about returning to the army. She disapproved of soldiering. Nothing to be done about that. Women might be cleverer than most men believed, but the feminine set would never understand the importance of a well-run army. The safety and freedom of every British citizen depended on a powerful military, from the highest-ranking general to the meanest foot soldier.

He smiled to himself. Interesting. The *Gael Forss* was halfway to America and he hadn't thought much about the army until today, a topic that usually consumed much of his leisure time. What post did Robertson have in mind for him? A garrison in Ireland? That would be acceptable. His family would approve, as it would be close enough to home. India? Now, that would be exciting. Traveling halfway around the world to an exotic land rich in trade goods. He might even be able to establish a lucrative connection for the *Gael Forss* partnership.

Then again, he'd heard rumors about a growing conflict in the Crimea. Should he and his men be sent to the peninsula, he could see heavy action. Or he could end up in Canada. Who knew? And what was the point of speculating? Wherever or whatever Robertson assigned him, he would have achieved his goal of returning to the army. After that, he would methodically make his way up in the ranks. Ian's father would be proud.

And like that, his mood darkened. How could he have forgotten? He had a son. When he returned to Edinburgh, he would take on the responsibility of the boy's care, his education, his future. He couldn't raise a son, a six-year-old boy, while stationed at a garrison or fighting in the Crimea. Ludicrous.

The boy—Rory—must stay with his gran. Ian would provide generously for the lad. Rory wouldn't suffer from Ian's absence. After all, they hadn't even known the other existed until a few weeks ago. Ian would visit the boy once or twice a year, send gifts on his name day and Hogmanay. Ian's sister Maggie could be relied on, too. She'd make certain he was well and happy.

Ian finished straightening the objects on his desk, counting the quills in the box, and squaring the furniture in the room. "There now," he said to himself and surveyed the cabin. His things were in their proper place, his problems were sorted, and he could breathe again.

Shirtless, bootless, stockingless, he held a lamp to his library shelves and searched for something to read. Something light. Something to lessen the weight of his impending future. He paused on *A History of Tom Jones, a Foundling* and smiled. Peter was a foundling. He'd loaned this book to him when he was sixteen and the lad had taken it to heart. He was, forever after, chasing skirts.

Foundlings.

His cousin Magnus and wife Virginia collected foundling children. Last time he'd seen them, earlier this spring, they'd had one of their own making and five more fostered. Virginia adored them, of course. They were fine lads. All of them. What surprised Ian was that Magnus also loved the fostered boys, claimed them as his own.

"They were born legitimate," Magnus had explained. In three cases, both parents had died. In the other two, the mother had died and the father had been arrested and sent away as an indenture with little hope of ever returning. "I would adopt them, but they have names. They're no' bastards."

Bastard.

No one liked a bastard. People treated them as if it were somehow the child's fault the parents had not conceived in wedlock. Ian's boy was a bastard. Not the boy's fault. It was Ian's fault, yet the boy—Rory—would suffer for it. Ian would take all the blame, if he could. He'd gladly erase the word and free Rory from the stigma. But it wasn't possible. It wasn't fair. Ian had committed the injury, and Rory would forever bear the scar.

He pulled a book from the shelf without looking, hung the lamp over his bed, and dropped his head on his pillow. He would do everything he could for Rory, everything a father should do. He would provide for him and for the boy's gran. He would pay for his schooling and, in the event of Ian's untimely death, Rory would receive a sizable insurance payment. In that way, he was a responsible sire.

But could he love the boy? Could the boy love him?

Memories of his own father mingled with his thoughts. Laird John, the hours he'd spent patiently showing Ian how to bait a hook, hold a sword, fire a gun, ride a horse, clean a rabbit, track a deer—hell. His da had been a soldier once, but had left that life to raise a family. Had his father set aside his ambitions to raise his sons properly? Guilt gnawed little bites from Ian's bowels.

He tossed the book aside and rose. Something was out of place again. Something needed righting, straightening, squaring before he could sleep. He touched every object on his desk, the pen box, ink, sander, blotter, all aligned and balanced. Next, the book spines. A few had shifted. He straightened those. The box on his chest of drawers, it was crooked. He squared it with the top. Yes. No. That didn't do it.

Something was still out of place. Shite. Where was Miss MacQuarie? He flung on a coat to cover his shirtless body and ran, barefoot, outside and down the steps to the lower deck. Startled heads popped up from the table. He must appear a madman.

"Where's Miss MacQuarie?" he demanded, unable to quiet his breathing.

"In her cabin, sir," Will said. It sounded more like a question than an answer.

"Are you sure?" Ian went to the door and knocked. "Miss MacQuarie?"

No answer. He flipped the latch and pushed open the door, on the verge of exploding into a million pieces if she wasn't—

The lass sat up in bed, hair tousled, eyes blinking. She was here. The gnawing sensation in his bowels stopped, the world righted, and Ian could breathe again.

She brushed the hair from her face. "What's happened?"

She looked so beddable it made his todger grow heavy. "Nothing, I—I was just checking. You left so suddenly."

"I'm fine. Really." She sniffed and swiped at her eyes.

"Have you been weeping?"

"You needn't concern yourself, Captain."

He left the door open and cautiously stepped into her cabin, feeling like a trespasser, yet needing to know what had upset her or he would not be able to sleep. "Did the talk of soldiering unsettle you, lass?"

"A little." She pulled the bedcovers up to her chin. His presence was making her uncomfortable. He should leave.

"We'll discuss it tomorrow. Perhaps I can put your mind at ease."

"Very well."

"Good night, Miss MacQuarie." He made a slight bow and realized his coat was hanging open and his bare chest was visible. He buttoned the top button. "Sorry."

"Good night, Captain."

He walked back to his cabin dazed, as if he'd been clubbed in the head with a war hammer. Where was his brother Alex when he needed him? Alex would have told him to stop acting like a numpty weeks ago. And Declan, plague take him, had better have a different dream about the woman in trousers or Ian would have to drown his cousin. Declan's wife, Caya, wouldn't forgive him, but Alex and Magnus would understand.

...

Louisa stared at Captain Sinclair's back as he departed. *What was that about?*

Mairi entered the cabin and asked the same question.

"Dinnae ken."

Mairi folded her arms and narrowed her eyes. "A man barges into your room half crazed with fear that he may have *misplaced* you, and you dinnae ken why?"

"Well…" The burden of her dilemma was too much for her to shoulder alone. And it was, after all, their shared secret. Mairi was as much a part of this folly as Louisa, even though Louisa was entirely to blame. "You'd better sit."

Mairi lowered herself onto her berth. "You're scaring me. What's amiss?"

"Tonight, at supper, Captain Sinclair told me that my da has promised him a commission in the army as a reward for seeing that I get to Connecticut and wed Mr. Kirby."

Mairi glanced at her gown hanging on the wall.

"Dinnae fash yourself, Mairi. I willnae change my mind. You'll be the one to wed Mr. Kirby. It's just that once Da finds out about us, he'll take it out on Captain Sinclair."

"I see. And you're feeling sorry for him."

"Aye."

"And guilty."

"Aye."

"Me, too."

"You? But it was all my idea. You shouldnae feel guilty."

"But I do." Mairi started to blubber. "Every time the reverend says my name I feel like I told another lie. And I realized that's what I'll be doing forever. My entire life will be one big lie."

Louisa went to Mairi and tried to comfort her. "It's all right, Mairi. We're doing this thing for love and that cancels out the sin. Besides, after you and Mr. Kirby are married, you'll love your husband and your children so much, God will forgive you for everything."

Mairi sniffed and wiped her nose on her sleeve. "Promise?"

"I promise. You'll see. Everything will work out fine." Louisa sounded more confident than she felt. More lies added to the pile. Soon she would drown in them.

The next morning after breakfast, Louisa went for a walk on the quarterdeck. She had hoped to escape Captain Sinclair's notice, but no such luck.

He bounded up the steps to meet her. "Good morning, Miss MacQuarie."

"You've come to talk to me about the army, I suppose? Put my mind at rest?"

"Aye. I wanted you to understand that having a strong military is important for the stability of the government."

Oh, for all God's glory, did he think her head was filled with feathers? "I know that."

"Of course, you do. What I mean to say is that soldiers always face the possibility of danger. It's their duty to fight—"

"Fight, yes, soldiers fight." *Exasperating man.* "Captain Sinclair, despite the fact that I am a woman, I know what soldiers do. I know the importance of a well-trained army."

Captain Sinclair put one hand on his waist and clamped the other over his mouth, turned full circle, and paused. He took a few moments to prepare himself before he spoke. He even made a few false starts before he said, "Miss MacQuarie, often when we converse, I get a good feeling, as if things are pleasant between us, but eventually I always say or do something that upsets you, and I have to start all over again, as if we're strangers."

Regret for being so impatient weighed heavy on her conscience. He was trying hard to be a good captain.

"Please. It's not what you say or do, it's how I react. The fault is mine, not yours."

"Could you not tell me what upsets you? Do you not trust me enough to confide in me?"

"Some things are private."

"Aye. That much is true. But I wish you would consider me a friend."

His words soothed and hurt at the same time. His opinion of her mattered. Very much. But if he knew all her secrets, he would hate her and think her the worst person in the world. She would be his enemy, not his friend.

He let his head drop. She'd disappointed him by not accepting his offer of friendship immediately, and it made her heart ache to think she'd caused him more pain. "I do think of you as a friend, sir." His head bobbed up and their eyes met. "I only hope I can be as worthy a friend as you are to me."

His eyebrows dove together and he let his eyes slide sideways. "I confess that sometimes I think of what it would be like to be more than friends." His eyes found hers again.

Honesty. He had made a gift of honesty. The least she could do was return it. "I have had similar thoughts."

Captain Sinclair drew in a long, ragged breath and exhaled on a smile so broad, so sunny, it brought tears to her eyes.

She smiled through them and shook her head. "I think you are a flirt, sir."

"An honest flirt," he said, still grinning that irrepressible smile. He shot a look at the sky and said, "It's hot out here. Come inside the captain's mess. It's cooler, I think. You can help me figure out where the devil we are."

Once inside the mess, Louisa removed her sunbonnet and set it on the bench under the window that faced the back or aft.

"Do you mind if I remove my coat?" he asked.

"Not at all."

He smirked as he did so. "Once again, I wasnae dress properly when I visited your cabin last night. I hope I didnae shock you."

"Not at all. I have brothers. I ken perfectly well how men are made."

Captain Sinclair had a sudden coughing convulsion. She stood and gave him a few sharp thumps on the back. "Better?"

"Aye," he croaked.

"You look like you're choking to death."

He let out a strangled, "Went down the wrong pipe." He coughed again and recovered. "I'm fine now." He went around to the map and placed his hands on the table to support himself. "I've taken my readings, and I estimate we're in the middle of the Sargasso Sea."

"Sargasso Sea. Sounds exotic." She joined him at his left shoulder. Rather than stepping aside to make room for her, he turned out, opening a space between himself and the map, welcoming her to occupy it. His right index finger tapped a spot halfway between the western coast of Africa and a group of islands southeast of the Floridian peninsula. "But we're so far south of Connecticut."

"We're riding the ocean currents. They circle down and around. Once we reach this mark"—he tapped a spot above the islands—"we'll catch a ride on the Gulf Stream. It's strong and fast. Barring any unforeseen weather, it'll swing up along the American coastline to Connecticut in no time. You'll see."

Louisa was achingly conscious of his body curling behind her, giving off heat, and a delicious scent of cloves. She tapped the spots of land on the map. "I've heard these islands are thick with pirates."

"Pirates cannae catch us. They've tried but never succeeded. The *Gael Forss* is far too fast."

"You're awfully confident."

He spoke low and easy, his lips caressing her right ear. "I would never let anything happen to you."

Had he simply spoken the words outright, she would have taken them at face value. But the rumble of his just-right voice carried a hidden meaning, and though she wasn't clear what that hidden meaning was, the mystery of it made her shiver.

"Captain Sinclair, are you trying to seduce me?" she asked, sounding far, far too breathless.

"Do you want to be seduced, lass?" He slipped his hand around her waist and drew her backside against his hips.

The sensation robbed her of her reason, her strength, and every thought in her silly head. She closed her eyes and leaned back against his chest. "Yes, please."

He gave a deep chuckle, spun her around, and covered her lips with a searing kiss.

Louisa Robertson was going straight to hell.

• • •

She was so tempting. He tried to resist. God knows he tried. He resolved every morning not to give in to his base desires, not to subject Miss MacQuarie to his ravenous need to touch her, taste her, consume her, but she called to him like a siren, and if he didn't lash himself to the mast, he would crash on her rocky shore.

The part of his tiny brain—for it had shriveled considerably since leaving Edinburgh—hoped she would stop him because he didn't have the strength of will to pull away. But she was clutching at his shirt, pulling him closer, her delicate tongue venturing past his teeth, touching his, and withdrawing quickly as if he might bite. Her inexpert kisses made him smile. She'd exaggerated her experience with men, too.

"Lass," he said trailing light kisses along her jaw. "What do you want?"

"More," she whispered.

"More of what?" He nipped at her ear.

"More of you—oh."

Her exclamation of pleasure made him go hard as brass, demanding that he take her. Now. He could do it, too. She was ready to lie down for him. He could feel her yielding even now. He knew how to bring her to the brink, to make her scream his name, to wrap her legs around his hips and dig her heels in his ass while— *Shite.*

He lifted his head from the tops of her breasts that were plumping up with each heaving breath. "Do you have any idea where this will lead, lass?"

Her eyes were closed in reverie, and if he could pay someone to paint a picture of her just like this, he'd nail it to the ceiling above his bed.

She groaned her answer, "No."

He stole another kiss, as hard and as explicit as he could make it. "Disaster."

It cost him dearly, but he pulled himself away from her. She wilted for a moment, and he steadied her, holding her upright by her shoulders. He realized he'd backed her against the table and pinned her there, her bottom shoved up onto the map. Christ, he was a frigging animal.

"Why?" she asked. It was a plea really.

Because I want to toss you to the floor, spread your lovely legs, and mindlessly pound into you until I spill my anger into your body.

He took a moment to clear his head enough to form a civil sentence. "Because I will ruin you."

"But—"

"No more fabrications about all the men you've kissed. I dinnae believe you."

Her fingers fluttered to her lips. "Was it that awful?"

"God no. Yours are the sweetest kisses I've ever tasted."

"Then why will you no' kiss me?" She was close to tears, and he hated himself even more.

"Because," he shouted. He reined in his temper when she flinched. "Because I cannae stop at kisses, lass. I would take everything from you, and give you nothing in return."

Miss MacQuarie, proud and stubborn Miss MacQuarie, lifted her chin. "I dinnae want anything from you."

"You should. You deserve a prince. I'm nothing but a beggar." He thought she might leave then. March out of the dining room like she always had when he'd disappointed her or angered her. But she stood her ground.

"You." She jabbed her bloody finger in his chest. "You started this conversation, sir. You. Not me. You."

He stepped back, an instinctive response to her attack.

"You wonder why we start each day warm and end it cold. You wonder why I dinnae trust you, why I dinnae tell you what troubles me." She continued stabbing away at his chest, digging a hole in his left nipple. He took another step back and fetched up against the wall. "You are the reason why, sir. You are more changeable than the weather. What is the meaning of kissing me like that and then stopping? It's wrong, I think. A cruel kind of tease." She gave him one last poke.

"Ow." He rubbed at the spot.

Miss MacQuarie, outraged and looking more beautiful than ever, like some fearsome avenging angel, jammed her lethal fists on her hips and growled. "I have no intention of trapping you into an unwanted marriage, if that is what you fear, Captain. As I've told you before, I dinnae want a husband. I especially dinnae want a soldier husband who marches in and out of my life when it suits him, fathers children and then ignores them, leaves them to grow up without his love or attention." She made a sound of disgust and turned away.

Surprisingly, she didn't leave. They remained in those positions, motionless, for what seemed like forever, the sound of her angry breathing filling the room, drowning out the other ship's sounds, drowning out his fear.

"Is that what your father did?" he asked as gently as possible.

She took her time answering and when she finally spoke, it was to the window seat. "Even when our father did come home, he wasn't truly with us. We were like furniture to him. He ignored our mother, too. He'd lock himself in his office for hours or bury his head in the newspaper at the table." She sighed then, picked up her bonnet and sat on the window seat.

Without drawing too much attention, he leaned a hip on the tabletop.

"Once, my brothers and I wrote a little skit and performed it for him after his homecoming supper. We reenacted a scene from the battle at Quatre Bras." She glanced up. "Not that he told us anything about the battle. We learned about it from an account we'd read in the newspaper." She leaned back against the window. "I think we thought that if we were good little soldiers, he'd love us." She gave a bitter laugh. "He neither appreciated us nor our little skit."

"It's hard for soldiers to talk about battle. Especially

with family." Mercifully, no one had asked Ian about the war when he'd returned home and he'd never spoken of it. "War is not pretty and despite what people write in the newspapers afterward, there is nothing glorious about it."

She turned wounded green eyes up at him. "Then why did he not come back to us when it was over?"

Ian shrugged. "Dinnae ken." He cocked his head. "Your da fought at Quatre Bras? What regiment?"

Her eyes widened. "Were you there?"

"Aye. I would have died there, too, but Miss Robertson's da carried me off the field. I owe him my life."

She stood then, fixing to leave him. "Thank God for General Robertson." She paused at the door. "I should like to read more of the play to the crew after supper, if you have no objections."

"None at all. I may join you, if there's room at the table. You draw quite a crowd."

Good. He'd made her smile.

After she'd gone, he could swear he could still feel her, smell her, hear her, as if she'd left a ghost of herself behind to keep him company. Christ. Her father had been at Quatre Bras. He might have even fought alongside the man. MacQuarie. He wasn't in Ian's battalion. Probably one of Gordon's Highlanders. They'd taken more casualties than the 42nd that day.

The man's neglect, intentional or unintentional, had had a profound effect on Miss MacQuarie. What had she said about a soldier husband? He fathers children *and then leaves them to grow up without his love or attention.* In a way, he was like her da. He'd left his son, albeit unwittingly, to grow up without a father's love or attention which, to Miss MacQuarie, was a great sin against his child.

Too late to go back and make that right again. As a lad, whenever he'd done something stupid, broken something or hurt his sister's feelings, his father would say, "Some things, once done, cannot be undone, but one can atone."

For the rest of his life, Ian would atone.

. . .

Louisa flopped back on her berth and let her hammering heart slow to a dull throb. She had to stop talking to Captain Sinclair lest she reveal too much. But he had a way of wheedling things out of her with his blue-gray eyes and his blasted kisses. God, why did he have to kiss her? And worse, why did he have to stop kissing her?

I will ruin you.

So-bloody-what? She was an actress. People expected actresses to have loose morals. No one expected them to be virginal. Better to be ruined by Captain Sinclair's sure hands than by some clumsy, fumbling oaf. Didn't he know that?

She'd begged him to ruin her without consequence. Still he refused. There must be something wrong with her. She wasn't the most attractive woman in Edinburgh, but men often looked appreciatively at her. And he had seemed to like her kisses.

Yours are the sweetest kisses I've ever tasted.

Louisa didn't want sweet. She wanted passion, lust, and wickedness. Captain Sinclair's body had vibrated with desire, and for a moment, while he was kissing the top of her breasts, she'd felt very wicked. Perhaps she hadn't been wicked enough.

Do you have any idea where this will lead, lass?

He'd said kisses would lead to disaster as if it was a bad thing. Her body had told her disaster would be deliciously sinful. Her body had reacted similarly when she'd snooped among her brother Connor's belongings and found a book with drawings of men doing ludicrous things to women, sticking parts of their bodies into parts that ought not fit...or did they? It would have been disturbing but for the looks of pure rapture on the faces of the caricatures. Obviously, this kind of activity was pleasurable beyond measure.

Had the artist drawn from memory, or did he have real live models performing these acts specifically for the purpose of the manual? She closed her eyes and pictured Captain Sinclair's handsome face and well-formed body in place of the rotund fellow in the drawing and her face and body for the voluptuous Venus figure.

If the captain was as ardent as the man in the drawing, if he hadn't stopped himself this morning, he would have shoved her skirts up to her waist, unbuttoned the fall of his trousers and...would his look like the one in the drawing? She'd seen her brothers' dangly bits when they were boys, but the solid column of manhood Ian had pressed against her had been much, much larger.

Mairi appeared at the cabin door. "There you are."

"Were you looking for me?"

"No' very hard. After all, ye cannae have gone far." Mairi rolled her eyes at her feeble jest. "Will's right behind me with water for the wash."

"Miss," Will grunted and carefully sidled through the door sideways, trying not to splash any of the overly full buckets of water on the floor. He was not entirely successful. "Sorry."

"Just set them down. I'll return the buckets later," Mairi said.

After Will left, Louisa rose and closed the cabin door. "Actually, I wanted to ask you something."

She collected her dirty shift, stockings, and pantalettes and dropped them in the bucket of warm water along with Mairi's things. She'd never had occasion to wash her own clothes before this journey. Mairi'd shown her how to do it using the Castile soap she'd brought with her instead of the irritating lye soap they had on board. It wasn't difficult or objectionable work. It just took time, which she had a lot of.

"What did ye want to ask me?"

"After you and Mr. Kirby marry, do you expect there to be passion? In the marriage bed, I mean."

"Aye, I ken what ye mean," Mairi said flatly. "There best be passion in our marriage bed. I'll make certain of it."

"It's up to the woman?" It never occurred to Louisa that women were the ones to create the passion.

"It's best when both are eager, but sometimes, if the man isnae, em, *ready*"—Mairi drew the word "ready" out as if it was especially significant and continued—"the woman might have to work harder."

"What did you mean by *ready*?"

"You know, when his todger is..." She used her index finger to point straight up.

"Oh, yes of course. And by work harder, what is it that you do?"

Mairi giggled. "I dinnae ken. I never had to. The coal man was always ready for me."

"What if the man is ready but doesnae want to be passionate with me—I mean the woman?"

One of Mairi's eyebrows jumped up. "Did the woman offer herself to the man?"

Louisa had trouble looking Mairi in the eyes. "Well, she didnae tell him to stop."

"But the captain stopped himself?"

"Aye." Louisa dropped the pretense. "Oh Mairi." She abandoned her washing and flounced down on her mattress. "It was a disaster. He kissed me and it was..." She sighed. "It was wonderful, and he said things that made my legs wobbly." She sagged. "And then he stopped. He refused to ruin me." Louisa pounded a fist on her thigh. "Blast that bloody man."

At half eight Will knocked on their door, presumably to collect their supper tray. "Come in," Mairi called. Captain Blue-Eyes opened the door.

He held her copy of *The Taming of the Shrew.* "Your audience awaits." He grinned that crooked smile of his, as if he'd won some sort of game they were playing, which infuriated her. It also made her laugh in spite of herself. He glanced at the undergarments hanging to dry in the corner. His eyebrows reached for his hairline and he blushed. She'd never seen the captain blush before. He hooked a thumb over his shoulder. "Em, I'll wait out here." He withdrew to the corridor.

On their way through the galley, Captain Sinclair said, "They drew straws, ye ken. The losers pulled duty up top. The winners are waiting for you in the crew's mess for an hour's performance."

The smile in his voice was warm and generous. At the risk of recalling their previous altercation, she asked, "Why are you allowing me to read to your crew?"

They paused in front of the door leading to the mess, his hand resting on the latch. "You caught me unawares last time and I reacted badly. I apologize. Reading is a healthy diversion for the men. As long as I'm present, I approve."

He opened the door and she was met with applause. *Applause,* and she hadn't even begun. The sensation was glorious, exactly like she'd experienced on stage. All eyes on her, listening, eager for her to speak. And like before, a tremor of excitement or nerves—she couldn't distinguish—danced a crazy jig inside her stomach. This was her entrance.

She gave them an abashed smile and curtsied low, evoking nervous tittering from grown men. One of them, a man she recognized from the last time she'd read, a sailor with the leathery brown skin of an old man and the sparkling bright eyes of a youth, said, "We thank ye for gracing us with your lovely presence this evening, miss."

"It is my honor, sirs."

"You were never so complimentary when *I* read to you," Captain Sinclair barked, causing a round of laughter.

"Yer no' as pretty, sir," a young man in the back shouted, doubling the hilarity.

Good natured as he was, Captain Sinclair laughed along with them. She examined the men illuminated in the lamplight, open smiling faces turned up to their captain, their leader. They adored him. But, of course they would. He led them with a firm but just hand, demanded discipline, rewarded their loyalty and good work. Exactly the sort of man her father the general would like. Exactly the sort *she* would like.

He motioned for them to quiet and said, "Right then, one hour. Everyone on their best behavior for the lady," and added the specific warning, "No bawdy remarks, Lewis." He offered her his hand and indicated a chair set on top of a crate, a makeshift stage of sorts. Using him for balance, she stepped up onto her perch and began where she'd left off.

Captain Sinclair stepped back out of the circle of lamplight, melting into the shadowy corners of the compartment, but he was still there. She sensed him. Watching her. And she loved it.

She finished Act II to a round of applause and bowed. To her gratification—probably too much to her gratification— Captain Sinclair shouted, "*Brava! Brava!*"

The next two evenings, Louisa read Acts III and IV. Captain Sinclair escorted her to the crew's mess after supper, remained there until she'd completed her reading, and returned her to her cabin afterward. The crew had even welcomed Mairi and Reverend Wynterbottom, making room for them at the much-coveted bench nearest the front. It was all so perfect, their appreciation, their adoration. Just as she imagined life would be like as a celebrated actress.

Perhaps what brought her the most satisfaction was the crew's animated discussion after her readings. In the morning, as she strolled around the deck taking in the air and exercising her legs, she could hear the men discussing the play as they went about their chores, assessing the worth of Bianca's suitors, deliberating over whether Baptista was a good father, and speculating whether Petruchio wanted Kate for a wife or if he was using her for sport.

The fourth evening, as she was reading the final lines of Act V, the men were more attentive than usual, leaning forward, eyes wide, mouths open.

She read Petruchio's line, *"Why there's a wench: Come on, and kiss me Kate."*

The men released a collective, "Ooooo."

She stifled a chuckle, and continued with the next three lines. She could not, however, resist a glance at Captain Sinclair when she read Petruchio's line, *"Come Kate, we'll to bed."*

The line, of course, drew a swell of, "Aaaaah," from the men, followed by a round of self-conscious laughter. She read the final lines, closed the book, and stood to thunderous applause—well, thunder, because the men were stomping their feet.

"Will ye sing us a song, Miss MacQuarie?" one sailor asked. Several others joined in with, "Aye, a song, if you please."

She'd never sung in front of an audience before. She rifled through her memory for an appropriate tune, and all she could think of was "The Maiden of Bashful Fifteen," a rather bawdy song her brothers often sang. She looked to Captain Sinclair. "If the captain has no objections?" He shrugged.

"All right then, I'll give it a try.

"Here's to the maiden of bashful fifteen,
Here's to the widow of fifty;

She received smiles of recognition on the very first line.

"Here's to the flaunting extravagant queen,
And here's to the housewife that's thrifty.

A few of the men started swaying and clapping.

"Let the toast pass, Drink to the lass,
I'll warrant she'll prove an excuse for the glass."

Some joined her for the second round of the chorus. It was then she saw Captain Sinclair cover his eyes and peek through his fingers. Did he not like the song? Was she singing poorly? No matter. She had an audience and she was going to finish. After the fourth verse, everyone was on their feet, swaying and waving their tankards. She finished the last line of chorus on a flourish and met with raucous applause. She bowed several times, until Captain Sinclair stepped forward and formally thanked her for her outstanding performance. He treated her like a real actress. He believed in her.

As the mess area cleared, Captain Sinclair asked, "Would you care to take the night air before you retire, Miss MacQuarie?"

"Yes. Thank you." Once on deck, she asked, "Did you not like the song, Captain? You didnae sing along."

"First, you ken perfectly well, I cannae sing to save my life." She laughed. "Second, no one expected a bawdy drinking song from a lass like you, least of all me."

"First," she said. "I dinnae mind your singing at all. I particularly like your voice. Second, what do you mean a lass like me? Do you think I'm so innocent I wouldnae understand the innuendo?"

He coughed like he was choking on something.

"Are you all right, Captain?" she asked, knowing full well she had managed to shock him just a little.

He recovered and said, "Aye. I mean to say, nae."

They took the steps up to the quarterdeck and were quiet for a while, enjoying the balmy tropical breeze. "Do you think Kate was a shrew?" she asked.

"She was battling to be who she was, not what others wanted her to be. I dinnae see that as being a shrew," he said.

"But at the end of the play, when she bends to Petruchio's will, do you think he has broken her?"

"Nae. I ken Petruchio recognizes he's found his match, and Kate kens he sees her as his equal."

"You are unlike any man I've ever met before, Captain."

He turned to face her. "And you are unlike—"

Peter trotted down the gangway and called up to them. "Captain, sir."

"Aye, Mr. Peter."

"Mackay's spotted a ship off starboard."

Ian's head snapped left, tension gripping his body.

She scanned the horizon where the stars met the black ocean waters. Nothing.

Peter bounded up the steps in three leaps to join them on the quarterdeck. "There, sir. Eleven o'clock."

Following the direction of Peter's outstretched hand, she saw it. Like stars riding on the horizon, only yellow in color instead of white. Two of them so close together they looked like one. Running lights.

"Tell Mackay to keep an eye on them. We'll stay our course until we can determine their heading." Captain Sinclair's orders were firm but calm. Purposefully calm.

"Aye, Captain." Mr. Peter pounded down the stairs and strode away.

"Pirates?" she asked, probably sounding like a ninny.

"Occasionally, we encounter other ships. It's rare, but it happens. More than likely, it's another cargo vessel headed for the West Indies." He sounded as though he was reassuring her that there were no monsters under her bed. "We'll know by morning if they're friend or foe."

"And if they're foe?"

"I willnae let anything happen to you or Miss Robertson. After all, my future depends on getting your friend to Connecticut in one piece." He laughed as if he'd told her something hilarious. In truth, his words, like a carving knife, stabbed deep into her belly.

Chapter Eight

Ian sent Miss MacQuarie to her bed, then ordered the running lights extinguished and had the crew quietly pass the word to load and prime their weapons. He ordered the gun crew readied, as well. He spoke the truth when he told Miss MacQuarie it was unlikely the ship they spotted was a pirate ship, but Ian was no fool, and he wasn't about to get caught with his trousers around his knees. The *Gael Forss* held twenty-one souls. His chief responsibility was to ensure twenty-one souls reached the Connecticut coast alive.

Mr. Peter wisely shortened shifts. They needed the crew well rested and ready for battle should the need arise. Sleep eluded him, even though he tried. He lay in his cabin sifting through potential dangers and the strategies for avoiding encounters with hostile forces. Every time he closed his eyes, they would bounce open with a new threat and all the possible outcomes therein.

Eventually, he gave sleep up for lost and prowled the ship, taking time to have a word or two with every crewman, answering questions, making a casual joke, providing reassurances. Peter had set Will and Danny to lashing down anything not bolted to the deck. A direct hit by a cannon could easily send the heaviest of objects flying. He touched everything, his men, the guns, even Turk's pots and pans. Everything must be in its proper place. Everything.

Shite. Where the hell is Miss MacQuarie?

She had better be in her cabin. Asleep. Or he would… have a stern word with the maddening woman, his actress, his star. He reached her door in a matter of seconds. Closed. He put his ear against it. No sound. Tried the handle. Locked. He could knock but then he'd wake her and have to deal with the meddlesome baggage when he was already plagued with worry.

He started off toward the stairs when a door opened behind him.

"Captain Sinclair?"

He froze in place. It was her. He responded without turning around. "Aye, lass."

"Did you need something?"

He turned and saw her standing in the corridor, lantern in hand, wearing her shift. He took her in. All of her. Bare feet, bare arms, dark hair tumbling down her front, splaying where her breasts proudly protruded, breasts freed of their corseting, he registered.

"I was just checking…" He'd better leave now. His todger was growing heavier by the second.

She dipped her chin and made an effort not to smile. "Were you making certain I was where I was supposed to be?"

Jee-*sus*. How did she know him?

He started toward her. She set her lantern down and stood her ground until he reached out one long arm and hauled her slip of a body against his. He sank the fingers of his other hand into her hair, tugging her head back. Her eyes closed and her lips parted. He had to claim her mouth now, quick, before it was too late. The thing inside him that signaled when things were out of place warned him, *Don't let this one slip away. Capture her, tether her to your soul, keep her forever.*

"I'll see that you're safe," he rasped.

"I trust you," she said and rose on tiptoe.

He kissed her deep and hard and fast, like he wanted to take her. He palmed one round buttock and pressed himself into that lovely cleft where her thighs met. Where, if he could slide into her, everything in the world would be in its proper place.

Footsteps on the stairs. Someone was coming. He released her and whispered, "Get back in your cabin and stay there until you hear otherwise."

She stood at attention and saluted, "Aye, sir." He watched her prance back to her berth.

"Dawn, Captain," Peter said from behind him. "We can see the ship."

"Coming," he said, and followed Peter topside.

With dawn at their backs, their bodies slanted tall shadows across the deck. Ian used the glass to get a better look. "War sloop," he said. It had more guns and, depending on how much the ship was carrying, it might be faster than the *Gael Forss.*

"She's got Bermuda rigging," Peter said.

Mr. Purdie joined them. "Could be a post ship."

Ian handed Peter the glass. Between the three of them, the lad had the best eyes. "Can ye see their colors?"

Peter peered through the glass, his right eye closed so tight it pulled his mouth into a snarl. "They're heaving to... hoisted a wheft tied in the middle. Looks like Gran Colombia colors, sir." He lowered the glass. "They're in distress."

"Anything wrong with their rigging?" Ian asked.

Peter shook his head. "Cannae tell at this distance."

"Could be a trap," Purdie said.

"Aye." Ian weighed his choices. Sail on, possibly leaving men stranded to die at sea? Or risk being boarded, his crew slaughtered, and the women…shite. The safest option was to sail on, but what if it were the *Gael Forss* in distress? Could he pass the ship knowing he might be sentencing men to death? Could he live with that decision?

"What would you have us do, sir?" Peter asked.

His humanity won out. "Prepare to heave to. We'll see what they're about. Open the gun ports and run out the guns. Everyone else on deck with firearms ready. I want their captain to know we will defend ourselves."

"Aye, sir."

"And Mr. Peter, be prepared to run at the first sign of danger."

• • •

Louisa leaned out of her door and called to Will. "What's happening?"

He reached the bottom of the stairs and said, "It's a ship in distress. Captain's going in to see what's to do. You're to stay in your cabin, miss."

Louisa closed the door. Like hell she'd hide in her cabin. Captain Sinclair kissed her as if it were their last. They were in danger. She knew it. That could be a pirate ship out there, waiting in ambush.

Mairi yawned and stretched. "What's amiss?"

"Get dressed. And hurry."

She didn't have to ask Mairi twice. She bounded out of bed and they both dressed as quickly as possible.

"Why are you wearing your trousers?" Mairi asked, tying the closures of her own gown.

"Captain Sinclair is investigating another ship in distress." Louisa braided her hair into a queue and slipped her coat over the tail of it to hide its womanly length.

"Pirates?" Mairi gasped.

"No one knows, but I'm no' taking any chances. Go wake Reverend Wynterbottom. Tell him to get dressed and come wait with you in our cabin."

While Mairi fetched the reverend, Louisa dug through the items in her trunk until she found her pistol case. As she'd practiced many times, she methodically cleaned and prepared her firearms. Made for a woman, they had once belonged to Gran. Matched Samuel Nock flintlocks, five inches in length, lightweight, balanced, yet lethal at close range. At Louisa's insistence, Gran had taught her how to use them. From the very first time she'd held the gun in her hands, she had been transformed. Stronger, braver, bolder. And for the first time, she had understood how it must be for a man to know such power, the power to take another man's life.

Mairi returned and gave a start when she saw the pistols on the mattress. "Is it that bad?" she squeaked.

"Dinnae ken, but I'll be ready no matter what." She stuffed one pistol in her coat pocket, a cast off of Connor's from when he was fourteen, the year before he'd shot three inches in height. It had taken another three years before he'd gained the weight to match his build.

Reverend Wynterbottom arrived at their door. "Where are you going?"

"I'll be in the corridor. You and Miss Robertson lock the door behind me. Will and I will guard this section of the ship."

"I can't allow you to risk your life like that," he said.

"It's all right, Reverend," Mairi said. "She's a crack shot."

Louisa handed Mairi one of the two pistols. "Use this only if you must."

"Luck to you, sister," Mairi whispered, and shut the door.

Louisa stood in the darkened corridor and waited for the *snick* of the latch. She sucked in a lungful of courage and peered up the staircase leading to the upper deck. Will stood at the entrance, one foot on the deck, one on the top step, staring intently over the starboard rail. She heard Captain Sinclair shout something, a greeting of sorts that was followed by a distant reply.

"What's happening?" she asked Will.

"Captain asked the ship to report its distress."

"And what did they say?"

"Dinnae ken. They're talking in some other language."

"What language?" Louisa removed the pistol from her pocket.

Will said, "Captain's asking does anyone speak Spanish."

"I speak some." Louisa ran up the steps.

"No, miss. Ye've got to stay down." Will tried to block her, but she shoved him aside.

"I speak a little Spanish, Captain," she shouted. "Enough to get by."

Captain Sinclair aimed a pair of furious gray eyes her way. His mouth flattened into a white line. "Get below—"

"Let me try."

He glanced back at the other ship, before turning his steely gaze her way again. "Come," he barked.

She reached his side in a half dozen strides, using the same swagger she'd used as Viola, thinking it best the other ship didn't know the *Gael Forss* had females aboard.

Captain Sinclair raked her up and down with a glare and growled low, "What the devil are you about? And where did you get that pistol?"

"It's mine. What do you want me to say?" The ship floated a good one hundred yards away. It was bigger, had an additional mast, but it wasn't unlike the *Gael Forss*. A black-haired man stood on the ship's rear deck with his hands clasped behind his back. He wore a long coat and an oddly shaped black hat trimmed with white. His coat was fashioned like a uniform with epaulets and gold braid.

"Ask them the nature of their distress."

Louisa didn't know the exact translation for that phrase. She was able to recollect a few words from her rudimentary Spanish and assemble them into what might not be conjugated properly but communicated the essentials. She shouted, *"Por qué lloras por ayuda?"* Why do you cry help?

The man fired back a rapid stream of Spanish. She understood not a word.

"Hablar despacio!" Talk slow.

"Timón roto! Timón roto!" he shouted back.

"What did he say?" Captain Sinclair demanded. She heard the tension in his voice. This was serious. They were drifting ever closer to the ship.

"I'm sure *roto* means something like broke or broken, but I have no idea what *timón* means."

"Could it be they've a broken rudder, sir?" Mr. Peter asked.

Captain Sinclair swallowed hard and narrowed his eyes. She looked in the direction of his gaze. She could see the other man's face more clearly now. A stony scowl. Not the expression of friendship and relief she would expect from the captain of a stranded ship.

"Go below, lass." Ian's words held an ominous tone she'd never heard before.

A loud *thunk* resounded from the direction of the bow of the *Gael Forss*. One of the men cried out, "Captain, sir!"

Someone from the Spanish ship had tossed a grappling hook on board. Its pointed iron tines sank deep into the wooden railing. The rope attached to the hook ran back to the Spanish ship where a sailor lashed it to a belaying pin.

They were anchored to the other ship.

"Cut that line now!" Captain Sinclair shouted.

Then another *thunk* resounded from the rear deck. Suddenly the other captain shouted in English, "Run! Run!" Another man rose up next to him, pointed a pistol and fired. Louisa jumped when the man's head exploded into bloody bits.

Captain Sinclair yelled, *"Fy-aaaaaaar!"*

A great series of explosions rocked the ship, making her stagger backward. Captain Sinclair called for someone to cut them free of the aft line. Through the haze of stinging gun smoke, she saw one of the *Gael Forss* crew hack at the line with an axe.

Captain Sinclair shouted something at her but she couldn't hear anything through muffled shouts and cracks. All she knew was that chaos had erupted, everyone on board was firing their guns in the direction of the other ship, and a flurry of activity swirled around her as the sails on the *Gael Forss* unfurled.

Captain Sinclair shoved her to the deck just as the railing in front of her exploded into splinters. When she hit the boards, the pistol flew from her hand and skidded across the deck. The crewman who had been hacking away at the thick rope connected to the grappling hook screamed in agony and fell. He'd been shot in the leg.

Louisa called to Will, "Help him. You've got to stop the bleeding." Meanwhile, someone had to finish the job the crewman had started. With no one else about, the job fell to her. She collected the axe from where the crewman had dropped it and flailed away at the hemp braid. They had to get free. She glanced back toward the bow. Another two grappling hooks sailed through the air and sank into the railing. Men from the Spanish ship, pirates probably, began to climb across the lines like rats. They were going to be boarded if they didn't get free.

She hacked at the line harder and faster. The line vibrated. Dear Lord. A pirate was creeping toward her, his body hanging under it, legs wrapped around the rope at his knees, pulling himself toward the *Gael Forss* hand over hand. Fast. He would be upon her any second. And there were two others following him.

Her pistol. Where was her pistol? She searched the deck floor. *There.* Louisa reached down and grabbed it, and with no time to check the firing mechanism, she cocked and aimed at the pirate pulling himself over the railing. One shot. One chance. She fired.

But the pirate didn't stop. Had she missed? She couldn't have. And yet he scrambled onto the deck, a satisfied-looking grin on his face, as if he knew all along he'd best her. Her gaze flicked down to the widening bloodstain on his chest and back to his eyes again. The smile slipped from his face a few seconds before he collapsed.

With no time to think about having just shot someone, Louisa found the axe she'd been using and returned to the task of hacking through the line. All the while, volleys of shots sang through the air, deafening blasts shook the ship, and gun smoke stung the inside of her nose. At last, the line frayed and broke, dropping the two pirates clinging to it into the sea. Thank God.

She peered through the smoke on deck, searching for a glimpse of Captain Sinclair. Ian. Was he all right? Yes. There he was. Standing tall. Sword drawn. Jaw clenched. Calm as can be. A true soldier. Her warrior.

"Hard to starboard. Full sail," he shouted.

She sensed the ship change course, turning away from the other ship. The cannon blasts hadn't stopped and both crews continued to load and fire their muskets across the widening gap between the ships, but the *Gael Forss* was freed and too fast for the other lumbering vessel to catch. Then, in the middle of shouting another order, Captain Sinclair fell. His whole body slammed to the deck, his head hitting the boards like a cannonball. Her ears had stopped working, but she heard herself cry out his name from inside her head. Ian didn't move.

She ran to him, grabbed the shoulders of his coat, and started dragging him in the direction of the captain's quarters. Above her head she sensed bullets whizzing by. Out of the corner of her eye, one of their crew faltered to his knees. Will came to her aid, and together they pulled the captain inside his cabin. Another round of cannon fire shook the ship. They'd been hit, and to her mind, the explosion was right outside the captain's window.

But none of that mattered at the moment. She needed to find what had brought down Captain Sinclair. The light inside the room wasn't enough. "Will, light the lamp so I can see what's happened." She opened Ian's coat and saw no dark blotches of blood staining his shirt. "Will, where's that light?"

Will was struggling, hands shaking violently.

"Give it to me."

He brought her the flint and oil lamp. With a calm she was surprised she possessed, she lit the lamp on the second try, covered it with the glass and turned it up.

"It's his arm, miss."

His arm. Not his heart, not his head, his arm. A person could live without an arm. Using Captain Sinclair's dirk, she cut a hole in his right coat sleeve and tore it until she could cut the whole thing off. Next, she cut and tore away his shirtsleeve. A ball had entered his upper arm on one side and exited on the other. Had the bullet entered the right side of his chest? She scrabbled to push away the side of his coat. Her heart hammered until she felt every inch, assuring herself it had not.

"Give me your neckcloth, Will."

He tore it off and she wound it around Ian's arm just above the bullet hole stemming the flow of blood. Fortunately, there wasn't much. Why did he not open his eyes? She recalled the way he'd hit the deck, slipped her fingers under his head, and felt a matted and sticky mess. Louisa pulled her hand away covered in blood. He'd hit so hard, he'd been knocked unconscious.

After an agonizing half hour, the gunfire and explosions dwindled and grew more distant. Mr. Peter entered the cabin and announced that they'd outrun the ship and that Turk, the ship's cook and surgeon, was seeing to the crew's injuries—two minor and one severe.

"Is he alive?" Mr. Peter asked with a hitch in his voice.

"Yes, but he hasn't spoken. He fell and hit his head hard."

"I'll send Turk in to tend to the captain right away."

"The pirate that boarded the ship, the one I shot, is he dead?"

"Aye. Dead."

The back of Louisa's neck burned and guilt gnawed a hole in her chest. She'd shot and killed a man. She'd taken a life. Carrying the damned pistols had made her feel brave, powerful. Yet, taking a life, even the life of a bad man, made her feel awful.

"You'll feel bad for a while, Miss," Peter said. "I know I did. But you'll come to understand that you saved more lives by taking the one, and God will forgive you."

"Thank you, Mr. Peter. I appreciate your kind words."

Shortly after Mr. Peter left, Will returned with the hot water and clean rags she'd ordered. By then, she'd removed Ian's ruined coat and neckcloth. She proceeded to wash and wrap his wounded arm and head. When she finished, he remained motionless on the cabin floor. Only the slow rise of his belly indicated he still breathed, he still lived. Blows to the head were taken seriously. Her neighbor had been hit in the head and killed by a loose roof tile, one that had weighed no more than a pound, but it had fallen from such a height it had practically caved the top of the man's head in. Or so Mairi had told her. Mairi was one for gruesome details.

Mairi.

"Will, have you checked on Miss Robertson and Reverend Wynterbottom?"

"Aye. They're helping Turk with the injured."

Just then, Turk appeared at the cabin door. He knelt at Captain Sinclair's side and examined him while she explained what had transpired since the moment he'd been hit.

"Ye done well, miss. Will, help me get the captain to his bed." Louisa cradled his head in one hand while Turk and Will carried Captain Sinclair by the shoulders and feet to his berth. "The ball went through the fleshy part of his arm. That's why there's no' so much bleeding. The cut on his head is small but there's swelling. There's not much more I can do for the noo. Keep the wounds clean, dress them once more using this." He placed an earthen jar of salve on the desk. "And make him as comfortable as possible. I'll be back before supper."

"Will he be all right?" Will asked.

"Too soon to tell, son." And Turk left.

Tears streaking his dirty face, Will gently removed Captain Sinclair's boots one at a time.

"Captain Sinclair is a powerful man," Louisa assured him. "A wee ball cannae stop him. You ken that."

Will dashed away the tears and nodded. "Aye. He's the best man I ever know'd."

Throughout the day, Louisa and Will kept vigil at Captain Sinclair's side. The captain had many visitors, Mr. Purdie, Reverend Wynterbottom, and the worried faces of every crew member but the wounded. Apparently, Mairi and

Danny had taken on the responsibility of feeding the crew while Turk tended to the injured.

Mr. Peter reported the ship had received some minor damage to the aft but that it had already been adequately repaired. She left the room once while Mr. Peter and Will removed the rest of Captain Sinclair's clothing and another time when Turk came to examine him again. Other than that, she remained at his side. She refused to consider, even for a moment, that Ian Sinclair would never wake up. He had to. She needed him. The ship needed him. Everyone needed him.

He had to wake up because he needed to choose another book for her to read to the crew, and she daren't touch his precious system. And he hadn't finished showing her how the blasted chrono-something worked. Who would steer the ship if he didn't wake up to navigate? Louisa would be glad to see him wake if only to reprimand her for not staying below.

"Please wake up, Ian."

"What, miss?"

"Nothing. Go back to sleep, Will."

He curled back into a ball on the cabin floor. She covered him with what was left of Captain Sinclair's coat and returned to the chair next to Ian's berth. He was so still, frighteningly still.

• • •

A pale angel sat beside Ian's body sleeping. He supposed that was how it was done. After you died, your soul waited inside your body until an angel came to take you to heaven. Did everyone get his own angel? If so, his angel was asleep on the job. He could wake her and hasten his journey, but she seemed so peaceful slumbering in his chair, softly snoring, and wearing men's trousers.

"Bloody hell," he said. His personal angel stirred, the bothersome green-eyed baggage, Miss MacQuarie.

She blinked twice and her wide gemstone eyes shone in the moonlight. "You're awake."

What was it about her that engendered his anger and yet robbed him of his ability to rail at her? He gave her a feeble smile. "You're beautiful."

She sobbed and leaned forward, tears welling and dropping on her cheeks.

"I should have told you that before, but I was too proud," he said.

"I should have stayed in my cabin," she said.

"You disobeyed me, as usual. I would smack your bottom but my arm doesnae seem to work." He lifted his head and studied his arm. "My head hurts like the devil, too."

"You got shot in the arm and it knocked you to the deck. You hit your head hard, but Turk says you'll recover." She sniffed.

"Anyone else hurt?"

"Mr. Peter said Carson and Mackay have minor injuries, but Dougald Clyne might lose his foot."

He dragged in a breath. He might have avoided all this had he listened to his better judgement. "The ship?"

"Only minor damages and they've all been repaired."

"There's a bottle of whisky in the bottom drawer of my desk. Will you get it for me?" He was parched and in need of the healing properties of Declan's finest single malt.

She found the bottle, uncorked it, and helped him to sit up. He sucked in a few swallows, wiped his lips with his good hand, and lay back down. The sheet had slipped to his waist. She tugged it back up to his shoulders.

"You caught me naked again."

"How can you make light at a time like this, when I'm so worried for you?"

"Did ye look?"

Again, he surprised her into laughter. "No, I did not."

"Want a keek?"

"Stop your nonsense. Will's asleep on the floor. You'll wake him."

"Too bad for you."

She stroked his forehead, a welcome sensation amidst the rest of his aching body.

"Are you in a lot of pain? I can go get some laudanum from Turk."

"Nah. I've been worse." He stuck a finger in his ear and wiggled it. He had the ringing in his ears like he always did after battle, that high-pitched whistle that wouldn't stop. It had faded over the years but now it was back. Louder than ever. "I must have been out for some time, because I have to piss so bad it hurts. Help me stand."

"No, you cannae. I'll get the chamber pot, and wake Will to help you."

"I'm a grown man. I dinnae need help, but I cannae do it lying down. Help me to my feet."

"You are impossible, you know that?"

He grasped her right hand with his left, pulled himself to sitting, and swung his feet over the edge of the berth. He let the room stop spinning for a moment while Miss MacQuarie bent over, her lovely round arse in the air, and shook Will awake.

"Captain Sinclair needs your help with the chamber pot."

"Bloody hell. Hand me the pot and leave the room. I can manage."

She did as he asked, but not before making an interesting assortment of huffing noises, all of which he was familiar with as his mother, his sister, and his brother's wife used the same expressions to whinge. Was it a language common to all women? Were they taught from birth or was it something instinctive?

Ian got to his feet and leaned against the chest of drawers for support. Will stood in the shadows rubbing his eyes and yawning while Ian performed his business no-handed.

Once he'd finished, the boy took the pot from him brawly and set the cover on it. Offering his shoulder as support, Will helped him back to the berth.

"That was bloody humiliating." Ian sighed back on his pillow.

"Dinnae fash, Captain. She saw most of you, but she didnae see your pecker or your arse."

Ian sucked in his cheeks to keep from laughing.

As sober as a judge, Will carried the pot from the cabin like it contained the Crown Jewels and not the longest piss Ian had ever taken in his life.

Miss MacQuarie hurried back. The bedclothes had slipped to the floor when he stood and, of course, the moonlight illuminated the one part of him that had been better left in shadow. She assiduously averted her eyes, collected the sheet and tossed it over him.

"Sorry," he said.

"I doubt you mean that."

Seeing her march around the room in trousers stirred memories of this morning's brush with disaster. An image came to him of her swaggering down the gangway like a peacock. And then that heart-stopping moment when...

"Where did you get that wee pistol?"

"It's mine. My gran gave me a pair of them. I ken how to shoot. If you dinnae believe me—"

"Oh, aye. I believe you. Nothing you do surprises me anymore."

"I would have stayed below. Really. It's just that Will said you needed someone who spoke Spanish and I do, so…" She choked on her words and the tears that had been welling in her eyes rolled down her cheeks. "I shot one of the pirates. I killed him. I didnae—I didnae want to but..."

"It's all right, lass. It's over now. It was a brave thing you did, but try to forget about it, aye?" He sure as hell would like to forget about this entire day. "You were almost killed, do ye ken that?" he whispered, not wanting to speak the words out loud lest they come true.

She sniffed. "So were you." She stroked his forehead and raked her fingers through his hair. He remained quiet, enjoying the feeling. She said, "I thought about what happened. I thought a lot about the captain who spoke Spanish. I think pirates took his ship and forced him to lie to us."

"I think you're right."

"He gave his life to save us. He knew there was a gun pointed at him, still he warned us." The lass was working herself into a state. "And they shot him."

"Hush, now," he said. "He was a courageous man and we'll remember him in our prayers. But dinnae think about how he died, lass. Picture him in heaven with his family because that is surely where he is."

Miss MacQuarie sniffed and wiped her eyes. "You're right. That is what I'll do."

They were quiet for some time, disturbed only once when Will stole back into the room with an empty chamber pot and resumed his place on the floor.

"Should he not find his bed?"

"I asked him to—several times—but he insisted he had to be here with you," she whispered.

Ian closed his eyes. "My arm hurts. Will you rub my temples?"

"That's the remedy for your headache."

"You've got magic in your fingertips, lass."

"I feared you'd be so angry with me for disobeying, you

wouldnae want to speak to me."

He recited a line he recalled from *The Taming of the Shrew*. *"Sit by my side and let the world slip: We shall ne'er be younger."*

That got a chuckle out of her.

"You beetle-headed, flat-eared knave." She pressed her rose petal-soft fingertips against his temples and made those slow, bliss-inducing circles.

"There's small choice in rotten apples," he murmured.

"You three-inch fool," she whispered.

"Slow-winged turtle."

"Monster in apparel."

• • •

When she was certain Captain Sinclair was resting peacefully, Louisa returned to her cabin for some much-needed sleep of her own. The instant she entered their compartment, she was assaulted with something that stank of almonds, camphor, and rotten fish.

"Och. What is that smell?"

Mairi slathered an offensive substance on her hands. She had stuffed wads of cloth in her nose and so her speech sounded stoppered.

"Turk give it me for my cracked hands." Her brow buckled with real concern. "I'm afeard he kens what we're aboot."

Her words had a chilling effect on Louisa. She sat across from Mairi. "Take those things out of your nose and speak plainly. What makes you say Turk knows something?"

"Me and Danny was—were working in the galley making parritch for the crew. Turk come—came in, took my hand, and says, 'Those are no' the hands of a lady. What will yer husband say?' And then he gived me—gave me this manky goo and sent me awa'."

Louisa exhaled her relief. "Dinnae fash yerself. He didnae mean anything by that." She slipped off her coat and trousers and crawled under the bedclothes wearing only her shirt.

"But what if he's right? I hadnae considered my hands afore. Will Mr. Kirby ken right off I'm no' a lady when he sees my hands?"

"You can tell him you ruined your hands doing your own laundry on the voyage."

Mairi harrumphed. "More lies."

"Fine then," Louisa snapped. "For the rest of the voyage, I'll do all our laundry and you can let your hands pickle in that awful keech." She immediately regretted her outburst. They were both exhausted and Mairi needed careful handling. "Sorry," she said. "But it's important you dinnae tell anyone, now more than ever."

"Because of Captain Sinclair?"

"Aye."

"How is he?"

She flopped back down and covered her eyes with her forearm. "He'll do."

• • •

The following two weeks of their voyage were uneventful. So much so, Louisa yearned for something to happen to break the doldrums. Captain Sinclair had appointed Mr. Peter captain while he recovered from his wounds. The cut on his head had healed quickly. His arm was another matter. Louisa and Turk waged a constant battle to keep infection at bay. The smallest amount of suppuration could mean the loss of the captain's arm, an eventuality Louisa did not like considering.

Captain Sinclair had forbidden her to read to the crew

unless he could be present. Since Turk had forbidden the captain from leaving his quarters, saying, "Any number of contagion could be floating in the stale air below deck," Louisa had performed her dramatic readings for an audience of one.

This evening, she arrived at Captain Sinclair's door, book in hand, his favorite novel since childhood, *Gulliver's Travels* by Jonathan Swift. She found him propped up on his berth, his long legs stretched out and crossed at the ankles, his right arm in a sling. He was dressed in trousers and a shirt that had the right sleeve removed making it easier and more comfortable to change the bandage on his arm.

The procedure was not pleasant for the captain. The wound required some debridement, a thorough washing with hot water, and the reapplication of salve, painstaking for Louisa and painful for Captain Sinclair. On most days, Turk changed his dressing in the morning, and Louisa performed the duty in the evening. Each night, he would halfheartedly try to cajole her into skipping the redressing part. In turn, she would bargain, "No dressing, no reading." He would always acquiesce. Tonight, however, Captain Sinclair was being obstinate.

"Sit a while," he said, "and tell me of your plans to become an actress."

"We should change your bandage first, I think."

"Aye, lass. In a moment. First, tell me what you will do after Miss Robertson and Mr. Kirby marry."

"I travel to the Island of Manhattan where I will apply for work with a theater."

"You're confident you will find work with this place?"

"Oh yes. My previous employer has provided me with an excellent reference."

"I ken I should accompany you."

Accompany her? That was not an offer Louisa expected

nor one she could accept. Her references named Louisa Robertson, not Mairi MacQuarie. "But you have your own business, do you not?"

"Aye. Captain Peter is more than capable of taking our shipment to Boston and returning to New London for me."

"You are kind, but neither Miss Robertson nor I would trouble you, sir." She had started to lose control of her breathing and was growing more and more lightheaded by the second.

"It's no trouble. It's my duty. I've promised General Robertson I'd see his daughter delivered safely to Mr. Kirby. I reckon the general would want me to see his daughter's companion safely to New York, as well."

"But, but…" Oh, Lord. What to do? She hadn't foreseen this complication. Nothing was turning out quite like she thought. She hadn't anticipated meeting a handsome man like Captain Sinclair, nor had she ever imagined she would take such a liking for him and he for her, if she was interpreting his kisses properly. And she certainly hadn't guessed that her father had specifically asked the captain of her ship to bring her to her new husband as a personal favor in exchange for a choice commission in his army. And now this.

Captain Sinclair used the sleeve of his good arm to wipe his forehead. It was then she noticed he was perspiring. Sweat dripped down the sides of his temples and the front of his shirt was damp. A new kind of panic set in. The kind that filled her with dread. She held the back of her hand to his forehead and snatched it away as if she'd been burned. Fever.

She bolted from the cabin and called down the hatchway. "Will. Go fetch Turk. Hurry!"

She returned to Captain Sinclair's side, fumbled with the sling, and pulled away the dressing. The hole on the outside of his arm had almost healed. She turned his arm out to check the other side and cursed.

"*Tsk-tsk*," he chided. "Such language, Miss MacQuarie."

A light green pus oozed from the wound on the inside of his arm. All their work, two weeks of vigilance, had come to this. "Bloody bollocks."

"Sorry," he said, his voice but a ghost of a whisper.

Louisa met his gaze. His dark eyebrows, those two gleaming smudges that graced his handsome brow, drew together with such a plaintive look, it made her want to cry.

After examining Captain Sinclair, Turk took Louisa aside. "The ball must have left a piece of shirt inside his arm and it's taken this long to fester. I'll need to remove it."

"Now?" Fear had her by the throat and the word sounded strangled.

"The sooner the better." He turned and called, "Will, send Mr. Peter to me."

She heard Will shout, "Aye, sir," from just outside.

"What should I do?" Louisa asked.

"Best go below and wait. This is no business for women."

Sudden sharp fury burned away her fear. "This *is* my business, and I will not go to my cabin."

Turk's left eyebrow slowly crept upward and Louisa thought he'd put up a fuss. "Right then. Fetch hot water from the galley and bring it to the surgery."

By the time she reached the surgery with the kettle of hot water, Turk and Mr. Peter had the captain's long body stretched out, his feet hanging six inches off the foot of the table. Her chin wobbled at the sight of his big bony feet, naked and vulnerable. If this surgery didn't work, Turk may have to take his arm and still the captain could die of infection. If the surgery did stop the infection, there was a chance Turk would leave the arm mangled, crippling Ian for life.

The room was small and close and that old panicky feeling was inching up her spine. *Please. Not now. Not when he needs me.*

Turk strapped Ian's legs and arms to the table. He did not look good. His eyes had half closed, his jaw had gone slack, and his normally nut-brown face appeared waxy and lifeless. She had to turn away.

She edged by Mr. Peter and poured the scalding water into the basin.

"Fetch my knife and pinchers from the cabinet, Miss MacQuarie, if ye please," Turk said.

Just as she pulled the bundle of metal objects down from the shelf, Mr. Peter jostled her arm. She fumbled and dropped them into the basin of screaming-hot water. Without thinking, she reached into the basin to retrieve them. Only after she removed the objects and handed them to Turk, did the searing pain set in.

"You all right?" Turk asked.

"Y-yes. I'm f-fine."

Turk stuffed the leather sheath for his knife between Ian's teeth and said, "Bite." But Ian was too groggy to hang on to it. "Hold it there for him, lass. He'll bite down when I start. Then hold his head still, aye?"

"Yes."

Turk was quick. That much she could say. But the torture Ian endured etched itself on her heart. His efforts not to cry out made it only worse. She wiped away his tears and whispered over and over, "Breathe. Breathe. It's almost done. Almost done."

She didn't watch the procedure because she was too afraid she might be sick or swoon. She'd never liked the sight of blood. Turk pulled a wee piece of what he thought was cloth from Captain's arm, but he couldn't be certain. All they could do was wait and watch and pray. They gave him laudanum and carried him back to his cabin so he could sleep in comfort.

Once again, she and Will kept an all-night vigil by Captain

Sinclair's side. The fever clung to him like a devil. And rather than allowing peaceful sleep, the laudanum plunged him into apparent distress. He tossed about, mumbled words she couldn't understand, and shouted names she'd never heard. As dawn approached, she had one moment of terror when she thought it was the end for him. She had leaned over to wipe his forehead with a cool cloth when he opened his eyes.

He looked frightened, desperate. He said, "I've lost him. He was too small and I've lost him."

"Who?"

"Rory."

"It's all right, Ian. We'll find him," she reassured, even though she had no idea who Rory was.

Ian nodded as if he'd heard her, understood her, believed her, and closed his eyes.

. . .

The only thing worse than the pain in his arm was the bloody awful taste in his mouth. Had someone fed him cow dung for breakfast? He worked up enough spittle to speak. "Whisky." A cloud of lavender settled over his head, and he opened his eyes to meet a lovely pair of green ones.

"You're not having whisky for breakfast."

She lifted his head and held a cup of cool water to his lips. He drank a few sips before trying to sit up on his own. He'd had quite enough of this lying around like an infant. They grappled with each other but in the end, he won. Or she let him win. He didn't care. He was sitting, naked again, of course. Did she remove his clothing on purpose?

"How is your arm?" She secured the bedclothes over his lap.

"It's still there. What happened?"

"Your wound got infected, and Turk had to remove the

bit of lint that was causing the problem."

He scratched his head with his good hand. "That would explain why I dreamed I was being crucified." He thought for a moment and then asked, "Did you wipe my nose?"

Her green eyes slid sideways. "Maybe just a little."

He sighed. "Am I not allowed any dignity?"

Her back went ramrod straight, indignant, as if he'd insulted her. "I'll have you know you endured the procedure valiantly and with very little protest."

"You mean I didnae cry for my mother?"

"Not even once." She smiled then, a bashful smile he'd never seen before. He should stop being an ogre. She looked weary and had, no doubt, lost sleep on his account. "Who is Rory?" she asked.

Ian's heart thudded in his chest. "Who?"

"You said you lost Rory."

He swallowed hard. Denying Rory's existence did not sit well with him. Nor did discussing the child.

"Never mind," she said. "You were heavily drugged with laudanum at the time. I'm surprised you didnae talk aboot unicorns and fairies." She laughed then and Ian laughed halfheartedly.

To change the subject, he said, "I'm hungry."

• • •

Three days later, he was well enough to dress himself and take his meals at the table like an adult. He and Peter had finished taking their readings, and they estimated they were about ten miles off the coast of Georgia.

"Another week perhaps?"

"If the weather holds," Peter said.

"When we get to New London, I want you to take the ship to Boston as we planned, and then return for me."

"What will you do?"

"I will escort Miss Robertson and Miss MacQuarie to Mr. Kirby's home."

"Do you never find it odd?" Peter asked, his normally smooth brow deeply furrowed.

"Do I find what odd?"

"Miss Robertson and Miss MacQuarie."

"What's odd about them?"

"They seem…reversed."

"What the hell are you talking about, man?"

Peter held both hands out, signaling him to calm. "It's just that Miss Robertson is supposed to be from a good family and Miss MacQuarie, well, she's an actress."

"So?"

"Would you not expect Miss Robertson to be the one to have the manners of a gentlewoman?"

Calling into question Miss MacQuarie's station rankled Ian. "I'm surprised by you, Peter. Of all people. Just because Miss MacQuarie has her sights set on a life in the theater doesnae mean she's of low birth."

"Sorry, I didnae mean to imply—"

"I should hope you did not." Ian straightened the map and moved the compass to the right corner. Peter's comment aggravated him more than he'd like to admit. He'd had similar misgivings, but for reasons he didn't like to examine too closely, he'd set them aside.

"Em, you were saying, sir," Peter said. "You'll be escorting the ladies. And who will go with you?"

"No one. I'll be fine on my own."

Peter cocked his head to the side and gave him that look.

"What?"

"Am I still captain of the *Gael Forss*?"

"Aye. You've done a fine job in my stead. I knew you would."

"Good. Then, as captain I insist you take another crew member with you as escort."

Ian opened his mouth to object, and Peter cocked his bloody head again.

"Fine," Ian bit off. "I'll take Will. Miss MacQuarie is fond of him."

"And are you fond of Miss MacQuarie?"

"I beg your pardon." He took a menacing step around the table.

"Did your cousin Declan not dream you'd marry a lass in trousers?"

Ian did not like Peter's tone.

"And was Miss MacQuarie not wearing trousers the day we battled the pirates?"

Ian pointed a cautionary finger. "Tread carefully, sir."

Peter had the audacity to laugh at him outright.

"Ye'd better run," Ian growled, "or yer going to lose those pretty white teeth of yours."

Peter fled but paused at the doorway and shot back, "Ye ken Declan's dreams never lie."

Ian hurled a stale bannock at Peter's head. He ducked and it hit Miss MacQuarie between the eyes. "Och!"

"Sorry," Peter said and bolted, leaving Ian red faced and seething.

"I believe this is yours," she said, handing him the bannock.

"One day I'm going to lose my patience with that loon and give him the thrashing of a lifetime."

A merry chuckle bubbled up from deep inside her. God, she looked lovely—lovelier than usual—and the sight of her made him forget his anger.

"How is your arm?"

"Fine." To demonstrate, he gave it an experimental flex, the range in motion twice what it was yesterday.

"Then you're well enough to come below while I read to the crew?"

The answer to her question was yes and she knew it. But he wasn't ready to share her with anyone just yet. He feigned fresh pain. "My arm gets to aching as the day wears on. I ken I need your tending after supper. Your voice is a tonic to my suffering."

"If that is what you wish," she said, and lowered her lashes, hiding her green eyes from him.

He caught a hit of her lavender scent and knew he needed to touch her. "Come here to me."

"I dare not come closer, as I think you have more vigor than you admit to."

He crept a step closer to her. "Nae, lass. I'm as weak as a kitten. No threat to you."

"Sir, by the look in your eyes I would say I am in more danger than ever."

"What you see, I fear, is a fever. Put your hand to my head and check." He stepped closer still and lifted her silky palm to his forehead.

"Oh, aye. That is a fever, but no' the kind of fever any medicine will improve."

He slid his good arm around her slender back, pulled her close, and spoke low in her ear. "Tell me what is the cure, my sweet lass, and then give it me."

She kissed him then and his body hardened. He was sick with want and he would have his cure splayed on his floor, bent over a table, sitting on his lap—it mattered not how, other than he needed her naked so that he could lick every inch of her skin, kiss every freckle, stroke her in all the places that made her gasp with delight.

She pushed away. "No. No more kissing. I must speak to you about something first."

"And then kissing?" he asked, grinning at her like a fool.

She huffed. "This is serious."

"Sorry. Proceed."

"Reverend Wynterbottom will accompany Miss Robertson and me to Mr. Kirby's home. She's grown rather attached to him and wishes for him to attend her wedding breakfast." She prowled around the perimeter of the room like a cat. "After the ceremony, the reverend will see me to New York."

"The reverend is a fine man when he's sober, but he's no substitute for a skilled soldier."

"Must I remind you that you have only one functioning arm and that arm is, I'm guessing, not your sword arm?"

He didn't like that reminder, but she was wrong. They could take his arm, his legs, and his ears and he'd still be twice as lethal as the next man. "By the time we reach New London, I will be fit to be your protector."

"Ian," she said and the velvety sound of his name on her lips made him burn. "We must part. You know that."

"Aye."

"Better to make the cut quick and clean and spare each other pain, is it not?"

He swallowed hard. She was right. He didn't like that she was right, hadn't let himself imagine what life would be like once she was no longer aboard the *Gael Forss*, but she was right, and it made the thing inside him itch for order. He straightened the map on the table, pushed a chair back into place, and turned the handle of the teapot to the right. "That's a problem, you see. Because I find I need to see that you arrive safely in New York."

"It would spare my heart if you would not," she said, and Ian saw her eyes glisten.

"It would soothe my heart if I would," he said.

Chapter Nine

They sailed into port at New London, Connecticut, on August 21st exactly as Captain Sinclair had promised her to the day. She hadn't exchanged many words with him since she'd asked him to abandon the notion of escorting her to New York. The few times they had spoken, she'd hinted at it, but he'd remained unmoved. Unlike the many previous disagreements they'd had, Captain Sinclair didn't seem angry. His demeanor was melancholy, if she were to guess. Perhaps that's how a long voyage affected some people. Especially when you'd grown friendly with passengers you might never see again.

Mr. Peter told Louisa and Mairi it would be hours before they could go ashore, so they took their time with their toilette. During the crossing, fresh water had been too precious to waste on bathing. The ladies had had to stand in shallow tubs and sponge themselves from a basin of water. But once they weighed anchor in the calm waters of the Thames River—for like the port city of New London, its river had been named after its English counterpart—Will hauled a hip bath to their cabin and filled it with hot water.

Heaven.

They used their time luxuriating in the bath, applying powders and scents, dressing in their best gowns, pinning their hair into intricate whirls and curls, and finally adorning their heads with their best bonnets. Will knocked on their door and announced that the time had come.

"I'm going to miss you, Will," Louisa said. "You've been very kind to us."

"Oh, ye willnae miss me yet. I'm to travel with the captain as his personal *ay-dee-kam*."

Louisa ran *ay-dee-kam* through her head a couple of times before retrieving the translation. "Do you mean his aide-de-camp?"

"Aye. That."

"I see. Well, are you washed and ready to go?"

"Captain checked, but you can check, too, if ye like." He bent his head and pulled the flaps of his ears forward so Louisa could inspect behind them. The fact that Captain Sinclair had checked tugged at her heart. He would be a good father and a good husband. It's too bad he had to be a soldier. And it was very unfortunate that he would suffer when her father discovered her lie. Because General Robertson would find out. Maybe not right away, but eventually. She would do anything to change that. She'd even give up her own ambitions if she could change Captain Sinclair's outcome to something that would make him happy.

She and Mairi followed Will up on deck and joined Reverend Wynterbottom who was shaking hands with Danny Sinkler and Turk. She didn't see Captain Sinclair anywhere.

Mairi hung over the railing and scanned the dock, which looked and smelled like the Leith Docks in Edinburgh where they'd started their voyage. "Do you think he's here?" Mairi asked.

"Who?"

"Mr. Kirby, a' course." Mairi continued to search. Would she be able to pick him out of a crowd based on the painted miniature alone?

"I doubt he'll know to meet us."

"That's him." Mairi shook Louisa's shoulder. "That's him." She pointed to a tall gentleman wearing a short top hat, a dark brown cutaway coat and waistcoat, black tied neckcloth, and turned-down boots over tobacco-brown trousers. He removed his hat revealing a mop of loose light brown curls. He lifted his open face to the ship. Mairi leaned out and waved her hand high. "Mr. Kirby!"

The moment Mr. Kirby connected with Mairi, his face lit up with an astonished smile. He waved his hat high above his head. "Miss Robertson!"

Mairi grabbed Louisa's hand. "He sees me," she squealed with delight. "He's here and he's waiting for me." She turned to Louisa, tears in her eyes. "I've never been so happy in my life. Thank you."

Louisa embraced Mairi and they both wept, the feelings of the moment too overwhelming for them to sort.

From behind them, Captain Sinclair said, "Are you ready to meet your fiancé, Miss Robertson?"

"Yes," Mairi said.

Captain Sinclair offered Mairi his hand and escorted her down the gangway. Louisa waited and watched. The dock was too noisy for her to hear their conversation, but it was clear from the look on Mr. Kirby's face, Mairi had mesmerized him immediately.

Mairi lost her balance for a moment and wobbled. Captain Sinclair had warned them they would be unsteady on their feet once they disembarked, but it would only last a few minutes. Mr. Kirby was delighted to catch Mairi and hold onto her. He cradled her in his arms as if holding a life-sized doll made of china. Had she just watched two people fall in love? And did Mr. Kirby know how very lucky he was to have Mairi and not her for a wife?

Captain Sinclair strode back up the gangway and called to her. "Coming?" He reached out a hand. She was tempted to slip her gloved one in his. She had a fleeting desire to repeat with Captain Sinclair the scene Mr. Kirby and Mairi had just played out. But that was not the drama in which she and Captain Sinclair had been cast. Mr. Kirby and Mairi were cast in a comedy. Louisa and Captain Sinclair's play was a tragedy.

. . .

She didn't want him to come along. Too bad. That wasn't her decision. Ian was in charge, and he didn't bloody care what Miss MacQuarie wanted. She might be done with him, but he wasn't done with her. Not by a long chalk.

He offered her a hand thinking she might appreciate some help to shore. But no. The bothersome hen shooed him away. *She shooed him away.* Well then, fine. She could steady her own goddamn self down the gangway.

It always took Ian a moment to find his land legs. However, he neglected to keep in mind that Miss MacQuarie was not at all prepared for solid ground. As soon as they stepped off the planking, he heard Miss MacQuarie utter a very unladylike curse word.

When he turned to find her crumpled on the ground, he uttered the same curse word only louder. "Oh, Christ, lass. I'm sorry." He scooped her up, set her back on her feet, and held her there while she tottered from side to side.

"Bloody hell. The land stays still, but I cannae stop moving." She clutched his bad arm for support.

"Ow." He peeled her gloved hand off his arm one finger

at a time. "Dinnae panic. It'll go away in a second."

She swatted him with her purse thing. "I'm no' panicking and stop manhandling me."

He released her and she immediately teetered backward. Ian caught her with his good arm and righted her again. He growled in her ear, "Stop fighting me."

He felt her body sag against his.

"Sorry," she sobbed.

He stared down his nose at her. She was obviously out of sorts. He didn't know why but he deeply regretted being so impatient. "I'm sorry, too." He waited for a moment, then said, "Can you stand on your own now?"

She stepped away from him, sniffed and took a brave breath. "Yes. I think so."

"Good. Let's go find Mr. Kirby and Miss Robertson. They said they'd wait by the dray with the baggage."

He forged a path through the crowd of people standing on the dock and did his best to shield Miss MacQuarie from being jostled about. When at last they reached the dray, he got that uncomfortable itch. Something wasn't right. Shite. Where the hell was Will? He shouted his name.

"I'm here, Captain." Will waved to him from the back of the dray. The lad had made a sort of nest for himself among the trunks and baggage.

"Good lad. Stay with the luggage. See that it gets to the house safely."

"Aye, sir."

"Here." He handed Will a few American coppers. "In case you need 'em."

"Do ye ken we'll be attacked by Indians, sir?" Will asked gravely.

Ian kept a straight face. "Perhaps. But I trust you'll handle them brawly."

Will puffed out his narrow chest. "Aye-aye, Captain."

The driver snapped the reins and the dray pulled away. Ian waved farewell.

Miss MacQuarie said, "Why ever did you let Will think there would be Indians?"

He smiled down at her and shrugged. She might grasp the fundamentals of navigation, read Shakespeare, and speak Spanish, but wearing trousers didn't make you think like a man. She'd never understand Will's need to be one today.

Oblivious to the rest of the world, Mr. Kirby and Miss Robertson stood gazing into each other's eyes wearing soppy grins that made them appear to Ian like twin dafties. He shook his head in disgust and asked Miss MacQuarie, "Do you want to interrupt them, or should I?"

She made a gracious sweep of her hand. "You may do the honors, Captain."

Ian stepped forward and cleared his throat. Twice. No response. He called to Mr. Kirby, a shout that startled other people milling about, but had no effect on the smitten kittens. He asked Miss MacQuarie, "Do you want to take a crack at it?"

She slipped her arm through Miss Robertson's and said, "Darling, is this your Mr. Kirby? You must introduce us."

At last the lovebirds awoke from their stupor. Miss Robertson made introductions, and Mr. Kirby stammered through what must have been a welcoming speech he'd rehearsed.

"How did you know we'd arrive today?" Miss MacQuarie asked.

Ian knew the answer before Kirby owned it.

"I didn't, actually." The man dipped his head. "I've come to the docks every day for the last week…hoping."

He knew in his head he should be happy for the man. Kirby had applied for a wife, and a wife had been delivered to him. A bonnie wife and from the looks of her, a willing wife. Yet a part of him resented the man's good fortune. What had Kirby done to deserve Miss Robertson? Then he remembered: they called her the General's Daughter from Hell. Miss Robertson had been nothing but biddable during the crossing. Had she reformed, or was she saving her worst for after the wedding? Perhaps he should feel sorry for poor Mr. Kirby.

Reverend Wynterbottom joined them. Ian had completely forgotten about the man.

After introductions, Mr. Kirby said, "My carriage is right this way if you'll all follow me." Kirby offered Miss Robertson his arm. The loon was going to walk into a wall if he didn't tear his eyes away from Miss Robertson and look where he was going.

Ian offered Miss MacQuarie his arm, but not because he needed to attach himself to her like a lovesick puppy. He did it for purely practical reasons. The streets were crowded and rutted and it would be just his luck she would turn an ankle.

"Does your arm pain you?" she asked.

"Only when a certain someone sticks her thumb in my wound."

She snorted. *The bloody wee bizzum snorted.*

"You find that amusing?"

"Me? No." Was she feigning innocence? Was she acting again?

"It's a serious matter, ye ken. It could have been worse. As it was, I nearly died." How did she manage to get at his spleen?

"I know and I am sorry. You're in a delicate state, and I promise to handle you gently from now on."

He clamped his mouth shut and bit back a curse. When he had his temper under control he growled, "Miss MacQuarie, when I get you alone I'm going to—" Something occurred to him, a sudden thought which blossomed into a full realization. He smiled his bitter satisfaction. "I see what you're doing."

"What? What am I doing?"

"You're trying to make me so angry, I'll return to the ship."

She gasped and sputtered those female sounds, the ones that meant she thought he was being ridiculous, but it was all an act.

"I'm not trying to—that's utter nonsense. I dinnae ken where you get such notions."

They didn't speak again until they reached the carriage, a smart-looking coach and four. Mr. Kirby must be doing well for himself. Ian held the reverend's stick for him and gave the older clergyman a boost up into the carriage.

While Kirby helped Miss Robertson inside, Miss MacQuarie turned to him and announced in full voice, "Well, this is goodbye then, Captain Sinclair. You've executed your duty splendidly. Miss Robertson and I are safely delivered into the capable hands of Mr. Kirby." She was acting up a storm. He knew it. She knew it. He suspected Miss Robertson knew it, too. "I thank you for your service and do wish you a good voyage home." Mr. Kirby was, however, unfamiliar with Miss MacQuarie's talents.

"Captain Sinclair, I insist you join us. There's plenty of room in my house. You'll be an honored guest at our nuptials. We can be wed within a fortnight." He turned to the Daughter from Hell. "That is, if you desire it so, Miss Robertson."

Miss Robertson gave him a pretty blush. "I do, Mr. Kirby." Could women make themselves blush whenever they wanted to? He knew he couldn't control his own color. Perhaps that was a skill taught only to women.

"Captain Sinclair has very important business awaiting him in Boston," Miss MacQuarie insisted.

"Thank you, Mr. Kirby. I accept your gracious offer as it is my fervent wish to see you wed so that I may report the details to Miss Robertson's father."

He experienced a euphoric rush when his pistol-wielding, trouser-wearing actress slumped her shoulders in defeat.

Chapter Ten

Louisa resisted calling the captain a bad name and climbed inside the coach. Why did he have to insist on coming along for the wedding? He'd done his job, fulfilled his obligation. Now it was time for him to go back to Scotland and report to her father. She could imagine how that would go. Captain Sinclair standing at attention in front of the general, glowing with the satisfaction of a job well done, and fully expecting his hard-earned commission.

Delivered the goods just as you asked, sir. A few minor incidents at sea. Nothing out of the ordinary. Chased by a hurricane and shot by a pirate. Nothing I couldnae handle. What's that you ask? Any problems with the Daughter from Hell? None at all, sir. Quiet as a mouse, she was. Stayed in her cabin like a good girl the entire time. It was her companion that was the real problem. A blasted actress. Wore trousers and carried pistols with her. Nearly got me killed.

And then her da would know. The Tartan Terror would fly into a rage. If he didn't kill Captain Sinclair on the spot, he'd put him in irons. At the very least, he'd dismiss him, disgrace him, leave him dishonored and disbarred from the army forever.

Oh God, what have I done?

"Are you feeling unwell, Miss MacQuarie?" Mr. Kirby asked. He and Captain Sinclair were seated facing Mairi, Reverend Wynterbottom, and Louisa in the sumptuously appointed carriage. The interior was lined with velvet and trimmed in polished brass. Even more impressive, the seats were upholstered with plush leather squabs.

"I fear she has the land sickness," Captain Sinclair said. "Odd because she didnae have the sea sickness at all. I ken the lady was made for the sea."

Louisa wanted to smack the smirk off the captain's face. How could he be such a beast after she'd chased away his migraine and nursed his wound for weeks?

Mr. Kirby leaned a concerned face Mairi's way. "Was it a difficult journey for you, Miss Robertson?"

Mairi batted her bloody eyelashes. "Och, dinnae fash yourself, Mr. Kirby. I didnae have any trouble with the seasickness. I come—came to like the sea just fine."

Mr. Kirby glowed. "Charming." He turned to the captain. "Isn't she charming?"

"Oh, aye," Captain Sinclair said, sounding bored. He leaned an elbow on the open window and pretended interest in the scenery. Impossible man.

"I don't know if your brother Nathan told you, but I'm English. Well, my mother was a Scot, but I was raised in the Lake Country near Penrith."

"Beautiful country. I know it well," the reverend said.

"Do you know it, Miss Robertson?" Mr. Kirby asked. Mairi stared blankly, and he gushed an apology. "No, of course, you wouldn't. I'm sorry for babbling. I'm just so... happy."

She sent him a dazzling smile, the one that never failed

to slay any man she targeted. "As am I, Mr. Kirby." She held him in her blue-eyed gaze. Even the big bounce the carriage took when it hit a particularly deep rut didn't shake the man loose from his trance.

Captain Sinclair lifted his chin from his fist to examine Mr. Kirby, then darted a look Louisa's way. He was probably thinking the same thing as she: *Poor Mr. Kirby is done for.*

"How much longer?" Louisa asked.

Mr. Kirby came to and answered, "Oh, em, not much longer. Another mile, I'd say. I hope you like the house. We call it Quaker Hill. It's in desperate need of a woman's touch."

"I'm interested to see your foundry," Louisa put in, if only to change the subject. It worked, too, because Mr. Kirby and Captain Sinclair launched into an involved conversation about furnaces, Fahrenheits, ingots, and iron. She turned her attention to Mairi. "You look very happy," she said and squeezed her hand. "Is he all that you hoped for?"

"Aye. And more. So much more."

Even though her grand idea had become something not so grand, at least she'd done one thing right. Mairi was happy—blissfully happy—and so was Mr. Kirby. Once Louisa began her acting career, she'd be happy, too. If only there was a way to make things right for Captain Sinclair. He was the only person to suffer from her deceit.

That wasn't exactly true. When she'd hatched this idea, changing identities with Mairi and running away to be an actress, she had hoped that her father and her brothers would regret their cruelty. If she was perfectly honest with herself, she'd hoped they would suffer from guilt for sending her away.

She'd imagined a scene, a sort of tableau, with her father weeping and her brothers at his side, hats in hand and heads bowed low, all three grieving for the loss of their beloved sister. Years later, she would arrive in Edinburgh as a celebrated actress, and her fathers and brothers would come to her beautiful hotel suite, kneel before her, and beg for forgiveness. She would, of course, forgive them because she was a kind-hearted person.

She now knew those scenarios to be pure fantasy. Nothing like that would ever happen. Rather quite the opposite and much worse. Her father would shake his head in disgust and shout something like, "I expected nothing more from my Daughter from Hell." Her brothers would laugh and celebrate having seen the last of their ridiculous sister. She'd never be welcomed home. And Captain Sinclair. Oh God. How perfectly horrible for him. Would people laugh? Would he be ruined? Would he give up hope and—

"Miss MacQuarie. *Lass!*"

"What?"

Captain Sinclair narrowed his eyes at her as if assessing her health. "We've arrived."

Good heavens. The reverend, Mairi, and Mr. Kirby had exited the carriage and she hadn't even noticed.

"What's wrong, lass?"

"Nothing at all."

He slid out of the door and reached a hand back in to help her out. There was a mud puddle at the base of the step and Captain Sinclair lifted her by the waist and set her down on dry land. "My God, have you lead in your pockets?"

She felt her cheeks color.

"Bloody hell, woman. Are you carrying your pistols?"

"You can never be too careful."

He rolled his eyes. *He rolled his bloody eyes at her.* And to think, a moment ago she had felt sorry for the bastard. Well, not anymore.

"Give them to me," he said, holding a hand out.

"I will not. They're mine."

The carriage had stopped in front of the stable. The others were already halfway to the house, a three-story brick house.

Not palatial by any means, but a hundred times grander than Mairi could have hoped for had she remained in Edinburgh and married the coal man.

"Give them to me before you shoot off your foot."

The driver was staring at them, waiting for them to clear the carriage.

"You're making a scene," she hissed. The captain didn't move, just stared at her dull eyed. Damn. "Fine." She retrieved the weapon from her skirt pocket and handed it to him.

"Now the other one."

Bollocks. She pulled the second pistol from her other pocket. "I want these returned to me when I leave for New York. They were a gift from my gran."

"Damn it, woman. These are loaded."

"Well, they're not much good to me empty, are they?"

He tucked them in his coat pockets.

"I would also like our travel documents back, please."

"I gave them to Mr. Kirby after the harbormaster checked them."

"Why?"

"For safekeeping."

"We are not children. We are grown women—"

The driver interrupted. "Is there a problem, sir?"

"No. No problem," the captain called out. "Just sorting out a few details."

• • •

Ian had reached the end of his tether with the bloody woman. Actually, he'd thought he'd reached the end several times before, but each time his tether seemed to lengthen another yard or two. But really, this had to be the end.

He turned her about and ushered her toward the house. Mustering his last scrap of patience, he said, "You're exhausted from traveling. You'd best find your room and have a lie down."

She marched ahead of him at an angry pace. "The only thing that has me exhausted is an irritating captain named Sinclair."

"The only thing that has me irritated is the Daughter from Hell's infernal companion."

She froze in place for a moment before her head slowly turned on her slender neck a near 180 degrees, as if she were possessed. Even more terrifying was the look on her face. Just like a gorgon. Ian thought he might turn to stone. He couldn't believe it, but he actually heard himself say, "Oops."

She opened her mouth to fire some insult his way. He was spared by Miss Robertson.

"Come on, you two. Mr. Kirby's going to give us a tour."

Kirby hadn't exaggerated when he'd said the house was in need of a woman's touch. It had no touches at all. They stood inside the hallway, walls plastered, but void of any paintings, sconces, or embellishments. It was a good-sized entry, though nothing like Balforss House with its grand two-story hall and central staircase that was roomy enough to hold parties and family gatherings.

A sturdy woman about his own mother's age stood at the foot of the stairs wearing an apron and a pleasant smile.

"Everyone, this is my housekeeper, Mrs. Foley."

Mrs. Foley said, "Welcome to Quaker Hill. Or should I say, welcome to America."

"This is Miss Robertson's companion, Miss MacQuarie, Reverend Wynterbottom, and Captain Sinclair," Kirby said, and then, in a honeyed tone, "and this is my fiancée, Miss Robertson."

Miss Robertson curtsied, which was slightly odd. Looking confused and probably not knowing what else to do, Mrs. Foley curtsied in return.

Kirby picked up the lost thread. "Em, Mrs. Foley and her husband, Mr. Foley—my driver, you met him—they pretty much run the place. Since it's just me, she does all the cooking."

"Will you no' be overburdened with all the house guests, Mrs. Foley?" Miss Robertson asked.

"Not at all. My two nieces have come to help out," Mrs. Foley reassured her.

"I'm giving everyone a tour of the place," Kirby said.

"Of course. I'll have tea ready in an hour." Mrs. Foley added, "I hope you like fish cakes. They're Mr. Kirby's favorite."

At the mention of food, Ian's stomach made a loud sound.

Miss MacQuarie looked at him as if he'd done it on purpose, then said, "Sounds delightful, Mrs. Foley."

Kirby led them into what he called a "cozy little parlor." The echo of their footsteps bounced around the room. No carpet, no paintings, and no draperies. The only thing cozy about the room was that it was smallish. On the positive side, there were several comfortable-looking overstuffed chairs, a secretary, a settee, and a card table with four ladder-backs. The ceilings were high, too, and the two tall windows allowed in plenty of afternoon light.

Kirby waited anxiously while Miss Robertson strolled around the room. At last she turned to him radiating delight, and said, "It's absolutely perfect."

Mr. Kirby exhaled as if the judge had just announced, "No, Mr. Kirby, you will not hang today."

"I'll buy whatever things you need to appoint the room as you see fit, of course."

Too bad for Mr. Kirby, Ian thought. The poor besotted fool was headed for financial ruin.

"All it really needs is drapes," Miss Robertson said. "If you'll help me choose the fabric, I can make those."

Ian made a quick reassessment of Kirby's fate. Maybe the fellow was a lucky besotted fool.

Jealousy slid its long knife into his chest much the way he'd seen his cousin Magnus sink a fourteen-inch dirk under a pirate's armpit straight into his heart. Instant death. Only jealousy didn't kill a man. It just made him stupid. And Ian felt himself growing stupider by the minute.

"Shall we go look at the dining room, now?" Kirby asked.

"You all go on ahead without me," Miss MacQuarie announced. "I think I'll sit here and rest until tea."

"Sounds like a good idea. I'll join you," Ian said. "Dinnae let us hold you up. Miss MacQuarie and I have things to discuss."

They stood silently as Kirby, Miss Robertson, and the reverend's voices trailed away into other parts of the house. The fire had gone out of Miss MacQuarie's eyes. He was sad to see it go. He rather liked her temper. She was beautiful when she was angry. She was beautiful when she was happy, too. The only time she wasn't beautiful was when she was unhappy. Which was, of course, a lie. She was always beautiful. He was just bothered today because he suspected he was the cause of her unhappiness and he'd rather be the reason for her joy.

"Why are you here?" she asked. A simple question. Why was it so hard for him to answer her?

Tell her the truth, ye bampot. Tell her you're here because you couldnae bear to let her go. Tell her you wish you could take her home with you.

But he couldn't tell her that because then he would have to tell her that his carefully planned future had exploded into a million bits before they'd left Edinburgh, that he had a son, a six-year-old son he hadn't known existed until six weeks ago.

"I want you," he said. The words had spilled out before

he'd had time to calculate the risk in saying them.

"You want me to what?"

He shook his head and took a step closer. "You dinnae understand. I *want* you. I want to have you. Do ye ken what I mean, lass?"

It was plain Miss MacQuarie understood exactly what he meant. As plain as the blush on her cheeks and the perfect *O* on her lips. He'd never had such a pretty pink reception to one of his blatant advances. Unable to stop himself, he took advantage of her momentary silence and kissed the *O* from her lips. She kissed him back with a startling ferocity that made him rock hard. If she didn't take her wicked hands out from under his waistcoat immediately he was going to ruck up her skirts and have her against the—Jee-*sus*.

He pulled away and Miss MacQuarie teetered on her pins until she opened her eyes and stomped her foot. "You infuriating man. Why do you always stop?"

Ian sputtered. "It's, it's, it's the middle of the day and we're in a strange house." He gestured toward the door. "It's unlocked. Anyone could—" Bloody hell. A second ago he was in control.

She pointed that deceptively delicate finger at him. "You-know-what-I-mean." She punctuated each word with a jab to his chest. That made him angry.

He managed to keep from shouting, but his voice shook from the effort of holding back his rage. "I stopped because you fire a passion in me that I cannae control and I willnae take you like some animal." He paused to catch his breath and wipe the sweat from his brow. "When I have you, it will be in a bed, naked, and with full control of my body and my mind. I would have your first time—"

She tried to make a protest and he held up a hand to stop her.

"No matter what you say, I know that privilege will be

mine and I value it. Maybe more than you do." The look on her face softened, encouraging him to continue. "But I will make your first time one you will never forget." He sank his fingers into her hair. "One by which you will measure every man after me." He kissed her cheek and whispered, "And find them all lacking." He kissed her mouth until she leaned against his body and groaned.

"Ahem."

They startled and stepped away from each other. Ian turned toward the back of the room, aware that he was in a shockingly aroused state. Miss MacQuarie, brave lass, faced the intruder at the door.

"Will. Good. You've arrived safely. No Indians, I trust."

Ian sidled discreetly behind one of the wing-backed chairs. "Well done, lad."

"I brung Miss Robertson's trunk to the green room, and put Miss MacQuarie's trunk in the red room. Then I brung your bag to the blue room, sir."

"Where are you sleeping?"

"Mr. Foley says I can stay in their garret, but if you want me to sleep on your floor—"

"No-no. I want you to stay with Mr. and Mrs. Foley. I'm sure you'll be of use to them with all the wedding arrangements."

Will smiled broadly. "I never been to a wedding afore, sir."

He took in Will's shabby coat and trousers, aware they were probably the best he had. "We'll need to visit the tailor tomorrow and get measured for new clobber. Captain and his mate need to make a good show for Miss Robertson, aye."

"Aye, sir."

Mrs. Foley appeared at the parlor door. "Tea is ready in the dining room." She turned to Will. "And you, Master Will, I've got a slice of cherry pie that needs eating. Come with me." She put a hand on Will's head of hair and steered him out of the room. One afternoon in the back of a dray and the lad was already filthy again. Ian hoped she'd make him bathe before he took him to town for new clothes.

Two sets of heels clicked in the corridor and before anyone else could interrupt them, Ian whispered, "Expect me at your bedchamber door tonight."

She gazed at him with such...God...was it appreciation or anticipation? Whatever she was experiencing, he wanted to taste it, drink it, drown in it. Tonight. He could last for another six or seven hours, couldn't he? Shite. Which was the red room? Better get up there and sort it out now before all the doors were shut.

"I'll be back in a trice."

• • •

Louisa could barely breathe. Captain Sinclair had dashed out of the room leaving her dazed and, if truth be told, excited by his proposal.

Expect me at your bedchamber door tonight.

Tonight. It would happen tonight. Once everyone in the house was asleep, Captain Sinclair would come to her room, and she would give herself to him. After which, she would be perfectly and irreversibly ruined. As every professional actress should be.

"Are you coming, Miss MacQuarie?" Mairi called from just outside the parlor door.

"Yes, of course." She hustled to Mairi's side, and together they walked casually toward the dining room.

"Where's the captain?" Mairi asked.

"He went above stairs. He'll be right back." Louisa gave Mairi's arm a gentle squeeze and whispered, "I take it you are happy with your soon-to-be husband."

"Oh, I am. It's a bloody miracle. And do you know what?" Mairi gazed ahead at some imaginary horizon, her eyes unfocused, her enraptured expression like those in paintings of ecstatic saints. "Mr. Kirby said I was more beautiful than he had ever imagined and that the day we marry will be the best day of his life. He's so romantic."

Captain Sinclair hadn't wasted any romantic words on Louisa. He'd simply said, "I want you," and she had agreed to welcome him into her bed. No mind. Louisa didn't need flowery words. She wasn't marrying Captain Sinclair. They weren't silly romantics. They were practical people. They understood each other. A lasting relationship between them was out of the question. In fact, in a couple months, he wouldn't even like her. He would despise her for destroying his life. Perhaps, if she made tonight good for him, he might not hate her so very much. He'd promise to make tonight unforgettable for her. She must do him the same favor.

Mrs. Foley laid out a lovely tea—fish cakes, hot buns, and two kinds of cheeses—but Louisa had little appetite. Captain Sinclair had taken the seat opposite. Every time she glanced up from her plate, he was looking at her like he was a cat and she was his dinner. Come to think of it, the captain did have rather catlike eyes. Steel gray when he was angry and China blue when he was…well, whenever he was in whatever state he was in now.

"Sour pickle?"

She sat up straight. "I beg your pardon." Mr. Kirby held out a relish tray. "Oh yes, of course." She accepted the dish, skewered one green spear for her plate and handed it to Captain Sinclair. He accepted it with that wicked smile again, as though he could see right through her clothing.

Louisa had seen him naked—most of him, at least—and he was wonderfully made. Men would say he was "well set." Women would say he was beautiful. He must have worked many hours without his shirt because the sun had burnished the skin on his muscular chest and broad back to an appealing golden brown. She'd seen his arms and legs, too. Long and sculpted. He moved with grace for one so large. Even his fingers were elegantly formed. But it was his big bony feet she'd fallen in love with. Powerful enough to hold his towering frame erect, and yet so vulnerable looking when naked. She'd had a fleeting glimpse of his privates, but not a good enough keek to truly understand what they were about. Tonight, though, she'd not only get to see them, she'd touch them, his todger and his...

"Figs," Mrs. Foley said, placing a serving dish in front of Mr. Kirby.

"Ah, what a wonderful treat, stewed figs," he exclaimed.

"You'll want to feed up on those with your wedding so near, Mr. Kirby," Reverend Wynterbottom said. "I have it on good authority, figs are an excellent aphrodisiac."

The men chuckled at the reverend's uncharacteristically bawdy remark.

Mr. Kirby, who had turned red in the face, said, "Very well then. I'll take two." To which Mairi replied, "And I'll have three." Everyone had a rollicking good laugh at that.

When the dish of figs came the captain's way, he spooned two on his plate and winked at Louisa. She bit her lower lip and spooned two on her plate, as well.

• • •

It had been the longest eight hours of his life. One hour over tea stealing glances at Miss MacQuarie with her cheeks freshly flushed from his announcement that he would deflower her tonight. Three hours touring Edward Kirby's coach house, hay barn, dovecote, hot house, and garden—all, he had to admit, enviable. Another two hours over dinner, trying not to stare at the tops of Miss MacQuarie's breasts, the way they plumped up and made an inviting crease, a perfect place to put his—

Jee-*sus*. When had he become a degenerate?

And these last two hours, sitting in a room the size of a closet, ruminating on what he was about to do. His bedchamber, if one could call it that, had space enough for three bits of furniture: a narrow bed not long enough for his body, a ladder-back chair on which he hung his coat, and a washstand with basin and ewer. Will must have referred to it as the blue room because the bed had a blue counterpane. He pushed open the window to let in a light breeze, tugged off his neckcloth, and leaned back on his pillow to wait for the sun to go down.

Was he doing the right thing taking a virgin to bed? He had rules about that sort of thing. Always stay the middle course. No extremes. No virgins. No trollops. Only the married or recently widowed variety of female where the terms of commitment—or lack thereof—went unspoken, yet were clear. And never more than two nights in a row with the same woman.

He would be breaking one of his cardinal rules by taking Miss MacQuarie to bed. He'd broken one of those rules before. He'd spent seven nights in a row with Alice Crawford and the result had been fatal for her—and life changing for him. Damn. Why would he think of her now, at a time like this?

Guilt, he supposed.

Guilt. Bloody frigging guilt. It had always hovered in the back of Ian's mind when it came to sex. When he was in school, the vicar had told the boys they would go blind if they played with their peckers. He'd been so terrified that for months he wouldn't touch it even to piss. Fortunately, his da had set him straight on that matter, saying that it was more likely he'd go blind from *not* playing with himself.

During his time in the army, when he had been far too

promiscuous, he'd kept guilt at bay by creating his set of rules—no virgins, no whores, no more than two nights—as if that would make womanizing acceptable. At the time, he'd told himself he was a rake, but an honorable rake. He'd known it was utter bullshit, but his cock hadn't cared.

If he was a good man, a decent man, a repentant man, he would observe Alice Crawford's passing by denying himself any pleasures of the flesh for a year, at the very least. But he knew that was bullshit, too. No amount of abstinence would atone for Alice Crawford's death.

He was done with guilt. He wanted Miss MacQuarie, and she wanted him. He would have her tonight, bury himself in her slick heat and not feel guilty about it. Not even for a second.

He sat up. The sun was down, and he hadn't heard movement outside his door in quite some time. The women had retired first. Kirby had suggested a nightcap, and since the reverend was no longer drinking, he'd excused himself. Neither Ian nor Kirby had lingered over their brandy. They'd made a few tentative plans for the following day, said good night, and trudged up the stairs yawning and stretching and saying things like, "I'll be asleep before my head hits the pillow," and, "I'm dead on my feet," and, "The house could fall down around me before I woke up."

Right at this moment, Ian hadn't been this alive and awake in years. He was about to bed a woman. Jee-*sus*. He'd promised Miss MacQuarie he'd be the best lover she'd ever have. In a matter of minutes, he'd have to make good on that boast. He hoped he remembered how to do it.

He crept to his door only two steps away. Everything in the room was only two steps away. The door opened with a squeal that set his teeth on edge. He poked his head out and peered up and down the hall. Dark as hell. He couldn't see a damn thing. Fortunately, the hallway was carpeted.

When he'd done his reconnaissance this afternoon, he'd

determined that Mr. Kirby's room was on the far end of the hall on the other side of the staircase. The door to the red room was to the left of his, and Miss Robertson's directly opposite Miss MacQuarie's.

He left his door open rather than risk another deafening squeal, and slowly made his way down the hallway with his hand trailing the wall as a guide. When his fingers met the first doorjamb on the left, he leaned his ear against the cool wood. No sound. He rapped lightly and the door opened.

"Oh, Edward, I've been waiting."

"Miss Robertson?" Why was Miss Robertson in Miss MacQuarie's room?

Shite. Wrong room, ye dafty.

Ian tried to think of a plausible excuse for knocking on her door other than, "I thought this was Miss MacQuarie's room," when a door at the end of the hallway opened.

"Miss Robertson?" Mr. Kirby rasped.

"Actually, no," Ian said in a voice slightly louder than Kirby's.

The door behind him opened and Miss MacQuarie whispered, "Is that you, Ian?"

Ian felt as though he'd just stepped into some sort of farce. How had he made such a compromising blunder? And then the answer came to him. Bloody frigging hell. Will was color blind. "Sorry. I...em...got turned around."

"As did I," Kirby said, and quickly added, "I mean, I couldn't sleep and thought I'd...um...um..."

"I couldnae sleep, either," Ian said. "Another nightcap, perhaps?"

"Yes. Excellent idea. I'll find a lamp."

"Sorry for the disturbance, ladies. Please, go back to bed," Ian said to the dark, and then two doors shut with a click. He was going to strangle wee Will.

Chapter Eleven

Louisa struggled to keep her eyes open. She couldn't fall asleep on her wedding night—her almost-like-a-wedding night. That's how she thought of it. The only difference between her and a bride was that she wasn't actually married to the groom. That's the part that happened off stage, all the official nonsense with vicars and family and ceremony and documents, etcetera, all the unimportant parts. She was pretending that all those things had happened already.

The part that was about to happen, the coupling part, was the only bit that mattered. It's what bound two people together and made it real, the union, that is. The joining made it official because without sex, one wasn't truly married.

Where is he?

It seemed like hours since that mishap in the hallway. Surely those two had finished their nightcaps by now, yet no captain. She'd been listening very carefully and hadn't heard anyone come up the stairs. She opened her door a crack and stilled. From below, she heard the faint murmur of male conversation.

Bollocks. She had half a mind to go down there and insist they go to bed immediately. Nonsense, she told herself. *He'll be here any minute.*

She returned to the upholstered chair and curled up between the cushioned arms, big and comfortable like the captain's arms, roomy enough and cozy enough to sleep in. The room was to her liking, done in various shades of green and gold with a four-poster bed. The counterpane and bed curtains were a forest print. A braided rug covered most of the floor and the evergreen draperies were trimmed with gold fringe. The rest of the room was unadorned. No paintings, no objects aside from the washstand and ewer. One day, when she owned a house of her own, she would decorate her bedroom just like this.

Where the hell is he?

She launched herself out of the chair, tied her robe around her, and collected the candlestick—the third one of the night. Such a waste. She padded down the staircase to the entry hall. The men were in the parlor talking with the door ajar. She didn't eavesdrop exactly. That would be bad manners. She simply waited for the right moment to enter so that she wouldn't interrupt them. Interrupting was downright rude.

"I'll be honest with you, Captain Sinclair," Mr. Kirby said. "I wasn't in the hallway by accident. I had larceny in mind."

"Larceny?" the captain rumbled.

"Yes, well, I had planned to steal into Miss Robertson's room and, and, you know."

"Oh, aye."

"It's just…with her here, under my roof, sleeping two doors down from my own, it's so tempting to…to…"

"Enjoy the honeymoon afore the wedding?"

"Yes. I don't know if I can last another week."

The captain chuckled. "Dinnae fash. In any case, what would be the harm? If you lived in Scotland, you could handfast, take her to bed tomorrow, and have the vicar marry you after."

"Ha-ha! I've heard of that."

"And you're no' the only one that's tempted."

"What do you mean?"

"I confess..." Captain Sinclair hesitated for a second. Lord. He wasn't going to tell, was he? "I wasnae turned around. I thought I was knocking on Miss MacQuarie's door." Louisa inhaled sharply and covered her mouth. How dare he tell Mr. Kirby about his plan to bed her?

"I'm afraid I let my desire cloud my judgement."

Cloud his judgement? *Cloud his judgement?* Molten fury scorched her body. So, this whole evening had been a hiccup, a mistake, a case of poor judgement? Louisa picked up the hem of her robe and ran up the staircase. Her candle went out, but she'd always been able to see well in the dark. As she reached the top, she heard Captain Sinclair call, "Miss MacQuarie?" He thundered up the stairs after her, stumbled in the dark, cursed, and marched down the hallway to her door. "Lass. Open the door."

"Go away."

"Open the door and let me explain."

"I wouldnae want to cloud your judgement."

He was quiet for a while and then she heard him sigh. "Fine. We'll discuss this in the morning." And then in a soft voice meant only for her, he said, "Good night, love." His slow footsteps trailed away.

Good night, love.

Those three words doused her anger with joy. He called her *love.*

• • •

Ian barely slept. He couldn't. His body had been primed for something other than sleep and it would not let him forget it. Twice he slipped into erotic dreams about Miss MacQuarie only to wake at the penultimate moment.

Cooking smells drifted up from the summer kitchen in the backyard.

Someone rapped on his door. "I've got water for your basin, sir."

"Please come in."

A girl about thirteen years old, thin and freckly with large brown eyes peeking out from underneath a huge mobcap, slipped inside his chamber. She reminded him of Hattie, the upstairs maid at Balforss.

"What's your name?"

"Eliza Foley, sir." She dipped a quick curtsy.

"Mrs. Foley's your aunt?"

"Yes, sir. I'm to tell you breakfast will be waiting downstairs in the sunroom." She scurried out of the room. Probably awkward to keep her so long in a room with a naked stranger. Hattie had never thought twice. She was like a sister to him.

Balforss. He rarely felt such a sharp longing to be home among his family, sleeping in his old room, eating Mrs. Swenson's good cooking, knocking about with his brother and his cousins Declan and Magnus.

But things were different now. They all had families of their own. Declan with Caya and their brood living at Taldale Farm, and busy with his whisky business. Magnus and Virginia living in Latheron with their rabble of five— or was it six now? They collected foster children like strays. Magnus and his boys bred draft horses, some said the finest in Scotland.

And then there was his brother who helped their father run the estate and would one day be laird of Balforss. Alex was everything Ian wished he could be. Oh, his brother was a bit of a hothead, but that's what made him the best strategist and the most courageous soldier he'd ever known. Ian missed him the most. But Alex had been married to Lucy for eight years. They had a beautiful daughter, a fiery redhead named Jemima, the perfect combination of the two of them, a holy terror. Ian smiled. Their mam said Alex had gotten the child he deserved. Jemima was, no doubt, Alex's penance for all the trouble he'd caused their parents. What would she say when Ian brought Rory home? Was Rory the child he deserved?

Ian couldn't think about that right now. He had other matters to…smooth over. What was done was done, and there was no way to change it. What mattered was the present, and he was presently in hot water with Miss MacQuarie. He tossed off the bedclothes, washed, and dressed.

Last to the table, Ian took the seat across from his would-be lover who glared bloody daggers at him. He heaped a plate with scrambled eggs and seven slices of bacon and began eating. Wynterbottom, absorbed with slathering his toast with a quarter-inch coating of butter, was oblivious to anyone else. Kirby and Miss Robertson exchanged cretinous grins. How had they become so ridiculously and hopelessly smitten with each other in less than a day? It had taken Ian weeks to—

Best not finish that thought at the breakfast table.

He swallowed the last bite of egg and cleared his throat. He had to do it twice to get Kirby's attention. "I'd like to take Will into town with me. He's in need of a new set of clothes. Can you recommend a good tailor?"

"Absolutely. Harmon Brothers on Hill Street," Kirby said and smiled adoringly at the object of his affection. "I would come with you, but I've promised Miss Robertson a picnic by the water. I want to show her more of the property."

Ian didn't think that was all Kirby wanted to show Miss

Robertson. Was it his responsibility to make certain the General's Daughter from Hell maintained her maidenhead until her wedding night, or was his only obligation to see that she wed? He decided on the latter as he didn't think he could accomplish the former given how the pair were so determined to...do exactly as he planned to do with Miss MacQuarie.

Jee-*sus*. He couldn't even think about the act without his cock jumping to attention.

Not at the breakfast table, you mindless numpty.

"Miss MacQuarie," he said. Her sharp green eyes darted back to him. "I would consider it a great favor if you would accompany me to the tailor and help Will select the proper attire." The grim set of her mouth softened. "And if there is anything else you would like to do while we're there, I would happily accommodate your wishes." God, he sounded like a sycophant. Why the devil was he groveling?

"I'll agree on behalf of Will. He's a sweet boy and is kind to me always." Miss MacQuarie pushed away from the table. "Please excuse me. I need to prepare for our trip."

Bloody hell. He wanted to kiss that priggish smile off her face until she groaned for more, like she had done only yesterday.

"Excellent," Kirby said. "I'll tell Foley to get the carriage ready. Last I saw, Will was with him in the coach house learning to groom the horses."

Ian considered Will for a moment, a lad he cared for but hadn't thought a fully formed man as yet. Four years ago, while he'd been having a meal at the Crown Tavern in Wick Harbor, Peter had approached him with a filthy-looking urchin in tow and said, "His name is Will. His mam's dead, sir. He's got nowhere to go."

"What about his father?" Ian had asked.

"Never had one."

Ian had asked Will, "How old are you?"

The lad opened his mouth and tried to answer, but he had been shaking so hard, no sound came out.

"I ken he's aboot ten, sir," Peter had said. "We could use a cabin boy. Someone to see after the passengers, aye?"

Ian had asked Will, "Do you want to work aboard the *Gael Forss*?"

Will's eyes had opened wide with astonishment. "Yes, sir."

And that was how Ian had acquired Will. What would have happened to Will had Ian not agreed to take him on? For that matter, what would have happened to Rory if he hadn't had a grandmother to care for him? Ian shuddered at the thought.

He took one last sip of coffee and, noting what a fine brew it was, excused himself from the table. "No need, Mr. Kirby. I'll go talk to Mr. Foley about the carriage myself."

He poked his head inside the summer kitchen and thanked Mrs. Foley for a delicious breakfast. She might have blushed from the unexpected compliment. More likely she was flushed from the kitchen fires. She said, "I'll be sure and make more bacon for tomorrow's breakfast," and winked.

Inside the shade of the coach house, he heard Will talking to Foley. Ian let his eyes adjust to the dim, as he walked toward the voices.

Foley said, "Horses can sense when a human is uneasy and it unsettles them. If you remain at ease, the horse will calm because he knows he's safe."

"I'm no' afeart," Will said gazing up at the giant chestnut gelding. But Ian could tell by the tension in Will's shoulders he was more than apprehensive. He supposed the lad hadn't spent much time around horses. He knew Will to be fearless aboard ship, but the beasts must be a puzzle to him.

"His name is Henry," Foley said. "Feed him this carrot, speak to him in a gentle voice, and say his name. You'll be friends in no time."

Ian's braw cabin boy held out the carrot and said, "Good morning, Henry. My name is Will." Henry took the carrot and munched away. Will patted Henry on the neck tentatively. "You're a big fellow, but wait till you meet my captain. He's the tallest man you'll ever see in your life." Henry nickered, and Will laughed nervously, looking to Foley for confirmation.

"Morning, Captain Sinclair," Foley said, noticing Ian in the shadows.

Will spun around beaming. "Did you see me feed the horse, sir? His name is Henry. I petted his neck. I think he likes me."

"I saw, Will. I'm glad to see you like horses. You're good with them, I think."

"Do you like horses, sir?"

"As a matter of fact, I do. I had my own once, you ken. His name was Lightning for the white blaze on his head. A big bay. Sweet lad, he was." Ian felt that twinge of homesickness again.

"What happened to him?" Will asked.

"Horses dinnae live as long as us, Will. That's why we must treat them kindly for the short time they're with us."

Will glanced back at Henry with a worried look.

"Don't fret, son," Foley assured Will. "Henry will be with us yet for many years."

"You and I are going into town with Miss MacQuarie to see the tailor about some proper clothes."

"Sorry, Mr. Foley," Will said. "I cannae help with the horses this morning. My captain needs me."

"The carriage will be ready in thirty, Captain. Perhaps the boy can ride atop with me?"

"Would you like that, Will?"

One would have thought Ian had offered him a gold coin. "Oh, aye, sir."

. . .

Louisa took her time. He'd made her wait on him all night, he could bloody well wait for her all morning. The problem was that she was eager to go to town with the captain, not only to help Will at the tailor, but to do some shopping of her own. A visit to the milliner would be in order, as her best hat had been ravaged by the wind aboard the *Gael Forss*. Mairi had asked her to look for more soap. If time allowed, she might have a browse through the dry goods shop. Most importantly, she would like to visit a bookseller. Mr. Kirby said there was one not far from the tailor.

She sat in her bedchamber fully dressed in her sunbonnet and gloves with her reticule on her lap and waited and waited. The girl who'd brought her basin water this morning rapped on her door with, "Mr. Captain wants to know, are you coming soon, miss."

"Tell him I'll be down when I'm ready," she called through the door. Louisa had only counted to thirty when she heard his boots thumping up the stairs. She'd thought it would take forty-five at least.

He pounded on her door three times and announced in a firm voice, "Miss MacQuarie, the carriage is wa—"

She opened the door and shined a sweet smile up at him. "I'm ready."

He stood there with his mouth open, taking her in. She had made an effort, but she wasn't prepared for his appreciative stare. "You look—" He swallowed and straightened. "You look ready."

Outside, Will called to her from the driver's seat, his face alight with excitement. "I'm helping Mr. Foley drive the carriage, miss."

"Then we are in good hands, are we not, Captain?"

"Oh, aye."

As much as she had come to like Reverend Wynterbottom, she was disappointed to find him waiting inside the carriage. She'd rather looked forward to having Captain Sinclair's exclusive attention. Nevertheless, she nestled next to the clergyman and tried to avoid the captain's gaze which remained fixed on her all the way to town, a fact that pleased her immeasurably.

When the carriage stopped in front of Harmon Brothers Tailor and Haberdashery, the reverend reached for the door handle, and Captain Sinclair stayed his hand.

"Wait a while. Will wants to give us the full treatment."

Louisa warmed. Captain Sinclair, dear, kind, patient Captain Sinclair, was set on making this moment special for Will, a lad that was of no relation but for the fact that Will worked for him and, as Louisa knew well, worshiped him.

The carriage door opened. Will pulled down the step and reached into the carriage for Louisa's hand. She took it and stepped down. "Thank you, Will."

He sucked in his cheeks, clasped his hands behind him and rocked back and forth from one foot to the other. Reverend Wynterbottom congratulated him, as well. When Ian climbed out and simply nodded to him, as if Will did this all the time, the lad inflated with boyish pride. She felt compelled to put a hand on his shoulder to hold him down lest he float away.

"I have some business to attend to. Where and when shall I meet you?" the reverend asked.

"Is three hours enough time, do you think, Miss MacQuarie?"

"Four would be better."

Captain Sinclair called up to Mr. Foley, "We'll meet you back here at half three."

At the tailor's shop, the proprietor, Mr. Harmon, was happy to receive their business and mentioned several times what an important and well-respected man Mr. Kirby was in the community. While the tailor measured Ian, she chose a burgundy wool for Will's coat, a gray silk for his waistcoat, and black linen trousers, as she and Captain Sinclair agreed they would show less dirt should the lad accidentally come in contact with the ground.

While Will endured the poking and prodding of the tailor's measuring tape, Captain Sinclair selected fabric for himself. He'd chosen a dark gray for his coat and was deliberating between a gold or blue silk for his waistcoat.

"The blue, I think," she said. "Unless my opinion matters not."

"Your opinion matters very much to me, Miss MacQuarie."

"*Hmph.*"

"I'm sorry for last night."

"What on earth were you doing at Miss Robertson's bedchamber door?"

"Will told me your things were in the red room. I found out the hard way Will's color blind."

"*Hmph,*" she said again.

The captain lifted two bolts of green fabric. "Will, which one of these is red?"

"The one on your starboard side, sir."

"You see?" Captain Sinclair said, sounding all too smug.

"Still, I can never forgive you for telling Mr. Kirby"—she stumbled—"what you had no right to tell him."

"You are correct. But if you had seen him, how he was suffering, you would have done the same. I only told him so he wouldnae feel so bad about himself."

"You said I was a mistake," she hissed.

"I phrased it that way so that it sounded like my idea alone." He whispered, "Will you give me another chance, please?"

Louisa regarded him for a few seconds, trying to determine if he was sincere. If he was not, he was a better actor than she. "I'll think about it."

Will approached them and sighed deeply. Apparently, the chore of standing still long enough to be measured had exhausted him.

Mr. Harmon said, "We'll have you and your son's garments ready for a final fitting by Monday, sir."

Louisa expected Captain Sinclair to correct the man. He didn't. Instead, he thanked the man and led Will out of the shop.

"Come along, Will," Captain Sinclair said, patting the lad on the back. "There's more shopping to do, I'm afraid."

"That man thought I was your son," Will said.

"Easy mistake to make. You do look a lot like me."

"Why did you no' tell him I was just your cabin boy?"

"I suppose I dinnae mind him thinking you're my lad," he said. "Do you?"

Will smiled. "No, sir." Will gave his eyes a swipe with his forearm.

At that moment, Louisa witnessed what was, to her, a true expression of love between a father and a son, and the captain wasn't even Will's father. And at that precise moment, Louisa fell in love with Captain Sinclair.

Blast the man.

· · ·

Ian had prepared himself for a long, tedious afternoon of following Miss MacQuarie about while she examined every basket, bauble, and button she came across. He was surprised, therefore, when she announced she had completed her shopping after entering only one shop and buying one item, a cake of soap. And it wasn't even for her. It was for

Miss Robertson.

"Are you hungry, Will?" she asked. Silly question. When was the wee heathen not hungry?

"Oh, aye," Will said with an expression that reminded him of his father's herding dogs when they would sit outside the kitchen waiting for scraps. And why didn't she ask *him* if *he* was hungry? Grown men get hungry, too, and he was famished.

She pointed toward a cart parked near an open area on the riverbank. "That woman is selling what looks like meat pies. She's attracted quite a crowd so they must be good." She strode off in the direction of the pie lady with Will at her heels, following like a puppy. He followed, too. Like a dog.

The pie lady had cleverly situated herself next to what looked like a sort of public garden. While they waited their turn to buy their dinner, Ian watched people strolling along the bank, ladies chatting, children playing tag, and a few men casting lines into the river. He wondered idly what was biting today, when he noticed Will had focused on a group of boys about his age.

"What are they doing?" Will asked.

"Playing some sort of game," Ian said.

Miss MacQuarie looked in the direction of the boys. "They're playing Annie Over."

"What's that?" Will asked, now very keen.

While Miss MacQuarie explained the general rules of the game, Ian purchased three golden crescent pies that looked a lot like the ones Declan's Cornish wife made. He asked the pie lady, "Are these pasties?"

She returned a brilliant smile. "Come from Cornwall, do you?" She wrapped the three pies in an old newspaper.

"Nae, we're all Scots, but I have a Cornish friend who makes meat pies like these, and yours smell every bit as good."

She pocketed the coins Ian gave her and wished him and

his family a pleasant afternoon. Again, he didn't address the mistaken perception that Will and Miss MacQuarie were his, and again he was aware of how uncharacteristically pleased it made him to let the mistake go uncorrected.

Had Miss MacQuarie heard the lady? If so, she hadn't objected.

"I see a spot under that oak that looks shady. Let's sit there and enjoy our meal," she said.

Will finished off his pie before they reached the tree and remained standing, watching the boys play the Annie Over game. Ian finished his pie in three bites. They were delicious but too small. Perhaps he should buy more. He turned to ask Miss MacQuarie, but was distracted by the sight of her sharp white teeth sinking into the pie. Her eyes closed as if savoring the meaty filling. A bit of flaky crust clung to her bottom lip. The last time he'd spotted something on her lip, he'd had the same impulse then as he did now, to lick it off and kiss her until she gasped his name. God, he loved to hear her say his name.

"Go on, Will. The teams are uneven. They could use another man," she said. "You ken the rules. Go and play with them."

Will looked to him for permission. "Go on, then," he said, and thought, *have fun for a change.* How much fun had the lad actually had in the last four years? Was he working the boy too hard?

"Do you want the rest of my pie?" she asked him, having eaten only half. "I cannae finish."

"You sure?" She nodded and handed it to him. "Thanks," he said. She was seated on the soft carpet of grass, her legs tucked to the side under her bottom and her skirts arranged around her. She'd taken off her gloves to eat and hadn't put them on again. It was too hot for gloves, was it not? "We're in the shade. You can take off your hat."

She did. She didn't even argue. Not a word of protest. He tested her again to see just how agreeable she was.

"Would ye mind if I take off my coat? It's awfy hot, even in the shade."

"I wouldnae mind at all."

He removed his coat, folded it carefully and placed it on the grass next to her thigh.

"Would ye mind if I lie down and close my eyes? I didnae sleep at all last night."

"Go right ahead. I'll keep an eye on Will."

Well now, why not toss in all your chips, laddie?

He repositioned himself, legs stretched out, boots crossed at the ankle, hands clasped over his chest and reclined...with his head in her lap. Her only reaction was a short, audible intake of breath. Ah. This was grand.

He closed his eyes and said in a low voice, "Miss MacQuarie?"

"Aye?"

"Would ye mind rubbing my temples like ye did before?"

"Does your head hurt?" she asked with sincere concern.

"Nae. I just like it."

She made a deep chuckle, the kind women made in the bedroom, and touched her magic fingers to his brow. "Do ye like it more than meat pies?"

"Oh, aye," he sighed. "I like it more than whisky."

Her laughter made his heart pump hard and strong, as if the sound infused him with the godlike power to do anything, be anything, say anything— "Did you mind people thinking we were married?" Jee-*sus*. What the hell did he just say?

"Nae. Did you?"

"Nae." He waited for a half second to catch his breath. His mouth seemed to have a mind of its own. "Would ye mind so much if it was true?" *Bloody buggering hell. What am I doing?*

"Nae." She swirled her cool fingers in circles.

Christ. Had he just asked her to marry him hypothetically? And was her "nae" a hypothetical "yes"? She slid those velvety tips over his forehead, down the bridge of his nose, and around his eyes, and his whole body sank three inches into the ground.

"Me, too," he sighed. *May God strike me mute before I say another daft thing.*

"We can never marry because I'm going to be an actress in New York, and you're going to be a soldier in...wherever the King sends you. But I dinnae mind pretending." In a shy, almost inaudible voice, she said, "If you like, you can come to my bed tonight and show me what it's like to be married to you."

His cock leaped to attention, and he flipped over, scrabbling to his hands and knees. "Thank God," he said and kissed her.

She pulled away laughing and swatting him in the chest. "Not in public, ye loon." She aimed those gorgeous green eyes at him, and he realized he'd felt this way all along, ever since he'd seen her in the bookshop, when he hadn't even known her name. She cut him a look. "And you'd better get the right room this time."

Chapter Twelve

It was time to go. Louisa anticipated difficulty having to coax Will away from the game and his new friends. He was having so much fun. But the captain called to him once, and, like a dutiful member of his crew, Will responded immediately. The lad, generally not one given to long speeches, gave them a running commentary of the entire game: the names of the other boys, their ages, their levels of skill and speed, and how they measured up as players. Nonstop chatter all the way back to the carriage where Mr. Foley waited. It was half three, just as they had planned, but no sign of Reverend Wynterbottom.

"Where did he say he was going?" Louisa asked.

"He said he had business to see to. Since he didnae say what business, I thought it was none of mine," Ian said.

She asked Mr. Foley, "Have you seen the reverend?"

"Not since he entered the Pettibone Tavern about three hours ago."

Louisa glanced at the captain to confirm her suspicions.

"You and Will stay here with the carriage," Captain Sinclair said. "Mr. Foley, would you mind leading me to the

Pettibone Tavern?"

Less than half an hour later, Reverend Wynterbottom came staggering down Main Street, the captain and Mr. Foley propping him up on either side.

"Oh dear," she said to herself.

Will said, "I ken the reverend's going to have to start all over again."

Captain Sinclair poured Reverend Wynterbottom into the carriage amid his repeated apologies for his unseemly condition. They let the man curl up on one bench while she and the captain sat on the other.

"It's my fault. It's all my fault," the reverend kept repeating. "God will never forgive me for abandoning them."

"I hope he stops talking," the captain said.

"I hope he doesn't vomit," Louisa said.

"I left them. I left them," the reverend said between sobs. "All my little chicks, I left them."

Wynterbottom ceased his nonsensical chatter, fell asleep, and snored all the way back to Quaker Hill. The captain ordered Will to stay with the horses and carriage while Louisa led the way, opening doors as Mr. Foley and the captain carried the reverend into the house and up to his room to sleep it off.

"His head will hurt like the devil tomorrow morning, but my missus has a tincture to cure that," Mr. Foley said and excused himself.

"I wonder where Mr. Kirby and Miss Robertson are," Louisa said, standing in the hallway with the captain.

Captain Sinclair scratched the back of his neck and averted his gaze. "Perhaps you should have a rest afore supper?"

"But I'm not tired."

One side of the captain's mouth kicked up in a rakish grin. "Aye, but ye will be once I'm done with you."

Louisa went to her room and removed her lightweight summer gown. While she washed the heat of the day from her face and neck, she considered the comment Captain Sinclair had made. It bothered her. He'd meant it as a jest, yet there must be some truth in it.

He'd implied she was going to be tired when he was done with her. What on earth did that mean? Kissing made her breathless and a wee bit weak in the knees, but it wasn't what she would call strenuous. She lay on her bed wondering how coupling could exhaust her. Surely all that naked nonsense with parts inserted into other parts etcetera wouldn't be the sole cause for collapse. What else did he have in mind and just how debauched *was* Captain Sinclair?

Eliza woke her some hours later and announced supper would be ready in thirty minutes.

"Has Miss Robertson returned?"

"Yes, miss. About an hour ago. She and Mr. Kirby are in the parlor with the captain."

"Please tell them I'll join them soon."

She dressed and tidied her hair as quickly as possible. Louisa needed to talk to Mairi. In matters of the bedroom, she was experienced, at least more experienced than Louisa. Mairi would know what Captain Sinclair meant by her being tired "once I'm done with you."

Louisa thought she'd be able to pull Mairi aside before supper. No such luck. She'd attached herself to Mr. Kirby like a barnacle and would not let go. Even at supper, she kept reaching over and holding his hand. Didn't she know the man needed two hands to eat? At this rate, she might starve Mr. Kirby to death before she got a chance to marry him. If only she could find a moment to pry the woman off of the man.

"Mr. Kirby and I are going for an evening stroll," Mairi announced as they rose from the dinner table.

"Actually, could you spare a few minutes to talk about

some wedding details?" Louisa asked sweetly.

"All the wedding plans are set, are they not, Mr. Kirby?" Mairi said. "Dinnae fash yourself."

Mr. Kirby beamed. "I love it when you say those charming Scottish expressions."

Louisa stole a glance at Captain Sinclair who looked like he was about to squash Mr. Kirby like a bug.

"Yes, well, there are a few additional things I need to discuss with you. *Alone.*" She leaned forward, opened her eyes wide, and stared deeply into Mairi's, hoping she would catch on. She didn't.

Before Louisa could object, Mr. Kirby wrapped a shawl around Mairi's shoulders and swept her out of the house. Damn. She'd missed her opportunity.

"Come. We'll have a brandy, aye?" The captain ushered her across the entry into the parlor.

She arranged herself on one end of the settee while Captain Sinclair poured the brandy. He handed her a tiny glass of the spirit and settled next to her. The settee was meant for two, but he seemed to be crowding her on purpose, one arm draped over the back behind her, his leg crossed and his boot nudging her leg slightly.

"What were you so desperate to talk to Miss Robertson aboot?"

"As I said, wedding details."

He chuckled that deep, rich baritone, the one that was just right. "You get red patches on your cheeks when you fib."

"I do not."

"Aye. Ye do." He ran the back of his finger down the side of her face. "Right here."

"Maybe it's none of your business what I was going to ask Mairi—Miss Robertson, I mean." Dear Lord. She needed to calm down or she'd make a dreadful mistake.

He gave her an odd look, then took in a deep breath and

let it out slowly. His face was so close to hers, she felt it on her neck. "Lass, dinnae fash aboot tonight. I'll go slow. Slow and gentle."

"But what…" She stopped herself from finishing. He'd only think she was foolish and ignorant.

"Dinnae look to little Miss Robertson for answers, lass. Believe me. She can tell you nothing aboot what you and I will share tonight."

She could stand the suspense no longer. "What did you mean when you said you would make me tired?"

For a split second, she registered surprise on his face. Then he did the worst thing. He laughed.

She shot to her feet. "Stop laughing at me." She punched him in his sore arm on purpose.

"Ow!"

"You're a bloody imbecile, Ian Sinclair."

He launched himself at her, giving her no time to escape. He wrapped his long, muscled arms around her, hauled her against his chest, and kissed her with such ferocity, it made the private spot between her legs hot and damp and tight. Oh Lord, he was grinding his body against hers, his muscles trembled, and all she wanted was… What was it she wanted? Why didn't she know?

He dragged his lips to her ear and growled. "When a man wants a woman like I want you, the passion between them will spark a fire that will consume them, incinerate them, leaving nothing but ashes. I plan to love you all night, make you come apart in my arms over and over until you are spent and boneless. Do ye ken what I mean now, love?"

"Aye. I do."

"Say my name," he rasped.

"Ian."

"Again."

"Ian."

He squeezed her tighter. "*Again*."

"Oh God, Ian. Kiss me. Please kiss me."

• • •

Ian was going to have to kill Reverend Wynterbottom. The reeking sot had stumbled into the parlor and interrupted them at the best part. Well, maybe not the very best part, but close to it. He was about to ruck up Miss MacQuarie's skirts and have her up against the wall. He'd always found that a fun and satisfying way to—

Damn. He was a frigging animal. Literally. He'd promised slow and gentle. Instead, he was about to roger her in the parlor. He should thank the reverend for barging in on them.

"Did I miss supper?" the bleary eyed clergyman asked.

Miss MacQuarie straightened her gown and discreetly drew the back of her fingers across her lips. "I'm afraid so, Reverend, but Mrs. Foley left you a cold plate in the pantry."

"Ah. Thank you." He waved a hand. "Carry on," he said and toddled off.

They stood there, six feet apart, staring at each other and still breathing hard from their close encounter, until Ian said, "Forgive me for forcing myself on you like that. I had planned to go slow and—"

"Oh dear, I'm out of breath." She swallowed and put a hand to her chest. "I understand what you mean, now. About the fire and the ashes." She smiled, and his body went hard as a rock. "I, em…" She pointed to the door. "I'll go to my room now and…wait for you."

Ian had another brandy, fortification for the long night ahead, before retiring to his room. He thought it best to go above stairs before Kirby and Miss Robertson returned to the house lest he find himself in an extended conversation with his host as he had the night before.

Like last night, he removed his coat, waistcoat, and neckcloth. Tonight, however, he removed his boots. For stealth, he told himself, stealth and ease of trouser removal. He lay on his bed with his member straining to be released. He was so hard, that if he opened his drawers, he was certain his cock would point to the sky on its own like a flagpole.

Soft scratching on his door made him think of a cat, and he rolled out of bed to see. He opened his door to the dimly lit hallway and a gossamer sylph slipped inside his room.

"Lass?"

"I couldnae wait any longer," she whispered, and reached up to pull his face down to hers. Her kiss, filled with the unskilled passion of an innocent, threatened to undo him. He would spend in his trousers if he didn't slow the hell down. He swept her into his arms, carried her to his bed, and laid her there gently.

"Let me lock my door and light some candles," he said.

And let me gather my wits and cool down before I embarrass myself.

He'd had this fantasy ever since he was fourteen, the one where a beautiful woman comes to his room and asks him to bed her. He'd replayed it in his head a thousand times, all the things he would do and say. The woman never had a face, only a body with silky skin, plush breasts, and a plump, round bottom. And in the fantasy, he was a masterful lover. He said things that made her sigh, stroked her until she came, and plunged inside of her over and over until she called out his name. A thousand times he'd brought himself off to the daydream and yet, as he lit the last candle and took her in, he couldn't remember a single clever thing he'd said or done.

She'd taken off her shift and was sitting naked in the center of his bed, her legs tucked under her bottom, her ample breasts pert, the nipples tiny tightened beads pointing at his cock. Her hair tumbling about her shoulders and so long, it reached her narrow waist. And her hands, those birdlike, velvety magic hands, were clasped demurely over her lap to hide her thatch of curls.

"Aren't you supposed to be naked, too?" she asked.

His mouth had gone dry. Fortunately, his flask of whisky sat on the floor next to his bed. He took a long pull and replaced it. He tugged the shirt over his head, unbuttoned his fall and shoved his trousers to the floor. Next, he loosened the string on his drawers and let them drop. Finally set free, his cock waved joyfully at her nipples.

"Oh, Ian," she said, raking her eyes up and down his body, "you are beautiful."

He climbed onto the bed, facing her, one leg tucked under him, the other leg dangling off the side. He looked at her, every inch of her gorgeous body, especially those breasts. He'd imagined they would be on the large side, the way he liked them, but hadn't imagined the shape of them would be so...perfect. And the nipples like two brass bullets. He would have to kiss those, lick them, suck them, tweak them. But that would wait. Right now, he needed to see everything. He unclasped her hands and drew them away from her lap revealing the dark triangle of curls. He resisted slipping a hand between her thighs to see if she was ready for him. There would be time for that, too.

"What's next?" she whispered.

"This," he said. Leaning forward and bracing himself with one fist on the mattress, he slipped his other hand through her hair around the back of her neck. He kissed her. She opened to him, let him play with her tongue and tease her lips. She slid her hands up his chest and paused to rub her fingers over his nipples. Jee-*sus*. He sucked in a breath and stilled her hands.

"What?" she asked.

"We're going to play a game," he said. She tilted her head

quizzically. "We're going to take turns kissing each other's bodies. First, you lie still on the bed while I kiss and touch every inch of you to my satisfaction."

"And then I get to do it to you?"

"Aye. That's the way it's played."

"How do you tell who's the winner?"

"Oh, you'll know, love. You'll know."

• • •

Louisa thought there wasn't anything more thrilling than wearing trousers on stage. She was wrong. The most thrilling thing in the world was wearing absolutely nothing in Ian Sinclair's bed. Dear Lord, the way he looked at her made her feel as if she was the most interesting, the most beautiful, the most desirable woman he'd ever seen. It was a deliciously wicked feeling. Did that mean she was a wanton woman?

Gran had always said there was nothing sinful about sex, and women who maintained a distaste for the marriage bed were either lying or unsatisfied with their partner. Apparently, pretending to be prudish about the subject was a sign of virtue. Louisa wanted no part of that. Men could be rather prudish, too. Captain Sinclair more so than most, always pretending to shield her from seeing his body, but she knew better. He wanted to show off for her.

Well, he wasn't shielding his body from her view now. He stood before her in all his naked glory, proud as a peacock. And he had a right to. Shoulders, arms, chest, belly, all perfectly sculpted with muscle. She let her eyes fall to where his sun-brown chest met his pale white nether region just below his belly button. Her gaze traveled even lower to the wild nest of auburn pubic hair. Oh, for the love of God. Even his ugly bits were beautiful. Elegant. Longer and thicker than she'd ever imagined that part of a man could get. It bobbed as if it had a personality of its own.

"Oh, Ian. You are beautiful."

He slid one knee onto the bed and sat. Was she supposed to do something now? Was he waiting for her to…to do what? Were there other things that came before the connecting parts business? She should probably ask, but she didn't want him to think she was stupid. He pulled her hands away from her lap. She hadn't even realized she'd clasped them there. Up until now, he'd been preoccupied with staring at her breasts. His interest had shifted to her lower anatomy.

The anticipation was too much. "What's next?" she asked.

"This," he said and kissed her. She didn't have other kisses to compare with his, but she was certain Ian Sinclair was a more than competent kisser. Like when he'd kissed her before, she became a little dizzy, and her nipples tightened into painful knots. The lazy, languid way he kissed her seemed to indicate the way in which he planned to take her. He did, after all, promise slow and gentle. She was also growing more and more aware of the spot between her legs that often tightened and throbbed when he kissed her. Tonight, it was very insistent, demanding attention, touching. So wicked. She was going to hell.

She put her hands on his belly, his hard, tight belly and slid them up toward his shoulders, but got distracted when she encountered his nipples, tiny beads of flesh that delighted her touch.

He hissed and took hold of her wrists. Did she hurt him? Maybe his nipples ached as much as hers? Didn't he know touching them would help with the ache?

"What?"

"We're going to play a game," he said.

A game? Why would he want to stop in the middle of all this thrilling business to play a bloody game? But once he explained the rules, the game made a kind of wicked sense. Hadn't she heard it referred to as bed-sport? Of course. Sex was meant to be fun. And not just for men. Why would women pretend not to like something that was fun?

Without him having to ask her twice, she unfolded her legs and got into position. "On my back?" she asked.

"Aye, and tuck your hands under your bottom. When it's my turn, I get to touch you, but you cannae touch me."

She nodded and slid her fingers under her hips.

"Close your eyes and no peeking."

"Can I talk?"

He chuckled deep in his chest. "You can make all the little sounds you want, love. Just dinnae be too loud, aye?"

"Loud?"

"No screaming."

That was alarming. "Is it going to hurt?"

"Nae, it's going to feel so good, you'll want to cry out."

"Oh."

"The next time, I'll make sure we're all alone so you can scream as much as ye want, I promise."

There would be a next time? He straddled her legs and braced himself with a palm on either side of her. She inhaled, surprised at how big and dominating his dark figure looked looming over her.

"Close your eyes, love. The game begins now."

The first flood of sensation came when he buried his nose in the crook of her neck, and groaned, "God, you smell good." His full day's growth of raspy beard prickled her skin and made her turn her face into his silky hair and inhale.

"*Mm*. So do you."

She lay in a sort of delirium while he kissed her ears, cheeks, nose, chin, brow. Then opened her mouth for a deep kiss, his tongue dancing in and out, tangling with hers, teasing her lips. He paused, leaving his lips lightly touching hers, and then whispered. "My beautiful green-eyed sorceress, you've bewitched me. You are all I think about. All day I pictured you like this, naked, under me, letting me touch you." He trailed a kiss down her neck and over her shoulder. "In all my fantasies, you never tasted this good, or smelled this good..." He shifted on the bed and his cock grazed her thigh. He growled, "Or felt this damn good."

He covered her left nipple with his cool wet lips and sucked.

She cried out and her back arched at the shocking sensation.

"*Shhh*," he said. "Tell me quietly now, how does that feel, love?"

"Good," she panted, "so good, too good."

"Shall I stop?"

"Nae, dinnae stop."

He chuckled into her breast. "I wonder, does the other one taste as good?"

"Ah." She arched again. "You are a wicked man, Ian Sinclair."

He lifted his head. "If I am, you make me so."

While he sucked and nipped her right nipple, he cupped her left with his hand and squeezed. He pinched the hard nub and rolled it between his fingers. She moaned and pleaded for more, begged him not to stop. Her hips had started to rock and twist and squirm because she needed something—

He hooked his hand under her left knee and pulled her leg up, then snugged his thigh firmly against the spot between her legs. Yes. That's what she needed. Contact. Pressure. Something to rock against.

His big warm hand skimmed the inside of her thigh all the way up to her— "Oh."

"Christ, you're so slick and wet." He said it as if it was a good thing. Which was fortunate because that wasn't something she had any control over. In fact, she was losing control by the second.

Her eyes flew open when he slid a finger into the cleft of her womanly part. She lifted her head, but he didn't notice because he had bent his head to look at her parts. He scraped his teeth over his bottom lip and his tongue slipped out in concentration as he began to stroke her experimentally. He rubbed up and down, then in small circles. "Which feels better?" he asked.

"More," she gasped. "More. More. More. Oh God."

He slid one finger inside her and she thought she might fly off the bed and hit the ceiling, it felt so sinfully good.

"Keep your eyes closed," he whispered in her ear. "Concentrate on that spot, think naughty thoughts, whisper dirty words."

She did as she was told and concentrated on the burning, tightening, throbbing feel of his finger swirling circles around that wild spot on her body. His private part was the naughtiest thing she could think of. Even naughtier, she pictured her hand wrapped around it. She couldn't bring herself to utter the dirtiest word she knew out loud, so she mouthed it over and over.

"You're almost there, love," he whispered. "Say the word out loud and let yourself go."

"Please, please, oh," and then she said the word out loud.

The world splintered into a thousand shards of colored light and her body shuddered.

"That's it, love. Come for me." He slid his finger inside and her body pulsed around it.

"Oh, Ian, Ian, I didnae ken it was like that. Oh Lord. That was so wicked."

She wrapped her arms around his neck and buried her face in his shoulder. She felt like sobbing but she was too happy. No one had prepared her for how intimate this would be, sharing something like this, whatever it was called.

She lifted her head. "What was that?"

He settled next to her and stroked her belly with the back of his hand. "You had an orgasm. Did you never touch yourself before?"

"Was I supposed to?"

"When someone isnae in your bed to give you pleasure, you can always give yourself pleasure."

What an incredible idea. Ian wasn't nearly as prudish as she had originally thought. In fact, he was a wicked, wicked man. And she loved that.

"There are people who will tell you there is shame in it, but dinnae listen to them. There's no shame at all." He kissed her then, a long sweet kiss. A kiss so natural it felt like they'd kissed a thousand times before.

She suddenly remembered her recent wanton behavior and her hand flew to her mouth.

"What is it?"

"I said that word out loud." The back of her neck burned with embarrassment.

"Aye, ye did." He nuzzled her ear. "And now I ken your secret word, the word that brings you off."

• • •

Ian had brought many women to completion. He'd gotten quite good at it. It was the polite thing to do, after all. An exchange of favors. He'd felt obliged to give the woman pleasure before he took his. The more efficient he was, the quicker he could achieve his own and be on his way.

Never, never in all the years he'd spent swiving as many women as he could coax into his bed had he ever derived as much pleasure as he did watching Miss Green-Eyes open like a flower in his arms. And Christ, when she'd uttered that word—which happened to be his favorite trigger word, too—he'd nearly spent himself on her belly.

"Did I win?" she asked.

"Nae. The object of the game is to please the other. I believe I won."

"Is it my turn now?"

"I'm no' done with you."

She rolled onto her stomach and propped herself on her elbows. "What's next?"

"My bed's too small for what I have in mind. Shall we make a dash for your room?"

They semi-dressed and snuck down the hallway one at a time. His heart thundered in his chest with the possibility of being caught, but he doubted Kirby would think poorly of him since he had the same lurid intention of debauching Miss Robertson. Once inside Miss MacQuarie's chamber, he locked the door behind him and skimmed off his trousers and shirt. His vixen was already lighting candles.

"Wait," he said. "Take off your night things. I want to watch you walk about the room naked." He hopped onto her bed, stretched out his legs, and folded his arms behind his head.

She lifted one elegant eyebrow. "Comfortable?"

He smiled. "Very. Begin the performance."

She swept off her shift and very casually—as if a debauched ex-soldier with a cock as hard as brass wasn't watching her—draped the item over a chair. She lit a taper off the burning candle, then went about the room lighting six more, just as natural as can be. Not a self-conscious tic or twitch.

She was a performer.

Finished, she looked to him for more. He twirled his finger in the air. Miss MacQuarie gracefully turned full circle and curtsied low for him.

He sat up and mimed clapping his hands, whispering, "*Brava, brava.*"

She burst into giggles, trotted to the bed with breasts and curls bouncing, and jumped in next to him. He gathered her into his arms and planted kisses on her head, cheeks, ears, neck, anything within reach of his lips. She straddled his hips and sat back on his thighs.

"Do ye ken you have a very fine arse, Miss MacQuarie?"

"I do now." He reached for one of her breasts and she batted his hand away playfully. "What did you want to do that required a bigger bed?"

"That comes later."

"Then is it my turn now?"

He pushed himself up to sitting. "Just let me feel them one more time." She leaned forward and stuck out her chest so that he could cup them with his hands. "These are the most perfect breasts I've ever seen in my life. I'd insist they should be displayed in an art museum, except I'd have to kill any man who looked at them." Jee-*sus*. Where did that come from? He sounded like a jealous lover. He leaned back on the pillow and refolded his arms behind his head. "Right. I'm closing my eyes now. Do your worst. But remember, I'm ticklish."

She remained still for a long minute until he was compelled to open one eye. As far as he could tell in the dim lighting, she was inspecting his arms and chest. He felt the skin on his body flush. "Eyes closed," she said. The heat of her body left him and the bed dipped.

"Where are you going?"

"Dinnae move. I have a candle in my hands."

"Why?"

"I need to see you better." Her cool hand trailed slowly down his chest and belly, and he tensed with anticipation. No fannying about for her. The lass was going directly for the prize. To his dismay, her hand took a detour down his flank, over his hip and thigh, and paused on the ugly scar. "What happened here?"

"Saber cut. That's what brought me down at Quatre Bras. Nearly killed me."

"But my—but General Robertson carried you off the field."

"Aye." He opened his right eye enough to see her bend and kiss the angry red ropey-looking thing. Standing at the side of the bed—instead of in it with him as she should be, as he wanted her to be—she continued her close inspection. When her hand reached his foot, he flinched. "I told you. I'm ticklish."

"Do ye ken you have a very fine pair of feet, Captain?"

His belly bounced with silent laughter. "Feet?" He whispered. "Of all the parts of me, you choose to comment on my feet?"

"But they're beautiful."

"Come here, ye daft woman." He sat up, took the candle from her and set it back down on the table next to the bed. She climbed back in and resumed her straddle. His cock stiffened and jumped between their bellies, drawing her attention.

"Did you do that or does it move on its own?"

He laughed again and wrapped his arms around her back. Ian couldn't remember having this much fun with a naked woman before. "Most of the time, I can control it, but no' when it comes to you."

"Because I'm naked?"

He kissed her quick. "Because you smell like lavender, and you have emerald-green eyes that flash when you're angry, and you have magic hands that take away my pain." He licked her neck. "And ye wear trousers under your kirtle, and put loaded guns in your pockets."

"But I thought those were the things that made you

angry."

"Anger. Desire. My cock doesnae ken the difference." He cupped one heavy breast in his hand. "And ye have the bonniest chebs I've ever seen." He trailed more kisses down her shoulder.

She arched into his touch with a gasp. "But what about the game?"

He paused between kisses. "I concede the game. You are the winner." He wrapped one arm tightly around her waist and using his other for leverage, spun them both around so that her back was on the mattress and he was on top of her. She let out a little sound of surprise. He snugged himself between her legs and the thing inside his head—the itch that constantly reminded him when things needed to be straightened, or squared, or counted, or put back into place—calmed. This is where she should be. Under him.

"Is this when our parts go together?" she asked. He detected a hint of trepidation.

"If that is what you want, love. Do you want me inside you?"

"Will it hurt? You're awfully...big."

"A quick pinch, but after that, pleasure. And I promise you, I will fit."

His balls had drawn up so tight they began to ache. *Please say yes, please say yes.*

"I want you inside me, Ian. Now."

Thank Christ.

As he had promised, he went slowly, gently, mustering every ounce of control. His cock screamed for him to close his eyes and thrust. But the one corner of his sanity still functioning kept his eyes open, monitoring her for discomfort. Any time she winced, he withdrew an inch. Two steps forward, one step back, until he was halfway—the point of no return.

"Are you all right, love?"

"Aye."

"Shall I make it quick, then?" She nodded and he buried himself to the hilt. She let out only a little gasp. He stilled until he got himself under control, and her breathing quieted. He moved experimentally, a short withdrawal and back.

"Oh. Is this the pleasure part?" she whispered.

"Aye," he groaned, on the very edge of losing it. He began a slow incremental rhythm.

She uttered in a high-pitched, surprised, "Oh." And then a low, "Oh. Oh, Ian, that is nice. That is—oh. I had no idea. Oh."

Her words encouraged a faster pace, longer thrusts, harder thrusts. The thing inside his head began to uncoil, releasing tension he'd grown so used to, he hadn't known it was always present. At last. *He* was in *his* proper place. This was where he was supposed to be. Inside her.

"Oh, Ian, Ian, it's happening again."

It was happening for him, too. He was close, so close. His trigger word formed in his head, traveled to his tongue and he opened his lips to speak it…but instead of his word, it came out as, "I love you, lass. Oh God, I love you." The first pump of release brought him satisfaction like he'd never known, a glorious, overwhelming sense of peace and joy. The second pulse jolted him back to his senses and he pulled out, finishing himself on her belly.

Dazed from the power of his release, he collapsed in a sweating, heaving heap, completely oblivious to the woman under him.

"Ian, you're squashing me. I cannae breathe."

He rolled off, still panting, and draped his forearm over his eyes. Had he really just told Miss MacQuarie he loved her? Had she heard him? Another thought, darker than the first: he'd pulled out too late. Some of his seed was in her. It could be taking root even now.

A sickly sensation overcame him. A soup of guilt, shame, and regret. Bloody hell. Why did he always let his basest desires undo him? Was he doomed to repeat his same mistake?

"Are you all right?" he asked, unable to look at her.

"Yes. Are you?"

He got out of bed, padded to the basin, and dampened a towel. Returning, he said, "Sorry. It's a bit cold," and attempted to clean her belly.

She took the towel. "I'll do it."

"I should probably go back to my room. God knows what time it is." He searched for his trousers.

"It's not late. There's hours and hours left. Must you go?"

He winced. "We both need sleep, lass."

"Ian," she said, sounding grave. "Are you sorry it happened?"

He punched his way into his shirt. "I hope not, lass," he said, and left her.

Chapter Thirteen

The door latch clicked behind him. Lying on her bed, Louisa wept silently, letting the tears trickle out of the corners of her eyes and pool in her ears. The captain was sorry. Maybe not about the bedding, but he was sorry he'd told her he loved her. He couldn't even look at her afterward. Why did he have to ruin it? The best, most wonderful, most exciting and erotic night of her life, and he ruined the whole thing for him *and* for her with that one stupid comment.

I love you, lass. Oh, God, I love you.

Those words had burned their way into her heart—a slow searing pain. She'd never forget the sound, as if it had tortured him to say *I love you.* Was it true, or was it something he always said at the last...before he reached that ecstatic moment? If he spoke the truth, if he really loved her, Louisa's betrayal would be all the more devastating for them both. No wonder her father sent her away. How could he love her? She was a horrible, hateful, selfish person. She was truly the General's Daughter from Hell.

Louisa wished it didn't hurt her heart to destroy Captain

Sinclair's life. The truth was, she was in love with him. If he weren't counting on the commission her father would award him, things wouldn't be so complicated. Instead, they had become a twisted tangle she could never undo. What a fool she was to encourage his attentions, to think that giving herself to him would lessen the blow when he discovered her treachery.

She could imagine what tomorrow would be like. He'd tell her he didn't mean the words. He wouldn't look at her when he said it. And he'd probably never touch her again, never call her lass, never laugh for her, never put his head in her lap and beg her to rub his temples. How could she bear it?

• • •

He hadn't seen the look on her face, but he had heard the pain in her voice. He was a bastard of the first order. He was the one to lose control, to say a stupid thing like *I love you*, to come inside her, even a little, and yet he'd punished her like it was her fault.

As he passed Miss Robertson's bedchamber, he heard female laughter and a deep voice. Lucky for them. They were meant to be together. Why did things work out so nicely for everyone else but him?

He knew the reason. It was waiting for him in Edinburgh. The boy. His son. A child he'd fathered through careless, callous, thoughtless behavior. He'd walked away never knowing of the child's existence—for six years. And because of his ignorance, he'd lost his opportunity to make his own son legitimate. He would live this perdition for the rest of his life. No mercy. No joy. Every attempt at love would be snatched away at the last moment most cruelly.

Once inside his room, he put the latch on the door and crawled into bed without undressing. Lavender. His bed, this place, this nest where she'd shared her secret word with him, smelled of her. He drank what was left of the whisky and closed his eyes.

And what of Miss MacQuarie? He'd broken her, ruined her, he might have even left her with his child. It was possible. It had only taken one lapse in judgement to get Alice Crawford pregnant. If he'd known, if the letter had reached him, maybe he would have been there. Maybe she wouldn't have died, and he would have made things right for his son. But he'd been six years too late.

His head began to throb.

Dear God, not now, not now.

It wasn't too late to make things right with Miss MacQuarie. He could make it right. He would make it right.

The next morning, the thing in his brain woke him. Chaos. He'd allowed his well-ordered, well-disciplined world to fall into chaos. His ship, his books, his things were miles away in Boston. His crew, out of reach and out of his control. He'd debauched Miss MacQuarie, allowed Kirby to debauch Miss Robertson, Reverend Wynterbottom had fallen off the wagon again, and Will had had his first taste of fun yesterday. Had Ian kept the lad close, he'd have never known what he'd been missing. He'd never have known what a life on board the *Gael Forss* as a cabin boy cost him.

He made a vain attempt at appeasing the itch. He washed, folded the towel perfectly and hung it next to the washstand. Dressed meticulously. Tied and retied his neckcloth three times. Made his bed with military corners. Straightened the fringe on the counterpane and made certain the bed curtains were evenly pleated before he went below stairs.

When he entered the breakfast room, he found only Reverend Wynterbottom. Apparently, no one else had risen.

"Morning," the reverend said between bites.

Ian poured a cup of tea from a samovar, helped himself

to buttered brown bread, and sat. "I apologize for yesterday, reverend. You are freshly sober and vulnerable to temptation. I should have remembered that and taken more care."

"My dear, captain. You are kind to say so, but the blame falls squarely on my shoulders." The reverend dashed away a tear. "I'm only grateful my host and Miss Robertson didn't see me in my sorry condition."

"Nor shall they hear of it." Ian smiled.

Miss MacQuarie entered the room with, "Good morning." He and the reverend rose. She didn't look at him like she usually did. Why would she, and how could he expect her to?

"Good morning, Miss MacQuarie." Fortunately, he stopped himself from the automatic *did you sleep well* question. Any answer would have been awkward.

Having finished his breakfast, the reverend excused himself. "I am preparing a few words to share with Miss Robertson and Mr. Kirby on their wedding day. Not a sermon, mind you," he chortled. "Just a few words."

"That's lovely, Reverend," she said. "Miss Robertson will be especially pleased."

The reverend left them in an uncomfortable silence. He looked at her, stared at her, willed her to look at him. She kept her eyes on her damn teacup, blast her.

He heard himself blurt an angry, "You have to marry me." Ha! There. That got her attention. Her green eyes flashed bloody murder at him. It was a good thing he still had possession of her pistols.

"Have you lost your wits?"

"Possibly. But you have to marry me." His heart was banging away in his chest. Was he going to have an apoplexy?

"I most certainly will not."

"Don't be stupid. You could be carrying my child."

She laughed out loud. "I never took you for a romantic,

Captain Sinclair." Her words dripped with sarcasm.

"Very well, I'll get on my knees, if that is what you require." He was good at sarcasm, too.

"Do you honestly think marrying me will assuage your guilt for having ruined me last night?"

He'd bolted to his feet. "Morning," he shouted over Miss MacQuarie's words but it was too late. Miss Robertson and Mr. Kirby entered the breakfast room. They'd heard.

Miss MacQuarie flushed crimson.

"Shall we continue our conversation in the garden?" Ian was careful to imply it was a command and not a suggestion.

She pinched her lips together so tight they turned white, then threw her serviette on the table, stood, and marched out of the room.

"Excuse me," he said to the couple, whom he hated right at this moment because they were so obviously infatuated with each other.

He rushed after her, which of course fueled his anger. He'd never chased a woman in his life. He caught the back of her skirt just as she was about to run upstairs to her room. "Not so fast. We're having this out. You can do it where everyone can hear us or you can come to the garden wi' me. Which will it be?"

"If you'll recall, Captain, I do not like to be ordered about." She was breathing fire now. Why did that excite him?

"Is that since this morning? Because, last night, ye didnae mind at'all."

She slapped his face so hard, he had to blink to see straight. "You are a monster!" she hissed.

"Right then." He wrapped his good arm around her waist, heaved her onto his hip, and headed for the front door. She kicked and flailed and protested, but not hard enough to hurt him. Not hard enough at all.

Halfway to the garden, she demanded, "Put me down.

I'll walk the rest of the way myself. I promise." They were far enough away from the house to speak comfortably anyway, so he set her on her feet. She sputtered and huffed and jerked her bodice back into place. While he waited, the gravity of what they were about to discuss set in.

"Sorry," he said. "I should have asked you, not told you."

Mollified—temporarily, at least—she said, "Even if you had asked me, my answer would be the same. No."

The word *no* jabbed him in the gut like a dull knife. How could a word so small hurt him? "Please be reasonable, Mairi."

"I asked you not to call me Mairi." Tears welled in her eyes. He needed to proceed with more caution.

"Lass. I'm no' sorry last night happened. I'm sorry the way it ended. I got carried away and…well, I forgot myself. Even if the chances are slim, I cannae leave you here knowing that you might be carrying my child."

"And what of the last part?"

"Which part?"

"You know. The words of love," she said. "Did you mean them?"

He swallowed hard. "What if I did?"

"I would…" she began and averted her gaze. "I would tell you to save those words for someone worthy of your love."

• • •

Louisa was close to tears, though whether from disappointment or pain she couldn't tell. She held her throbbing right hand in her left. "I'm sorry I slapped you." A red splotch had bloomed where her hand had connected with his cheek.

"Did you hurt your hand, love?" he asked.

Bollocks. Why did he have to be so bloody decent about everything? She preferred it when he was being an ass like at breakfast. Demanding and ornery. She did not like his blue puppy-dog eyes. Not one bit. They made hers water and she hated crying like a ninny.

"No," she squeaked.

"Let me see." He took her hand and she didn't resist. "Och, lass," he said, grimacing at her pinkish palm, then he kissed it.

"I'm sor—I'm sor—I'm sorry—" A kind of hysteria overcame her, leaving her sobbing and hiccuping uncontrollably. The more she tried to hold it in, the worse it got. Captain Sinclair wrapped her in his arms and hugged her tight against his hard chest. She buried her face in his perfectly tied neckcloth and disintegrated.

He held her, rocking ever so slightly, alternately rubbing and patting her back, laying kisses on the top of her head. So bloody sweet and understanding. Damn him.

"It's all right, love. You're overwrought. It's a lot to take in, but, once you've had time, you'll see I'm right about this. We have to marry."

"I cannae marry you." With her face planted in his neck, her words came out muffled.

"What?"

She pulled away and wiped her eyes with the tail of his neckcloth. "I said I cannae marry you." She sniffed.

"I ken you had your heart set on being an actress, but—" He craned his head around. Someone was calling.

"Captain! Captain!" Will came racing across the yard waving his hat, his face alight with excitement. He practically barreled into them. Captain Sinclair steadied Will by the shoulder.

"Easy lad, what's amiss?"

"Mr. Foley's taking Mr. Kirby into town, and he said I could come along and visit the park with the other lads so long as you gave your permission. Can I go, sir?"

Captain Sinclair looked at Will with such despair it made Louisa's heart ache. What had upset him? With great effort, he choked out, "Aye. Be sure and help Mr. Foley if he needs you."

Will's eyes became even rounder. "Thank you, sir," he said and tore off toward the coach house.

The captain watched him for a moment, his hands on his hips, his mouth working. He turned away from her suddenly and dipped his head.

"What troubles you?" She walked around to face him, but his head was lowered, one hand rubbing his brow shielding his eyes from her. "What is it, Ian?"

He lifted his head, eyes glistening, face rippling with grief. "He's a boy. He should have a mother and father. He should have brothers, friends. He should have fun. But he works for me on my ship and has since he was ten. *Ten!*" He poked himself in the chest. "Do ye ken what I was doing at ten? I wasnae carrying water and food and slops all day, that's for damn sure."

"Ian, Peter told me he found Will starving and filthy, but you took him in. You saved his life, and the lad worships you for it. He loves you as much as any boy could love a father. You *are* his father."

He broke away from her and shouted, "I'm a horrible father. I'm a monster. You said so yourself."

"And I was wrong. You are not a monster."

"And I'm not a father. I'm—" He stopped himself. "I'm raving." But Louisa got the impression he was raving about something other than Will.

She tried to reach for him again, but he put up a hand to stop her and turned away. "I'll wager you had a wonderful father," she said. "One who loved you very much. Spent time with you."

He nodded. "Aye. He's a great man."

"Children can have family, a home, an easy life even, and still have no love. Will has love. He has you. That's more than most."

When he faced her again he had regained his composure, but his eyes had shuttered. They'd taken on that dull quality, masking his thoughts and emotions. "We'll talk more about marriage later. Meanwhile, consider my offer. You'll come to see I'm right."

He walked toward the coach house with long determined strides, back rigid, fists clenched. Something was wrong. He was hiding something from her. She longed to know what it was, to smooth away his grief like she had his migraines. But revealing intimacies always required an exchange, and she'd revealed too much of herself already. Every time he asked her to marry him, it was harder to say no. And every time she said no, the pain of regret grew more difficult to manage. Perhaps it was time to leave this place.

Mairi greeted her in the entry. She was a beautiful lass, but this morning she looked absolutely radiant. "What's got you so pleased?"

"We've decided not to wait. Mr. Kirby asked the reverend to marry us tonight."

"Tonight? What about the wedding?"

"We'll still have the wedding feast. Edward—Mr. Kirby has already invited the guests and Mrs. Foley's ordered the food from the market and hired the staff. But Reverend Wynterbottom will marry us this evening before supper." She hugged Louisa then. "Oh, it's all so romantic. It'll be just you, the captain, Mr. and Mrs. Foley, and the reverend, of course. All the people that matter. You'll be my maid of honor, yes?"

"Of course."

"Where's the captain? I want to ask if he'll give me away."

"I saw him go to the coach house. I'm sure he'll be back soon." Louisa wasn't altogether certain about the time of his return. He may have intended on going into town with Will and Mr. Kirby. "Is there anything I can help you with?"

Mairi ticked off items on her fingers. "My dress is finished. Mrs. Foley knows to make a cake. Mr. Kirby's gone to town to collect the ring..." Her eyes darted up. "Would you help me make my wedding bouquet?"

Louisa smiled through happy tears. "With joy, my darling friend."

· · ·

He'd accompanied Kirby to town under the pretense of requiring masculine company. The truth was, he felt compelled to look after Will. The lad was his responsibility. Yet, as he sat in Kirby's fine carriage, he realized what he really wanted was to witness Will's fun, experience his joy vicariously, taste what it would be like to be a real father. Did he have the patience and the heart to be a father? Was he as selfless as his own da? And, more importantly, would Rory want him as a father?

Ian hollered for Will to slow down, but it was no use. The lad sprinted halfway up Huntington Street before Ian made it out of the carriage. He and Kirby parted company with plans to meet at the Pettibone Tavern for food and refreshment shortly after the noon hour.

Ambling down the main thoroughfare toward the public park area, Ian paused outside a bookseller, and debated for only a moment before stepping inside to browse. He'd never been able to pass up an opportunity to look at books. He perused the shelves for a quarter of an hour—the shop was small and not particularly well stocked. He asked the shopkeeper if he carried vol. 2 of Southey's epic poem, *Madoc*. When the man replied in the negative, he bid him good day. On the way out of the shop, his gaze fell upon *Moll*

Flanders.

That morning in the bookshop came back to him vividly—that first moment he'd set eyes on her—the cloud of lavender, the roses blooming in her cheeks, the perturbed set of her lips, the angry flash of her green eyes and, of course, the book she'd clasped protectively to her breast.

At the time, he'd been shocked that a young gentlewoman would be so bold as to open such a novel, much less enjoy what she read. That was before she'd swaggered into his life wearing trousers and carrying pistols. Before she had held his head in her lap and smoothed away his migraine. Before they'd shared their bodies and their pleasure. Now, of course, he knew this was exactly the book for his green-eyed lady.

Some minutes later, Ian sat under the same tree he and Miss MacQuarie rested under yesterday. Was that only yesterday? It seemed like a week ago, so much had happened. Yesterday, she was an innocent. Today, she was ruined. And possibly pregnant. By him.

Bloody frigging hell.

As he watched Will and his new friends play, he recalled himself as a youth about Will's age, spending all day with his brother Alex, and cousins Magnus and Declan. He remembered the games they'd played in Mam's bee field—Attack the Keep, and Capture the Brigands—games they'd invented to hone their battle skills by pretending they were warriors, games in which they tested their mettle by imagining real danger.

How had Rory gotten on without a father or an older brother all these years? Did he have friends to play games with? He and his gran had looked healthy when Ian had met them on the docks. They were well clothed, well fed. Though not wealthy, Alice Crawford's husband had left her with a modest income which would have passed to Rory and been managed by his gran. But Ian should have been the one supporting them. He should have been the one seeing to their needs. If only he had known, things would have been different for the boy.

He picked a long blade of grass from the ground next to him and examined it. The leaf was wide and brilliant green, just like the grass that grew in Scotland. Ian had lived his childhood carefree. Completely ignorant of hunger, cold, and sickness. Balforss House had been his home, a fortress of love and protection built a century and a half ago when safety and security were never taken for granted. And his father had been the one to teach him and his brother how to be good men. What kind of men would they have become had it not been for Laird John's gentle but firm education?

Ian positioned the blade of grass taut between his thumbs, held it to his mouth and blew, producing the duck call he and his father would use when hunting. The call was loud enough that Will and his friends paused in the middle of their game, searching for the source. He blew again. Like the Pied Piper, the boys were drawn in.

"How did you do that?" the tallest lad asked.

"Sit down, and I'll show you," Ian said.

"Are you really a captain?" another one asked with skepticism.

"I'm captain of the merchant vessel, the *Gael Forss*. Will is a member of my crew."

Will gave the skeptic a bland eye. "I told ye."

The collective interest in whistle-making with a blade of grass became feverish, and Ian patiently, contentedly, gratefully spent the next hour demonstrating how to perfect a grass-whistle duck call.

On the carriage ride back to the house, Kirby showed Ian the ring he'd purchased. "Do you think she'll like it?"

The gold band held a sizable oval-cut ruby in the center surrounded by small diamonds. "She will love it. I have nae doubt."

Kirby flushed with relief, placed it back in the small velvet bag, and tucked the bag into his coat pocket. "I neglected to tell you before, we've asked Reverend Wynterbottom to marry us this evening. We couldn't wait any longer. We'll still have the wedding feast as planned, but tonight will be our wedding night."

"What about the banns?"

"Not completely necessary here, in America, and the contract has an open date so, not to worry."

"I see."

"Do you think I'm being unwise? Am I being unfair to Miss Robertson?" he asked anxiously.

"Not at all. I have it in mind to marry as well."

Kirby grinned at him. "Miss MacQuarie?"

"Aye."

"Have you asked her?"

His answer came uneasily. "More than once. She's refused me every time." Kirby looked upon him with pity. God, he must seem like a besotted fool. "But she'll come around. She's just not used to the idea yet."

But would she accept his child as her own or would she reject the notion of a cuckoo in her nest? She had a kind heart. It seemed she liked children. Surely, she would like Rory. Perhaps, one day, she'd come to love him.

Upon their return to Kirby's house, Ian was disappointed to find that Miss MacQuarie and Miss Robertson had sequestered themselves above stairs in preparation for the evening's ceremony. He had looked forward to presenting the book he'd purchased to the lass in hopes that a gift might help smooth things between them. He penned a short note and tucked it inside the front cover.

He spent the rest of the afternoon trying to keep memories of the night before at bay. They were deliciously erotic, the stuff of fantasies, really. Unfortunately, they were marred with the veneer of guilt and frustration. Guilt because he should not have taken her to his bed and frustration because she would not let him make things right.

On the positive side, he had another eight days before she planned to leave for New York, which meant he had eight days to change her mind.

Chapter Fourteen

Louisa placed the last pin in Mairi's hair when a knock rattled on the bedchamber door.

"If that's Edward, dinnae let him in," Mairi said. "I'm no' ready."

Louisa went to the door and called, "Who's there?"

"It's me, Eliza. I've got something for you." Louisa opened the door to the girl, and Eliza held out a book. "Captain asked me to give this to you, Miss MacQuarie."

"Thank you, and please tell Mr. Kirby and the reverend we'll be ready in a few minutes."

Louisa closed and latched the door after Eliza departed.

"What is it?" Mairi asked.

"A book." Louisa smoothed her finger over the lettering on the spine and smiled. *Moll Flanders.* He remembered. The very book she'd wanted most of all, and he had purchased it for her. She swallowed hard and fought back tears. The gift felt intimate and forgiving. It felt like...love. She opened the cover and a note slipped to the floor. She picked it up and read:

I may be a monster, but I am your monster.

Her heart skittered. It was as if he could see inside her mind, a terrifying thought, as she had too much to hide from him.

"Is ought amiss?" Mairi asked.

"Oh, Mairi. I'm so afraid."

Mairi rose from the dressing table to sit next to Louisa on the edge of the bed and comfort her. "Is it because we've both fallen in love with the wrong man?"

"That doesnae frighten me. I dinnae mind loving him. I'm frightened he will hate me when he finds out who I really am."

"Dinnae fash yourself about it. After all, he may never discover the truth. What are the chances your father or brothers will come here? Scotland is a long way away."

"Aye. You're right." Louisa sniffed away tears. "Tell me something, does Mr. Kirby call you Louisa?"

"Aye, he has."

"Does it trouble you?"

"It did at first, but now he mostly calls me darling."

Louisa smiled. "You're a beautiful bride, dearest. And my heart is full of joy for you and Mr. Kirby."

"We did the right thing, did we not?" Mairi asked.

"I'm sure of it." Louisa went to the door. "If you're ready, I'll go fetch Captain Sinclair, and we'll both walk you down the stairs."

She didn't have far to go. Captain Sinclair was waiting at the upstairs landing, looking so hopeful, it almost broke her heart. She went to him.

"Do you like it?" he asked.

She realized she was holding the book to her heart. "You know I do. Thank you."

"I mean to marry you, Miss MacQuarie, and I shall not leave you until you say yes."

"Captain Sinclair, I think perhaps you have a secret that you are unwilling to tell me." He blinked, and she knew she was right. "We both have secrets," she continued. "I dinnae see how we can marry when we keep secrets from each other."

If Louisa *was* getting married, which she wasn't, she would plan a ceremony exactly like Mairi and Mr. Kirby's. But of course, she wouldn't because she wasn't getting married. Even if she *wanted* to marry, which she didn't, and even if she *could* marry, which she couldn't, she would marry Captain Sinclair. But, no matter what Captain Sinclair said or did, she wouldn't, couldn't, shouldn't marry him.

Captain Sinclair disrupted her nonsensical rumination. "Do you think they'll be happy?"

Louisa surveyed the parlor: Mr. and Mrs. Foley in their Sunday best, the new Mrs. Kirby in the wedding gown she'd lovingly made and embellished with gold stitchery, Mr. Kirby in a fine suit of gray summer wool, Reverend Wynterbottom in clerical blacks, Captain Sinclair with his perfectly tied neckcloth and snug-fitting breeches, and herself, the actress playing the role of Mairi MacQuarie in a calico day dress.

"I believe they will be blissfully happy, Captain," she answered.

Mr. Foley made another toast to the couple's eternal happiness, and they raised their cups. Reverend Wynterbottom's cup was filled with cider, of course.

"Is the only reason you reject my offer of marriage because you want to be an actress, Miss MacQuarie, or does it have something to do with your secret?"

Her heart thumped at the mention of her secret, but she was spared the need to answer when Mr. Kirby peered outside the parlor window and announced, "Looks like we have a visitor." Mr. Kirby held up a hand. "No, no, Mrs. Foley. Stay here. I'll go see who it is."

Captain Sinclair leaned down to whisper in Louisa's ear. "I thought she might give me problems."

"Who?"

"The bride. People call her the General's Daughter from Hell, ye ken. Even her brother Connor said she'd be difficult. But she's been no trouble at all." He gave her a crooked smile. "You, on the other hand, have been a thorn in my side since the first moment I saw your wicked green eyes."

Louisa felt herself flush with an odd mixture of happiness and trepidation.

Laughter echoed in the entry hall, drawing her attention away from Captain Sinclair. Mr. Kirby burst into the parlor beaming at his new wife. "Darling, I have the most wonderful surprise for you."

Louisa's heart stopped beating the instant a tall, dark, and very familiar-looking man swept in, arms outstretched and smiling. "Louisa."

Her first surge of panic was for her friend whose world was about to collapse. Mairi's smile contorted into a mask of horror. And Edward Kirby's face flickered from elated to confused when his best friend, Nathan Robertson, walked right past his new wife.

Nathan clapped his hands around Louisa's shoulders and laughed. "Sorry, Lou. Looks like I just missed the wedding. Let me be the first to congratulate you." He kissed her on the cheek.

Numb with fear and shock, Louisa chanced a look back at Captain Sinclair. His buckled brow was rapidly hardening into something dark and dangerous.

She shoved her brother in the chest. "What are you doing here? You're supposed to be on the Continent."

Nathan took a deep breath. "I know, I know. I felt guilty

about how things had unfolded for you," he explained with his hangdog face. "I came to see that you were happy, Lou."

"You ruined everything!" She spun back to Captain Sinclair, the full realization of her betrayal in his stony gaze. "I'm sorry Ian, I never meant to—"

Unable to bear the look on his face, unable to witness Mairi's dream crumble, and unwilling to explain her deceit to her brother, Louisa fled the house and kept on running.

. . .

Ian remained suspended in a haze of disbelief as he watched a distraught Miss MacQuarie dash from the room. Was this some kind of elaborate joke Kirby had arranged? Some bizarre wedding custom unique to America?

Reverend Wynterbottom was the first to speak what his fear did not allow him to believe. He pointed to the empty doorway. "So, *that* one is your sister?" His finger shifted to the bride. "And this one is…?"

"My sister's maid, Mairi," the visitor helpfully clarified. Shaking his head, he continued, "I'm sorry. Would someone mind telling me what's going on here?"

The sobbing bride was next to flee the room. Mrs. Foley followed her.

"I'll go stable Mr. Robertson's horse for the evening." Mr. Foley finished his whisky, set down his cup, and hurried out of the parlor.

Like rats fleeing a sinking ship, Ian thought, his temper simmering somewhere deep in his belly.

The new visitor turned to Kirby for an answer. The groom would be of no help. His face had turned gray. Ian had seen similar looks in the eyes of men skewered in the gut with a sword. And Reverend Wynterbottom had his head bowed in fervent prayer. Once again, the burden of sorting out this mess fell to Ian. Damn. Why was it always him?

He inhaled a deep breath and extended his hand to Robertson. "I'm Ian Sinclair, Captain of the *Gael Forss*."

"Nathan Robertson." They shook. "Why is my sister so upset?" Robertson asked, his face hardened and his words clipped. He looked a hell of a lot like his father, the Tartan Terror.

"It seems the ladies have exchanged identities. Miss MacQuarie just married your friend Kirby."

Robertson's face went blank. "But why—how did you not—" In a matter of seconds, the man managed to sort out what Ian and Kirby hadn't seen until this moment. Nathan Robertson's face twisted into a frightening scowl. "That blasted little— I'm going to thrash her."

"Get in line," Ian snarled and strode out of the room.

"Where are you going?" Robertson shouted after him.

"I'm going to find her."

The task proved harder than he expected. She wasn't in her room, nor anywhere in the house, nor was she in the summer kitchen. It was full dark now. She wouldn't have strayed into the woods or the fields. That left the coach house. A pale light shone from the open door. Mr. Foley was inside stabling Robertson's horse. As Ian entered, Foley handed him a lantern.

"She's in the back," Foley said in a low voice. "The boy is with her."

Ian walked to the end of the row of stalls and peered into the loose box. He held the lantern up, and its golden glow illuminated Miss Mac—Miss Robertson curled up in a mound of hay, head buried in her arm, sobbing. Will, like a steadfast hound, crouched at her side.

"It's all right, miss," he said. "The captain is here now. He'll make everything all right. You'll see."

Her sobbing increased to a wail at the mention of his

name.

"Go find your bed, Will," Ian said, his voice laced with barely contained rage.

Will gave her one last pat and left the box. Ian hung the lamp on the wall. He needed both hands free to strangle her. He paced inside the loose box. The stifling heat only provoked him further. He tore off his coat and tossed it down.

"Sit up," he growled.

She slowly lifted her head, wiped her swollen eyes, and hiccuped.

"A *secret*?" he said, beginning to shake. "You call this a *secret*? This, Miss Robertson, is a crime!" He wiped the spittle from his lips. Christ, he could barely see straight. "Do you understand—can you even begin to understand what you've done?"

"I'm s-s-sorry."

"Lives, Louisa. You played with people's lives. There are consequences." He spun away from her and held his head. It was beginning to throb. *Not now. Not now.* "My life, my future, everything. It's all gone." He leaned down and cupped her chin in his hand so she would look at him. "You knew what was at stake for me, and still you did this. Why?"

"You—you wouldnae understand," she said, and resumed her crying.

He released her and backed away. "You're right. I will never understand. But you *will* tell me. I will know the reason for your trickery." When she didn't reply, he glared down at her and shouted, "Now!"

She startled and for a half second, he was sorry he'd frightened her. Then the tide of his anger rushed back.

"We planned everything bef—" She gulped. "Before we left Edinburgh. Then I met you and you were so kind and—and good. And when I found out about your plans, it was too late." It took effort for her to grind out her words. Each one rode on the crest of a fresh sob. "Mairi, she's more than my maid. She's my f-friend. She wanted to—" She sniffed and took a breath. "She wanted to marry Mr. Kirby and I wanted to-to-to…"

"To be a goddamn actress."

"To punish my da!" she blurted. She gave way to her sobs and cried uncontrollably. "He doesnae love me. He doesnae want me. I wanted him to hurt. I wanted…" She collapsed on the hay again.

Ian sighed. Exhausted from having spent every last drop of his anger in this past half hour, the storm inside his body had started to calm, and the nauseating feeling of having his life upended had abated.

"Louisa."

Ian spun at the unexpected voice. He hadn't heard Nathan Robertson approach. How long had he been standing there?

Robertson entered the loose box, knelt, and gathered his sister in his arms. She let her head rest on his shoulder.

"I'm sorry, Nathan."

"God, Lou. Of course Da loves you. He's only ever wanted what's best for you. He doesnae ken how to show it, but he's always loved you most." Nathan rose and carried his sister back to the house. Though every muscle in Ian's body objected, he reminded himself Nathan had a right to carry Louisa. She was his sister. Ian was only—

Bloody hell. What was he to her now? Jee-*sus*. Would her brother make her marry Kirby? Would Kirby insist on an annulment of the first marriage and wed Louisa? They had a contract. Shite. Of course, that would happen.

And there wasn't a goddamn thing he could do about it.

He waited in the parlor while Robertson carried Louisa up to her bedchamber. Kirby was in there looking like hell. The reality of what had just happened had hit him. Reverend Wynterbottom, a good man despite his weakness for spirits, stood behind Kirby's chair, one hand on the disappointed groom's shoulder comforting him with aphorisms like *God has a plan for us all* and *Everything happens for a reason.* Utterly useless words in this case.

"I'll sit with him. You go on to your bed, Reverend."

The man nodded and left the parlor. Ian poured himself whisky. He needed something to steady his hands as well as something to dull the pain of what was to come. Kirby held up his cup without a word, and Ian refreshed it. He took the seat across from Kirby.

"I'm sorry."

Kirby lifted his head, his eyes narrowed at Ian.

"If you're thinking I was part of this, you're wrong," Ian said. "I found out when you did. I'm just as appalled." But then, that wasn't the whole truth. Somewhere in the back of his mind, he'd known Miss MacQuarie wasn't who she said she was. Her manners, her speech, the occasional misspoken name, her refusal to let him call her Mairi. Peter had suspected, too. He'd even brought his suspicions to Ian's attention and he'd chastised him for it.

Kirby groaned like a wounded animal. His eyes, his mouth, his shoulders, his whole body sagged with the weight of defeat.

"You love her, I know," Ian said gently. "If it helps, Miss Robertson told me they concocted the plan because Miss MacQuarie wanted very much to marry you. She may have lied about her name, but I dinnae think she lied about her feelings for you."

Kirby nodded slightly and took a deep swallow of whisky. Ian looked at his cup. Whisky was for celebration. Tonight felt like a funeral.

Robertson entered the parlor. "How is she?" Kirby asked.

"Which one?"

"My— Miss MacQuarie."

Robertson went to the drinks trolley and helped himself to a cup of whisky. "The housekeeper gave her a draught of something to calm her and put her to bed."

"And Miss Robertson?" Ian asked.

Robertson paused and eyed him speculatively. Just long enough to make Ian's insides squirm. "The housekeeper is doing the same for my sister."

"What's going to happen?" Kirby asked.

Robertson emptied his cup and poured himself another. "What should have happened in the first place. You're going to marry Louisa."

Kirby bolted to his feet. "It's too late. I've already married the other."

The tall dark Scot, who looked so much like the man Ian had fought alongside seven years ago, seemed to consider Kirby's words for a moment. "It's not too late. Ye havenae taken her to your bed."

Kirby flushed crimson, and Robertson read the guilt on his friend's face immediately. "Bloody hell, man. You thought that was my sister and you took her to your bed before the wedding?"

"You don't understand—"

"No matter, Edward. The marriage is void. You were deceived."

Kirby doubled over as if punched in the gut.

Ian rose to face Robertson knowing what had to come next. He took in a lungful of courage and announced, "Your sister cannae marry Kirby. She's been compromised, as well."

"You bloody bastard!"

He saw the murder in the man's eyes a half second before Robertson's fist connected with his face. Ian staggered backward, crashed into a table, and toppled over, his head smacking into the wall before his body crumpled to the floor in a heap. Jee-*sus* that hurt. Checking his nose experimentally, he determined it was still attached to his face, not broken, but was bleeding profusely. He wiped his face and got to his feet, still a little rattled from the blow. Ian had seen it coming and did nothing to block it—he'd deserved it after all. However, he derived a measure of satisfaction when he saw Robertson shake out his hand.

"I suppose it's pistols at dawn, aye?"

"Nae." Robertson pulled a sickly smile. "I'll leave the pleasure of killing you to my da."

. . .

She promised Mrs. Foley she'd take the sleeping draught right after she said her prayers. As soon as the woman closed the door behind her, Louisa poured the contents of the glass into the chamber pot. She had to leave. If she stayed, her brother would make her marry Mr. Kirby, and that would only create a bigger disaster. She packed lightly, only what she needed for the next few days. The rest she could send for once she'd reached her destination.

While the men were still below stairs discussing her future without consulting her, she stole into Captain Sinclair's room and found her pistols. Mr. Kirby had placed their identification papers in his safe. There was no retrieving those. At least she had her letter of recommendation with her.

It didn't take much stealth or effort to escape the house. Everyone thought she and Mairi were drugged and asleep. Lucky for her, the moon was bright enough she could see the road. If she kept up her brisk pace, she'd make it to town in time to take the first coach out.

Louisa tried not to think about the look on Captain Sinclair's face. He'd been angry, of course. She'd expected as much. She hadn't anticipated how much the truth would hurt him. He had been close to tears. She'd shattered his dreams.

It didn't matter to him that she hadn't planned on hurting him, that she had intended to make people happy, not ruin lives.

Lives, Louisa. You played with people's lives. There are consequences.

She'd known there would be consequences. She just hadn't known they would be hers. That she would hurt, as well.

• • •

Ian rolled out of bed with the sun, his head pounding from too much whisky, staggered to the basin, and finished washing away the crusted blood he'd missed last night. He peered at his reflection and groaned. With both his eyes slightly blackened, he looked like a pine marten. It would get worse as the bruises turned purple, then green, then yellow. Jee-*sus*. This was his wedding day. Not at all how he had planned. In fact, not what he'd planned at all.

He selected a clean shirt and trousers from his bag and noted absently that his things were out of order. He hadn't remembered leaving his bag in disarray last night, but then he hadn't remembered much about last night other than receiving a blow from Robertson that had nearly sent him crashing through a wall.

Once dressed, he sat on the edge of his bed and examined his hands. They were shaking, as were his legs. Was he ready for this? Absolutely not. Was he going through with it? Absolutely. He'd insist on it. It was the right thing to do, the honorable thing to do. Christ, yesterday he had practically begged Miss Mac—*damn*—Miss Robertson to marry him. Of course, that was when he'd thought he'd ruined her. But God had played him a fool once again. It was she who had ruined him.

The only thing that could have made this entire trip worse would have been to watch Louisa marry Kirby. At least he'd been spared that. Had he not ruined her, he'd be attending Kirby's wedding today and not his own. Ian refused to spend time examining why that fact somehow made things more bearable. The point was moot.

He was the first guest to the breakfast room. Mrs. Foley was laying out the sideboard with plates of ham, eggs, toast, and roasted potatoes. He poured himself some tea, sat at the table, and waited. Reverend Wynterbottom waddled in next mumbling "good morning" and "what a fine day" and "God's good grace" and this and that and so on. Ian uttered sounds he hoped would be taken as agreement.

Kirby entered next looking only marginally better than Ian. He said nothing, and the reverend was wise enough not to open a conversation with him. The thump of footfalls fast approaching had them all halfway to their feet when Robertson charged in.

"Where's Louisa?" he demanded, looking straight at Ian.

"She's not in her room?"

"No."

Mrs. Foley entered with more food.

"Have you seen Miss Robertson this morning?" Robertson barked.

Startled, she fumbled with the plate of eggs. "I haven't seen either of the ladies today."

Ian bolted for the exit at the same time Robertson made to leave, their shoulders creating a logjam in the doorway. They struggled for a moment before Nathan got the upper hand and shoved past Ian. Ian caught up with the arsehole at the staircase, yanked him back, and bounded up the stairs three at a time.

He pounded on her door. "Louisa! Louisa!"

"She's no' there, ye numpty," Nathan said. "I told you,

she's gone." He pounded on Miss MacQuarie's door. "Mairi, open your door and tell me where Louisa's gone to."

Mairi opened her door a crack and Nathan stormed inside. He towered over her and shouted, "Out with it, girl. Where is she?"

Kirby pushed past Ian. "Leave her be, Nathan." Mairi had started her sniveling again, and Kirby scooped her into his arms, consoling her.

Ian tried a calmer approach. "Mairi, some of Louisa's things are gone. She seems to have disappeared. She could be in danger. Did she say anything to you about leaving?"

She pointed to a scrap of parchment lying on her dressing table. Nathan pounced on it, and read the few words out loud. "Be brave, my dearest friend. Mr. Kirby needs your love now more than ever."

Ian thought for a moment. She would want to get to New York as soon as possible. She didn't know how to ride, and she couldn't have taken Kirby's carriage. "The post coach," he said. "She's walked to town to catch the post coach to New York."

With Kirby's permission, Ian and Nathan saddled his two best horses and raced into town. Ian flung himself from the saddle and strode into the coaching inn where Kirby had said they sold tickets. "Has a coach left for New York today?" he asked, out of breath from the ride.

The man behind the counter scrunched his face as if thinking caused him pain. "Um. Hang on." He wandered into a back office, saying, "Hey, Albert, is there a coach to New York this morning?" Ian heard someone, presumably Albert, say, "Um. Hang on."

Ian growled. "It's urgent."

The man poked his head out and put a hand to his ear. "What'd you say, son?"

Ian schooled his patience. "A young woman is missing—"

"My sister," Nathan broke in.

"—and we suspect she's headed for New York City," Ian continued. "She's about so tall, pretty green eyes, a fine figure—"

"Shut up about my sister's figure," Nathan shouted.

Ian closed his eyes and tamped down his temper. "Has anyone matching that description purchased a ticket to New York this morning?"

"No."

Good. Perhaps she hadn't left New London as yet.

"She boarded this morning's coach to New Haven," the man behind the counter said helpfully.

Nathan cursed.

"What time did it leave?" Ian asked.

"Um, three—no four—no three hours ago, maybe? What time is it now?"

"Never mind," Ian said. "Which way is New Haven?"

Chapter Fifteen

Louisa was rather pleased with herself. She'd made it to the coaching inn in time to catch the first coach out of town. Unfortunately, it wasn't headed directly to New York, but rather New Haven, Connecticut. Her limited knowledge of American geography left her at a disadvantage. However, according to the very nice man behind the counter, New Haven was a major stop on the coaching route. From New Haven, she could board a coach to Hartford, Boston, or New York City.

Pressed by the need to leave town immediately, before she was discovered missing, dragged back to the house, and married off to Kirby, she purchased a ticket to New Haven and boarded the coach along with a woman and her two children, a fashionably dressed gentleman with silver hair, a mustache, and a walking stick, and a young man whose tall slim stature and fair coloring reminded her of Mr. Peter. Thoughts of Mr. Peter, of course, reminded her of Ian.

Ian, with his just-right voice rumbling in her ear, his long, elegant fingers raking through her hair, and his hot sweet kisses on her breast. And then she remembered the look on his face the moment when he realized she had deceived him, the barely contained rage when he'd stood over her in the stable demanding to know why. He knew why, but he would never *understand* why and, therefore, he'd never be able to forgive her. They would never marry.

That last bit, she told herself, mattered not. All that mattered was that she didn't marry Mr. Kirby. Hence, the need to flee Quaker Hill. She would have rather said a proper goodbye to Mairi, but once she was established with the theater in New York, she would write and explain. Mairi would understand. Perhaps she would write to Captain Sinclair, though she doubted her apology would change his feelings.

To keep the pain of last evening at bay, she struck up a conversation with the other woman in the coach. The remarkably well-maintained roads, along with the well-sprung coach and good weather, made the ride to New Haven surprisingly pleasant. The lady's name was Mrs. Davenport. Her seven-year-old boy, John, sat between them fidgeting as boys do, while Annalise, her two-year-old, slept in her lap. The three were on their way home to Old Saybrook after visiting her mother in New London.

The young man, Mr. Eaton, was returning to his school in New Haven where he was studying the law, hoping to follow in his father's footsteps and run for office in the government.

The silver-haired gentleman never introduced himself. Instead, he tipped his hat over his eyes and slept the majority of the trip. They stopped at coaching inns to change horses every two or three hours. When Louisa parted with Mrs. Davenport at Old Saybrook, the coachman paused long enough for her and the other two occupants to purchase a light repast. According to Mr. Eaton, Old Saybrook was approximately halfway between New London and New

Haven.

"We've another twenty-five miles or so to cover, but if the weather holds, we should make it there before night fall. You'd best take the opportunity to eat now, Miss Robertson."

Her traveling bag was stowed on top of the coach. It contained a change of clothes and other necessities. Her jewelry and money she kept in her reticule looped safely around her wrist and tucked close at all times. She still carried the currency she used in Scotland. A good deal of it, actually. No one in the shops in New London had commented when she'd used English coppers to buy things. But the man at the coaching inn in Old Saybrook turned up his nose.

"We don't take those here. We're no longer subjects of the Crown."

"The scars of our wars with England run deep, I suppose. I'll change coin with you, Miss Robertson," Mr. Eaton offered. "They are, I believe, of equal value."

"Thank you, Mr. Eaton. You are very kind." She purchased a wedge of cheese, a small loaf of brown bread, and a mug of ale. What she didn't finish in the coaching inn, she wrapped in her handkerchief and stowed in her reticule. She and Mr. Eaton, and the silver-haired man, who had yet to introduce himself, continued on. She tried hard to stay awake, but the strong ale and her sleepless night worked against her, and she dosed intermittently for the remainder of the journey.

Someone shook her awake with, "Miss. We've arrived." The silver-haired gentleman loomed over her.

"Thank you." She gathered herself and stepped out of the coach. "Where's Mr. Eaton? I'd like to say goodbye."

"He got off two stops ago," the man said.

"Oh, well, could you recommend a suitable—" Louisa lifted her wrist, the one on which she carried her purse. "My reticule. It's gone." She climbed back inside the coach and searched everywhere. Icy white panic set in. Everything was in there, her money, her recommendation, her jewelry. "Oh, dear Lord, no."

She asked the coachman, "Did you see anyone take my reticule, my purse, I mean?"

"No, miss."

She chased after the silver-haired man. "Sir, someone must have taken my reticule? Did you see?"

"No. I..." He paused as if trying to remember. "I left the coach at South Lyme only briefly. The young man said he'd watch over you. When I returned, he was leaving the coach. I asked him if I should tell the driver to wait, but he said no this was his stop, and he bid me good journey."

"But I thought he was a student."

The silver-haired man tipped his head to the side. "Not everyone is who they say they are. I'm afraid that is a lesson you've learned the hard way."

"What shall I do?" she asked, feeling helpless and stupid.

"I can drop you at your destination, if you like. The hack stand is right over there." As if remembering, he said, "Forgive me. I never introduced myself. Mr. Charles Daggett."

"Miss Robertson. How do you do." She felt light headed and the ground seemed to tilt. Mr. Daggett steadied her.

"All right, Miss Robertson?"

"Yes. But I hadnae planned to stay in New Haven. I'm going to New York. I think."

"What is your business in New York? Perhaps we can send a message."

"I plan to work in the theater. I'm an actress, you see."

Mr. Daggett straightened and smiled almost as if he recognized her. She was admittedly flattered. "Of course, you are. I know exactly where to take you. There is an establishment here in town I visit frequently. Reputable and very popular. One at which actresses of your...quality perform regularly. I understand it pays quite well. I know the manager, and I'll see that you have an opportunity to demonstrate your talents."

How incredibly fortuitous. A direct connection to the theater and he'd been in her coach the entire trip. "Thank you. You are so very kind."

· · ·

They were lost. Again. Ian shouted a stream of curses long enough to call into question Nathan Robertson's parentage, his capacity for thought, and his love for sheep. Robertson in turn accused Ian of various and sundry debauchery on par with such infamous varlets as Genghis Khan and Ragnar Lodbrok.

Every mile they had to spend backtracking put Louisa in another hour of danger. The only hint that they were on the right trail had come hours ago at the Old Saybrook coaching inn where the publican had said a lady tried to use her English coin.

"I told her we didn't take that dirty blunt here. It's got the blood of my father and his brother on it."

Ian had managed to keep Robertson from climbing over the bar and breaking the man's neck. He dragged him out of the inn, changed horses, and they went on their way. It was now close to six o'clock and Ian was certain they had taken a wrong turn somewhere. He insisted they stop at a place called Guilford Tavern. "I'm going inside to inquire," Ian said.

"You're wasting time," Robertson called. "We're on the right road. I definitely heard the man say North Branford at the last stop."

Ian went inside and inquired anyway.

"No. Coach to New Haven doesn't stop here," the tavern owner said. "This is the road to *North* Branford. You want the Boston Post Road to Branford about a mile back."

Ian stormed outside. "We're on the wrong goddamn road!"

They didn't speak until lights in the distance indicated they were close. Fortunately, the ferryman who took them across the Quinnipiac River was helpful. He gave them specific directions to the inn where the evening coach from New London would terminate.

"The city's laid out so it's easy to find your way," the ferryman said. "Just follow Chapel Street to College Street. It's the Cook's Inn you're looking for."

They found the Cook's Inn just as the ferryman had said. He and Robertson split up. Robertson went inside to question the keeper, and Ian headed for the coach house to grill the grooms and coachmen. Ian had little success and was about to join Robertson inside, when a coachman approached him.

"One of the grooms told me you're looking for me. I drove the coach from New London. What do you want?"

"There was an attractive young woman aboard."

"Yes, I remember. She lost her purse. Claimed one of the other passengers took it."

Ian's heart stuttered. Not only was she alone, she most likely had no money. "Did she say where she was going?"

"Said she was an actress and another one of my passengers, the fancy man, said he'd take her to a theater."

Ian lost control and grabbed the man by his coat. "Where? Where did he take her?"

"Easy," the coachman said. Ian released him. "I don't know but there's only two places in town where ladies perform on stage. The Lyceum and the Grand."

Robertson trotted toward them. "Did ye find anything?"

"Where are these theaters?" Ian asked.

"Oh, I ain't never been to those kinds of places. My missus would skin me alive."

Ian staggered sideways, as if the coachman's words had been a blow. What kind of a place was that "fancy man" taking her to?

"Come on." Robertson grabbed him by the arm. "We'll find the answer inside the inn."

They extracted the locations of the two theaters from the innkeeper. To save time, Robertson took the Grand and Ian the Lyceum. They stabled their horses at the coach house. The Grand wasn't far away. Robertson could run there faster than a hack could carry him.

Ian grabbed the first conveyance he could find, a battered contraption drawn by a gray-muzzled nag. "How long will it take you to get me to the Lyceum?"

"About twenty minutes, I'd say."

"Make it ten and there's an extra guinea in it."

The hack would have to backtrack to the river as the Lyceum was located near the docks. Another bad omen. In his experience, docks in any port city were a dangerous place to be at night. He had no weapons. Not even his *sgian-dubh*. Louisa was better armed than he was with her wee pistols. Why didn't he think to bring a dirk with him at the very least? No matter. He'd trample on any man who got in the way of finding Louisa. *His lass.*

They were stalled by a long line of carriages blocking the narrow road. "What's the holdup?" Ian called.

"It's Saturday night, sir. Everyone's going to the Lyceum."

Ian exited the creaky box, paid the man, and raced down the line of carriages. No doubt he'd find the theater at the end. His heart sank when the pool of light from the theater shone on a crowd of men. This was no regular theater. This was a show for gentlemen only. He tried to push through but was shoved back with shouts of, "Get in line," and "They're not letting anyone in yet."

He investigated the side of the building. Theaters had

back entrances for the actors, didn't they? Maybe he could buy his way inside, find her, and haul her out of there before... Before what?

The flat-nosed giant standing guard at the door was not interested in Ian's coin or his pleas. "Buy a ticket like everyone else. You can meet your little lady after the show."

"Would you give her a message for me?"

"Do I look like an errand boy?"

Rather than press his luck, he did as the giant suggested. He returned to the front door, waited his turn, and bought a ticket. A chalk sign on the lobby wall read:

Tonight's Featured Performances
Titian the Magician
The Ravishing Ginny Tumble
Daring Dancers Do
Elsa the Sultry Swede

A man ran up to the sign and hastily chalked in, *Lulu the Sassie Lassie*, in a sloppy scrawl. Bloody hell. The Sassie Lassie. Well, they got that right, but for the wrong reason. She was here. Now how to reach her? The security was tight and he could understand why. The show hadn't even started and the men were already half drunk and restless.

No such places like this existed in Scotland that Ian knew of, but he had heard of theaters in London that featured performances catering to...male appetites. Bloody hell. *Bloody frigging hell.*

He took advantage of a lull in activity and pushed his way through the crowd toward the stage. His eyes burned from the smoke. It seemed as though everyone in attendance was puffing on a cheroot. Low-hanging chandeliers provided very little light. No chairs and tables in this place. Standing room only. Evidently the management's objective was to cram as many paying customers as possible into every show.

A lad was performing tricks with his dog on a dimly lit

raised stage in front of tall red curtains trimmed with gold fringe. No one was paying any attention to the boy's act. Ten feet was as close as he could get to the stage. Ten feet of gaping pit lay between him and his pathway to Louisa. The stage was elevated so that everyone in the room could see the performers. More than likely, the height was intended to protect the performers from anyone spanning the breach and making off with one of the ladies, which had been his original makeshift plan. He had to think of another way. A distraction maybe?

Someone drew aside the curtain and a roar of appreciation rose up from the men. Ian swallowed his heart.

• • •

Everything was happening so fast. One minute Mr. Daggett was helping Louisa out of the carriage, and the next she was being hustled into the theater by a strange man with a ridiculous mustache.

"But I didnae get a chance to thank Mr. Daggett."

"You'll get your chance. He'll be around after the show. You can thank him then."

The way the mustache man smiled unsettled her. There was some added meaning behind his words she couldn't decipher. He more or less dragged her through a shabby-looking, smelly theater with a raised stage and no seats.

"Tell me, what play will you present this evening?"

Mustache Man laughed.

"I ken my showing up at the last minute like this is inconvenient, but I'm a quick study. If you give me the sides, I can—" The man opened a secret door made invisible by the way it was painted to look like the rest of the proscenium wall. "Where are we going?"

"Backstage." His grip on her arm tightened, and he

shoved her into a dark corridor. "Can you sing?"

"I'm told I have a pleasant voice."

He opened another door to a well-lit hallway. People bustled in and out of rooms, paced up and down the hall, and chattered with each other. From behind a door, she heard a woman vocalizing scales. Her heart thumped hard in her chest, and she got that same thrill she'd had while waiting in the wings of the Grass Market Theatre.

Mustache Man said, "Wait here and don't make a move." He entered a side room and closed the door behind him. A muffled argument between two men raged for a few seconds and ended abruptly.

A wee man came out of the room immediately afterward. He, too, had a crazy, twirly mustache and his hair had been parted in the middle and slicked down. She estimated he was four feet tall if he was an inch. He wore a brilliant green coat, matching green trousers, and a yellow neckcloth tied under his chin. He scowled at her and jammed his hands on his nonexistent hips.

"What's yer name?" he barked.

"How do you do. I'm Louisa Robertson."

He made a face. "We're gonna have to come up with a better name than that. Karl says you can sing."

"I never had the opportunity to sing on stage before, but—"

"What are you, English? Irish?"

"I'm from Edinburgh." When he looked at her blankly, she added, "I'm a Scot."

He fiddled with the curly ends of his mustache. "Lulu the Sassie Lassie. That's what we'll call you. What song are you going to sing?"

Things were happening at such a pace, Louisa was having trouble keeping up. "Em..." She remembered the song she sang on board the *Gael Forss*. It had pleased the crew enormously. "How about 'The Maiden of Bashful Fifteen'?"

His scowl changed to a broad smile. "Exactly. An innocent Scottish lassie straight off the farm. They're gonna love you."

Louisa returned his smile, encouraged by his faith in her as a professional actress.

"This way," he said, and she followed the diminutive figure down the hall to a room filled with ladies in various states of undress. She expected them to scream in protest when the wee fellow entered, but they took no notice of him. "Hey, Ginny. Meet Lulu. We're gonna bill her as the innocent lassie from Scotland. Find her something to wear and tell her what to do."

Ginny was a beautiful woman with a pile of blond curls on top of her head. Her generous bosom was overflowing her corset and the only other articles of clothing she wore were pantalettes, stockings, and shoes, all in pastel blues, pinks, yellows, and greens. "Sure. Come on in, Lulu."

Louisa stepped around the other six ladies. They all wore the same outfit, black corsets and knee-length black petticoats trimmed with a rainbow of ruffles. Ginny pawed through a rack of frocks and pulled out a pink polka-dot gown with long sleeves and ruffles along the hem and cuffs. It was sweet but looked more like something she'd worn when she was ten years old.

"Here, you can wear this."

"Thank you. Are you a singer, too?"

Ginny smiled. "You could say that."

"Where shall I go to change?"

Ginny's eyebrows drew together. They'd been darkened with charcoal. Her lips and cheeks were heavily rouged, as well. "Right here. You're in the dressing room, dearie."

Louisa glanced around. "In front of everyone?"

Ginny laughed. "Your first time?"

"Oh, no. I've performed on stage in Edinburgh. The Grass Market Theatre. I played Viola in Shakes—"

"Good for you, dearie. Now get changed. You're on after Titian the Magician and before my act. Be sure and get the boys riled up for me."

"Riled up?"

"You know, a little tease. Take down your hair. Show them some ankle and maybe a bit more. If you take off your garter and throw it into the crowd, they'll love you."

She was speechless. Show her ankles? On purpose? Remove her garter? Outrageous. She glanced around the room. The other ladies weren't putting on any gowns over their undergarments. She supposed she was lucky. At least she hadn't been asked to wear one of the black corset costumes.

"Hurry up," Ginny said. "You're on in five minutes."

Louisa stepped behind the rack of costumes, unpinned her gown, and wriggled into the childlike frock. One of the black corset ladies, a dancer she guessed, offered to tie the bow in the back for her. She asked the lady, "Does the management pay us at the end of the evening?"

"Sometimes. If the take at the door is good and if the boys love your performance." She finished the bow. "Wait. You need something else." She rubbed rouge into Louisa's cheeks.

"Oh, I dinnae use that."

"Quiet." The lady dabbed more on her lips. "There ya go. You look great. Stage is to the right and up the stairs."

The stairs led to the stage left wing. The noxious smell of tobacco filled her nostrils and her stomach rolled over. *Dear Lord. I can't be sick. Not now.* Not right before her American debut.

A man on stage was performing magic tricks to an audience that wasn't impressed. In fact, they were so busy talking amongst themselves, they didn't pay any attention.

A few audience members shouted for the magician to finish already, and one called, "We want Ginny Tumble. Where's Ginny Tumble?"

Ginny Tumble, the pretty blond lady who'd helped her choose a costume, must be the star.

Assuming he was the stage manager, she approached the man standing in the wings.

"Does the orchestra have the music for my song?"

"Music?"

"Yes. I'm singing 'The Maiden of Bashful Fifteen'."

The stage manager laughed. "Yeah, sure. Harvey will give you a musical intro, and then you start singing. He'll follow you."

The wee Green Man found her. "Ready, Lulu?" The name Lulu, what her brothers sometimes called her, didn't sound right coming from a stranger. He made the name sound...rude.

She stared down her nose at him and nodded. "I'm ready."

The magician took his bows to a smattering of applause and carried his things off as Green Man waddled out to center stage.

On the way past Louisa, Titian the Magician said, "Careful. They're out for blood tonight."

· · ·

Ian figured, based on the magician's reception, things did not bode well for tonight's performers. The men were here to see ladies. More than likely, they were here to get a keek of flesh, too. It better not be Louisa's. And what the hell was she going to do? Read Shakespeare to this crowd? Jee-*sus*. That would not go over at all.

A wee man toddled out on stage and introduced himself as Larry the Leprechaun. "I've got a special treat for you tonight." He used a singsong tune as if cajoling children. "Now settle down and behave yourselves, gentlemen. Our next performer is a sweet little girl just arrived from Scotland. She's as innocent as milk and pure as the driven snow."

Bloody hell. Ian's insides churned. The wee one's words said one thing, but his tone implied the opposite. He glanced around the theater again, searching for ways to scale the stage and rescue her if necessary. His only consolation: if he couldn't get up there, no one else could.

Larry the Leprechaun held out his stubby arm. "Straight from Scotland, Lulu the Sassie Lassie."

Hoots and howls and rude shouts erupted from the crowd and penetrated the smoky haze. A woman in a pink dress with cherry cheeks and a rosebud mouth walked hesitantly to center stage. Was that Louisa? She clasped her gloved hands tightly at her waist. Had it not been for those wide green eyes, he wouldn't have recognized her. Good God, she'd let her hair down. He was going to have to kill her.

The pianoforte started up, and the raucous crowd simmered down. Louisa glanced at the musician in the pit, looking puzzled. She mouthed a few words as if starting to sing but nothing came out. The musician started his intro again. Oh, Christ. She was shaking. The poor lass was terrified. And no wonder. The crowd hadn't given her a chance. They were already grumbling and shouting, "Louder, Lassie! We can't hear you!" and "If you're not going to sing, show us some leg."

Ian's impulse to find the arseholes responsible for those remarks and beat them bloody was quickly doused when he realized he'd have to fight every man in the room.

She started and stopped and tried again, searching for the key. Her voice was thready and weak. Not at all like the bold voice she'd used aboard the *Gael Forss*. She was singing the same song, too. Ian could just pick it out among the cacophony of catcalls. "The Maiden of Bashful Fifteen."

Christ, why did it have to be that tune? Why not a church hymn or something?

"Shut up!" he shouted to the men next to him to no effect. He roared, "Pipe down, ye bastards. Give the little lady a chance, goddamn ye!"

Surprisingly, the crowd did quiet, and Louisa's sweet voice cut through the smoke.

"Here's to the charmer whose dimples we prize,
Now to the damsel with none, sir,
Here's to the girl with a pair of blue eyes,
Now here's to the nymph with but one, sir."

She hadn't won them over yet, but they'd stopped their catcalls. He joined in the chorus with a full voice.

"Let the toast pass. Drink to the lass,
I'll warrant she'll prove an excuse for the glass."

"Come on, sing, ye bastards!" he yelled. A few men joined him for a repeat of the chorus. Ian doubted she could see him. He was close to the stage but, like the rest of the audience, he stood in near darkness. Just as well, if she spotted him or recognized his voice, she might falter. As much as he wanted to snatch her off the stage and hide her from the leering gazes of two hundred men, he wanted her to succeed, to triumph. She wanted this. She'd crossed the ocean for this.

By God, she was a braw lassie. It took courage for her to stand up there and face the restless, raucous crowd, to hold her ground. Hold her ground like a warrior. And Ian was proud of her.

By the time she started the third verse, the hem of her skirt had stopped trembling, she was in full voice, smiling, and confident. She *was* the Sassie Lassie and she was loving her moment on stage. Ian loved her, truly loved her, and with a deep pang of sadness, he realized that although Louisa might love him, she loved the theater more. Could he let her go? Did he love her enough to let her go?

Someone grabbed his shoulder. "What the bloody hell is she doing on that stage?"

Shite. Her brother. Nathan surged forward, but Ian held him back, shook him and growled in his ear, "Let her do this. If you drag her off, you'll humiliate her. Let her do this once. Just once."

Louisa came around to the chorus, and Ian sang along. So did half the men in the audience. Ian punched Nathan in the arm, encouraging him to join in. With reluctance, Nathan managed to harness his anger long enough to belt out the second round with Ian.

"Let the toast pass. Drink to the lass,
I'll warrant she'll prove an excuse for the glass."

On the fourth verse, Louisa was in her element. She glowed in the footlights, swaying and waltzing side to side on the stage. By the chorus, every man in the room sang along and the chandeliers shook with their voices. She finished to thunderous applause and, "More, more. Give us another!"

She made a low and graceful curtsy, stood, stepped to the side and made another. Then she turned her back to the audience and bent over. Bloody hell, what was she doing? When she turned back around, she had her goddamned garter in hand and tossed it, along with a kiss, into the sea of men. A fight broke out as a dozen drunkards clawed and punched and wrestled to grab it.

When Ian glanced back at the stage, she was gone. His entire body relaxed. It was over.

He hoped.

Ian dragged Nathan out into the lobby, deafeningly quiet compared to the madhouse they'd just escaped. He bought two shots of whisky from the barman. "*Slainte*," they said without thinking and tossed the fiery spirit back. They both made gasping sounds and faces.

"God, that is piss-poor whisky," Nathan spat.

"I'm no' even sure if it *is* whisky," Ian said, trying to get the taste out of his mouth.

"Why did you let her do it?" Nathan demanded. "Why did you let her...flaunt herself up there?"

Ian shook his head. "She wants to be loved. She doesnae think her family loves her. So, she wants to make the world love her instead."

"We love her," Nathan said, horrified by Ian's remark. "My father loves her most of all. And Connor loves her to bits. I frigging sailed across the Atlantic Ocean to see she was happy," he said, growing agitated. "What more does she want?"

He shrugged. "She wants what you have, the freedom to choose what her future will be."

"Well, her decisions are shite, if ye ask me. Look how she's bolloxed up her life."

"Ye mean because she has to marry me?"

Nathan cut him a look as if to say, *That's exactly what I mean, mate.*

"If you dinnae mind my advice—"

"I do, but you'll give it to me anyway."

"I will marry her. I want to marry her. But I suggest you let her choose. If you make her, she'll feel trapped like the feeling she gets in small spaces, ken?"

Nathan glared at him, but he seemed to consider what Ian said. After a moment, he nodded his agreement, albeit reluctantly.

"Let's go 'round to the backstage door and find your sister. There's an ogre guarding it, but I think between the two of us we can take him."

Chapter Sixteen

Louisa practically floated off stage. She'd done it. For all God's glory, she'd actually *done it*. She'd sung the song and everyone had clapped. They loved her. The stage manager man was first to congratulate her. The wee Green Man made a comment as he passed. Something like, "You've got a place in tomorrow's show." And the black corset girls patted her back and said, "Well done," and "Good for you, girl."

She went downstairs to change into her own clothes. Louisa shuddered to think how close she'd come to making a complete fool of herself. The room had been smoky and the audience so loud, she hadn't been able to hear the musicians, couldn't find the right musical key. For a moment, she hadn't been able to find her voice. How very lucky for her a man in the audience had started singing along, a Scot by the sound of him. He couldn't carry a tune, but he'd been loud. And then everyone had joined in and it had been just like singing with friends.

Karl the Mustache Man met her outside the dressing room door. "You did good," he said. "Better than I expected.

If you can do that again tomorrow night, you've got a job."

"Thank you," she said. "Can I get paid for tonight?"

"Didn't I tell you? First time's free." Karl smiled a sickly grin, as though he really didn't know how to smile. It made her stomach go sour. He hooked a thumb toward the dressing room. "Mr. Daggett's waiting inside. I'm sure he'll give you something."

Mr. Daggett was, indeed, waiting inside. He was reclining in a chair with his feet up on the dressing room table, his hands clasped over his belly. He stood when she entered. "It's the Sassie Lassie. What a delightful little ditty. 'The Maiden of Bashful Fifteen,' was it?"

"Aye. My brothers used to sing it. I picked it up from them." Mr. Daggett took a few steps toward her, perhaps closer than was necessary for two people to converse in a small room. She backed away. "I dinnae ken how to thank you for recommending me to the manager."

He closed the door to the dressing room. That old panic arose in her chest. Was the door locked? Was it the only way out? He leaned one arm against the door, half caging her in. "I can think of a number of ways you can thank me," he said.

Why was he being so different? He hadn't been like this earlier. She'd thought he was a kind, older gentleman who looked upon her like a daughter, like he was concerned for her welfare. That's not at all how he acted at the moment. And he'd been drinking. She could smell it on his breath.

"Yes, well, I'd better change out of this costume. If you'll excuse me." She tried sidling out from under his arm. He blocked her way and her heart spiked. Out. *Out!* She had to get out. Get away, before… She fumbled with the door. Why wouldn't it open? "Take your hand off the door, sir. You're holding it closed. I need to get out. I need air."

Mr. Daggett seemed to have grown another foot. He spun her around, held her against the door with both hands, and pushed his lips into her face. She tried to scream, but he smothered her cries with his mouth. When she tried to kick her way free, her knee made contact with his bollocks and he released her with a curse. She inhaled and let out a loud cry, "Help!"

Louisa flung open the door. Two men, looking harried and wild eyed, skidded to a stop in front of her. Nathan and Ian. "You're here." She fell into Ian's arms. Her brother went inside the dressing room, dragged Mr. Daggett out, and tossed him down the corridor as if he weighed no more than the wee Green Man.

"Are you all right, Lou? Did he touch you?" Nathan asked. "If he did, I'll kill him."

"She's fine," Ian said. "I ken she's just fine." He held her close and patted her on the back. "Let's go afore the ogre at the door rouses."

"My bag." She pointed to the dressing room. "Behind the rack of clothes."

Nathan rummaged on the floor until he found her traveling bag. The three of them hustled out of the theater through the back way. Outside, they had to step over a big man sleeping on the ground in front of the door. Only when she got a better look at Ian and Nathan under the streetlamp did she notice their disheveled hair, bruised faces, and scraped knuckles. Had they been fighting with each other?

"What happened to your face, Ian?"

"Your brother and I had a disagreement."

She rounded on her brother with an appalled, "Nathan."

"*Humph.*" Nathan turned away, shoved his hands in his pockets and shrugged.

The two of them were eerily quiet. Even more perplexing, Nathan didn't object to Ian holding her close. Ian flagged a hack and they climbed inside. Still, Ian kept his arm around her, yet Nathan said nothing apart from giving the driver directions. Her brother sat on the bench opposite. It was dark, but when they passed a streetlamp and the light flashed across his face, she thought he looked sad. She didn't dare provoke either of them with chatter about her performance. In any case, Mr. Daggett's frightening advances had taken the shine off her short-lived elation.

Ian pulled his handkerchief out, licked it, and wiped the rouge off her cheeks and lips. She'd forgotten how they'd tarted her up for the stage. She inhaled sharply and turned to Ian. "It was you. You were the one who started singing along."

"Aye."

"Why?"

"I like that song."

"No, really. Why did you do it? Wouldn't you rather have seen me fail so you could say I told you so?"

"I would never want to see you fail, lass." His words were so sincere, so earnest, they made her eyes water. Such a strange state to be in, happy and sad at the same time. Oh, dear Lord. They'd seen her toss her garter to the audience. Everything she'd experienced in the last half hour—elation, fear, anger, relief, shame, guilt—it all swirled into an unendurable bog of emotion and she was drowning in the mire.

Ian wiped away her tears with a thumb. "What's amiss, lass? Everyone loved your song."

"I dinnae want to be an actress anymore. I want to go home. I want my da." She sobbed into her gloves.

After a moment, she felt Nathan's hand on her knee. "It's all right, Lou. Everything will be fine."

"N-Nathan, I'm sorry I ran away. It was stupid. I feel so foolish." She hiccuped and blubbered like a child, which only made her angrier at herself. "I'm sorry, Ian. I'm sorry for lying and for ruining your life."

The carriage left them at Cook's Inn on Chapel Street.

Nathan arranged for two rooms, one for her and one for him and Ian. Ian must have sensed how hungry she was because he said, "I'm going to see if I can get us some scran."

Before she closed her bedchamber door, she asked Nathan, "Are you going to make me marry Mr. Kirby?"

"Nae. I'm no' going to make you marry anyone. I'm taking you home."

"Da's going to make me—"

"I'm not going to let Da make you marry, either. That will be your decision, aye?"

She flung her arms around her brother's neck and squeezed him tight. "You do love me." She kissed his cheek. Smiling through fresh tears, she asked, "What changed your mind?"

Nathan tipped his head toward Ian who had appeared in the hallway with a tray of food and drinks. "Him."

* * *

Physically exhausted and emotionally drained, they arrived at Quaker Hill by nightfall the following day. Kirby and Mairi waited for them in the parlor. Mairi's eyes were nearly swollen shut as though she'd been crying for two days, and Kirby looked like a man about to be hanged.

Ian noticed the reverend then, sitting in a corner deep in thought, both hands propped on the handle of his walking stick, his mouth set in a grim line.

A wave of uneasiness washed over Ian. He had expected smiles and expressions of relief. After all, they had found Louisa relatively free of damage. She'd lost her money and her jewelry. He could replace both. But she still had her travel documents and her blasted pistols.

Robertson must have been equally perplexed by their welcome. He clapped Kirby on the back and asked, "Why the long face?"

Kirby went even paler. "I've consulted with my attorney. It seems that my marriage to Louisa Robertson is legitimate. The contract is valid."

"We determined that before we left," Robertson said with forced joviality. "Your marriage to Mairi will stand, and Louisa will marry—" Robertson censored himself no doubt remembering the promise he'd made to his sister. "Louisa will marry whom she pleases."

"You don't understand," Kirby said. "The marriage to *Louisa* is valid. The law considers Mairi a proxy. As long as the names were stated, the marriage is legal."

The news made Ian's stomach heave. Kirby must be mistaken. There had to be a loophole, a way out. He chanced another look across the room, and met Louisa's emerald-green eyes, her brow dimpled with concern. "No," he shouted. "No. You were tricked, Kirby. Robertson said so. You're free to ask for an annulment. Robertson, tell him."

For once, Nathan Robertson seemed at a loss for words. "I...I confess, I'm not as familiar with the American legal system. It's possible the marital laws are different."

Desperate, Kirby glanced around the room as if he could find an answer under a cushion or behind a table. "We can just forget about it. The only people that know about the marriage are in this room. We can deny it ever happened."

"It's too late for that now," Nathan said. "Mr. and Mrs. Foley were there. Eliza knows and she's told her whole family, no doubt. And your attorney knows. Hell, half the village probably knows by now."

Ian's body vibrated with an urge to grab Louisa and run. He needed to be alone with her, speak to her privately. Fear for her safety had burned away his anger at what he had thought was betrayal, but had come to understand was an ill-conceived plan gone horribly wrong. He still wanted to rail at her for it, get it out of his system. First, though, he needed to appease that nagging, crawling feeling inside his head. The one that warned him things were not right, not in their proper place, and that he needed to straighten them, square them, put them in order. Then they could discuss love.

"I refuse to marry Mr. Kirby," Louisa stated firmly. "I beg your pardon, Mr. Kirby. You are a fine man, but I dinnae love you, and I will not dishonor my friendship to Mairi." She looked to Ian when she said, "I insist on an annulment."

Relief spread across Ian's chest, until Robertson added miserably, "I'm not certain that's possible, Lou."

"We have to do something," Ian said.

"But what?" Kirby asked.

After a long pause during which the only sound was Mairi's sobbing and Louisa's quiet reassurances that Captain Sinclair would see that everything would turn out right, Reverend Wynterbottom rose from his chair and excused himself. "I do beg your pardons, but I must retire."

A round of offhanded "good nights" and "sleep wells" circled the room and then quiet again. Louisa turned pleading eyes his way. Why was he responsible for sorting this mess out? Why was he *always* the one people turned to? *Damn.*

"First thing tomorrow," he said, inventing a plausible plan of action as he went, "we'll visit a judge." All eyes had fastened on him, the pressure to produce a miracle growing. "I recall some mention about marriage in America seen as a civil rather than a churchly matter."

Hope animated Kirby's face. "Yes. Yes, that's exactly right. We'll go see Judge Owen tomorrow, the three of us, you, me, and Robertson. He's sure to grant us the annulment when he understands what's happened."

Robertson continued to look dubious. "I have no doubt he will, Edward. But these sorts of things often take time." He looked directly at Ian. "I'm afraid it may take months before anyone can get married."

Sleep eluded Ian once again. Robertson's words still rolled around inside his busy brain. "It may take months before anyone can get married." He tossed onto his back and stared up at the ceiling faintly illuminated by blue moonlight. Shite. The *Gael Forss* would be back at New London Harbor within a week. He could hardly ask Peter and the crew to linger until he was certain Louisa was freed from any marriage contract. Could he take her back to Edinburgh with him, and leave her brother behind to sort things out?

A light breeze skimmed his naked skin. The night had been so hot and still, a cooling rainstorm would be welcome. Lightning flickered and, like he did when he was a lad, he counted. He reached five when thunder rolled in the distance. The storm was five miles away. He heard another sound outside his chamber. He rose and wrapped the bedsheet around his waist and opened the door to the dark corridor.

When lavender tickled his nose, he reached out and hauled her against his body with a thump. He shut the door, put it on the latch, and circled his arms around her. Ian wasn't as surprised by her visit as he was the first time, but he was just as pleased, if not more. A part of him worried she might accept her marriage to Kirby, or that Robertson would change his mind and insist. It might be Mairi MacQuarie he brought back to Edinburgh and not Louisa.

He bent and dragged his lips across her cheek searching for her mouth. He paused when he encountered tears along the way. It was then he realized her body was stiff and trembling. "Dinnae fash yourself. You'll have your annulment. I'll see to it."

Louisa sniffed and swallowed audibly. "But if I marry

Mr. Kirby, you'll get your commission."

"You would do that? You would marry Mr. Kirby so that I could get my commission? You would do that for me?"

"I've ruined your life."

"Nae. Miss MacQuarie will marry Kirby and that's final."

"But what about your commission?"

"That's my concern, lass." Now was the time to tell her. To tell her about Rory, about not wanting the commission. Now was the time to tell her he loved her. He gathered her up and carried her to the bed where he sat with her on his lap in front of the window. The breeze smelled of impending rain and bathed them with cool air.

"I've ruined your life," she repeated. "You said so."

"I said that in a fit of anger and I'm sorry. What you and Mairi did was reckless and daft and I'll never understand it, but I ken you didnae do it on purpose to hurt anyone. Not even your da, Louisa."

She buried her face in his neck. The thing inside his head had become peaceful, and he experienced a rare moment of serenity. Now was the time. If he had the courage, he could say the words now. But the memory of what had happened the last time he spoke words of love kept his mouth still.

The first splats of raindrops hit the windowsill. He would like to stretch her out on his bed and bury deep inside her, rut until they were both spent and satisfied. Common sense demanded he wait until they were well and truly wed, preferably on Scottish soil, but the condition of his body argued that was too long for a mortal man to abstain.

· · ·

She'd come to learn the signs of his arousal. Pulse quickening, breath ragged, and the most obvious proof pressed against her right thigh. She shifted in his lap, and his hold on her

tightened possessively as if to say, *you're not going anywhere.*
To assure him she was here to stay, she pressed a kiss on his
neck. That tiny action provoked an instant upheaval. For one
dizzying moment, her world spun around her. In the next, she
was lying on her back, and he was settling his big, naked body
tight against her side.

Oh yes, please. Please do it all again.

Propped up on one elbow, Ian placed his palm on her
thigh and gathered the hem of her night rail. Slowly dragging
it up over her hips to her belly, he alternately kissed her face
and murmured, "Never run from me, love. Promise you'll
never run from me again. I need you. I need you with me. I
need to watch over you."

She sank deeper into a delirium of his making. "Yes, Ian.
Yes."

He kissed and nipped her taut nipples through the thin
cotton of her night rail. Twining his leg with one of hers, he
nudged open her thighs and stroked her curls until he made
her hips rock against his hand.

Lightning flashed across his handsome face bent over her
hips in concentration, working on that part of her that was
drawing all her senses into a spiraling free fall. The more she
panted, the more she became light headed, and the closer she
inched toward glorious oblivion.

"That's it, love," he said. "You're almost there." He leaned
closer and whispered her secret word in her ear, sending her
crashing over the edge of reason. He had to cover her mouth
with a kiss to silence the stream of words spilling from her
lips. It was so much more intense than the last time, the
pulsing so strong. This time she'd very nearly left her body
altogether. *Wicked, wicked man,* she thought, and raked her
fingers through his silky hair.

A crack of thunder and lightning lit up the room and the
face of the beautiful man in the bed with her. He smiled down

at her, his eyes darkened, half lidded, and dream soaked.

He kissed her then. A long fierce kiss. A determined kiss. A kiss that said, *I will have you.*

"You'd best get back to your room," he rumbled in her ear.

"But we've not finished. You havenae—"

He pressed a finger to her lips. "Listen to me, love. You were willing to marry Kirby so that I could get my commission. You were willing to do that to make me happy. Thank you for giving me that choice. But if you married Kirby, I would be miserable." He brushed another kiss across her lips. "I would like to give you a choice, too. Sometime in the next month, we'll know if I've made you pregnant. If you are not with child, then you will have a choice. In the meantime, I cannae take any more risks. Especially if you dinnae want me for a husband."

What was he saying? Choice? Risk? "Are you withdrawing your proposal?" Hot tears threatened. Captain Sinclair was having second thoughts. Rather than err on the side of caution, he'd wait for confirmation. He'd wait to find out if she was pregnant. If not, well then, no reason to buy the cow when the milk is for free. "You're still angry with me."

"Listen to me," he said. "I wasnae honest with you before. It's true, you might be carrying my child…" He put a warm hand on her belly. "And that would make me very happy, by the way." She detected a smile in his voice. He inhaled deeply, as if what he was about to tell her took courage. "You see…the truth is…if you were pregnant, I wouldnae have to tell you that I *want* you to marry me."

She touched his cheek. "Ian, I—"

"Nae." He stilled her hand. "Dinnae say anything. Not until…God, I cannae even believe I'm telling you—it's just easier to tell you these things in the dark." He took another shaky breath. "The damned truth is that I want you more than I want a commission in the army. I didnae ken it until I saw you on that stage. I dinnae want you to *have* to marry me. I want you to *want* to marry me. And so I would give you a choice. Do you understand, love?"

"Aye, I do, Ian."

"There are many issues—obstacles really—that must be..." Ian swallowed audibly. "That must be addressed before either of us can make any decisions. The least of which is this blasted marriage contract. When we get back to Scotland— that is, if you choose to return to Scotland with me?"

He seemed to be waiting for her answer so she nodded adamantly.

He huffed a stifled laugh. "When we get back to Scotland, I've got to face your da. I dinnae ken what the Tartan Terror will do, but I ken he willnae be happy wi' me."

The next morning, she arrived at the door to the breakfast room and found Mairi, Nathan, and Ian already breaking their fast.

"Good morning, everyone."

Nathan and Ian rose from the table, swallowing and wiping their mouths.

"Morning, Lou," Nathan said.

"Good morning, Miss Robertson," Ian said.

Louisa went to the sideboard and the men lowered themselves into their seats again. "Where's Mr. Kirby this morning?"

"He's gone out to ask Mr. Foley to get the carriage ready," Mairi said.

Louisa returned to the table, her plate heaped with eggs, sausage, toast, and roasted potatoes.

"You've got quite the appetite this morning," Nathan

said.

"Indeed." She leaned back and inhaled deeply. "I always do when I get a good night's sleep." She looked pointedly at Ian. "You look as though you didnae sleep at all, Captain."

He sent a warning look her way. "As a matter of fact, I did not." He stabbed a bit of sausage and brought it to his mouth.

"I'm so sorry. Was something keeping you awake?" she teased. "The storm, perhaps? Or maybe the heat?"

Ian choked on his sausage and Nathan gave him a good thwack on the back.

Edward entered the breakfast room looking more out of sorts than usual.

"Is something wrong?" Mairi asked.

"I'm not sure," he said. "The carriage is gone. When I asked Mrs. Foley about it, she said Mr. Foley drove the reverend into town. It seems he's left us."

"Without saying goodbye?" Mairi didn't make any attempt to hide her distress.

"I'm sure Mrs. Foley must be mistaken," Louisa said. "The reverend wouldnae leave us. Especially when everything is so unsettled."

Edward pulled a folded parchment from his coat pocket. "He gave this to Mrs. Foley to give to you, darling."

The furrow between Mairi's brows deepened as she read. She shook her head slightly. "I dinnae understand this, Edward." She handed him the parchment and he read aloud.

"Dear Miss Mairi,

I write because shame prevents me from speaking these words to your lovely face. I am a man unworthy of forgiveness and yet I ask for your understanding. I, too, am not who I seem to be. Like you, I left Scotland under a false identity. Unlike you, my motives were not true. I left my wife and children behind rather than face the consequences of my dishonorable conduct. I chose this time to leave you because revealing myself will resolve your current dilemma. I am not nor have I ever been a clergyman. I was, until late, a banker. Or should I say an embezzler. I will not give you my real name, lest duty compel Captain Sinclair to apprehend me. Know that I could never anticipate how my assumed identity could complicate things for you, my dear girl. I never meant to cause you harm and hope that this belated confession can set things to right again.

My best wishes for a long and happy marriage to you and Mr. Kirby.

Anonymously yours."

The room was completely silent for what seemed like a long, long time. Finally, Mr. Kirby said, "So...so he's not..."

"He's not a real..." Nathan ventured.

"Clergyman," Ian finished.

Again silence, as if no one dared believe what this revelation implied.

"The ceremony wasn't real." Excitement bubbled up inside Louisa. She wasn't married to Kirby by proxy. She wasn't married to anyone. "It was a rehearsal. It didnae count. It was just a rehearsal!" She was free.

In an uncharacteristically impulsive gesture, Kirby swept Mairi into his arms for a kiss.

Nathan burst into peals of laughter. She hadn't heard her brother laugh that way since they were children. Ever since he'd become a man of business, he'd been so serious he almost never smiled.

She chanced a glance at Ian and was pleased to find him laughing as well. Their eyes met, his glittering with mirth. Was he thinking the same thing as she—that they had cleared the first and most formidable obstacle?

• • •

Ian gazed back at those dancing green eyes and grew more confident. He knew he would have to fight hard for Louisa, but he had a strategy to win her heart. He'd anticipated it would be a long and messy business to break Louisa's marriage contract with Kirby, but as it turned out, the battle for Louisa's freedom had been less than a skirmish, thanks to Fake Reverend Wynter-whatever.

His next battle would be with the Atlantic Ocean. He had to get her safely back to Scotland with him. Once on Scottish soil, he would take the offensive with the Tartan Terror. That would, no doubt, be the bloodiest conflict. He would take all the blows General Robertson dealt to shield Louisa from his wrath. But the final battle, the one he feared most, the one with the highest stakes, would involve a six-year-old boy. He loved Louisa and he would do anything within his power to make her his, but for Rory, he would fall on his own sword.

Ian was spared further contemplation of the hell that awaited him in Scotland when the jangle of an approaching carriage reached them. Everyone moved toward the front door and spilled out into the morning sun.

As soon as Mr. Foley pulled the brake, Will hopped down from the driver's bench smiling from ear to ear. "Got a surprise for ye, Captain." The lad opened the door and a familiar lanky form slid out of the coach.

"Peter!" Ian strode directly to his quartermaster, gave him a fierce embrace and slapped him on the back. "I didnae expect you for another three days at the least."

"We completed our business in good time. Rather than let the crew idle in Boston, I thought we might find a better price on beer and entertainment in New London." He turned his mop of blond hair toward Louisa and executed his formal bow. It never failed to please the lassies. "Good morning, Miss Robertson."

Louisa returned a deep curtsy. "I take it Will has filled

you in on our folly?"

"Oh, aye. I got an earful. My head's still spinning."

"Mr. Peter, this is my brother, Nathan Robertson."

Peter shook Nathan's hand. Anyone who didn't know Peter well would never have detected the slight tic of his almost invisible blond eyebrows when he looked Ian's way. But he read Peter's thoughts as clearly as if they'd been written on the lad's forehead. *Bloody hell, man. I cannae believe you're still alive.*

Ian asked, "How did you find Will?"

"Will found *me*. Spotted me coming out of the general store. I'd gone in there to find out where Mr. Kirby lived."

"Did you get a good price for Declan's whisky?"

"Aye. One buyer took it all. And if the exchange of silver for sterling stays the same or goes up—"

"Please," Louisa said. "You can talk about business later. Mr. Peter, come inside with me. Miss MacQuarie will be delighted to see you again, and I want you to meet Mr. Kirby."

"We'll join you shortly," Robertson said. "I want a word with Sinclair." He draped a chummy arm over Ian's shoulder.

Shite. Robertson probably needed to burn off some anger with a fistfight. Ian was far too tired for fighting, but if he must, he must. As soon as Louisa and Peter were out of sight, Ian sloughed off Robertson's false embrace, and sighed. "I let you have one free shot the other night because I owed it to you. But if you try it again, I'll knock you on your arse."

"*Humph.*" Robertson swept a doubtful gaze up and down Ian. "Save it for another time. There's something else I want to discuss."

• • •

Louisa was more than a little put out when the men locked

themselves in the parlor for a "private discussion." In her experience, private discussions were often tactical in nature. Since America and Great Britain were no longer at war, Louisa could only assume she and Mairi were the enemy. She put her ear to the parlor door to listen.

"What could they be talking about?" Mairi wrung her hands in her skirts as if she were wearing an apron, an unconscious habit she'd yet to break.

Louisa flapped her hand to shoo her away. "I cannae hear when you're talking." The heavy clip of boot heels echoed from within, and she skipped clear of the door, whispering a frantic, "Get back. Someone's coming."

The parlor door opened, and the men filed out. With little to no explanation, they found their hats and headed toward the front door.

"Wait. Where are you going? Mr. Peter just got here."

"Business in town," Mr. Kirby said, and slipped out the door.

"Yes. Business," Nathan said, and followed.

"Will and I have an appointment with the tailor," Ian said, and flashed her a roguish grin. What was he so happy about?

Mr. Peter was much more polite. "Thank you for your kind hospitality," he said, sweeping a graceful bow. "It has been my pleasure to spend time in the company of—"

"Mr. Peter!" Ian shouted from outside the door.

"Good day, ladies." Mr. Peter flashed them a charming smile. Dear Lord. Women must fall at his feet.

She and Mairi spent the rest of the day trying to shake their agitation. After all, the worst of it was over. Their secret was out and no one had expired. And Mairi and Mr. Kirby were to be married as originally planned. He'd forgiven Mairi and told her he didn't care what she'd been before he met her. He'd said, "You could have been a chimney sweep and I would not have loved you less."

The carriage rumbled into the yard around six o'clock that evening. Louisa remained curled up on the settee with her *Moll Flanders*. If Ian wanted to talk to her, he could damn well come and find her. Male voices and boot heels echoed in the entry. Mr. Kirby called out to Mairi and thundered upstairs.

The parlor door opened. Louisa lifted her head from her book as if surprised by the disturbance.

"We're back," Ian said.

"I see."

"Like the book?" he asked.

"Oh, aye. It's quite…bracing."

"Good," he said.

Her brother Nathan marched into the parlor, announcing in his usual dictatorial manner that their departure from New London would take place on the morrow.

Louisa dropped the book and bolted to her feet. "But Mairi's wedding."

"You've already attended Mairi's first wedding. The second will be no different."

"Can we not stay until Saturday? It's a difference of four days," she pleaded.

"The longer we stay, the more likely we are to meet with storms at sea," Nathan said. "Sinclair has made the arrangements. I'll have no more discussion." He spun on his heel and left the room.

"Ian," she implored. "Do something."

"Your brother and I have found something upon which we can agree. Savor the moment. I doubt it will happen again anytime soon," Ian said, and exited.

She clenched her fists and growled, "Men."

After a tearful morning packing her things, Louisa and Mairi said their goodbyes. Louisa had known the day would come when she and Mairi would part, but she had always imagined it would be on different terms and that they would, at the very least, live on the same continent, not on opposite sides of the Atlantic Ocean.

"You will write to me," Louisa said, holding Mairi's hand from inside the carriage.

"I promise." Mairi sobbed. "Thank you, my dear friend. Thank you for everything." Mr. Kirby wrapped a possessive arm around her waist and drew her back.

Mr. Foley whistled and the team pulled away from the house. Louisa leaned out the carriage window and waved until she could no longer see Mairi.

When they arrived in town, the carriage paused near the park where Will had played with his new friends. Will hopped down and raced toward the group of boys.

"I promised Will we'd say goodbye," Ian said, and climbed out. "He'll only be a minute."

Ian waited by the carriage for Will's return. Louisa sensed Ian was tense by the set of his shoulders. True to his word, Will returned breathless and smiling. "Told 'em I'd see 'em next time we made port, sir."

Ian rested a hand on Will's shoulder. "You know, you can stay here if you prefer, Will. You can stay with the Kirbys, work for them, go to school, have friends. Would you rather do that, lad?" Louisa heard a hitch in Ian's voice. It had cost him to make the offer.

Will gazed up at him, confused. "You mean leave you and Mr. Peter?"

"Aye."

"The *Gael Forss* is my home, sir. I'll never leave."

Ian's shoulders relaxed. He must have been holding his breath. He ruffled Will's mop of curls. "Right then. Up ye go." Will clambered up to the driver's seat with Mr. Foley, and Ian climbed back in the carriage.

When he sat back in his seat, she noticed Nathan's knee bouncing impatiently.

"What?" she asked.

"Let me tell you both how things will be on board the *Gael Forss*. You two will not eat together, drink together, walk together, or talk together unless I am present. I expect you to abide by my word during the entire crossing. In exchange, I will speak on Sinclair's behalf when he makes his report to the general. One infraction, and the deal is off. Am I understood?"

"That's six weeks," Ian protested. "At night, she's bothered by the small spaces below deck. I allow her to read in the captain's mess," he pleaded. "You must grant her that freedom, at least."

Nathan turned an unsympathetic shoulder on Ian.

"If you promise you willnae let Da harm Captain Sinclair," Louisa said, "I'll stay below at night, no matter what."

"Louisa," Ian said, his brow buckled with concern. "How will you manage your fear?"

She tilted her head and smiled sweetly. "I'll do just as you showed me. I'll close my eyes and let you take me dancing."

Chapter Seventeen

Five weeks, five days, and eight hours later, Leith Docks, Edinburgh, Scotland

Ian stood on the quarterdeck as Mr. Purdie guided the *Gael Forss* into Edinburgh Harbour. He should feel a sense of victory. He had, after all, won his battle with the Atlantic without any casualties. Even Dougald Clyne's foot had healed well enough he could walk with a crutch. And he'd met Robertson's challenge. He had not spoken to Louisa or been within ten feet of the lass without the presence of her brother—a difficult thing to do given the length of the voyage and the size of the ship. Harder still because every minute of every day he ached to wrap his arms around her, feel her heat against his body, smell her sweet scent.

He hadn't given a toss about Nathan's promise to speak on his behalf, but it was very important to Louisa, so he'd agreed. What was more, Louisa seemed to have won the battle with her own demon. The small spaces on board ship no longer caused her panic and that pleased him. For that matter, the itch inside Ian's head had miraculously calmed, leaving him relatively free of his tics.

Today, the ban on Louisa's company would end the instant they set foot on Scottish soil. The prospect should thrill him. Yet, he felt only apprehension. Two weeks after they'd departed the shores of Connecticut, Louisa had left a note under his cabin door.

I can confirm, a marriage is not required.

The implication of her note was that she was not pregnant. The knowledge should have brought him a sense of relief. Instead, he was downcast for days. *A marriage is not required.* Did that mean a marriage was not desired?

Added to that concern, his final two battles loomed ahead. More than likely, he would have to tackle them both today. First, General Robertson, a full-on assault. If he survived, then he would tell Louisa about Rory. He would have few defenses for that fight, and even less ammunition. Endurance would be his strategy. If he could stay on his feet, he might have a chance.

Robertson and Louisa came up on deck and went to the railing. This late in the season, a biting wind ripped through the docks. She was well cloaked, wore a hat and woolen gloves, and when the wind picked up the hem of her skirts, he saw the trousers. He liked to think she felt him smile because she turned then and smiled back.

She said goodbye to Will and Danny and the cat they had named Brandy. She had talked about taking the feline with her, but Will and Danny had become attached to the thing and she didn't think her old cat would like a companion.

"Mr. Peter, have the cargo unloaded and stored in the warehouse."

"Aye, sir."

"Will, take Danny with you and see that the Robertsons' trunks are delivered to this address." He handed the lad a note and a bag of coins. "And get yourselves something to eat."

Will beamed. "Aye, sir."

"And you, sir?" Peter asked.

"I'm going to Castle Rock to report to the Tartan Terror."

"Do you need a second?"

"Nae. Robertson will fill that role, but let's hope it doesnae come down to a duel, aye."

Nathan waited with Louisa dockside while Ian found them a carriage. They were silent the entire way to Edinburgh Castle. At the esplanade, they got out and Ian paid the driver. The last time he'd stood facing the castle, he'd been so certain of success, he could taste it. This time, he tasted nothing but a cold disquietude.

"Are you sure the general will be here?" Ian asked.

"He said he'd be in Edinburgh the entire month of October," Nathan said.

All too quickly, they were escorted to the Governor's House.

"Do you want me to go in with you to meet my father?" Nathan asked.

Ian straightened his waistcoat. "Nae. You and Louisa stay here, in the hall. I'll see him alone."

"Stop," Louisa said. She fussed with his neckcloth, a wifely thing to do. "There," she said, and patted his lapel. The gesture emboldened him.

He knocked.

"Come."

Ian entered the lion's den and shut the door behind him. He waited at attention as he always did in front of the man. General Robertson stood at a window looking out over all of Edinburgh, his hands clasped behind his back.

"Sir."

Without turning, the big man said, "You delivered my

daughter to Connecticut?"

"Aye, sir."

"Kirby met with your approval?"

"Aye, sir."

In a voice clouded with emotion, he asked, "You saw Louisa marry Kirby?"

Ian swallowed. This was when things would get ugly. "No sir."

Robertson turned, his furry white eyebrows coming together. "What?"

"Your daughter, Louisa, did not marry Mr. Kirby, sir. Miss MacQuarie married Kirby."

Real concern etched Robertson's brow. "And Louisa?"

"I brought her home, sir."

General Robertson seemed to inflate to twice his size, which Ian would expect from a warrior about to swing a killing blow, but the man was grinning like he'd won a high-stakes pony race. "Where is she?"

Very cautiously Ian pointed to the door. "Outside, sir?"

"Louisa!" the general roared.

The office door swung open and Louisa burst inside. "Da!"

Ian stood with his mouth hanging open as the two hugged and sobbed and rocked and murmured endearments.

Nathan strolled in smiling with satisfaction, as if he'd known this would happen all along. "Close your mouth, Sinclair. Ye look like a numpty."

"What the bloody hell?" Ian whispered.

"I told ye," Nathan said. "He loves her best."

Robertson released Louisa, took out a handkerchief, and unashamedly wiped his eyes. "Thank God, Sinclair. I knew the instant she was gone I'd done the wrong thing. I've been miserable. But you've brought my girl home to me. Thank you."

"Does that mean you'll grant Captain Sinclair his commission, Da?" Louisa asked.

"Yes, yes, of course. Come back and see me tomorrow, Sinclair. I'll have it for you then."

The general turned his back on him and continued his chatter with Louisa. It seemed as though Ian was being dismissed. Well, bloody frigging hell, he was not finished yet.

"General Robertson, sir," he boomed.

All three Robertsons stopped mid-sentence to look his way.

Ian straightened to his full height. He may not possess the highest rank in the room, but he was the tallest. "I would like to offer for your daughter's hand, sir." His words ricocheted around the stone walls of the room. He remained still, rooted to the ground, eyes fixed on his target. No retreat.

General Robertson's face went a dangerous red.

"Now, Da," Nathan soothed. "I can speak for Sinclair's character."

The general took one step forward and Louisa flung herself between them. "No, Da. Dinnae touch him. He's mine. I love him."

He tried not to take his eyes off the Tartan Terror, tried not to move, tried not to smile at her words. *She loves me.*

"Louisa, Nathan, step aside," Ian said, using the most commanding voice he could muster. "I'll speak to the general alone."

"Ian, he might kill you," she whispered.

"Dinnae fash yourself, lass."

Nathan and Louisa withdrew and shut the door. Ian braced himself for a fight.

"You've got balls, Sinclair. I'll give ye that," the general growled.

"Ye ken she'll marry me whether you want her to or no'."

The big warrior narrowed his eyes. "Then what are you

asking me for?"

"She requires your love and approval. She'd never be happy if you frowned on our union."

The general seemed to weigh Ian's words. After a moment, he nodded, and broke his stance. He started to move, then stopped himself, as if he had a second thought. General Robertson gave him a puzzled look, as though Ian had gone off his nut. "Are you sure aboot this, son? Ye ken she's an impossible woman."

"Aye. She's a bloody nightmare. But I love her all the same."

"And you think she'll have you?"

Ian shifted. He and the general had just waded into dangerous waters. "Well, that's the next battle, sir."

The general tipped his head to the side considering.

"What is it, sir?"

"It's just that, everything I've ever told Louisa to do, she's done the opposite. All I have to do is endorse you, and she'll have none of it." The man showed his teeth and it was obvious how he'd gotten the name Tartan Terror.

Ian sighed. "Then I ken it's best we fight for her. I'll let you have one free swing."

"You'll *let* me?" The general laughed.

Ian got a sick feeling that this was going to hurt.

• • •

As soon as Louisa and Nathan were out of her father's office, she punched her brother in the arm as hard as she could.

"Ow," he said, rubbing the injury. "What was that for?"

"You know perfectly well what that was for," she said, punctuating every other word with a *thwap* to his chest. She stopped and put an ear to the door. "I dinnae hear anything. Do you think he's strangled him?"

"Dinnae be daft."

"You said you would speak for him. You promised. Six weeks I kept to myself. Do you ken how hard that was?"

"Aye. I was amazed, actually." Nathan had the nerve to laugh.

A crash of furniture, curses, thumps, grunting, and more falling items rumbled from within.

"Get back in there and save him. Now!"

Nathan flung the door open in time for Louisa to witness Ian picking himself up off the floor, and her father dabbing at a bloody lip. Both were breathing hard from the short but violent scuffle. She rushed to Ian's side. Ian kept his fierce gaze on her father, but allowed her to check his face for injury. Nathan had already caused damage to Ian's nose. It would be criminal if her father left a mark on his otherwise perfect countenance.

Outraged, she rounded on the general. "How could you behave in such a beastly manner to the man who saved my life?"

Ian looked down at her, surprised. "I thought it was you who saved my life."

Touched by his comment, she said, "We saved each other." She laced her arm through his. "Come Ian. You may take me home now."

They strolled calmly out of the Governor's House, around the old stone buildings, through the portcullis, and across the long esplanade. Once they found a carriage and climbed inside, Louisa turned his face toward the light to check it for bruising.

"Are you sure you're all right?"

He looked at her with sleepy eyes, the irises narrowed to light blue rings around dark pupils. "Are my lips hurt?"

"No. They look undamaged."

He closed the shades in the carriage. "Good. Because

I've been waiting a long time to do this." He kissed her then. A long, passionate kiss, one to make up for the span of time since the last. He tried to pull her closer and when frustrated by their positions, he hauled her onto his lap and kissed her until she grew dizzy. When he stopped, they were breathless. He rested his forehead against hers and closed his eyes. "You love me."

Still reeling from his kiss, she murmured, "Do I?"

"Aye. You told your da you loved me."

"That's right. I did say something like that."

"I remember your words exactly. You said, 'He's mine. I love him.'"

A squeeze to her bottom made her inhale sharply. "Is that what I said? I'd forgotten."

"For as long as I live I'll never forget a word of it." He kissed her sweetly again. "Do ye ken what I told yer da?"

"What?" she whispered brushing her lips over his bristly cheeks.

"I said you're a bloody nightmare, but I loved you all the same."

A surge of white rage burned up her spine. She shoved both palms against his chest. Laughter bubbled up from somewhere deep inside Ian. She couldn't believe it. The most romantic moment of her life, and he was laughing at her. "You *are* a monster. I'm quite sure someone took the worst parts from my da and my brothers to put you together." She thumped a fist on his shoulder.

"Come on and kiss me, Kate," he said, echoing Petruchio's line near the end of the play. For some inexplicable reason, it diffused her sudden wrath. It was as if he were saying, all that business that just happened was a play, a scene we acted in front of the world to show them that we are a match, equal and complementary.

"Marry me, Louisa."

She bit her lip. *Why is it so hard to say yes?* "Put me down so I can think."

He gently shifted her onto the seat across from him then waited patiently.

He took one of her hands and tugged at the glove one finger at a time until it slid off. He raised her hand to his face, kissing each finger reverently. "Your fingers were the second part of you I fell in love with."

"What was the first?"

"Those green eyes of yours." He turned her hand over and kissed the palm. "But when you asked me to choose a book from my library for you, I knew my life would never be the same."

"How odd," she said. "When you chose *The Taming of the Shrew,* I knew you were different from any other man in the world."

Ian leaned back in his seat and made a pained face.

"What?"

"That wasnae the book I would have chosen. I was looking for *The Beaux' Strategem.*"

She laughed out loud. "That moldy old thing?" She could tell by the set of his mouth she'd hurt his pride just a little. "Still, you let me have the Shakespeare."

"I thought it was, perhaps, too bawdy for a lady and you would think I was being impertinent."

She inhaled deeply. With the carriage shades closed, his manly scent had filled the cabin, it having grown stronger with his arousal, a fact that had become obvious. "My dear Captain Sinclair, impertinent does not even begin to describe your perfectly outrageous behavior in the bedroom."

"I think we are well matched in that respect."

Louisa felt the heat pool between her thighs.

"Why do you hesitate, Louisa? Are you afraid I'll treat you differently? That I willnae allow you the freedom you require?"

"A little."

"You dinnae like that I would take a commission in the army?"

"That and..."

"And what?"

"Ian, why do you want to marry me?"

• • •

Why did he want to marry her? A thousand reasons rushed from his brain to his mouth at once.

"Because I love you."

"Why do you love me?"

He thought for only a second before answering. "I love you for the same reason you love wearing trousers," he said. "It feels wonderful."

Her jaw dropped open. A look of pure delight broke out all over her face, and he couldn't believe he was the lucky one to receive it, much less cause it. She flung herself at him with a force that knocked him back in the seat. Arms twined tightly around his neck, she kissed him. He loved kissing her. Even more, he loved when she kissed him, because it was different somehow.

But there was something he had yet to do. Something important that had to be done, even at the risk of losing her. With his heart hammering in his chest, he said, "Before you give me your answer, I need to tell you something."

The coach stopped. They had arrived at the Robertson town house on George Street.

Louisa laughed and said, "You've already told me you love me. What more do you need to say?"

"Much," he said gravely.

"Come inside, then. You can tell me over tea."

"No. I need to tell you now."

The expression on Louisa's face changed. "Ian, you're scaring me. What is it?"

He took her hands in his and inhaled deeply. "I should have told you before. Weeks ago. But I've only come to terms with it recently."

She squeezed his hands. "Go on."

"Two days before we left Edinburgh, I was told I have a son."

Louisa went very still. The coachman called out and Ian replied with, "Bide a while."

"You said you werenae married." Her voice was barely a whisper.

"I'm not. Nor have I ever been. I had a brief affair with a woman seven years ago, before I left for Flanders. I never knew the woman was pregnant. Apparently, she died in childbirth. It wasn't until the boy was six that his gran found me to tell me."

Her brow furrowed as if pleading with him. "You have a six-year-old son?"

"Aye. His name is Rory."

• • •

Louisa sat back in the seat abruptly. Rory, the name he'd repeated when he was delirious. All this time he'd known he had a son, and he'd never told her. He could have no reason to hide the fact from her, other than shame.

"Did you love her?" She didn't know why she asked the question, it just seemed important to know that answer.

"No. I barely knew her. Which makes my indifference all the more criminal."

The coachman called again and Ian growled, "A moment!"

The interior of the coach had grown small and stifling. She needed out. When she reached for the door, Ian stayed her hand.

"Louisa, please."

"Out! Let me out. Now!"

He climbed out of the coach and helped her down. She started toward the door to the town house and Ian called to her with a voice she'd never heard. One filled with hurt and uncertainty.

"Please. If you love me, could you not love the boy, too? He needs us, Louisa. He needs a father and a mother."

Gripped with a new and horrifying thought, Louisa whirled around to face Ian. "Is that why you want to marry me? To be your son's caretaker? Did you plan to leave me with Rory while you saunter off to your military career? Did you imagine I'd sit at home wondering when you might visit, pat us on the head like well-behaved dogs, and then disappear again for months?"

"No. No, that's not what I—"

"I'll not be that woman, Ian. I'll not spend my life married to a ghost. I will not."

The door to the town house opened and she ran inside.

"Wait," Ian cried out, but she didn't hear the rest of what he said, as the door closed behind her.

• • •

Ian stood staring at the closed door, his mouth open, and his limbs numb. Defeat. Utter annihilation. He'd come to the battle woefully unarmed and she had surprised him with cannon fire. One blast and he'd lost the war.

The coachman cleared his throat, and he woke from his temporary stupor, paid the man, and waited until the coach drove away. Without any plan for where he was going, he began to walk. He had intended on making this visit with Louisa at his side. She would have known what to say, how to behave. She would have smoothed the way for him. Instead, he would have to go it alone.

Before long, he found himself paused by an oak tree at the edge of St. Andrew Square directly across from the Crawford house on St. David Street. Something unusual was happening. A constant stream of men carried bits of furniture out of the house and deposited them into a large cart waiting in front. Bloody hell. Had the old lady decided to move and not tell him?

He crossed St. David Street and stopped one of the laborers. "What's going on here?"

"Emptying the house," he said, and wiped his brow with a filthy rag.

"Why? Is the family moving to a new residence?"

The man shrugged and gave him a crooked smile. "If you can call the hereafter a residence." He chuckled and started toward the door again.

Panic catapulted Ian forward. He grabbed the man and spun him around. "Are you telling me the occupants of this house are dead?"

Unhappy with Ian's rough treatment, the man groused, "Here, here. Leave off. I just do as I'm told."

A bone-thin woman wearing an apron and a face full of wrinkles crossed her arms and leaned against the front doorjamb. "Old Mrs. Crawford passed a month ago. What's it to you?"

"The boy, Rory, what happened to the boy?" he asked, trying not to sound as crazed as he felt inside.

"He's at his school, far as I know." She turned and shouted for the men inside to have a care, then turned back to Ian. "Some benefactor's looking after the wee one. Poor lad doesnae have a soul in the world."

"What school? Where?"

"How should I know?"

Ian staggered away, the thing inside his head gnawing at his brain reminding him that *it* was in command. Not Ian. Everything had gone to hell. Nothing was in its place. Nothing was right. He'd lost all control over everything and everyone in his life. *Bloody frigging hell.* He'd lost his son. What kind of a father lost his son?

The ache in his head began then. A dull thud at first, but he knew what was to come. Sickening, debilitating pain. He needed Louisa. Only Louisa could help him. But he'd lost her, too. He'd lost everything.

The attorney. His solicitor. He hoped that was his connection. Perhaps Old Lady Crawford had given him instructions in the event of her death. Christ. Did she ken she was dying when he saw her in the spring? Is that why she insisted he take Rory?

He stumbled out onto the main thoroughfare, Princes Street. He remembered the address of the attorney, but got confused about the direction. Sunlight stabbed bolts of pain through his eyes and into his brain. Just like the spiteful Scottish sun to choose this day of all others to shine like the blazes.

A hack stopped in front of him. Blasted Nathan Robertson leaned out the cab window and laughed. "Turned you down again, did she? Poor sod."

Ian shaded his eyes and swayed. It was becoming more and more difficult to see properly.

"Something wrong, Sinclair?" When he didn't answer, Robertson got out and ushered him into the hack with him. The hack provided blessed shelter from the sunlight. "Where are you going, man? I'll take you to the address," Robertson said.

What seemed like an eternity later, Robertson helped

him out of the hack. "Are you certain this is the right place, Sinclair? It's a solicitor."

"Aye," Ian said. "This is the right place."

"Will you be all right? You dinnae look well."

"I'll be fine. Thanks."

Ian barreled through the door and pounded up the stairs to the office of Andrew Carlisle, Esquire. "Carlisle," he called. "Open the door. It's Ian Sinclair. I need…" He rested his forehead on the cool wood of the door and gathered the strength to call again, the sound inside his head only amplifying the pain. "I need to talk to you."

The door opened. "Captain Sinclair. You look unwell."

"Where's the Crawford boy? Rory? Where is my son?"

Carlisle helped him to a comfortable chair and got him a brandy while he explained the key details of what had transpired over the last three months. Yes, the Crawford woman did suspect she was dying. No, the boy had not been informed of her passing. Yes, she'd made arrangements for the bulk of her property to be liquidated and held in trust for the boy. No, the boy has no other blood relatives who have laid claim to him.

"Rory has been at the Danderhall Academy since the first of September," Carlisle said. "It's what the Crawford woman wanted and, therefore, what I assumed you wanted."

"Is he well?"

"As far as I know, yes. The headmaster has been instructed to send quarterly reports to my office."

"And he has no one?"

"No one. Mrs. Crawford did state in her will that she wished for the boy's natural father to assume full custody."

Ian nodded. The beast inside his head settled, his headache ebbed, and he could breathe normally again.

"When I met with Mrs. Crawford, I assured her that your intention was to claim the boy. She said my assurance gave her great comfort."

"Did she." Carlisle recognized Ian's question as a statement and did not answer.

"The Danderhall Academy has an excellent reputation. I know the headmaster personally. You may, of course, leave the boy there with confidence or..."

"Or?"

"Or you can collect Rory and take him into your household."

For the first time, the thing that made his brain itch spoke to him with words. Or maybe it had always spoken to him and Ian had never listened until now. It said in loud capital letters, *Rory's place is with you.*

"Today? Can I get him today?"

"You can remove him anytime you like."

An hour later, he reached for the knocker on the front door of his sister's house and, with a healthy measure of dread, he let it fall. His brother-in-law Mark Pendergast answered the door.

"Ian. You're back. Good to see you, man," Mark said and hauled Ian inside. "Come on in. Maggie will be glad to see your face."

Ian heard Maggie call his name before she trundled down the stairs with open arms to greet him. After a fierce embrace, she pulled away and examined his face carefully. "What's happened?"

"Sit down. I have something to tell you, sister."

Chapter Eighteen

Late that afternoon, Ian stood before the headmaster of Danderhall Academy for Boys with one hand crooked behind his back, and a book clutched to his chest with the other. He waited more or less at attention while the bespectacled, berobed, and bewildered headmaster read the document from his solicitor. Ian felt like he was fourteen again and in deep trouble. Any minute, the headmaster would ask him to hold out his hand for a tawsing.

At last the headmaster peered over his spectacles and said, "Master Rory has only been with us for a month, hardly time to adjust completely, but his performance thus far appears promising. Are you absolutely certain this is the wisest course of action?"

"I believe the age of six is young to be separated from family, sir."

"From what I know, you are a stranger to the boy."

A trickle of sweat ran down Ian's temple despite the chill in the air. "I would like the chance to put that right, sir."

"There is the additional trauma of finding out his

grandmother has expired," the man said.

"Aye. I know. All the more reason he needs family."

The headmaster sniffed in a lungful of air through his long beaky nose and returned to the letter. After another interminable minute, he said, "You understand my hesitation is born only from a concern for Master Rory's well-being."

"Of course, sir." The wait had begun to test Ian's patience. The matter was clear. Ian had the power to take his son whenever he wished. If the perverse pedagogue continued to stand in his way, Ian would walk over him to get to Rory.

At last the headmaster rose and gestured to a chair. "You may have a seat. I'll return with the boy in a few minutes."

Left alone, he set down the book he'd purchased for Rory, one of Ian's favorite stories as a lad. The muscles in his arms and legs cramped and trembled very much like they would before battle. This wasn't a battle, he told himself, but lives were at stake, his and Rory's.

His gaze drifted over the bookcase, desk, globe, and mismatched chairs positioned in corners of the room. The wood-paneled study was awash with afternoon light streaming in through a large bay window. Outside, at least two dozen boys of various ages ran about on a field playing tag. The younger lads had no chance, but seemed to enjoy the game no less than the older ones. Was one of them Rory? Would he be able to pick him out from the rabble?

He heard voices, and Ian spun toward the door. The headmaster entered, nudging Rory inside saying, "This is Captain Sinclair. He would like to talk to you. I'll be just outside if either of you need me."

Ian stood speechless, drinking in his son—lean, wiry, with hair cropped shorter than the last time he'd seen him at the Leith Docks. Rory wore the short pants and coat that was the academy uniform. His socks had fallen and bunched around his ankles and his left knee was skinned. Had anyone been there to comfort the boy?

Rory watched him with dispassionate gray-blue eyes so like his brother Alex's it made Ian's heart hurt. He reached out a hand and said, "Do you remember me, Rory?"

With a solemn face, Rory placed his small hand in Ian's and shook. "Aye, sir. You're the captain."

Ian smiled ruefully. "Aye." He took a deep breath. "I have some difficult things to tell you. Do you think you're old enough to hear them?"

Rory's brow buckled slightly and he made a tentative nod.

"Did your gran ever talk about your da?"

"She said he got lost after the war but one day he'll find his way home and be my da. That's why I didnae want to come here. If he comes home, he might not know where I am."

Ian didn't know whether to curse or bless the woman for the fabrication. He bent to one knee to be eye level with the lad. "I found you, Rory. I'm your real da."

Rory's brows drew together, the thin dark arches identical to his own. "Why did you not tell me before? When we met on the dock? Did my gran scare you? She scares a lot of people."

Ian almost smiled at Rory's concern. "No, son. I wasnae scared. I had to go away. It was a long voyage. I'm sorry I didnae get here sooner."

Rory smiled. "It's all right. You're back now."

"Thank you." He choked on the words. Of all the reactions Ian had expected from Rory, mercy was not one of them. Swamped by emotion, he struggled to maintain calm. Steeling himself, he said, "Now I have to tell you the hardest part, Rory."

Rory looked at him long and hard, his chin dimpling. In a small voice, he asked, "Did my gran die?"

"Aye, son."

The boy's face rippled. Ian reached out with one arm, and

Rory fell against his shoulder. Ian held him, his palm nearly spanning the boy's narrow back. He hadn't known until this second how much he wanted to hold his son. The thing inside his head uncoiled and the rightness of the moment spilled over his whole body. Ever since he'd learned of his existence, Ian had, in some sense of the word, loved Rory. Now, he knew he would love the boy with a full heart and forever.

Playtime was over, and the raucous mob of boys tumbled into the hallway outside the office. Ian gathered his son into his arms and walked to the far corner of the room where Rory's grief would be his own. He sat in a chair, stood Rory on his feet in front of him, and waited. When it looked as though the boy had recovered somewhat, he retrieved his handkerchief, and handed it to him. "Take this and blow."

Rory dutifully obeyed, and returned the handkerchief. As Ian pocketed the thing, he asked, "Do you like it here?"

Rory shrugged one shoulder noncommittally. At Ian's doubtful look, he said. "Nae."

"Would you like to come live with me?" Ian held his breath, waiting for Rory's answer.

On the carriage ride back to Edinburgh, Ian gave Rory the book he'd purchased for him before he left for Danderhall. Rory read the fly page out loud, mispronouncing some of the words and stumbling over the more difficult ones. "The Life and Strange Surprizing Adventures of Robinson Crusoe, of York, Mariner: Who lived eight and twenty years all alone in an un-inhabited island on the coast of America, near the mouth of the great river of Oroon...Oroon..."

"Oroonoque," Ian assisted.

"Oroonoque; having been cast on shore by shipwreck, wherein all the men perished but himself. An account of how he was at last strangely delivered by pirates."

"Well read."

Rory smiled at the praise. "Is that what happened to you?"

Ian considered his earnest question. "Sort of. I wasnae shipwrecked, but I did feel like I was all alone. And I wasnae rescued by pirates."

"Who rescued you?"

"A pretty lady with green eyes who likes to wear trousers."

Rory's eyes opened wide. "Is she a fairy?"

So bittersweet was the moment, Ian laughed even though it hurt to do so. "Nae, son. She does remind me of a pixie, the kind that causes all sorts of trouble, but she's a real lady." She was a real lady that had, for one glorious hour, been his, and then he'd lost her. But he'd found his son. If there was one thing he'd learned from Louisa, it was that his son needed him. And, if he was completely honest with himself, he needed his son.

• • •

Louisa regretted her harsh treatment of Ian almost immediately after he left. Ian had been furious with her when he'd discovered her deception but he'd given her an opportunity to explain herself. She hadn't even given him that. Had she leaped to the wrong conclusion? Was Ian's reason for marrying as he had said, that he loved her? Had she been too hasty to think that he'd only wanted a mother to care for his son? She went to her room and stayed there for the rest of the day, refusing to see anyone.

The next morning, Nathan told her about meeting Ian on Princes Street in a sorry state. "What did you say to the man, Lou? He looked like hell."

Louisa knew then she had been terribly wrong. She had

to find him. Despite his protests, Nathan took her to where he'd left Ian, the office of a solicitor by the name of Carlisle. The man claimed she was asking for information that was confidential. He was of no help at all. A trip to the Leith Docks also proved fruitless as the *Gael Forss* had already left port. Had Ian gone away, as well?

Days passed and with each one, her anxiety grew. Nathan's and Connor's pointed questions regarding Captain Sinclair's intentions had only sharpened her unease. She wouldn't tell them about her quarrel with Ian. Their opinion of him had soured and discovering he had a son would only further complicate matters.

On the morning of November third, Louisa stirred to the sound of the upstairs maid refreshing her basin water.

"Morning, miss," Constance chirped. "That captain fellow you were expecting just arrived."

Louisa bolted upright in bed with a gasp. "He is?"

"Aye. He's talking to Mr. Nathan in the parlor."

Heart beating with a combination of relief and anticipation, she bounded out of bed. "Quick, Connie. Help me dress."

Louisa's impatience to see Ian made dressing and putting her hair in order twice as difficult. Partly because Constance was not a lady's maid and had no idea how to assist, but mostly because Louisa's sudden, jerky movements only complicated the ordeal.

When she deemed her reflection presentable, she raced down the corridor. The front door closed as she reached the top of the stairs. Nathan stood in the entry.

"Did Ian leave?" she asked glaring down at him. "Did you send him away?"

Nathan's expression hardened. "Captain Sinclair came to formally withdraw his offer of marriage."

"What?" Louisa picked up her skirts and tore down the

stairs. She shoved past Nathan and reached for the front door.

"Lou, wait. Dinnae go do that—" Nathan called.

She ignored her brother. He'd do and say anything to hurt Ian and spoil her happiness. Outside on the front steps, she spotted Ian climbing into a hack, and shouted to him. When he didn't turn to acknowledge her, she ran to the carriage door and flung it open. Ian's face lifted, startled by her intrusion.

"Ian Sinclair, get out of this carriage and face me like a man," she shouted. When he didn't move, she hiked her skirts up and made an unladylike leap into the carriage. She settled in the seat across from him, chest heaving, hair and skirts in disarray. "How dare you speak to my brother without talking to me?"

His expression was so laden with conflicting emotion, she couldn't read it. Sorrow and happiness, desire and reserve, anger and relief. Her tears started then.

Ian was quiet for a long time. He handed her his handkerchief, which she took, gratefully. She would have rather he held her, but he seemed determined not to touch her.

At last he said, "Your brother thought it best I not speak to you directly."

"My brother is an arse," she blurted.

A smile flashed across his handsome face and faded. "I made a mess of things. I'm sorry."

"So, you dinnae want to marry me anymore?"

"I want you, more than you will ever know. But my son needs me. His gran died. He has no one, and—"

"May I meet him?" she asked.

Ian cocked his head, as if he didn't understand the question. "You want to meet him? Why?"

"Because he's your son. He's a part of you. Of course, I would want to meet him."

"You're no' angry wi' me?"

"I'm furious with you. I cannae believe you would ask me to marry you without telling me about him, but..." Louisa inhaled a shaky breath. "Oh, Ian, I miss you so much. Will you hold me?"

He scooped her into a tight embrace and buried his face in her hair. "Give me another chance, Louisa. I need you. I love you."

"Take me to Rory."

She trembled in his arms. Ian must have thought she was shivering, because he released her suddenly and said, "Where the hell is your cloak? Are ye daft? You cannae go out in November without a coat." He launched himself out of the carriage. "Wait here. I'll fetch your things."

He returned five minutes later with her ermine-trimmed cloak and gloves and gave the coachman an address. They settled next to each other and were quiet for a while, as the coach rumbled through the cobblestone streets of Edinburgh and over the North Bridge.

Ian asked, "What made you change your mind?"

"Once I had time to think, I realized you didnae mean to deceive me any more than I meant to deceive you. It just happened. I'm sorry I didnae give you a chance to explain. I was too quick to think the worst of you."

"You were wrong, you know. I would never leave you alone. How could I when I only want to be with you? But you were right about one thing. I do want you to be Rory's mother. He needs a mother, and I dinnae ken how to be a father."

The carriage made a slow, winding journey through the old part of the city until the buildings and crowded streets opened and gave way to hedge-lined fields, an area Louisa had never been to.

"Where are we going?" Louisa asked.

"King's Park. My sister Maggie has taken the children for a picnic."

His sister. She would meet his sister and her brood, as well. Somewhere in the back of her mind, she knew marrying Ian would mean that his family would become her family, yet she hadn't fully envisioned the setting where she might actually meet them. Her vague image of the event involved champagne or tea and cakes, at the very least.

The carriage paused at a footpath leading into a forested area.

"We're here." Ian studied her. "Are you sure you want this?"

"I'm very certain, but I sense you are not. Are you worried Rory willnae like me?"

"I want what's best for him, but I'm not certain what that is."

She took his hand in hers. "I vow that, no matter what happens, I will put Rory's concerns before my own."

Ian swept her into his arms again with such ferocity, her bonnet slipped off and dangled by the ribbons. The kiss was bruising, penetrating, unlike any other. The desperation was almost frightening. The driver called out, and he released her lips, his breath roaring in her ear.

"God, I've missed you. The only thing that keeps me alive is knowing the boy needs me. But my heart cannae take another day without you." The driver called again, and Ian shouted a terse, "Soon!"

Louisa saw the tear streak on his cheek then and swiped it away with her gloved thumb. She gave him what she hoped was an encouraging smile. "Let's go see your son."

The scene was nothing short of idyllic. Edinburgh residents taking advantage of what might be the last sunshine before winter. Groups of picnickers bundled against the chill dotted the meadow, blankets spread on long grass, ladies in their bonnets and furs, men in top hats and mufflers, children running wild, tumbling, shouting, squealing. One group of children caught her eye, the same one on which Ian's hawklike gaze was riveted. One of them was his. She wondered if she could pick him out of the rabble. Ian ushered her closer to the bunch.

"Are you ready, love?" he asked. At her nod, he shouted, "Rory."

One head popped up, a mop of dark brown curls with sparks of red glinting in the sun. The look of delight he sent Ian's way made her gasp. It was Ian's smile, the one that had made her heart stutter so many times before. Rory ran to Ian yelling, "Da! Da!" When he leaped into the air, Ian caught him and spun him around, as though they'd practiced the acrobatic trick a thousand times. Ian chuckled at Rory's squeals of delight.

"I've someone I want you to meet," Ian said, and set Rory on his feet in front of Louisa.

Before Ian could make the introduction, Rory cocked his head to the side, his eyebrows buckled together, an expression stunningly like his father's. "Are you the pixie lady what likes to wear trousers?"

Louisa flashed Ian a look. His hand went to his heart, and his face scrunched in mock agony as if he'd been shot. Obviously, he'd said something about her to his boy. She gave Rory a warm smile. "How did you ken it was me?" she asked.

"You have green eyes. Da said you had the greenest eyes he'd ever seen."

"What else did Da tell you?"

"He said you rescued him." He glanced down at her hem. "Are you wearing trousers right now?"

Ian burst out laughing, then sobered instantly at Louisa's admonishing glare.

"I'm not wearing trousers now, but I do wear them on

occasion."

"What occasion?" Rory asked, slightly awestruck.

"Whenever I play Pirates and Sea Captains."

"Do you and Da play Pirates and Sea Captains?" Rory asked, half in disbelief and the other half delighted.

"It's our favorite game," Ian said and slanted Louisa a heated gaze, one so hot it set her own insides ablaze.

Just then, a woman in her mid-thirties approached. She was elegantly slender and nearly as tall as Ian.

Rory ran to her, took her by the hand, and dragged her to them. "Auntie Maggie, this is the Pixie Lady. She and Da play Pirates and Sea Captains. It's their favorite game. Is that not right, Da?"

Auntie Maggie's golden-red eyebrows lifted with an amused look. "Who plays the pirate and who plays the sea captain?" she asked Ian.

The features on her breathtakingly beautiful face were so like Ian's, introductions were unnecessary, but Ian obliged.

"I'm very pleased to meet you, Mrs. Pendergast," Louisa said, inclining her head.

"I assure you, Miss Robertson, I am pleased beyond measure to meet you." She indicated their picnic blanket several yards away. "Come join me. I can tell you all about the Sinclair family, things my cloth-heid brother Ian would never dream of telling you." She laughed and winked at Ian. "You should be apprised of all our darkest secrets before you make any permanent decisions, aye?"

Several hours later, snugged inside a cramped hack, Ian sat next to Louisa with Rory asleep on his lap like a wet sack of laundry. They were on their way back to Louisa's house on George Street. She asked, "Where have you been these last weeks?"

"Spending time with Rory. It's been an adjustment for the lad. We'll stay with my sister's family until my business here is complete."

"And then what?" she asked.

"I dinnae ken. Rory needs me. I cannae raise him on board a ship and I won't be getting that commission. My parents want us to live with them at Balforss until I figure out what to do." He made a disgusted sound and dipped his head. "I can hardly expect you to marry a man with no home and no prospects."

"Stop being ridiculous," she said, irritated that Ian would doubt himself when she had complete confidence in him. "You are the most capable man I've ever known. And that includes my father. You can do anything you set your mind to, and you know it." Her exasperated huff brought a smile to Ian's lips. "At any rate, you insufferable man, you can have that commission if you want it. You've only to ask, but…" She glanced down at the sleeping boy held tightly in Ian's arms.

"But what?" Ian asked. "Finish what you were going to say."

"But things have changed, aye? I know because I was so certain I wanted to be an actress. Then things changed and being an actress didnae hold the appeal it once had. I think maybe being a soldier doesnae appeal to you so much anymore, either. Am I right?"

"You are." The carriage stopped in front of her house, and Ian placed a hand on her knee. "All I want is you and Rory to be with me, as a family. That's what feels right to me. But I dinnae ken how to do it. Will you help me?"

Will you help me? Potent words to Louisa. Infused in them were respect and trust and partnership. Everything that comprised true love in Louisa's mind. Ian loved her exactly the way she wanted to be loved. As an equal. As his Kate to her Petruchio.

"What do you love to do the most? Aside from sailing and soldiering, that is." He gave her his most rakish grin, and she felt a deep blush creep up her neck. She added, "Aside from sailing, soldiering, and that other thing."

Ian kissed her quick and shrugged. "Reading books, I suppose."

She leaned back and examined him thoughtfully. "Yes. Your system."

His eyebrows dove together and he opened his mouth, presumably to ask her what she meant, when a sudden wash of understanding crossed his face. "A bookshop?"

Chapter Nineteen

Three weeks later, aboard the Gael Forss

With the exception of a few trusted crew members for security—the ship was, after all, tied to the dock in Leith—he and his new wife were completely, blissfully alone. Ian had supplied the balance of his crew with plenty of coin to keep them at the tavern until dawn, allowing him enough time to thoroughly enjoy his wedding night with Louisa aboard the *Gael Forss*.

Ten minutes after he shut the door to his cabin, they lay in a tangle of limbs and bedclothes, spent and gasping. Their coupling had been quick and desperate. He'd waited, it seemed, for an eternity to have her again. In truth, it had only been a little over three months since that first time but for him, wanting Louisa was the same as needing her, requiring her. She was as necessary to him as the air he breathed.

"Sorry," he whispered, his chest still heaving up and down.

Louisa stirred and stretched. "What must I forgive you

for this time, husband?"

He chuckled. "I sort of raced to the finish."

She sat up and arranged herself so that she straddled his hips. His cabin berth was too tight to sleep the two of them comfortably and far too cramped for lovemaking—or at least too cramped for the kind of lovemaking he wanted to engage in on their wedding night—so he'd made up their bed on the floor. Moonlight slanted in through the cabin window and colored her skin pale blue like a fairy. Her wedding gown was twisted around her waist, the skirt rucked up and the bodice yanked down, those gloriously plump breasts in full view. The memory of how he'd just taken her made his cock jump back to life. He'd never recovered so quickly.

She switched her hips in a circle over his hardened member and he hissed with pleasure. "I'll make you go slower this time," she said.

Although he'd removed his shirt before he'd taken her, he still had his boots on and his trousers around his knees. Under any other circumstances, he might feel at a disadvantage. But, at this moment, with her lowering her pretty thatch of curls onto his mast, their state of semi-undress served only to heighten the tension.

She was slippery but tight, her cunny like a fist around his cock. Fully seated, she leaned down and kissed him. The instant he slid his tongue inside her mouth, her insides squeezed and he surged upward. They both gasped.

"Is that good?" he asked.

"Oh, aye. Dinnae stop, Ian."

"Never," he said. Her breathing grew ragged, punctuated with soft moans and whimpers. She rode him like that until she was close. So close. "Say it, love. Say the word."

She moaned the word *cock* and cried out his name. Her cunny pulsed around him as strong and satisfying as a good stroking. He bucked hard, and called out, "I love—I love—

oh, God, I love you."

Ian had no right to feel so chuffed. After all, it was his duty as a husband to please her. Still, he couldn't help but congratulate himself on a job well done, as he watched Louisa slumbering peacefully. He, on the other hand, was wide awake. A stroll on deck was in order. He pulled up his trousers, buttoned the fall, and slipped on his coat. The November nights had taken on a chill.

The two crew members he'd retained to watch the ship sat at the bow, a polite distance from his cabin, offering him and Louisa the privacy they required. He lifted a hand, and the shadowy figures acknowledged him. The docks were deserted, quiet. Even the harbor was calm, lifting the ship gently up and down rather than rocking it side to side.

So much had changed for him since June. And the agent of that change had come in a small lavender package with fierce green eyes. In hindsight, it was all so clear. Yet at the time, he had been like a man with a blindfold tied 'round his head. So many clues ignored. The thing inside his head had known, but he'd been so used to silencing that itch, he hadn't picked up the signals.

General Sir Thomas Robertson and his sons Nathan and Connor had given token resistance to his proposal of marriage. He'd won Nathan's respect somewhere between New London and New Haven, Connecticut. Ian suspected the general was simply relieved his beloved daughter would remain in Scotland, and Connor...well, the fact that he and Peter had become fast friends could be interpreted as good luck or bad news depending on one's perspective.

Louisa and Rory had formed a bond so tight, Ian often envied their closeness. She had taken to motherhood as easily and as naturally as she did wielding a pistol or wearing trousers. His son had been loved and cared for by his gran. Still, it wasn't the same as having a mother. They were a real family now. Ian had his own little family, something he'd thought he would never deserve.

The gentle breeze carried her lavender scent, announcing her presence before she spoke.

"Come to bed, husband." She tugged his sleeve.

He gathered her into his arms and growled in her ear, "How lucky I am to have a wife so eager for my bed."

She curled into him, soft parts molding to his hard edges. Holding her like this, he could have lingered for hours, but his soldier stood at attention and saluted, reminding him of his husbandly duty.

• • •

Once inside the relatively warm cabin, Louisa and Ian shed their clothes and huddled under the blankets. He captured her with one leg and one arm slung over her. In a matter of seconds, his body enveloped hers with heat. Tomorrow morning was a momentous day, Ian's last voyage as captain of the *Gael Forss*. They would collect Rory and sail to Caithness where they would open a bookshop in Thurso. She looked forward to the challenge. What made her fret was meeting Ian's parents, Laird John and Flora Sinclair.

"Do you think your family will like me?"

"They will love you. Everyone will love you. Caya and Lucy will smother you with their friendship and I will be jealous." He gave her a squeeze.

"Caya's married to..."

"Cousin Declan."

"And he's the one who had the dream about you marrying the lass in trousers?"

Ian groaned. "Oh, aye. I'd almost forgotten. I bet him a crown he was wrong. He'll want to collect."

"Rory will have plenty of cousins to play with."

"Oh, aye. Magnus and Virginia have six boys, I think. One is bound to be Rory's age. Declan and Caya have two young ones with another on the way—or maybe two. Declan claims he dreamed they would have twins, and Declan's dreams are frighteningly accurate. And Alex and Lucy have a daughter who's about Rory's age."

"What's her name?"

"Jemima, but everyone calls her Jemma. My brother calls her the Redheaded Tyrant. She reminds me a lot of you, actually. Wherever she goes, chaos follows."

"Ian, if you tell anyone about the General's Daughter from Hell, I will sit on you."

He roared with laughter. "I'll keep that bit to myself. I promise." He stroked her cheek. "Dinnae fash, lass. They will love you."

"Kiss me," she said. "I love your kisses, Ian." He kissed her with quick light taps, then his tongue slid along the seam of her lips parting them and sliding inside, reminding her of their recent joining. Pulse quickening, sex tightening, she twined a leg around his and slid her hand down his belly. As soon as her fingers wrapped around his silky, hard girth, he groaned and rolled onto his back, a move she interpreted as an invitation to have her way with him.

One of the more exotic illustrations she'd examined closely in the naughty sex book she'd found among her brother's things was entitled "Penelope Plays the Pipe." It depicted a woman on her knees with a man's private part in her mouth. At the time, she'd thought the act ludicrous. At this moment, however, she believed it was exactly what was needed. She scooted downward laying kisses on his belly. The closer she got, the louder he moaned.

Once faced with Ian's "pipe" she realized what monumental effort it would take to actually "play" it. But Ian lifted himself on one elbow, gave her gentle yet explicit directions until she understood what he needed. At the last, he pulled away, tossed her on her back, and brought them both to a roaring crescendo. He collapsed next to her wearing a big grin.

"I think you liked that very much, husband."

He chuckled and gasped out, "Oh, aye." When he'd recovered his breath enough to speak: "I didnae have the courage to ask you to do that. What gave you the idea?"

She confessed to him about her brother's naughty picture book. Ian doubled up and laughed out loud. "Dinnae laugh at me." She thumped him on the shoulder. "I was curious."

He wiped away tears of laughter and gathered himself. "Oh, lass, I love you. I didnae ken it was possible to love anyone like I love you."

Ian's confession swamped Louisa with the certain knowledge that she was loved by this man, the person who held her heart and her future in his hands, the one person who recognized and valued her assets, compensated for all her weaknesses, and accepted her flaws. That knowledge produced in her a joy so rare it was better than acting for an audience, better than the applause of a thousand people, better than wearing trousers on stage.

"Ian?"

"Aye, love?"

"You will still let me wear trousers from time to time, will you not?"

He pressed a kiss to her mouth and murmured, "My darling wife, I will insist on it."

Acknowledgments

Romance readers are special individuals. They are smart, they know what they are about, and they read twice as much as the next person. Most importantly, romance readers carry the belief that true love is possible, that our sons and daughters deserve to be loved and valued for exactly who they are, and that every woman can and should be the heroine of her own story. Love makes the world go 'round.

About the Author

Jennifer Trethewey is an actor-turned-writer who has moved her performances from the stage to the page. She would, if she could, live half of every year in Scotland. It's the next best place to home. She never feels like a tourist in Scotland "because the people there always seem like they are expecting you, like you are a long-lost cousin come to visit." Her love for Scotland has been translated into her first series of historical romance novels, The Highlanders of Balforss.

Trethewey's primary experience in bringing the imaginary to life was working for one of the most successful women's theater companies in the nation, where she was the co-founder and co-artistic director. Today, she continues to act but writes contemporary and historical fiction full-time. She lives in Milwaukee with her husband. Her other loves include dogs, movies, music, good wine, and good friends.

Don't miss the Highlanders of Balforss series...

TYING THE SCOT

BETTING THE SCOT

FORGETTING THE SCOT

Discover more Amara titles...

A Protector in the Highlands
a *Highland Roses School* novel by Heather McCollum

Scarlet Worthington flees her home in England to Scotland to help her sister run a school for ladies. There, Scarlet begins to rebuild her confidence by recruiting a fierce Campbell warrior to teach her and the students how to protect themselves. Burned in a fierce fire, Highland warrior, Aiden Campbell, has finally healed enough to take temporary command of his clan. That's where his focus should be instead of on the feisty, beautiful Sassenach.

A Lord for the Lass
a *Tartans and Titans* novel by Amalie Howard and Angie Morgan

Lady Makenna Maclaren Brodie is on the run from her clan for the death of her husband and laird. Even though she is innocent, she and her maid run to the only safe place she knows...and right into the arms of the handsome French lord she'd met a year ago. An unapologetic rake, Lord Julien Leclerc is focused on one thing—expanding his empire and increasing his fortune. However, when the widowed Makenna arrives on his doorstep in the Highlands, all bets are off.

How to Train Your Baron
a *What Happens in the Ballroom* novel by Diana Lloyd

When Elsinore Cosgrove escapes a ballroom in search of adventure, she has no idea it will lead to a hasty marriage. Now she's engaged to an infuriating, handsome Scottish baron who doesn't even know her *name*! But Elsinore is determined to mold her baron into the husband she wants. Quin Graham is a man with many secrets. If another scandal can be avoided with a sham marriage, so be it. Only his fiancée isn't at all what he's expecting. For reasons he's unwilling to explain, the last thing Quin needs is to fall for his wife.

The Devilish Duke
a novel by Maddison Michaels

Devlin Markham, the "Devil Duke" of Huntington, needs a woman. And not just any woman. If he can't woo eccentric bluestocking Lady Sophie Wolcott within the month, he can kiss his fortune goodbye. But he finds love a wasted emotion and marriage an inconvenience. And Sophie seems unmoved by his charm... When Sophie learns her orphanage is in danger, she'll do anything to save it. Even marry a ruthless rake. Even one targeted by a killer.